Girl, Serpent, Thorn

ALSO BY MELISSA BASHARDOUST

Girls Made of Snow and Glass

Girl, Serpent, Thorn

MELISSA BASHARDOUST

HODDER &
STOUGHTON

First published in Great Britain in 2020 by Hodder & Stoughton
An Hachette UK company

1

Copyright © Melissa Bashardoust 2020

The right of Melissa Bashardoust to be identified as the
Author of the Work has been asserted by her in accordance
with the Copyright, Designs and Patents Act 1988.

Designed by Anna Gorovoy

A CIP catalogue record for this title is available from the British Library

Hardback ISBN 9781529379075
Trade Paperback ISBN 9781529379082

Printed and bound in Great Britain by Clays Ltd, Elcograf S.p.A.

Hodder & Stoughton policy is to use papers that are natural, renewable
and recyclable products and made from wood grown in sustainable
forests. The logging and manufacturing processes are expected to
conform to the environmental regulations of the country of origin.

Hodder & Stoughton Ltd
Carmelite House
50 Victoria Embankment
London EC4Y 0DZ

www.hodder.co.uk

TO ANYONE WHO HAS EVER
FELT POISONOUS OR MONSTROUS
OR BRISTLING WITH THORNS

I am both the Sleeping Beauty and the enchanted castle; the princess drowses in the castle of her flesh.

—ANGELA CARTER, *VAMPIRELLA*

GIRL, SERPENT, THORN

PROLOGUE

Stories always begin the same way: *There was and there was not.*
There is possibility in those words, the chance for hope or despair.
When the daughter sits at her mother's feet and asks her for the
story—always the same story—her favorite part is hearing those
words, because it means anything is possible. *There was and there
was not.* She is and she is not.

Her mother always tells the story the exact same way, with the
exact same words, as if they were carefully rehearsed.

*There was and there was not a girl of thirteen who lived in a city to the
south of Mount Arzur. Everyone there knew never to go wandering too
close to the mountain, because it was the home of divs—the demonic
servants of the Destroyer whose only purpose was to bring destruction
and chaos to the Creator's world. Most people even avoided the sparse
forestland that spread out from the southern face of the mountain. But*

sometimes children who thought they were adults would go wandering there during the day—only during the day—and come back to boast of it.

One day, the girl wanted to prove her bravery, and so she went into the forestland. She planned to go just far enough to break off a sprig of one of the cedar trees that grew there, to bring back as proof. What she found instead was a young woman, trapped and tangled in a net on the ground, begging for help. It was a div trap, she told the girl, and if the div returned, he would take her prisoner.

The girl took pity on the young woman and quickly found a sharp rock to saw through the ropes of the net. When the woman was free, she thanked the girl, then ran off. The girl should have done the same, but she hesitated too long, and soon a heavy hand clamped down on her shoulder.

The girl looked up at the div that was looming over her, too terrified by his monstrous form to run or even scream for help. She thought her heart would stop from fear and save the div the trouble of killing her himself.

The div took one look at the empty net, the pieces of rope, and the rock in the girl's hand, and knew what had happened. "You stole something of mine," he said to the girl in a low growl. "And so now I will steal some-thing of yours."

The girl thought he would take her life, but instead, the div cursed her firstborn daughter, making her poisonous, so that anyone who touched her would die.

At this point, the daughter always interrupts her mother, asking—why the firstborn *daughter*? She doesn't need to mention that she is thinking of her twin brother with envy and perhaps a little resent-ment. It already shows on her face.

To which the mother always replies that the ways of divs are mysterious and unjust, unknown to anyone but themselves.

The div let the girl go after that, and she ran straight home, unwilling or unable to tell anyone of her encounter. She wanted to forget about the div's curse, to pretend it never happened. And it would be several years yet before she would have any children to worry about. In time, she did manage to forget the div's curse—mostly.

Years passed, and when the girl was older, she was chosen by the shah of Atashar to be his bride and queen. She did not tell him about the div's curse. She barely thought of it herself.

It was only when her children—twins; a boy and a girl—were born that she remembered that day in the forest. But by then, of course, it was too late, and three days after the birth, she discovered that the div had spoken true. On the morning of that third day, the wet nurse bent to pick up the daughter to feed her—but as soon as their skin touched, the nurse fell to the ground, dead.

And that is why her mother always agrees to tell her daughter this story, over and over again. She doesn't want her daughter to forget how important it is to be careful always to wear her gloves, to make sure never to touch anyone. She doesn't want her daughter to be reckless, as she once was, when she was only thirteen and wandered too far into the forestland.

At this point, the daughter always looks down at her gloved hands and tries to remember her nurse, who died because of her. *There was and there was not,* she reminds herself. It's just a story.

The daughter wants to crawl onto her mother's lap and lay her head against her mother's chest, but she doesn't. She never does.

It's not just a story.

1

From the roof of Golvahar, Soraya could almost believe that she existed.

The roof was a dangerous place, a painful luxury. Standing at the edge, she could see the garden spread out in front of the palace, lush and beautiful as always. But beyond that, beyond the gates of Golvahar, was the rest of the world, far larger than she could ever imagine. A city full of people encircled the palace. A road led south, down to the central desert, to other provinces and other cities, on and on, to the very edge of Atashar. Beyond that were more kingdoms, more land, more people.

From the other end of the roof, she could see the dry forestland and the dreaded Mount Arzur to the northeast. From every corner, there was always more and more, mountains and deserts and seas, hills and valleys and settlements, stretching on without end. It should have made Soraya feel small or inconsequential—

and sometimes it did, and she would have to retreat with teeth gritted or fists clenched. More often, though, standing alone under the open sky made her feel unbound and unburdened. From this height, everyone seemed small, not just her.

But today was different. Today, she was on the roof to watch the royal family's procession through the city. Today, she did not exist at all.

The royal family always arrived shortly before the first day of spring—the first day of a new year. They had a different palace in a different province for each season, the better to keep an eye on the satraps who ruled the provinces on the shah's behalf, but even though Soraya was the shah's sister, she never moved with them. She always remained in Golvahar, the oldest of the palaces, because it was the only palace with rooms behind rooms and doors behind doors. It was the perfect place to keep something—or someone—hidden away. Soraya lived in the shadows of Golvahar so that her family would not live in hers.

From above, the procession resembled a sparkling thread of gold winding its way through the city streets. Golden litters carried the noblewomen, including Soraya's mother. Golden armor encased the dashing soldiers who rode on horseback, led by the spahbed, the shah's most trusted general, his lined face as stern as always. Golden camels followed at the rear, carrying the many belongings of the royal family and the bozorgan who traveled with the court.

And at the head of the procession, riding under the image of the majestic green-and-orange bird that had always served as their family's banner, was Sorush, the young shah of Atashar.

Light and shadow. Day and night. Sometimes even Soraya forgot that she and Sorush were twins. Then again, the Creator and the Destroyer were also twins, according to the priests. One born of hope, one of doubt. She wondered what doubts had gone through her mother's head as she gave birth to her daughter.

In the streets, people cheered as the shah and his courtiers threw gold coins out into the crowd. Soraya understood why the people loved him so much. Sorush glowed under the light of their praise, but the smile he wore was humble, his posture relaxed compared to the rigid, formal stance of the spahbed. Soraya had long stopped imagining what it would be like to ride with her family from place to place, but her body still betrayed her, her hands clutching the parapet so tightly that her knuckles hurt.

As the procession moved through the palace gates and into Golvahar's vast garden, Soraya could see faces more clearly. With a grimace, she noticed Ramin in the red uniform of the azatan. He wore it proudly, with his head held high, knowing that as the spahbed's only son and likely successor, he had been born to wear red.

Her eyes gladly shifted away from Ramin to a figure riding a few horses behind him. He was a young man near the same age, his features indistinct from so far away, dressed not like a soldier in red and gold, but like a commoner, in a brown tunic without adornment. Soraya might not have noticed him at all except for one thing—

He was looking directly at her.

Despite the pomp of the procession, the lush beauty of the garden, and the grandeur of the palace ahead of him, the young man had looked up and noticed a single, shadowy figure watching from the roof.

Soraya was frozen, too surprised to duck away. That was what her instincts were telling her to do—*hide, disappear, don't let anyone see you*—but another instinct, one that she'd thought she'd buried long ago, kept her in place as she locked eyes with the young man, as she let herself see and be seen. And before she shrank away from the roof's edge and disappeared from sight, she silently issued two commands to this young man who saw what he wasn't supposed to see.

The first was a warning: *Look away.*

But the second was a challenge.
Come find me.

A beetle was crawling on the grass near where Soraya was kneeling. The sight of it froze her in place, her bare hands hovering in the air until it crawled a safe distance away from her. She shuffled a little in the opposite direction and went back to her work.

After watching the procession, Soraya had come to the golestan, needing something to occupy her thoughts and her hands. The walled rose garden was her mother's gift to her, along with teaching her to read. After Soraya had discovered as a child that she could touch flowers and other plant life without spreading her poison to them, her mother began to bring her a potted rose, as well as a book, when she visited each spring. As the years passed, Soraya's collections grew, and her garden was now teeming with roses—pink roses, red damask roses, white and yellow and purple roses, growing in bushes and climbing up the mud-brick walls, their scent as sweet as honey.

Like the much larger palace garden, the golestan was separated into quarters by tiled pathways that met in the center at an octagonal pool. Unlike the palace garden, there were only two entrances to the golestan—a door in the wall to which only Soraya had the key, and a set of latticed doors that opened from Soraya's room. The golestan belonged to her and her alone, and so it was the one place she didn't need to fear touching anyone or anything—except for the unknowing insects that found their way inside.

Soraya was still eyeing the retreating beetle when she heard the sound of stately footsteps coming from her room. She quickly stood and brushed the dirt off her dress, then put on her gloves, which she had tucked into her sash.

"Hello, Soraya joon," her mother said as she came to stand in the open doorway. Tall and regal, draped in silks, her hair glittering with jewels, Soraya's mother always seemed more than human. When the late shah had died seven years ago from his illness, Sorush and Soraya had been only eleven, and so it was Tahmineh who had become the regent, ruling in her son's stead until he was old enough to rule. And yet, with all that responsibility, she had never forgotten to bring Soraya the treasured gifts that lightened her daughter's burden. Even now, Tahmineh was holding a book under one arm and a clay pot in her hands.

With her gloves safely on, Soraya came forward to accept her mother's gifts, stopping a few steps away from her. "Thank you, Maman," she said, gently taking the potted rose. There was only a hint of green within the packed soil, just as Soraya preferred. She liked to see the roses bloom for the first time in her garden, by her hand. It was proof that she could nurture as well as destroy.

"I hope your journey wasn't too tiring," Soraya called over her shoulder as she found a temporary home for the potted rose until she could plant it. She hadn't had a conversation with anyone in so long that words felt clumsy on her tongue. Their greetings were always stiff and formal, since neither of them could embrace the other, but Soraya had seen the warmth in her mother's eyes, in the crinkle of her smile, and she hoped her own face showed the same.

"Not at all," Tahmineh answered. "Here," she said, holding the book out. "Stories from Hellea," she said, "since I think you already know every Atashari story that's ever been told by now."

Soraya took the book and leafed through the illustrated pages as her mother started to walk along the edge of the golestan. "These are beautiful," Tahmineh murmured to the climbing roses on the wall, and Soraya silently beamed with pride. She could never shine as brightly as her brother did, but she could still make her mother smile.

"There were more people in the procession today than usual," Soraya said, her tongue starting to loosen. "Are they all coming for Nog Roz?"

Tahmineh froze, her back so straight and still that she resembled a statue. "Not only for Nog Roz," she said at last. "Let's go inside, Soraya joonam. I have something to tell you."

Soraya swallowed, her fingertips cold even inside her gloves. She moved aside from the doors for her mother to enter first and then followed, still clutching the book in her hands.

She had nothing to offer her mother, no wine or fruit or anything else. Servants brought food to Soraya's room three times a day, leaving a tray behind the door for her. People knew the shah had a reclusive sister, and perhaps they all had their own theories as to why she hid away, but none of them knew the truth, and it was Soraya's duty to keep it that way.

The room was certainly comfortable, however. There were cushions everywhere—on the bed, on the chair, on the window seat, some on the floor—all with different textures, made from different fabrics. Overlapping rugs spread out across the entire floor, their vibrant colors a little worn from time. Every surface was covered with something soft, as though she could somehow make up for the lack of touch by surrounding herself with these artificial substitutes. Throughout the room were glass vases holding wilting roses from her garden, filling the room with the earthy smell of dying flowers.

There was only one chair in the room, and so Tahmineh sat on one end of the window seat. Soraya placed herself carefully at the other end, her hands folded in her lap, her knees held together, taking up as little room as possible so that her mother would feel comfortable.

But her mother looked anything but comfortable. She was avoiding Soraya's eyes, her hands fidgeting in her lap. Finally, she took a breath, looked up, and said, "The reason we have so many visitors is that your brother is going to be married next month."

"Oh," Soraya said with some surprise. From her mother's demeanor, she had expected to hear about a funeral rather than a wedding. She had known Sorush would likely marry sooner or later. Did her mother think she would be jealous?

"The bride is Laleh," her mother added.

"Oh," Soraya said again, her tone flat this time. It made sense, she told herself. Laleh was the spahbed's daughter, as kindhearted as she was beautiful. She deserved to become the most loved and influential woman in Atashar. Anyone would—*should*—be happy for her.

There was a loose thread on the edge of Soraya's sleeve. She took it between her finger and her thumb and pulled, watching the fabric slowly unravel. Her pulse was quickening with emotions she didn't want to have or name. Soraya took some slow breaths, the loose thread now wrapped several times around her gloved fingers. She wouldn't let bitterness or resentment overtake her. She wouldn't let them show on her face. Soraya took a breath, unwound the thread from her fingers, and looked up at her mother with a smile.

"They're a good match," Soraya said.

Her mother's smile was warm and genuine—and relieved. "I think so too," she said softly. Her smile faltered, her eyes flitting downward. "I may not have as much time to spend with you until after the wedding. It will be a busy time."

Soraya swallowed down the lump in her throat. "I understand," she said. The world would move on without her, as it always had.

"You know I love you."

Soraya nodded. "I love you too, Maman."

They continued to share pleasantries and bits of court gossip, but it was a mostly one-sided conversation. Soraya was too occupied with trying to control her emotions, sneaking glances down to make sure the light brown skin of her wrists was unmarred. By the time Tahmineh left, Soraya was exhausted from the effort.

Alone again, Soraya returned to the golestan to plant the rose her mother had given her. She ripped off her gloves, ignoring the lines of green that were spreading down her arms, and tried to let the sight of her roses soothe her. She cupped one of them in her palms and brought her face close to it, inhaling the scent as she let the edge of the petals brush along her cheek. So soft, as soft as a kiss—or so she imagined. She let her hands drift down to the stem, pressing the tip of her finger against one of the thorns, and that too was a comfort—knowing that something dangerous could also be beautiful and cherished.

But now she couldn't help looking down at her hands, at the insides of her wrists, where her veins had become a dark shade of green. She knew the veins running down her face and neck would be turning the same color, spreading out over her cheeks into a green web until she calmed and contained the tempest of her emotions.

They had all been inseparable once: Sorush and Laleh and Soraya, with Ramin often hovering over them. Laleh and Ramin were the only two outside of Soraya's family to know of her curse—an accident, but one that Soraya had been grateful for. She might never have had a friend otherwise. It had all seemed so easy when they were children. Tahmineh had been worried, but Soraya proved that she could be very careful not to touch anyone, and Laleh had always been well-behaved. Sorush had been there to make sure nothing went wrong. And for a time, nothing did.

But then the shah died, and even though his widow acted as regent, Sorush was suddenly under more scrutiny than before. Their mother kindly explained to her that he had less time for play, but over the years, Soraya figured out the real reason she never saw her brother anymore. Their family had a reputation to protect, and poisonous creatures belonged to the Destroyer. If Soraya's curse became public knowledge, the bozorgan might think the Destroyer had laid his hands on their family line. They would lose their confidence in the shah and his dynasty, and they would depose him.

And Laleh—how long had it been since she'd spoken to Laleh?

Was it three years or four? They had tried to keep in touch even after losing Sorush, but while two children could find time and space to play games or share candied almonds, it was much harder for two young women—especially when one of them was swiftly entering the world of the court that the other was forever barred from. Every year, they grew more distant, their time together shorter—and more awkward, both of them old enough now to understand how different their lives were and would always be. The spring Soraya turned fifteen was the first year she didn't see Laleh at all, and she hadn't been surprised. Laleh belonged to the same world as Sorush—a world of light, not shadow. Of open air, not narrow, hidden passageways.

Soraya bent down, digging with her hands into the soil to create a home for her new rose. From the corner of her eye, she saw the beetle still making its laborious way across the garden. Soraya watched it, this intruder to her sanctuary. And then she reached out and brushed one fingertip along its smooth back.

The beetle stopped moving, and Soraya went back to her work.

Five days after her family's return, Soraya was on the roof again. It was the night of Suri, the last night of winter, and Soraya was staring deeply into the heart of the bonfire, trying to feel some kind of connection with her ancestors. It was difficult in her case, though, because her ancestor was a bird.

That was the story, anyway. The first shah in her family's dynastic line, the shah who overthrew the wicked Shahmar and ascended to the throne more than two hundred years ago, had been a foundling child. His parents had cast him out, leaving him at the base of a mountain for the divs to take. But instead of divs, the simorgh—the legendary bird who served as the symbol and protector of Atashar—had found him and taken him in, adopting him as her son. Years later, after the Shahmar's defeat, the simorgh gave her newly coronated son one of her own feathers, which would keep him—and every reigning shah or shahbanu descended from him—safe from the Destroyer's forces. Though the simorgh's protection had no power over natural deaths, like that of Soraya's father, it protected the current shah from divs and the human sorcerers known as yatu.

The simorgh's protection had to be freely given by the simorgh herself, not won or taken by conquest, and so it was a great point of pride for her family, even though the simorgh had gone missing during the reign of Soraya's great-grandfather. Her family's supporters claimed the simorgh left because she wasn't needed anymore, while detractors argued that the simorgh abandoned the royal family in disapproval after Soraya's great-grandfather had entered a truce to end years of war with Hellea. Others believed the Shahmar still lived and had hunted and killed the simorgh out of revenge for his defeat. Whatever had happened to her, fewer and fewer people had lived long enough to remember ever seeing her.

And that was the ancestral origin Soraya was supposed to be honoring tonight. Tomorrow, on Nog Roz, the entire palace would celebrate life, but Suri was a night dedicated to the spirits of the dead. The bonfire blazing on the roof in front of her burned to welcome her ancestors, the guardian spirits who protected her family.

Every year, Soraya tried to feel her ancestors returning—some sense of continuity between this long line of shahs and her, the cursed shahzadeh standing alone in the dark. Or between her and the people of Atashar, who were all currently burning bonfires on their own roofs, welcoming their own ancestors. Her ancestors, her people, her country—these were a person's roots, the forces that bound someone to a time and a place, a feeling of belonging. Soraya felt none of it. Sometimes she thought she could easily float away from this life, like a tendril of smoke, and begin again, far away, without any regret.

Soraya turned away from the fire and wandered to the edge of the roof. Below, scattered throughout the garden, were several smaller fires in coal pits. Members of the court gathered around them, trying to seem solemn and respectful but probably gossiping over wine. If any of them looked in her direction, she would only appear as a dark, sulking outline against the fire.

Yes, she was sulking. After her mother's announcement, she had promised herself she wouldn't sulk—it would be too easy to sink into envy, to let that kind of poison into her heart as well as her veins. And yet here she was, alone on the roof once more, sulking.

Soraya sighed and leaned forward, her arms folded on the edge of the parapet. Whenever she was on the roof, she liked seeing the way her long dark brown hair spilled down against the wall, because it reminded her of one of her favorite stories. A princess had a secret lover who came to her window to see her. She let down her hair for him to climb and reach her, but he refused. He wouldn't harm a hair on her head, he told her, and he sent for a rope instead. Soraya had revisited that story over and over again through the years, wondering if she would ever look out her window and see someone waiting for her, someone like that young man, who would care more about her safety than his own.

A foolish thought. A pointless wish. Soraya should have known better by now than to indulge in such fantasies. She had read enough stories to know that the princess and the monster were never the same. She had been alone long enough to know which one she was.

Soraya started to turn away, but then something else caught her eye. A group of young soldiers in red were standing together, gathered around one man in particular. On a second look, she confirmed her initial suspicion—that the young man in the center was the same man who had noticed her during the procession a few days ago. He was now dressed in the red tunic of the azatan, a privilege most were born into. Elevation of a commoner to the azatan was customarily the shah's reward for those who performed great feats of courage in service to the crown. If this young man had joined the azatan, he must have performed such a feat.

Curious, Soraya took the opportunity to study him more closely. At first glance, he might have blended in with the other soldiers perfectly in their matching red tunics, but he wasn't built like them. The others were broad-shouldered, arms roped with muscle, while this young man was tall and lean. *Sinuous,* Soraya thought. There was a grace to him—in the tilt of his head, in his stance, in the way he held his goblet of wine—that the others lacked, like they were all as solid as heavy wood while he was shifting liquid.

"Soraya?"

Soraya straightened at once, turning toward the hesitant voice. She felt strangely guilty, as if she had been caught eavesdropping—but then she saw who had addressed her, and all thought of the young man left her mind.

"Laleh," Soraya said.

With the fire behind her accentuating the golden tones in her brown hair, Laleh appeared luminous, a dark red-orange sash the color of saffron draping down from her shoulder over the lighter hues of her gown. Of course Laleh was marrying Sorush—she already had the appearance and manner of a queen.

"I saw someone on the roof, and I thought it might be you," Laleh said. She spoke with the polish of someone who was used to making conversation, but there was a note of uncertainty in her voice as well.

"My mother told me the news," Soraya said. "I'm glad I have the chance to congratulate you in person."

Soraya didn't think she sounded particularly convincing, but Laleh smiled, her shoulders relaxing. She came to stand beside Soraya at the ledge, and Soraya felt a pang in her chest, because Laleh had made no effort to count the steps between them or to look down at where Soraya's hands were. Laleh had always been the only person to make Soraya forget she was cursed at all. Soraya turned her face so that Laleh wouldn't see her eyes.

"I was thinking the other day of how we met," Laleh said. "Do you remember?"

Soraya tried to smile. "Do I remember tumbling into your room by accident? How could I forget?" When she was a child, Soraya wasn't as adept at navigating Golvahar's secret passageways as she was now. She had miscounted a door once and ended up emerging from a secret door in the wall to Laleh's bedchamber, tripping over her feet in the process. Soraya still remembered the baffled faces of both Laleh and Ramin, the two of them bent over some game when a strange, gloved girl fell into their room out of nowhere.

"I didn't see you come in through the wall," Laleh said, "so I thought I was dreaming until Ramin went over to you." She shook her head in irritation. "And of course his immediate reaction was to try to confront you—as if an assassin would have sent a seven-year-old girl to attack us."

Soraya smiled thinly, but as much as she loathed to admit Ramin was right about anything, he wasn't entirely wrong to sense danger from her. While she had fumbled to open the wall panel again, Ramin had started coming closer and closer to her, asking her who she was. He had reached out a hand to her, and in her panic, she had told him not to touch her—that he would die if he did because she was poisonous. She wasn't supposed to tell anyone, but the words had rushed out of her before she could stop them.

"I was so scared he wouldn't believe me," Soraya said softly, looking down at her hands on the ledge. "I thought he might want me to prove it, and that I would have to kill something before he would leave me alone. But then you pulled him away, and you asked me if I wanted to join your game." Soraya looked up, determined to meet Laleh's eyes. "You were the only person who ever made me feel like I was the one worth protecting."

Laleh was silent, and Soraya traced in the slope of her mouth and the droop of her eyelids the way her thoughts went from pride to pity to guilt as she realized what Soraya had said—*you were,* not *you are.* Soraya hadn't realized it at first either, and she frantically thought of some way to lift the shadow that she had created. "You'll be a wonderful queen," she said. "Sorush is lucky."

That helped a little. Laleh's eyes were bright again as she thanked Soraya, and a mischievous smile crept over her face as she said, "You know, I used to wish that you and Ramin would marry."

Soraya blinked in astonishment. "Why would you ever wish such a thing on me?" she asked in mock seriousness.

Laleh burst into laughter at Soraya's offended look, one hand covering her mouth. "It was when we were all children and I still hoped you two might get along one day. I wanted us to be sisters."

Yes, Soraya remembered now. One morning, they had been lying under the trees in the orchard after stealing figs. They were side by side, their shoulders not close enough to touch, but not so distant that it seemed like they were not touching on purpose. Laleh had said that she wished they were sisters, and Soraya had considered the idea and said that she wished they could be married when they were older. Laleh had laughed, as if it were a joke, and Soraya had laughed too, even though it wasn't.

She wondered now if Laleh remembered that part—if she ever thought of it and still believed it had been a joke. But Soraya didn't want to see the shadow fall on her again, so she said, "I suppose your wish is coming true, then."

And there he is, the reason all of Laleh's wishes are coming true, Soraya thought as she found Sorush in the crowd below. From what she remembered of their father, the shah didn't often mingle with the crowd, except on Nog Roz, but Sorush was too young and lively to sequester himself away. *Don't sulk,* Soraya reminded herself.

But then she noticed the young man he was speaking with, and a small gasp escaped her lips. Laleh turned to her questioningly, then followed Soraya's gaze. "Ah, so you've noticed Azad."

Something about the sly tone in her voice and the knowing smile on her face made Soraya bristle with annoyance. Even if Soraya did harbor any feeling other than curiosity for this young man, did Laleh think anything could ever come of it? Or did she want to alleviate her guilt by believing that Soraya had someone else now to fill the void of their friendship?

"I noticed him the other day during the procession," Soraya said, trying to keep down her bitter thoughts. "I was wondering why he's in the uniform of the azatan now when he wasn't before."

"A few days before we started for Golvahar, we heard reports of a div raid in a nearby village," Laleh explained. "Sorush went himself, and one div tried to strike him from behind. But he has the simorgh's protection, of course, so before the div could strike, a young man from the village knocked the div unconscious. For his bravery, Sorush made him one of the azatan. The induction ceremony was yesterday, and Sorush asked him to remain at Golvahar until after the wedding."

Soraya processed Laleh's words, but more than that, she noticed the pride in Laleh's voice as she spoke of Sorush, the gratitude she felt for this young hero who had saved the man she loved. Though considering that Sorush had the protection of the simorgh and could not come to harm at the hands of any div, her gratitude did seem excessive to Soraya.

"Actually . . . ," Laleh began. She continued to stare down at the garden, but then she looked up at Soraya with determined focus, the firelight dancing in her eyes. "That was what I came here to talk to you about," she continued in a hushed voice. "The div that tried to attack Sorush was captured alive and is being kept in the dungeon. No one is supposed to know, but I overheard Ramin and my father talking about it."

Soraya shook her head, not understanding why Laleh was telling her this with such intensity, but then she heard the unspoken question behind Laleh's words, and the force of it made her knees buckle, her hand gripping the roof ledge for balance.

What if this div knows how to break your curse?

She almost let out a sob—not of sadness, but of relief. Of *hope*. Soraya had never seen a div in the flesh before, but her own flesh was itself a constant reminder of their existence, their power, their menace. It was a div that had condemned her and determined the entire course of her life.

Wasn't it possible, then, that a div might save her, as well?

3

Soraya opened the hidden panel into her mother's antechamber, and she instinctively held her breath as she stepped inside the empty room. Even as a child, she had always felt ill at ease in her mother's lushly furnished rooms. Everything here was impeccable—the gold embellishments on the furniture, the crystal and silver bowls of dates and nuts laid out on an ivory table in front of the low sofa, the rugs under her feet. Soraya held her hands stiffly at her sides, sure that if she touched anything, she would shatter this beautiful, pristine space that suited her mother so perfectly.

After thanking Laleh for telling her about the div, Soraya had come straight here to wait for her mother. She would need permission to visit the dungeon, but more than that, she wanted to see her mother's face alight with the same hope she was feeling now. Tahmineh tried not to show the strain Soraya's curse placed on her, but a thin line would form in the center of her forehead, growing deeper and deeper the more time she spent with her daughter. Soraya wanted to see that line smooth away.

Soraya tried to sit, but she felt too exposed, so she paced the edges of the room while waiting. When the door to the suite finally opened, she froze, wishing now that she had waited inside the walls instead. Her mother, wearing rich violet, stood at the threshold with her attendants—and they were all staring at her.

Tahmineh took control at once. She gave a small nod to Soraya, then turned to her attending ladies and dismissed them for the night. When they were gone, and the door was shut, she came toward Soraya with worried eyes, the line on her forehead beginning to appear. "Is something wrong?"

Soraya shook her head. "I have something to tell you—something that will make you happy." She should have begun by asking her mother how she was, or some other pleasantry, but she couldn't wait any longer. Without mentioning Laleh, she told her about the captured div, and that she wished to ask the div about her curse.

A moment passed in silence, and then another, and Soraya waited to see excitement replace the worry in her mother's face. But instead, Tahmineh's lips formed a thin line. Without saying a word, she turned and went to sit on the sofa, gesturing to the chair across from her. "Come sit, Soraya."

Soraya obeyed, feeling suddenly cold. Sitting across the table from her mother, she felt like she was going to be interrogated.

And she was right—the first thing her mother said was, "How did you find out about the div?"

She began to lie and say that she had overheard it when the full implication of her mother's question struck her. "You knew?" Soraya said, unable to keep the accusation out of her voice. "You knew and you didn't tell me?" She hadn't been surprised that Sorush hadn't told her himself—they rarely saw each other, and he had all of Atashar on his shoulders, so she was probably his last concern.

But her mother . . . Soraya would have expected to hear this news from Tahmineh before Laleh.

"I knew, but I didn't think it concerned you," Tahmineh answered.

"But the curse—"

"Divs are liars, Soraya. And they are dangerous. I'm not going to expose you to one of them."

"A div can't hurt me—especially in a dungeon."

Tahmineh's hands twisted the fabric of her skirt. "The danger is not always obvious. Divs can be manipulative. They can destroy you with a single word."

"Maman, please—I'll be so careful. Just let me talk to—"

"Soraya, this is not a discussion," Tahmineh said, her voice growing louder. "It's too dangerous, and you can't trust anything the div says. I won't allow it."

Soraya's cheeks went hot at her mother's sharp tone. She knew her veins were mapping out her frustration on her face, and she couldn't believe that her mother could sit and watch the poison spreading through her daughter and not allow her this slim chance to be free of it. Soraya shook her head, aware of the poison running through her veins, seeping from her skin, coating her tongue. "How can you say that to me when you—"

She stopped before she reached the one topic that always remained unspoken between them, but it was too late. Tahmineh's hand stilled in her lap, and her face went ashen, as if she had truly been poisoned.

Soraya had never accused her mother of anything. She had never before said, *This is my life because of you, because of a choice you made.* After all, her mother had been barely more than a child herself when the div cursed her future child. Soraya had never demanded an apology for what had happened, and Tahmineh had never offered one, either. Instead there was the line on her forehead, the weight of words unspoken.

Soraya bowed her head, her anger cooling into guilt. She would have bitten out her tongue if she thought it could undo what she had almost said. Her fingers sought out the loose thread on her sleeve. There was still a part of her that wanted to tell her mother that she couldn't accept her refusal, and that she had to speak to the div. There was a part of her that just wanted to scream.

But instead, she took a breath, like she was preparing to submerge underwater, and said, "I understand."

Soraya woke with a ragged gasp in the middle of the night. She'd had another dream about the Shahmar.

The dreams were different each time, but they always ended the same. The Shahmar would appear to her and raise one gnarled, scaled finger to point at her hands. Soraya would look down and see the veins on her hands turn dark green, but this time she couldn't stop them as they spread over her whole body in a final, irreversible transformation. A terrible pressure built inside of her, like something was about to burst out of her skin, but just when she couldn't bear it anymore, she would wake, the Shahmar's laughter still echoing in her ears.

The first story Soraya had ever heard was her own—the story of the div who had cursed her mother's future child. The first story Soraya had read for herself in a book stolen from the palace library was the story of the Shahmar: the prince who had become so twisted by his crimes that he had transformed into a serpentine div.

Soraya had looked in horror at the illustration of green scales growing along the young man's arms, and then her eyes had shifted to the green lines running down her wrist. She had slammed the book closed, promising herself that if she was very good and kept bad thoughts away, her curse would never warp her mind or transform her body any more than it already had.

There were other divs that may have been more frightening to a child—wrathful Aeshma with his bloody club, or corpse-like Nasu, who spread corruption wherever she went—but the Shahmar was the one she had revisited over and over again, horrified and yet unable to keep away. But soon she didn't need to seek out the Shahmar, because he began to visit her dreams, standing over her and laughing as his past became her future.

Soraya sat up, trying to erase the images from her dream and that feeling of pressure building under her skin. She had never told anyone about her fear of transformation, not even her mother. And maybe that was why Tahmineh couldn't understand Soraya's urgent need to find a way to lift this curse, or why it seemed so pointless to be afraid of a div. Soraya was far more afraid of herself and of what she might become.

In one hasty motion, Soraya rose from the bed and opened the doors to the golestan. The moon was a sliver tonight, but the embers of the fire on the roof still burned, giving the normally vivid and varied colors of her garden the same orange hue. The grass was cold, wet, and prickly against her bare feet as she padded across the garden to the door in the wall. She felt like a sleepwalker, taking one step and then the next as if compelled by something outside herself. She didn't care that it was the middle of the night. She didn't care that she was in her nightdress, her feet bare. All she cared about was the monster waiting for her in the dungeon beneath the palace.

There was no passageway that would take her down into the dungeon—that path had been blocked off before Soraya was born. Instead, she had to walk along the edge of the palace wall, moving down toward the far corner, where she knew she would find a small, unassuming doorway that opened onto a set of stairs leading down.

She was being completely careless, and not just because her hands and feet were bare, or her clothing inappropriate. She had no idea what she would do once she reached the dungeon. There would be guards, wouldn't there? How would she sneak past them?

And yet, she couldn't keep herself away from that shadowed doorway yawning before her. And as she reached it, as she stood at the head of the steps and stared down into the void below, she knew she would find a way—she *had* to find a way. Nothing else mattered to her, nothing else existed, nothing could stop her—

A harsh ringing sound to her right interrupted her thoughts, and she felt the bite of metal along the base of her throat.

"I wouldn't take another step," a familiar voice growled in the darkness.

She was lucky he hadn't killed her on the spot, but upon hearing Ramin's voice, Soraya felt truly cursed. Of all the people to catch her, why did it have to be him?

"It's me, Ramin," she said. The darkness swallowed up her voice, so she said again, louder, "It's Soraya."

Anyone else would have backed down at once—whether because she was the shahzadeh or because of her curse—but Ramin's sword lingered at her throat a breath too long, as if he were battling some inner temptation. Finally, he sheathed the sword, his hands going to rest on his hips. "Soraya. I wasn't expecting you." He took a step closer to her, forcing Soraya to take a step back.

"I was just—I wanted to see—"

Her voice was still too quiet, and so he started to approach her again, leaning in to hear her. She backed away, but he only followed, never letting her stay more than one step away from him. "You're too close," she whispered hoarsely.

He let out a derisive snort. "I'm not afraid of you, Soraya."

Her hands balled into fists at her side. *You should be afraid,* she thought. But Ramin knew from experience that she would rather fold herself into nothing than risk hurting him. As the son of the spahbed, it must have galled him to know that a timid, shrinking girl his younger sister's age was more dangerous and fearsome than he could ever be. And so he had always looked for ways to provoke her, as if in challenge. He would step in too close and gesture too widely near her, or speak to her in the most insulting and condescending tones. And every time, Soraya would tuck her hands away, lower her head, and try to ignore him, like a flower trying to force itself back into a bud.

"Tell me—what *are* you doing wandering around near the dungeon at this hour?" Ramin continued. "Have you spent so much time among the rats in the walls that you've forgotten how to sleep at night?"

Irritation made her blurt out, "We both know what's in that dungeon and why I'm here."

He frowned. "So you do know. Did Sorush tell you?" He paused in thought, and even in the darkness, she saw him bristle. "It was Laleh, wasn't it?" he said, his voice hardening. "You were always following after her. That will be over soon, though. Once Laleh marries Sorush and becomes the shahbanu, she won't have time for you anymore." He crossed his arms and aimed a pointed look at her. "Maybe then you'll learn to leave her alone, for the sake of your family's reputation if not for hers. I always knew you would try to hold her back—that's why I kept her away from you."

Those words nearly knocked the breath out of her as years of loneliness and disappointment came together to form a knot in her stomach. "*You* kept her away?"

"It wasn't difficult. Someone like Laleh doesn't belong hidden away. All I had to do was distract her with new friends at court until she finally forgot about you."

Soraya went still—except for the blood rushing through her veins like liquid fire. She had always found Ramin irritating, but she could ignore and push down irritation until it dissolved. The fire going through her now would not dissolve or fade away. It would eat them both alive.

You should be afraid, she thought again. But this time it was not a hopeless wish, the complaint of a girl who always gave in, but a realization, a truth she finally believed. It was also a threat. If he thought he could hurt her and boast about it to her face, if he wanted to test her limits, then he would have to face the consequences. In a way, she was relieved that all her formless frustration now had a name. A face. Something she could touch.

"But no matter how you found out," Ramin continued, "you're the last person I would allow to see the div, given what you are."

Soraya lifted her head, baring the deadly skin of her throat. "And what am I, Ramin?" She stepped toward him, the space between them so small now that one of them would have to retreat.

But Ramin didn't back away or even flinch, still unwilling to admit that she was more dangerous than he was. Soraya wondered what would happen if she reached up now and let her bare hand hover over his face—would he finally drop his stoic pose and surrender to her?

Her hand started to lift of its own accord, and a thought came unbidden to her mind: *If Ramin dies, Sorush and Laleh would have to delay the wedding.*

As quickly as the thought had come, another soon followed—a memory of Laleh's face, an expression burned into Soraya's mind since childhood. That same year she had first met Laleh, Soraya had convinced herself that the div had lied about her, or that the curse had worn off. She wanted to test her theory, and so one spring morning, she and Laleh had waited by the window until a butterfly landed on the sill, orange wings opening and closing. Soraya had reached out and gently brushed one fingertip along its black-edged wing. It was the first living creature she remembered touching. It was also the first living creature she remembered killing, its wings twitching once, twice, before stopping entirely.

But it wasn't the butterfly she remembered most vividly. It was the look of devastation on Laleh's face, her eyes watering, her lips pressed together as she tried not to cry. And Soraya understood that she had made Laleh sad by wanting something she couldn't have.

Soraya backed away from Ramin, realizing what she had almost done—to him, to Laleh, to herself—and wrapped her arms tightly around her waist, a familiar gesture of surrender. Her hands were shaking—and she couldn't help thinking that they were disappointed, cheated of their prize. But no, she didn't want Ramin dead. She didn't want to kill him or anyone else. She took no pride or satisfaction in her curse—she hated being dangerous, and hated the div that had made her this way. That was the only way she could be sure she was different from the monster in her dreams.

"Soraya?" Ramin moved toward her.

"Leave me alone," Soraya snapped, careful to keep her voice low. *You should be the one cowering away,* she wanted to say. But she couldn't speak in anger now. Anger needed a release. Soraya's arms tightened around her waist, her shoulders hunching over. Anger and shame fought for control within her, and so she forced her body into the position of shame, because it was safer. "Never mind," she said. "I shouldn't have asked."

With her head bowed, she couldn't see his face, but she heard him give an irritated sigh. "You're right about that. Besides, only the shah can decide who is permitted to see the div, so go back to your room and forget all about it."

She ignored the flash of anger at his dismissal and turned away from him, hurrying back to the golestan, to the walls that stopped her from wanting what she could not have.

Soraya rose and dressed on the morning of Nog Roz, the first day of the new year, with a sense of purpose.

On a day like this, Soraya would normally take extra care not to leave her room. Today, the palace opened its gates to everyone, the palace gardens teeming with people from all parts of society—including the shah himself. Though he would spend a portion of the day in the audience hall accepting gifts and offerings, he was also free to celebrate among the crowd.

But all night long, Ramin's parting words kept returning to her: *Only the shah can decide who is permitted to see the div.*

Catching the shah alone was difficult. He was often surrounded by guards, and more often accompanied by either the spahbed or Tahmineh. Even if Soraya tried to use the passageways to reach him, she would probably run into a guard first and have to explain why she was sneaking up on the most powerful and protected person in Atashar. But today was different. Sorush would still be well protected, but he would be out in the open and easier to reach. Plus, he would be in a good mood, and Nog Roz was a day for gift-giving, after all. Perhaps he would be moved to grant Soraya the only gift she had ever asked him for. Her mother had refused her, but Sorush outranked her, and so if he allowed Soraya to see the div, Tahmineh would have to agree.

Dressed in a finely made gown of green and gold brocade that she never had reason to wear, Soraya left her room through the golestan and made her way to the celebration in the garden, which was already full of people. Under the cypresses, children gathered around an old storyteller acting out the stories of brave heroes. She heard snatches of song from musicians and bards, singing both tri-umphant tales of legendary kings and sad ballads of tragic lovers. Directly in front of the palace were the four mud-brick pillars that were raised every year, one for each season. On top of the pillars were sprouting lentil seeds, meant to bring abundance for the year to come. Low tables were set up throughout the garden, holding golden bowls of fruit, candied almonds, and pastries, along with beehive-shaped bundles of pashmak—meant for decoration, but children kept sneaking handfuls of the sugary strands. Hyacinth and rosewater mingled in the air, creating the scent of spring.

Soraya had only ever seen this celebration from above, or heard it from afar. Being in the midst of all this color and light made her believe for once that the year was changing for her, too, the promise of spring's renewal fulfilled at last. She would have liked to have taken some almonds, but there were too many people gath-ered around the tables. Instead, she found a safe place under the magenta-blossomed branches of an arghavan tree where she ob-served the festivities from a distance.

She had thought the crowds would be difficult—and true, she did have to be especially careful of every movement, every step—but now she realized that only in such a vast and varied crowd could she hide without hiding. No one looked at her, no one glanced down at her gloves or asked her who she was, and yet she felt freer and more visible than she ever had before.

She might have forgotten her purpose entirely while standing under the trees, but an hour or so later, she heard a boisterous cheer roaring over the rest of the noise, and Soraya turned to its source. Sorush was passing through the crowd, a group of soldiers raising their goblets to toast him in his wake. He was dressed as one of them, in a red tunic that suited his black hair and bronze complexion, rather than in the more cumbersome robes of a shah. In the days before their father's death, they had celebrated Nog Roz together, along with Laleh. Sorush would steal pastries for them, and he and Laleh would bring them to Soraya's room to share.

Soraya peeled away from the shade of her tree and began to follow Sorush. She had to move slowly through the crowd, careful not to come too close to anyone, so she lost sight of Sorush in the line of cypresses that separated the four quarters of the garden. Still, Soraya kept winding her careful path forward, feeling a little like a serpent, unable to move in a straight line.

Once she'd passed through the cypresses, she caught sight of Sorush again, his red tunic easy to spot from a distance. Where was he going with such drive, such purpose? He barely looked around at anyone, moving through the crowd as though it didn't exist. Following more slowly, Soraya looked beyond him, to see where he was heading. Her eyes traced a clear path to one of the pavilions that offered shade and rest to the celebrants.

She stopped cold when she saw Laleh in the pavilion, waiting for her groom. Beside Laleh was Tahmineh, her forehead smooth now, her gaze fond.

Soraya ducked behind a flowering almond tree near the pavilion and watched Sorush join his bride and his mother. Together, the three of them were unmistakably a family. Laleh wore a brilliant smile, her eyes sparkling. *Someone like Laleh doesn't belong hidden away*, Soraya remembered as she watched Sorush take Laleh's hands, his thumbs softly stroking her knuckles. And Tahmineh beamed over them both, a son and a new daughter she could take pride in. Soraya had never seen her look so untroubled.

Soraya's gloved hands clutched at the bark of the tree. In the space around her mother, her brother, and the only friend she had ever had, she saw her own absence. In their glowing smiles, she saw the truth: that she always would have lost them, because they were meant to know joy. And no matter how much she wanted to deny it, Soraya knew that a part of her would always resent them for that joy, for having even the possibility of it.

Soraya slunk away, like a shadow disappearing when the sun was at its highest. But the crowd had thickened behind her, creating what seemed to her like an impenetrable wall of people. She tried to breathe and slow her quickening heartbeat as she sought a path through the crowd. But after only a few steps, something collided with her legs, and she jerked away in response, looking down at a little girl who had crossed her path. With visions of butterflies fluttering behind her eyelids, Soraya went cold with fear, almost waiting to see the girl fall dead on the spot. But the girl had only touched the fabric of Soraya's dress, and she skipped away without even paying Soraya notice.

Still, Soraya couldn't slow her pulse, and as she tried to keep making her way through the crowd, she was light-headed from the mixture of panic and relief. She kept her head down, knowing from the familiar heat in her cheeks that her veins were visible on her face, but as a result, she kept accidentally brushing against more people. Each time it happened, her heart would give another involuntary lurch, until her body felt exhausted and overwhelmed from the constant bursts of fear.

She was curling in on herself now, her shoulders hunching protectively, her head hanging forward, her arms going around her waist. She didn't even think she was moving anymore, but it was hard to tell when she was so disoriented. Her veins felt like they were straining against her skin. *Don't faint,* she told her swimming head, her pounding heart. If she fainted, then someone might touch her face or remove her gloves to find her pulse. *Don't faint, don't faint.*

A firm arm came around her shoulders. A hand clamped around her upper arm. Someone was trying to help her. "No," Soraya said weakly. "No, don't—" She lifted her head enough to see who had innocently come to her rescue without knowing that she was more dangerous than in danger. And through the curtain of hair spilling over her face, she saw a familiar young man dressed in red.

"Azad," she breathed.

He blinked at her. "You know me," he said, a note of surprised pleasure in his voice.

"You shouldn't come near me." She tried to draw away from him. "You don't understand—"

But Azad didn't let go. "Don't worry," he said. "I know you, too, shahzadeh banu."

Soraya froze under the weight of the young man's arm, repeating his words to herself. He knew her, he said. But what did he know? He had addressed her by her title, and so he clearly knew she was the princess. But did he know why she was wearing gloves on this warm spring day? Did he know why she was trying to hide her face? Did he know that only a layer of fabric separated him from death?

"You don't look well," Azad said. "How can I help you?"

Soraya pushed her questions aside. She was still in the middle of the garden, in the middle of a crowd, her head lightly spinning. "I need to get back to the palace," she said, her voice hoarse. Once she was inside, she could escape back into the passageways, their cool darkness never so appealing as now.

"I'll take you," Azad said. True to his word, he proceeded to lead her through the crowd, his arm around her shoulder both holding her up and shielding her from stray touches. Soraya's heart slowed, and her head settled. She felt weightless, all responsibility removed from her, like she was simply a passenger in her body.

But as they neared the palace steps, Soraya found something else to worry about—Ramin was standing in the shade of the wide ayvan that marked the palace entrance. If they went in now, he would be sure to notice her, and she wasn't ready to face him again so soon after last night's encounter.

Soraya halted suddenly, and Azad's brow furrowed with concern. "Not this way," she said to him. She veered to the right, and he followed her lead toward the trees of the orchard around the side of the palace. As soon as they were beyond the main garden's borders, the crowd began to diminish considerably, until they were finally alone. Even so, Soraya didn't move away from under Azad's arm. His nearness was no longer just a shield now, but a kind of luxury, a sip of heady wine that she would probably never taste again. Was it so wrong to linger?

It's wrong when he doesn't know what you are, or the danger he's in, a voice in her mind answered. He said he knew her, but he couldn't possibly know the whole truth, not when he had put his arm around her so comfortably.

Soraya halted somewhat abruptly under the shade of a pomegranate tree, causing Azad's arm to slip away. "Thank you," she said, "but I can go the rest of the way on my own."

"Of course, shahzadeh banu," he said with a small bow of his head. "You honored me by letting me assist you. Please tell me if I may help in any other way." He lifted his head from its bow, his dark eyes looking to her in expectation and . . . was it hope?

She opened her mouth to tell him that she didn't need any further help, but what slipped out instead was, "How do you know who I am?"

He looked down with an embarrassed laugh, and she tried not to notice the graceful slope of his neck, the pronounced dimples in his cheeks. *This is foolish,* she told herself. She should have dismissed him immediately.

"I knew who you were when I saw you on the roof a few days ago," Azad said. "You were exactly as I had pictured you." He was staring at her now as boldly as he had done when he had spotted her on the roof, and the longer he looked, the more real she felt, like she was taking shape under his gaze.

"What do you mean?" she asked.

He spoke softly, his tone almost reverent. "My father was once a merchant. He traveled all throughout Atashar and beyond, and when he returned, he would bring me stories from wherever he'd been. When I was no more than ten years old, he told me the mystery of the shahzadeh. No one outside the walls of Golvahar had ever seen her or heard her voice, he said. She was a secret, hidden away in the palace like a carefully guarded treasure."

Soraya couldn't help lifting an eyebrow at that. She wanted to remark that she was no treasure, but the way Azad was looking at her—that gentle, dreamy look, like he wasn't quite sure she was real—held her back.

"I was captivated," he continued. "I would stay up long into the night, wondering what you looked like and why you were kept hidden, imagining that I would ride up to the palace in a majestic horse to free you. I used to think that we'd . . ." He looked away, his cheeks coloring slightly. When he faced her again, his eyes gleamed with something that Soraya couldn't recognize. "Do you see now why I recognized you? You're my favorite story. I feel like I've known you for a long time."

Soraya drew in a breath, unable to speak. For the first time, she saw herself as Azad had imagined her—the heroine of a story, not the monster. It was only an illusion, of course, born from a young boy's uninformed romantic dreams, but for the space of a breath, she let herself enjoy it.

She didn't want to tell him the truth. She wanted his version of her to keep existing, if only in his mind. And so she knew what she had to do.

"Well, you did come to my rescue today, so now that you've lived out your dreams, I'll be on my way."

His face fell at once, a wrinkle of dismay forming at the center of his forehead. "Is there anything I can say to persuade you to stay and talk with me for a little longer?"

Soraya smiled sadly and shook her head. "Trust me. It's better that we—"

But before she finished speaking, a loud voice startled them both: "I thought I saw you in the crowd."

She and Azad both turned at once to see the approaching figure of Ramin. She took a hasty step away from Azad, but that only made her look guiltier.

"It's reckless of you to be out on such a crowded day." He looked at her with a significant arch of his eyebrow. "You've even made a new friend. Are you sure that's wise?"

All of Soraya's muscles tightened at once. He wouldn't dare tell Azad about her curse—to do so was to risk angering the royal family. Soraya was torn between the competing urges to shrink away, or step forward and show him she was unafraid. But her guilt from almost losing control the night before still lingered, and so Soraya simply said, "That's none of your concern, Ramin."

But Ramin wasn't even looking at her anymore—he was focused on Azad, who was standing stiffly, not moving or speaking. Ramin moved closer, coming to stand directly in front of him. Only then did Azad take a breath, his shoulders drawing back so that he was standing at his full height. There was a strange energy surrounding Azad, like clouds gathering before a storm, or the stillness of a snake about to strike. She couldn't take her eyes off him.

"You're that villager we brought back," Ramin said. He lifted his chin, his arms crossed, and nodded at Azad in approval. "You proved yourself to us all that day, so let me give you some advice, from one soldier to another: stay away from this one."

Azad tilted his head slightly, his long neck moving with slow, deliberate grace. "I don't think I need your advice," he said.

"Ramin, this isn't necessary," Soraya interrupted, trying to keep her voice calm.

Ramin looked directly at Soraya, disdain curling his lip, and said, "I don't need to hear from you, Soraya. You're not part of this conversation."

There was a sudden cracking sound—the snake had struck at last. Soraya barely even saw Azad's fist move, but it must have, because now Ramin was sprawled on the grass, rubbing his jaw.

And for the first time since Ramin had approached them, Azad looked away from him and turned to Soraya. "I'm sorry," he said at once, but his eyes were still burning with anger, his hand still closed into a fist.

Soraya felt that strange energy wrap around her now, the two of them practically trembling with it. And she realized that her hand was also a fist, like she had struck Ramin herself, like Azad had become an extension of her. He was the arm of her anger, lashing out when she could not. He was the force of her rage, unbound.

She looked Azad in the eye and shook her head. "Don't be," she said, with a firmness that surprised her.

Ramin pushed himself up from the ground, a dark bruise already starting to appear on his jaw. "That was a mistake," he said to Azad. Ramin started to charge toward him, but Soraya threw herself in between them, forcing Ramin to come to a sudden stop directly in front of her.

And now Soraya was the snake, her venom far deadlier than Azad's, and she wanted nothing more than to strike. She took a step toward Ramin, gratified when he took a hurried step back, a flash of fear in his eyes.

But the flash quickly transformed into a triumphant glint, and

Soraya knew what was about to happen even as she knew she couldn't stop it.

"Don't think me a coward," he said to Azad over Soraya's shoulder. "I would fight you right here, but you have an unfair advantage. This girl is poisonous—cursed by a div. If you ever touch her, you'll die."

All the blood drained out of her as Ramin spoke, and she felt like she was made of ice, cold enough to burn. Soraya was glad her back was to Azad, in case her veins were visible. Something familiar was bubbling inside her—the same cruel urge that had made her want to hurt Ramin the night before. And as she had done last night, she swallowed the urge down and tried not to choke.

Ramin smirked at her in satisfaction and walked away. *Laleh wasn't enough for him*, Soraya thought. *He won't be content until I'm completely alone.*

Even when Ramin was gone, Soraya couldn't face Azad. "It's true," she called back to him, the words scraping her throat. "That's the secret you've always wanted to know. The mysterious shahzadeh was cursed by a div when she was just an infant, and that's why she must be hidden away. If you touch me, you'll die."

She turned to him, knowing from the feel of blood rushing through her that her veins were etched dark green in her face. Azad was watching her, his face solemn, his eyes sad.

"Well," she said, holding her gloved hands out to him, "am I still your favorite story?"

5

In a way, Soraya was relieved that Ramin had told Azad her secret. She had liked Azad's version of her too much—it would have been hard to walk away from it. Let Azad be the one to walk away, then, and let him do it now, before she grew too attached.

But even as her half-taunting question still hung in the air, Azad didn't back away. He came closer to her, so close that she saw the stubble along his jaw. He tilted his head, brown curls falling over his forehead. "You're better than any story, shahzadeh banu . . . *Soraya*," he murmured. She barely heard him, but she watched his lips form her name. He gave a slight, disbelieving shake of his head, as if surprised by the depth of his emotion. "In my mind, you were only a shadow. But now, I can see you and know you for what you are, beautiful yet deadly. I can speak to you. I can touch you." Slowly, tentatively, he reached up to draw her hair away from her face, revealing more of the veins spreading out along her neck like vines. *Beautiful yet deadly,* he had called her. Somehow, he made one sound as sweet as the other.

But as intoxicated as she was by his words and his nearness, Soraya remembered herself and drew back from him, her hair spilling out of his hand. "Now you understand why you should keep away from me," she said, but she wasn't remotely convincing to herself, let alone to him.

She needed to put distance between them, so she turned and cut a path through the rest of the orchard, not looking behind to see if he would follow.

She hoped so much that he would follow.

"I'm not afraid to be near you," he called. "I'm only afraid that you don't want me to be." From behind, she heard his hurried footsteps catching up to her.

"It doesn't matter what I want," she said without stopping. "This is the last time you'll ever see me. I'm kept hidden away, remember? I shouldn't even have left my room today." She didn't voice her other thought, the one that was accompanied by what she had seen in the pavilion: *You'll leave me behind in the end, for one reason or another.*

The orchard curved around to the side of the palace, and so when she emerged from its trees, she saw the walls of the golestan up ahead. She would keep walking until she was safely inside those walls, and she wouldn't stop for anything or anyone.

"Then why did you?" he said. His voice was directly behind her now. He could have easily overtaken her, but he still remained a step behind, and Soraya couldn't help believing that it was out of respect, not fear.

"That's none of your con—" Her own thoughts interrupted her, and she halted abruptly. From behind, she heard Azad inhale sharply. When she spun to face him, he was too close to her, and so both of them took a hasty step backward. She looked him up and down, taking in the red soldier's uniform, remembering what

Laleh had told her about how he had earned it. *That's none of your concern*, she had begun to say, except that it was, in a way—he was the reason there was a div in the dungeon at all, and so he was the reason she had left her room today.

"Do you have access to the palace dungeon?" she asked him.

Her unexpected question made him frown. "I don't know. The rules of the azatan are still new to me."

Soraya tugged at her gloves as she thought. Even if he could access the dungeon, he might not be able to see the div. And even if he did—even if she sent him on her behalf—she would still feel cheated that she could not speak to the div herself. She shook her head. "No, it won't work," she murmured to herself.

She began to turn away from him again. "Are you thinking about the div?" he said. And now it was her turn to be surprised. When she looked at him again, she noticed a sly gleam in his eyes, as if he had known all along what she had wanted. "Do you think the div knows how to lift your curse?"

"I don't know, but I can't be at peace until I ask. I've already tried to enter the dungeon, but Ramin wouldn't let me pass. And I can't use the passageways."

"Passageways?"

It had been so long since she had spoken to anyone new that she had said it without thinking. "There are secret passages all throughout Golvahar. I use them to move through the palace without encountering anyone." She felt strangely embarrassed to explain herself—she didn't want him to think of her scurrying inside the walls like she was some kind of rodent. *Have you spent so much time among the rats in the walls that you've forgotten how to sleep at night?* "But the passage to the dungeon is blocked off," she continued.

He looked up at the palace, eyes narrowing in contemplation. "How is it blocked off?"

"A locked door," she said.

"Maybe we can break it down."

When he looked at her again, she felt a conspiratorial thrill pass between them. Her eyes swept down his arms, remembering the force of the blow he had landed on Ramin.

Soraya still hesitated, though. She had never brought anyone with her into the passageways. Even with torchlight, they were dark and narrow—close contact would be difficult to avoid. If her mother knew what they were planning, she would certainly disapprove. But then, she didn't want Soraya to speak to the div at all, and Soraya already knew that would be an impossible command to obey.

Music and cheerful voices carried from the garden in the front of the palace, filling the heavy silence between them. Soraya thought again of seeing her mother with Sorush and Laleh, of their uncomplicated happiness. *Don't I deserve to be happy too?* Didn't she deserve to take whatever chance of happiness was offered to her?

"Follow me," she said to Azad, and she didn't need to look behind her to know that he would obey.

She led him down a hedged walkway toward the front end of the palace—away from the dungeon. A large set of stairs jutted out from the palace wall, their sides carved and painted in bright colors depicting a line of feathers pointing upward, a testament to the simorgh's gift. Soraya bypassed the stairs themselves and walked to the green feather that was closest to the wall. The paint was dark enough that you wouldn't see the thin groove that went all the way down the feather, but Soraya knew it was there, and so she dug her fingers into that nearly invisible space and pulled to the right. The panel in the rock slid open, and she slipped inside, gesturing for Azad to follow.

It was strange to hear someone else breathing in these narrow tunnels, and to know she wasn't alone. She'd grown so used to these passages that she didn't need light to know where she was going, and so she hadn't realized how dark they were until she slid the panel shut again. In the thin beam of light that seeped in through the wall, Soraya examined her gloves to make sure there were no holes or tears before she tentatively held her hand out to Azad. She had planned to tell him he didn't have to take it if he didn't want to, but before she could even speak, he had taken hold of her hand.

She led him through the passageways, past stairways and doors that would open into different rooms in the palace, turning corners by instinct. When they reached the set of stairs that would take them down beneath Golvahar, she remembered to warn him to watch his step. Once they had descended, she let go of Azad's hand to find an unlit torch in its sconce, along with a piece of flint that she knew would be in a crack in the wall. She hadn't needed the torches in a long time, but she was grateful for them now as the fire illuminated their surroundings.

They were in a rounded chamber at the hidden heart of Golvahar, with three pathways leading onward—one straight ahead, one to the left, and one to the right, which was blocked by a door. Azad stood in the center of the chamber and looked around at the stone walls that encased them. Soraya flattened herself against the wall and tried not to look at the arch of his neck, the flicker of light and shadow caressing his throat.

"These tunnels run all through the palace?"

Her head snapped up to meet his waiting gaze. "Everywhere except for the newer wing on the other side. I've read that there used to be tunnels underneath the entire city, too—a way to smuggle in supplies in case of siege during the early Hellean wars—but they haven't been used in so long that I'm not sure they still exist."

"Who built the passageways in the palace?"

"No one knows for certain. The common theory is that a paranoid shah wanted to ensure he always had an escape route."

The corner of his mouth lifted. "Paranoid or clever?"

"Perhaps a little of both. But either way, I suppose I owe him my thanks. I would be confined to my room otherwise."

Azad gestured to the door. "Is that the way to the dungeon?"

Soraya nodded. "I asked my mother once why that door was locked, and she told me it was probably so no prisoners could escape."

Azad went to examine the locked door. After an experimental try at the handle, he backed away and threw his shoulder against the door. The wood didn't even budge, and so he tried again, and again, but ended up unsuccessful and breathless—*and probably bruised*, Soraya thought. It had been foolish to think they could break through a door that was meant to deter prisoners.

But Azad was still standing in front of the door, head tilting to one side. "I wonder . . ." he murmured.

He fell silent until finally, Soraya couldn't help asking, "What are you thinking?"

"If I were a paranoid yet clever shah with a network of secret tunnels at my disposal," he said, "I wouldn't keep a secret dungeon key on my person, where it could be stolen. I would hide it somewhere no one would think to look for it, but where I could easily find it."

"You think the key might be somewhere here?"

Azad shrugged. "That doesn't help us much. It could be buried or inside the walls. It would take anyone ages to find it, if it's even here at all."

But Soraya stopped listening when he said "inside the walls," because at hearing those words, an image flashed in her mind. Azad was right—it would take anyone ages to find the hidden key. But Soraya had grown up in these tunnels. She knew all their secrets, all their hidden grooves and notches, which meant that if there were any mysteries here, she would remember them.

Without saying a word to Azad, she went back toward the opening of the chamber and knelt on the ground. The colder months had always been difficult for her. Her golestan would wither away, and she would grow bored of her books, and so she had little else to do but explore the passages that belonged to her. When she was a child, she had noticed that one of the bricks here had an *X* carved into it. It would have been easily missed by anyone else, but at that age, the brick had been at her eye level. Now, on her knees, she found it again, running her fingers over the carved lines. A mystery she had never solved—until today.

The brick gave way under her hands, and she pulled it out. Inside the gap was a small silver key.

When she brought it back to Azad, he looked at her with something between awe and admiration. "How did you know it was there?"

She didn't answer, but only smiled and fit the key into the lock. Let him still have some sense of wonder about the mysterious shahzadeh.

Azad carried the torch behind her as Soraya led the way into the unfamiliar passage. There were no stairs or side passages here, which she hoped meant that this tunnel would lead them straight to the dungeon. She noticed, too, that the ground was inclined downward, taking them lower and lower beneath Golvahar.

Finally, they reached what appeared to be a dead end, but Soraya quickly found the edge of the stone slab in front of her and tried to push it to the side. It only budged a little, after years of disuse, and so Azad placed the torch in an empty sconce on the wall and came to help her. Soraya's breath caught in her throat as his arms reached around her, his hands on either side of hers against the stone. The slab moved more easily now, but Soraya was too worried about his proximity to her to feel any kind of excitement.

"That's enough," she whispered, her voice a rasp, when they had created a gap large enough for them both to pass through. She waited until he had moved away from her before she let herself breathe freely again.

"Let me go first," he whispered back to her, and she agreed, not for her own safety, but in case any passing guard collided with her as she emerged from the wall.

With fluid grace, Azad passed through the wall, and a few

moments later, he reached his hand through the gap for her. She took it and stepped out into a dimly lit corridor that smelled of sweat and stale air and something else that Soraya couldn't quite detect.

After replacing the stone slab in the wall behind them, Azad gestured to the left and said, "This way."

Soraya looked from right to left, both paths indistinguishable to her. "How do you know?"

"The ground."

Soraya looked down and saw that the ground continued to incline downward to their left, upward to their right. She nodded and they continued down the corridor.

The strange smell grew stronger as they walked, until Soraya finally recognized it. "Esfand," she murmured to Azad. The pungent smoke of burning wild rue seeds weakened divs, sapping their unnatural strength and making them lethargic. In a confined space like a dungeon cell, the smoke would be strong enough to manage a div in captivity. "If we follow the smell, we'll find the div."

The smell of the esfand acted as a beacon, and Soraya was thankful for it, because as they moved deeper into the dungeon, it became a labyrinth, full of twists and turns and dark hallways lined with doors that Soraya tried not to wonder about.

When the smell grew even stronger, and wisps of smoke became visible in the dim torchlight, Soraya knew they were close. "There," Azad said, pointing ahead to a set of stairs heading downward. The smoke was clearly coming from below.

They had to duck their heads in the narrow stairway, and as they neared the bottom, Soraya saw the glow of a torch. Accessing the dungeon had been her main concern, but now that she was here, Soraya remembered that there was a monster in that cell, and she was heading straight toward it.

The stairs opened into a chamber hewn out of the rock. Halfway into the chamber, iron bars stretched from the top of the curved roof to the ground, creating a cave-like dungeon cell. Hanging from a hook in the wall near the stairs was a brazier, where the thick scented smoke was emanating from, as well as a torch. The torch created a circle of light, but half of the cell was still in shadow, and from those shadows, Soraya felt something watching them.

Soraya took a breath of stale air before stepping forward. What would she find inside that cell? According to the priests, divs were pieces of the Destroyer sent out into the world, given monstrous form by the Creator so that people could recognize evil when they saw it. Soraya had seen illustrations of divs in the library, but they all took different shapes. Some were enormous, with horns and fangs and sharp claws; some were scaled and reptilian with skin like armor; some were deathly pale, while others had mottled fur.

Soraya peered into the cell, adjusting to the dim light until she saw the amber glow of the div's eyes. She watched as the figure slowly stood and stepped forward into the light. She braced herself for the monster's hideous appearance, and then she saw it—

It was a girl.

6

At first sight of the young woman, Soraya thought they had made a mistake, and this wasn't the div's cell at all. But then the young woman walked all the way up to the bars, her long black hair falling away from her face, and Soraya knew there was no mistake.

The div's skin had an odd pallor, with gray and brown patterns on her face like permanent shadows, and the amber glow of her eyes was unnaturally bright. At certain angles, they had a luminous sheen to them, like the eyes of nocturnal animals. Those eyes watched them now with a fierce stare that reminded Soraya of a hawk.

And now that Soraya was here, seeing a div for the first time, she didn't know what to say. "I'm—"

But she barely managed to make a sound before the div held up a hand, her fingers slightly longer than a human's. In a voice like nectar, a voice the color of her eyes, she said, "No need for introductions, shahzadeh. I know who you are and why you're here. But I won't speak to you unless you come to me alone. No guards . . . and no soldiers." At that last word, her eyes flitted to Azad, behind Soraya's shoulder. The div's eyes narrowed slightly at the sight of him, and Soraya remembered that he was the one who had stopped her from killing Sorush and allowed her to be captured.

Soraya turned to Azad, who was glowering back at the div. She brushed her gloved fingers against his arm, and he looked at her, his face softening. "Please," she said.

He hesitated briefly, then gave a curt nod. "I'll wait at the top of the stairs and keep watch. If you need anything, shout for me." He threw one last warning glare at the div, who waved good-bye to him with a smug grin, and retreated up the stairs.

Soraya waited until he was gone, and then, before she could change her mind, she slipped off her gloves and tucked them into her sash. If the div did know why she was here, she would understand the implied threat of that gesture.

The div's eyes darted from Soraya's bare hands up to her face, and she smiled, a flash of sharp white teeth. Her fingers curled slowly around the bars. "Isn't it better now that it's just the two of us? More personal. Now come, Soraya, and ask me your question."

The sound of her name on the div's tongue startled Soraya. The div hadn't been lying when she said she knew her. It bothered Soraya, though, that they should be on such unequal terms from the start, and so instead of asking the question the div expected, Soraya said, "Tell me your name."

Surprise flitted over the div's face, but then she answered, "Parvaneh."

Soraya flinched, as if that one word were an accusation rather than a simple answer to her request. *Parvaneh*—the word for moth or butterfly. Soraya held Parvaneh's gaze, almost certain that the div truly knew everything about her—every short, fluttering life that Soraya had stolen with a touch of her finger. The feel of air on the bare skin of her hands reminded her of death.

"How do you know who I am?" Soraya said, her voice wavering only slightly.

The div tilted her head, and the shadows shifted over her face, like something was moving under her skin. "All pariks know you, Soraya," she almost purred. "The human as dangerous as a div."

"What's a parik?" Soraya asked, ignoring that last remark.

"There are different kinds of divs," Parvaneh answered, "based on different aspects of the Destroyer. The drujes, the kastars, and the pariks, all with different skills and talents. Pariks look the most human, so it's easier for us to hide among you and work as spies."

At any other time, Soraya would have been interested to know more about the inner workings of the divs, but she didn't know how much longer Parvaneh would humor her questions. "If you know about my curse, then you must know how to end it."

Parvaneh shook her head slowly, disappointment on her face. "Why would you want that? You could wield such power."

Soraya laughed harshly. "You think I have power?" She stepped closer to the bars, and she felt the poison bubbling inside of her. Maybe it was because this dungeon, so far underground, felt a world apart from her well-ordered life above, or maybe it was because she was speaking to someone as deadly as she was, but for once, Soraya let her true feelings spill out.

"You think I'm here," she said, "in a dungeon, asking you to rid me of this curse because I'm afraid of power?" Another step. "My family hides me away out of shame. I spend most of my days in total isolation. If that's power, then I don't want it." She was standing only inches away from the bars now, close enough for the div to touch—and then a flicker of doubt made her almost back away again. Because part of her knew that the only reason she was standing so close, without fear, was her curse. The div was right— she did wield a kind of power. The power to make people afraid.

Hadn't she relished seeing that fear in Ramin's eyes today? Hadn't she briefly enjoyed it before shame coated her skin like cold sweat?

It was the shame she had to cling to, not the power. It was the shame that made her still feel human. She was a human as dangerous as a div, but unlike a div, she refused to enjoy being deadly or to revel in her monstrosity. That was the only thing that kept her on one side of the bars, while Parvaneh languished on the other.

She looked Parvaneh in the eye and said, "Now tell me: How do I remove this curse?"

Parvaneh studied her, not backing away from the bars. Her eyes began to move down Soraya's face to her throat, and Soraya knew that Parvaneh was watching the pattern of her veins as they changed color. And then, much to Soraya's surprise, Parvaneh reached a hand through the bars, her fingertips hovering a breath above the veins on Soraya's cheek and tracing them down Soraya's throat, all without ever touching her. "Such a shame. Such a *waste*," she said, biting off that last word as her hand dropped away.

Soraya's breath had grown shallow when Parvaneh reached her hand out, so close to touching her, and only now did it come rushing out of her. "Were you the one who cursed me?"

Parvaneh shook her head. "I had nothing to do with it."

"But you know who did? Did the pariks do this?"

Parvaneh's eyes gleamed with mischief and something else, something sharp. "They did and they did not. Isn't that the way all your stories start? I wonder what stories *you've* been told, Soraya. How did your curse happen? Tell me the truth, and I'll do the same—that sounds fair, doesn't it?"

Soraya hesitated, looking for the possible dangers in giving Parvaneh what she wanted. She felt like she was standing on the edge of a great cliff, and a div was telling her to jump—what kind of fool would she be if she listened?

A desperate one, Soraya thought. She began telling the story her mother had told her, of the div who had found her in the forestland south of Mount Arzur. She told it the same way Tahmineh always had—like it was just a legend, something that had happened to someone else, a long time ago. No names, no accusations. As a child, she had accepted the story without examining it too closely. She would demand it every time she saw her mother, always hoping for a different ending. But as she grew older, less able to distance herself from the words, she found the story too difficult to hear. It was even harder to finish the story now, but Soraya continued to the end, not letting herself look away from those staring eyes.

"Well?" she said when she was finished, her voice a little too loud. "That's all. Now tell me what you know."

"I promised you one truth for another," Parvaneh said. "What you just gave me was a story, not the truth."

"It's what my mother told me."

"Your mother lied."

Soraya shook her head at once, not even able to entertain the idea. Her mother wasn't a liar. Soraya's *life* wasn't a lie. And yet she couldn't help remembering how adamant Tahmineh had been when she'd refused Soraya's request to see the div. Was it possible that she feared what the div would reveal? Or was Parvaneh trying to throw Soraya's life into chaos with a simple suggestion? *Divs can be manipulative. They can destroy you with a single word.*

Soraya backed away from the bars. "You're toying with me. You would have said that no matter what I told you."

Parvaneh put a hand to her chest in mock offense. "You don't believe me? Let me ask you this, then: Why did the curse not manifest until a few days after your birth?"

Soraya sighed in frustration. "I don't know. So my mother wouldn't die from labor, so she would live knowing that she could never hold her daughter."

"And why the firstborn *daughter*? Why not simply the firstborn child?"

"Because divs are mysterious and unjust," Soraya snapped, but the question struck deep. It was under the surface of her thoughts every time she saw Sorush.

"And why would a div curse a child to be poisonous even to divs?" Parvaneh continued. "Why create a weapon that can be used against you?"

This time, Soraya had no answer, and Parvaneh wore a condescending smile that made Soraya's face burn. "And besides," Parvaneh said, "a curse like yours requires a more complicated process than simply saying a few words to scare a child."

Soraya resisted the urge to pick at the loose thread of her sleeve. "You're trying to confuse me."

"I'm trying to help you. You've been lied to, but not by me."

"I don't care!" Soraya shouted, her voice growing louder. She had spent so many years controlling her emotions, forcing them to submit to her will, and yet now she felt them all on the surface of her skin because of one smirking demon. She took a breath and reminded herself of the Shahmar, of those scales growing over his skin, and tried to calm herself. "I don't care how I was cursed. Just tell me how to get rid of it," she said more quietly.

Parvaneh's eyebrow arched. "If you don't believe me about something as simple as this, why would you believe me when I tell you how to lift your curse?"

Silence hung heavy between them, until Soraya trusted herself to say in a steady voice, "Then you *do* know."

Parvaneh opened her mouth to answer, but then she paused and tilted her head, listening to something. "Don't you hear footsteps, Soraya?"

She did, now that Parvaneh had mentioned it, along with the sound of arguing voices. Soraya whirled around to the stairs behind her in time to see the first guard emerging into the cavern. Two others followed, each holding one of Azad's arms as they dragged him down the stairs with them.

"Don't move," the first guard barked at Soraya, his sword already raised.

For one careless moment, Soraya thought to herself, *I could take them all.* From behind her, she heard Parvaneh snickering, as though she had heard Soraya's murderous thought. *Calm,* she reminded herself. It was dark enough that the guards might not be able to see her veins, but she couldn't take that chance.

"How did you get here without anyone stopping you?" the guard asked her.

Soraya's eyes flitted to Azad, and he gave a small shake of his head. He hadn't told them about the hidden passage, and neither would she. "I have a right to go anywhere I wish," Soraya said, trying to sound imperious.

The guard raised an eyebrow, his sword still pointed at her. "Is that so? And what gives you that right?"

With a quick glance at her hands to make sure her veins had faded, she lifted her hand, palm facing inward, so that the seal ring on her finger would show clearly. "My brother, the shah."

The guard inhaled sharply, and he came closer to peer at the ring, which bore the seal of the simorgh on it.

"Now please unhand my . . . my escort," she said, "and let us continue our business."

The guard frowned, probably unsure whether to believe that this strange girl in the dungeon was who she claimed to be. Still, his sword lowered slightly, and his tone was carefully respectful as he said, "Only a few people are permitted to see the div, and the shahzadeh is not one of them. I cannot let you stay."

Her whole body tensed in frustration, but she willed herself to be calm once more. If she argued with him, she would become agitated, and her secrets would show on her face. "Then see us outside, and we'll be on our way."

The guard shook his head. "I can't allow that, either. I'll need to take you somewhere until your identity can be confirmed. If you are indeed the shahzadeh, I'm sure you will understand."

Soraya's first instinct was to argue again, but then she stopped herself. Seeing Sorush had been her original purpose today, hadn't it? "I understand," she said. "Tell the shah I want to see him."

The head guard gestured to the other guards, and they ushered Azad back up the stairs. He threw a glance at Soraya behind his shoulder, and she nodded at him in reassurance.

"Please come with me, banu," the first guard said to her.

Soraya hastily put on her gloves, and from behind her, Parvaneh said, "Another time, then, Soraya."

"Do you really know?" she muttered to Parvaneh as the guard came toward her. She let him lead her away without resistance, too afraid that he might come in contact with her skin if she didn't comply.

But at the foot of the stairs, she turned back one more time. "Were you telling me the truth?" she called to Parvaneh.

And before she retreated back into the darkness of her cell, Parvaneh responded:

"Go ask your mother if I lied to you, and then come back and tell me her answer. I'll be waiting."

Soraya had only been in the throne room once or twice before, and so she had forgotten how grand it was. The massive domed ceiling was enough to impress, and then there were the carved stone reliefs on the wall, images of victorious kings in battle, and the painted tiles on the floor that formed the shape of the simorgh.

At the end of the room was a magnificent golden throne atop the dais, with the image of a great flame—the Royal Fire, which burned always in Golvahar's fire temple—painted in vivid reds and oranges on the wall behind the throne. One of the handful of times Soraya had seen her father before his death, he had been sitting on that throne, as distant and regal as ever, an intricate, heavy crown perched on his head. Soraya had been spying from behind the walls, opening the secret panel a crack to see the ceremony when her brother was officially named heir, and she wondered how her brother would ever be strong enough to wear that crown on his head.

But then she noticed something that was visible only from her close vantage point at the side of the dais. Hanging from the ceiling above the throne was a thin silver chain attached to the crown, holding it above the shah's head so that he only appeared to be bearing its weight. Soraya had told Sorush about it later, and he had laughed in relief.

He wasn't laughing now.

She'd tried to imagine what had been happening while she'd been waiting in an adjoining chamber. The dungeon guard had told one of the palace guards that a young woman claiming to be the shahzadeh wanted to speak to her brother. From there, the news must have gone up the chain of command, until one of the shah's personal attendants had found him in the garden and told him his sister had been caught talking to the div in the dungeon.

And Soraya might have felt sorry for causing him all this trouble on his one day of merriment away from royal duty, except that she was too irritated with him for bringing their mother, who was standing beside the throne with a severe expression on her face.

Soraya came forward, went down on her knees, and pressed her forehead against the cool tile, as was appropriate when addressing the shah.

"You may leave us," Soraya heard him say, and she thought he was talking to her until she felt the reverberation of the guards' boots against the floor as they all left the chamber.

Even when they were gone, she kept her head down until she heard her brother say in a weary tone, "Soraya, please stand."

She rose, and unsure how much formality he expected from her, she said, "I'm sorry if I've done something against your wishes, shahryar. I meant you no disrespect." She wasn't sure if it was the throne itself or the crown overhead that made the shah seem like he was an eternal fixture of the palace itself instead of her flesh-and-blood brother. Even in her mind, it seemed more appropriate to think of him as the shah than Sorush.

"There's no need to call me that," Sorush said, referring to his royal title. "I know you meant no harm. I only wished you had asked me first—"

"She asked *me*," Tahmineh said sharply. "And I forbade it. I'm surprised you would do something so dangerous, Soraya. I always thought you were more careful than that."

Soraya bit the inside of her cheek, her eyes stinging. For anyone else, that might have been a mild reprimand, but for Soraya, being careful was a matter of life and death.

"What did the div tell you?" her mother asked.

Go ask your mother if I lied to you.

Soraya studied her mother's expression, looking for some hint of fear or guilt, but her perfect mask never fell. Still, Soraya couldn't bring herself to tell them what Parvaneh had told her. For one thing, to accuse her mother of lying to her would be unforgivably disrespectful. But also, even if Parvaneh were lying, it was exactly the kind of manipulation her mother had warned her about, and she would be even more insistent that Soraya never speak to the div again.

"I asked her if she knew of a way to lift my curse. She told me nothing useful," Soraya answered, which she hoped was true enough not to count as a lie. "But I think it's possible that might change with time."

"You mean you wish to return?" Sorush said, a note of interest in his voice.

"Yes," Soraya said, "with your permission, of course."

"Absolutely not," Tahmineh said at once, turning to her son for confirmation. "It's too dangerous."

Both Soraya and her mother watched Sorush, waiting for him

to make his decision. Soraya could imagine her mother's frustration at knowing that her son could go against her wishes if he chose—and she, too, felt a prickle of annoyance at waiting for her twin brother's blessing to do anything.

But during her brother's thoughtful silence, Soraya noticed something other than frustration on her mother's face. It happened so briefly: The stony look on Tahmineh's face flickered, revealing something closer to fear or despair. It was like looking at a fine tapestry, its uniformity presenting a single image, and then, between one blink and the next, seeing every thread that held it together, ready to unravel at the slightest touch. For an instant, Soraya saw the fragility of the threads holding her mother together, and that was how she knew that Parvaneh was telling the truth.

Soraya's mother was keeping something from her. And whatever the truth was, she was terrified for Soraya to discover it.

"I agree with our mother's judgment," Sorush finally said. "I must ask that you not enter the dungeon or speak to the div again."

Soraya didn't trust herself to speak. Her mother said, "It's the right choice, Soraya," but Soraya kept her eyes down, unable to look at either of them.

"I'd like to speak to you alone, if I may, in a less formal setting," Sorush said. Soraya hated the way he phrased commands as if they were requests—as if she had any choice in the matter. It was as false a pretense as the crown floating a hair's breadth above his head.

"Of course," Soraya murmured.

"Please wait for me there," he said, stretching his arm toward a door to the side of the chamber.

Soraya walked with heavy steps to the door, which opened onto what seemed to be a council room. A long table took up most of the unadorned chamber, and Soraya paced its length as she waited for her brother to join her.

At last he arrived, looking smaller now without his crown and his state robes, an apologetic smile on his face. Soraya turned away from him and continued to pace. She should have wished him a happy new year, or congratulated him on his engagement, but she was sure that anything she said to him now would be laced with poison.

"I know you're probably upset with me, so let me say this first: I didn't mean any of it."

Soraya froze, turning her head toward him. "What?"

"I didn't want to worry our mother, but I think you *should* speak to the div."

Soraya turned to him fully now, forehead wrinkling in disbelief. "I have your permission?"

"Not . . . officially," he said. "You found a way into the dungeon without anyone stopping you—I'm guessing you could do so again?"

Soraya nodded, but offered no further explanation.

"Then I would only ask you to keep your visits discreet. I'll inform the guards that they shouldn't bother you, but no one else should know. And I'd like to ask you a favor in return."

Soraya started to tilt her head, but stopped herself, the gesture reminding her too much of Parvaneh. "What favor?"

Sorush went to a cabinet in the corner of the room and brought out a long roll of paper. He spread the paper out on the table in front of them, revealing a map of Atashar with red marks in various places. "Those marks," he said, "are where the divs have attacked in the last few years. The attacks have grown more prevalent recently, but my larger concern is that they've become more organized and united. Div raids are usually swift and brutal, with no end other than destruction, but these have seemed deliberate or planned, and they've been more interested in fighting our armies than in ransacking the villages. It's almost as if they're *practicing* for something."

His voice had grown more frantic as he spoke, his dark hair falling over his forehead, and he clutched the edge of the map as though he wished he could shake answers out of it. Gone was the polished image of the shah on his throne, no crown or burden too heavy. Now, Soraya saw only a boy who had become a king too soon.

"I need answers," he said more quietly. "I could do so much more for this country if I didn't have to keep worrying about the next battle." He took a breath and held it a moment before continuing. "After he fell ill, our father told me of his plans, the reforms he hoped I could finish for him one day. He wanted to lessen some of the bozorgan's control, to include commoners in higher positions of power, but he hadn't been able to do so during his reign. That was his hope for me, but I've barely *begun* to broach the issue because with all these attacks, the nobility is starting to lose faith in me and I can't afford to anger them, especially with the simorgh missing. Ever since she disappeared, there have been rumblings among the nobility that our family should no longer rule. That's why—"

He stopped abruptly, and Soraya finished for him: "That's why I'm a secret." A miserable silence stretched between them as Sorush kept his eyes on the table, so Soraya spared them both and continued. "But what makes you think I can bring you answers? Why would the div tell me their plans?"

He looked up at her, eyes bright with hope. "Because you won't be asking her for them. You have a completely different reason for being there, which means the div won't be as guarded as she is with the azatan. I don't want you to interrogate her, just to report back if she does reveal anything about the divs and their plans that we don't already know. Will you do it?"

Soraya nodded at once. She had been so angry with him, and now he was giving her this chance, this gift. She was torn between wanting to apologize and wanting to thank him—but her pride would not allow her to do either, so instead she offered him a gift in return.

"She's not just a div," Soraya said. "She called herself a 'parik.'" She told Sorush what Parvaneh had told her about the different kinds of divs, and that pariks were more human in appearance in order to work as spies. It wasn't the answer Sorush was looking for, but he listened raptly, any knowledge better than none.

"In a week's time, come to the fire temple at dawn," he told her. "We'll be alone, and you can tell me anything you've learned between now and then. And thank you, Soraya."

Soraya wondered if she was supposed to return the thanks, or to somehow acknowledge the friendship they had shared in childhood. But her throat closed up whenever she prepared to speak, and so instead she said, "The soldier who accompanied me to the dungeon—you won't punish him, will you?"

Sorush smiled. "Of course not." The smile grew strained as he added, "You will be careful, though, won't you?"

Soraya almost relished the question. It was easier to feel resentment than gratitude toward him. "I'm always careful," she said.

They stared at each other, the sun and his jealous shadow returning to their natural trajectory before Sorush quickly looked away.

The cell appeared empty, but Soraya knew better. She searched the shadows, looking for those hawk's eyes, or a flash of a smile.

Instead, she heard a voice: "I thought you'd be back."

Soraya had waited a few restless days before returning, enough time for Sorush to inform the guards to look the other way if they heard voices coming from the cavern. Now, Parvaneh stepped forward, her black hair and the patterns on her skin making her look like she'd been formed from the shadows themselves. "Do you still think I'm lying to you?"

The image of her mother's stricken face flashed through her mind, and Soraya said, "No, I believe you."

"Go on, then," Parvaneh said, her fingers wrapping around the bars. "Ask me."

Soraya swallowed, her heartbeat echoing through her body. Somehow—from the intensity of Parvaneh's stare, or from the feel of blood and poison rushing through her veins—she knew that if she asked the question, she would get an answer this time.

"How do I lift my curse?"

Parvaneh stared at her for what seemed like an eternity before she said, "What did your mother say, when you asked her if she was lying? Did she admit it?"

Soraya tensed. She felt like she was about to come apart. "Will you tell me or won't you?"

"If you want me to be honest with you, then you need to be honest with me. Did your mother admit it, or didn't she?"

"*No*," Soraya spat out.

"But you still knew she was lying. Interesting." Parvaneh leaned closer. "And I have a feeling you didn't tell her about our little talk. I thought humans were supposed to be the honest ones."

"*Please*," Soraya choked out, the last remains of her composure falling away. "Please, tell me what you know." She tried to breathe, to stop the spread of green she knew must be webbing across her skin, but she was so tired of secrets—tired of *being* one. If she had to hand over her dignity in exchange for the answers she wanted, then so be it.

Something hardened in Parvaneh's eyes, her voice grave as she said, "I'm trying to spare you. Once I tell you the answer, you won't know another moment's peace."

"I've never known a moment's peace. Tell me."

Parvaneh opened her mouth to speak, but then she turned away, walking the length of her cell along the bars. "What will you give me, if I tell you?"

Ah, there it was. Soraya should have expected this, but in her desperation she had forgotten that the div would likely want something in return. "What do you want?" she asked.

Parvaneh paused, one eyebrow raised as she looked at Soraya. "Would you grant me my freedom?"

"I could speak to my brother on your behalf," Soraya said quickly. "I could ask him—"

Parvaneh waved the offer away. "You and I both know that means nothing. You could free me right now if you wanted."

Soraya shook her head. "I don't have that power."

"No?" Parvaneh stretched one arm through the bars, her finger pointing at the lit brazier, still emitting its constant smoke. "All you would have to do is put out that brazier. I could do the rest myself."

Soraya looked from the brazier to Parvaneh and back again. Would she let the div go free in exchange for her knowledge? Would she be willing to endanger Golvahar—endanger her *family*—for the chance to save herself? She remembered again that Parvaneh had attacked Sorush. And how did she know that Parvaneh would tell her the truth? The risk was too great, the reward too uncertain. "No," she said at last, without any doubt in her voice. "I won't do it."

Parvaneh shrugged and resumed pacing. "I didn't think so, but I had to ask. But don't worry, I'm willing to negotiate." She stopped in front of Soraya again and said, "I want you to bring me the simorgh's feather."

She said the words as if they were simple, but Soraya felt hollow, like Parvaneh had reached inside and torn whatever remaining hope she had out of her body. It was unthinkable, the most disloyal act she could imagine—against both her brother and her people. She would still be a curse on her family if she did such a thing, only in a different way.

And besides that, no one but the shah and the high priest knew where the feather was.

"I can't do that," she said, her voice hoarse.

Parvaneh shook her head. "That's my only offer. Bring me the feather, and I'll tell you how to lift your curse."

Soraya's skin prickled. She was suddenly too aware of everything around her. The smell of esfand in the stale cavern became overwhelming, and the smoke blurred her vision. In the dim light, the div's eyes were too bright, too piercing. *I should never have come here*, Soraya thought. *I should never have trusted a div to tell me anything true.* Because this was a trap—she saw it now. Parvaneh would try to buy her trust by making her think her mother had lied, and then she would lure Soraya into betraying her family. Why else would a div ever agree to help her?

And the worst part was that she was still tempted to accept.

But she had to be wary. She couldn't let the force of her wanting overcome all reason. "How do I know you'll keep your end of the bargain? Or that you even have the answer at all?" She had meant to sound determined and authoritative, but she only sounded defeated.

Parvaneh hesitated, and then the lines of her face sharpened so that she looked like she was made of the same stone as the walls that imprisoned her. The cold blaze of her eyes shone as brightly as the torch, and in that moment, there was no mistaking her for human. "I swear on the lives of the pariks, my sisters, that if you bring me the feather, you will have the answer you seek."

There was nothing mocking or sneering in her voice as she spoke, and Soraya found to her surprise that she believed her— which made this impossible bargain even more frustrating. "Why do you even want the feather?" she demanded. "Are you planning to destroy it?"

"No, I have a use for it. Don't bother asking—I won't tell you."

"Would you be able to return it to me, when you were finished with it?"

"If I'm successful, then yes, I believe so."

Soraya shook her head. She shouldn't even have asked. She shouldn't be considering this trade at all or trusting anything Parvaneh told her. "It doesn't make sense. Why wouldn't you destroy it? You tried to kill my brother. Any div would want to destroy it."

"I'm not any div," Parvaneh snapped. "I'm a parik, and my purposes are my own."

The answer took Soraya by surprise, and she wondered if she could still emerge from this conversation with something useful. She tried to keep her voice light as she said, "And yet I heard the divs were more united than ever. Or is there discord among you?"

A slow, knowing smile spread over Parvaneh's face. "You heard that, did you? And I'm sure whoever told you that is currently waiting to see what answer you bring back. Is that why you were allowed to come back here?"

Soraya answered with silence, and Parvaneh nodded. "Well, I can't send you back empty-handed, can I? You're my favorite visitor. Here's something for you to take back with you—you're right that the divs are more united now than they have been. The question you should be asking is *who* united them."

"Who—"

"That's all I can tell you. But I want to make something clear. Whatever you choose to report back, you will not speak a word of our arrangement. If you tell *anyone* I asked for the simorgh's feather—your brother, for example, or certain handsome soldiers I've seen in your company—then the deal is off. And I promise you that I will know if you've told anyone, and I will never speak to you again. Understood?"

"Understood."

Parvaneh reached her arm out through the bars. "Shall we shake hands? Isn't that what humans do to seal a promise?"

She didn't mean it, of course—Soraya knew she was only teasing her. But still, the sly look in Parvaneh's eyes made her want to play along, to show Parvaneh that she wouldn't be rattled so easily. And so, holding her gaze, Soraya stepped forward and extended her gloved hand, close enough for Parvaneh to reach.

In a single movement too fast for Soraya to predict, Parvaneh's hand shot through the bars and grasped Soraya's, pulling her forward until she felt the metal of the bars against her shoulder. They stood face-to-face, both of them daring the other to be the first to back away. Her grip on Soraya's hand was relentless.

This close, Soraya more clearly saw the patterns on Parvaneh's face—the scalloped waves along her chin and jaw, the whorls on her cheeks, the stripes along her forehead, like a moth's wings were laid out over her skin. Soraya had the strangest urge to trace those lines with one fingertip, to see if her skin would be as soft as a moth's wing too. But then she flinched at the thought, remembering the last time she had touched a butterfly's wing.

Parvaneh noticed the way Soraya had recoiled, and she responded with a slight shake of her head. "Don't be afraid," she said. She wasn't looking Soraya in the eye, and Soraya realized that while she had been studying the patterns on Parvaneh's face, Parvaneh had been studying the green lines on her own face.

"I'm not afraid of you," Soraya whispered.

Parvaneh's eyes sparkled, not with their usual mockery, but with something like hunger. "Of course not," Parvaneh said. "You could kill me with a single touch. Why should you ever be afraid of anyone?" She peered closer, tilting her head. "No, it's only yourself that you fear." Parvaneh's hand slid out of hers—taking Soraya's glove with it. The unexpected feel of air on her bare skin always made Soraya's heart race, but her panic quickly subsided into irritation when she saw the victorious smile on Parvaneh's face as she dangled the glove out of Soraya's reach.

"Give that back to me," Soraya said.

Parvaneh shook her head. "You'll have to return for it."

And before Soraya could protest, Parvaneh had disappeared into the shadows again, taking a piece of Soraya with her.

8

A week after Nog Roz, Soraya met Sorush in the fire temple, as planned. The fire temple was not within the palace itself, but on a low hill behind the palace, so Soraya couldn't take any tunnel or hidden passageway to reach it. Instead, she woke early, well before dawn, and made her way in the darkness before anyone else had risen.

She hadn't returned to Parvaneh since receiving her impossible bargain. It was pointless—a dead end when the path had barely begun. She didn't know where the simorgh's feather was, and even if she did, she could never hand it over to a div.

She tried to put it out of her head, but every time she pulled on the new, unfamiliar pair of gloves that was slightly too large for her hands, she would remember the glow of Parvaneh's eyes, and the price she had demanded. And she knew that even though she couldn't move forward, she could no longer go back, either.

She could never return to a time before she'd spoken to the div, a time before knowing that there *was* a way to remove her curse.

I could ask Sorush, she thought for the hundredth time as she climbed the hill to the fire temple. Sorush knew where the feather was, and so did the high priest, who even now was probably in the fire temple. It made her want to scream a little, knowing she was about to be alone with the only two people who could tell her what she needed to know, and yet she couldn't ask either one of them without explaining why.

The sun was just rising as she reached the fire temple. Compared to the grandeur of the palace, the temple seemed misplaced in its simplicity: a round, domed roof over four stone columns forming a square, with an arch on each side. Soraya rarely came here, not only because of the location, but because of what had happened the last time she had come to the fire temple.

Shortly after the butterfly incident, Soraya had come by herself to the temple to pray—to apologize to the Creator for harming one of his creatures. The high priest at that time overheard her talking about her curse, and he told her that the Creator would not hear her prayers, because she did not belong to him— that anything venomous or deadly belonged to the Destroyer. His logic was too sound for her to disagree, and so she had never returned. It gave her some comfort to know that the priest had later been found guilty of some treasonous act and had been scheduled for execution, though he had escaped in the end, never to be heard from again. *Even* he *knows where the feather is*, Soraya thought bitterly.

The current high priest did not know about her curse, and so when she stepped into the temple, he simply smiled at her and bowed his head, his hair as white as his long robes. He and another, younger priest stood beside the Royal Fire, which burned in an urn on top of a stone pedestal in the center of the temple. There were many other sacred fires in many other temples throughout

Atashar, all honoring the Creator, but only the Royal Fire had been ritually created from several sources, including lightning sent from the Creator himself. An iron grate enclosed the pedestal, and only a priest was allowed to open the grate and tend to the Fire, which never went out. The younger priest poured some esfand onto the flames now, and the smell of it filled the air.

Soraya stood uncomfortably near the temple entrance, still hearing the former high priest's gravelly voice confirming all her worst fears. *You don't belong here in this temple,* he had told her. *You belong somewhere like the pit of Duzakh, where the Destroyer dwells among wicked spirits. Or even better—the dakhmeh, where the yatu seek refuge, where the vultures fly overhead, hungry for human flesh, where the div Nasu spreads death and corruption. Because isn't that what you do, shahzadeh? Aren't you made for death?*

The words kept playing over and over again in Soraya's head, and she was thankful when she heard Sorush's steps behind her.

Sorush approached the high priest and spoke to him in a low voice. The priest looked from Sorush to Soraya, then nodded, and he and the other priest stepped outside the temple, leaving the two of them alone.

With the priests gone, Soraya was better able to relax, and she came to join Sorush in front of the iron grate, the fire crackling inside it.

"Did you learn anything new?" Sorush asked her quietly, his eyes locked on the fire.

Soraya had already decided what she would tell him—and what she would omit. "I think there may be some kind of animosity between the pariks and the other divs—or at least between this parik and the others," she reported.

Sorush nodded. "That could be useful. I thought it was strange that I've never seen a div like her before on the battlefield. But if they're not all aligned with one another, that would make sense."

"There's something else," Soraya said. "She said it's true that the divs are more united now than they have been, but that the question we should be asking is *who* united them. She might be lying, though. She guessed that I was digging for information."

Sorush frowned in thought as he stared deep into the fire. "Did you learn anything else?"

"I tried asking what she meant by that, but she wouldn't tell me anything more."

"No," Sorush said, turning to look at her. "I meant about your curse."

She had hoped he wouldn't ask, so she wouldn't have to lie directly. But she couldn't tell him what Parvaneh had asked for, because then he would always wonder if she would accept those terms and betray him for her own sake. "No," she said, looking away from him. "I don't know if there's any point in going back."

From the corner of her eye, she saw him nod. "I understand if you don't. But if you do, and she tells you anything else, please send word to me."

"Of course," Soraya said, and to her surprise, she found herself disappointed that her mission would be over so soon. She would miss feeling useful.

Sorush began to walk away, their exchange having ended, and Soraya felt strangely cold, as if he had taken the fire's warmth with him. "Sorush?" she called to him. He turned, and before she could stop herself, she asked, "Do you remember the man who was high priest when we were children—the one who escaped execution? Do you know what ever happened to him? Why was he arrested?"

"He was caught trying to put out the Royal Fire," Sorush answered. "It turned out he was secretly a yatu posing as a priest. Why? Do you think he might be the one the parik was talking about?"

"No," Soraya said. "Being here again reminded me of him, and I was curious."

She remained in the fire temple until after Sorush left, even after the priests returned, staring into the fire until her eyes burned.

The former high priest had been a sorcerer, then. He had told her she belonged to the Destroyer, and she supposed he would know, being aligned with the Destroyer himself. But she couldn't afford to hold a grudge against him now, because he knew where to find the feather—and Soraya was fairly certain she knew where to find him.

From different parts of the roof, Soraya could look down at the entire city surrounding Golvahar like it was a map. Her eyes swept over the flat roofs of houses and shops, at the orderly streets that separated the city into its different districts. For years, that was how shahs had maintained a stable rule, with everything and everyone in its proper place. No wonder, then, that Soraya had to be hidden away like a stain on a tapestry or a weed in a garden. There was no place for her within these walls—just as there was no place inside the city for the dakhmeh.

Even without the memory of the false priest's words in her mind, Soraya would have avoided looking directly at the roofless, cylindrical shape of the dakhmeh where it loomed on a hill outside the city walls. It wasn't a choice so much as an instinct born out of fear and revulsion, the same way she would try not to look at a decaying animal. It was the same instinct, she imagined, that made her family avert their eyes from her. No one wanted to look at the face of death.

But Soraya had been caught unawares once. She had been on the roof, a few hours before sunset, and seen a funeral procession. She had watched as a family followed their dead to the dakhmeh, a priest leading the way with a brazier of esfand for protection against Nasu and other demons. The corpse-bearers took the body inside the dakhmeh—they alone were permitted to go inside, and they had to perform a rigorous cleansing ritual afterward. That day, Soraya had watched until she saw the first sign of vultures overhead, and then she turned away, wondering if the corpse-bearers would return later for the bones.

The dakhmeh—where the vultures fly overhead, hungry for human flesh, where the div Nasu spreads death and corruption.

Where the yatu seek refuge.

Every day since speaking to Sorush in the temple, she had come here to the roof to look out at the dakhmeh, searching for some hint that her suspicion was correct. Had the false priest run to the dakhmeh for refuge? It was the one place where the living dared not enter, the one place no one wanted to even think about, let alone disturb. Soraya had read that yatu used human remains, like hair or nail clippings, for their spells, and what better place to find such things than the dakhmeh? If she were a yatu, that was where she would hide.

But it had been years since the yatu had escaped. Even if he had gone to the dakhmeh at first, he might have moved on since then. He might even be dead. And even if he were there, and Soraya managed to travel through the city and cross the barren landscape beyond to walk into such a polluted place—would she ask him for the location of the simorgh's feather? She had told herself she would never accept Parvaneh's bargain. But then why did she still come to the roof, day after day, to look out at the dakhmeh and wonder?

Or maybe she didn't need Parvaneh or the feather after all. Wasn't it possible that the yatu knew the secret to lifting Soraya's curse? Perhaps he had known all along but didn't want to reveal his knowledge of such forbidden magic.

"I have to do this," she muttered to herself, surprised at her resolve. Now she just had to figure out how.

"Soraya?"

She jumped at the voice, but saw with relief that it was Azad emerging from the stairway. How long had it been since Nog Roz? Three weeks at least. She had been so occupied with demons and feathers and sorcerers that she had barely spared a thought for the young man who had helped her so much that day. He was tanner than when she had last seen him, his arms more defined—he had probably been spending time out on the training grounds, sparring with his fellow soldiers. She wondered if they had fully accepted him, or if they thought of him as a villager who had risen above his station. Perhaps he didn't fit neatly into Golvahar's structured world, either.

"You always know where to find me," she said as he came toward her.

"Because I always look," he answered with a grin. "Whenever I come or go from the training grounds, I look up and see you here, staring out into the distance. I came to see what you've been looking at." He looked over her shoulder, and Soraya felt a flare of panic, as if he would somehow know it was the dakhmeh that occupied her.

"How has my brother been treating you?" she blurted to distract him. "Well, I hope? I asked him not to blame you for what happened on Nog Roz."

"I haven't seen much of him," Azad answered. "I imagine he's busy preparing for the wedding tomorrow."

The wedding—Soraya had nearly forgotten about the wedding, let alone realized it was tomorrow. She had forgotten about everything other than her hopeless quest. But even now, the grounds below were bustling with people preparing for the wedding, setting out long trestle tables and rugs and tying crystal birds to the tree branches.

"Besides," Azad continued, his eyes locking on hers, "I think I prefer the company of his sister. I've thought of you often since Nog Roz."

A shiver went down her spine, not only because of the way his voice lowered into a caress, but also from the spiteful pleasure of knowing that someone preferred being with her over Sorush. *Nothing can come of this*, an insistent inner voice whispered. Even so, the novelty of Azad's attention was thrilling enough on its own. She still remembered the feeling of his arm around her from when he had helped her on Nog Roz.

The memory sparked an idea in her mind—if he had helped her navigate one crowd, couldn't he do so again? But could she ask this of him? He had already put his position at risk by helping her once.

"You're thinking about something else," Azad said. "I can see it in your eyes."

"I was thinking about Nog Roz," she said. "About what you did for me then."

"The div? Did she tell you what you wanted to hear?"

She took a breath, wondering how much to tell him, how much he deserved to know. But she remembered Parvaneh's warning not to tell anyone—including a certain handsome soldier. "No," she said. "I didn't like what she had to say. But I think there may be another way."

"What is it?"

Soraya hesitated again, but the pull to the dakhmeh was as strong as the pull to the dungeon. She hadn't spared Azad then, and she knew she wouldn't now, either—especially not when it provided such a perfect excuse to keep him close to her. "I have to go to the dakhmeh," she answered. "I'm hoping to find a yatu there who might have the answers I'm looking for."

She expected him to argue or stare at her in disbelief, but in the silence that followed, he only frowned in thought. Finally, he said, "I don't want you to go alone. Would you let me come with you?"

She almost laughed in relief. "I do need help getting out of the palace and through the city. I wouldn't ask you to come inside the dakhmeh—"

"You don't have to ask," he said. He took a step toward her, closing the already short distance between them, and clasped one of her gloved hands. "This is what I always wanted—to save you."

Slowly, never taking his eyes off her, he brought her hand to his lips.

His courtly action should have moved or thrilled her, but the dulled feeling of his lips on her gloved hand only sharpened the reality of their situation. *He still thinks this is a story, and I'm letting him do so for my own sake.* He was saying all the right words, making all the right gestures, almost as if he had practiced them in his head a hundred times—which he probably had. And even though Soraya knew better, she hadn't stopped him, letting him play the hero despite the risk to his safety and position in court.

"This was a mistake," she said, as much to herself as to him. She pulled her hand away.

He shook his head, a flicker of worry in his eye. "What do you mean? Have I offended you?"

"Not at all," she said. "But you can't save me, Azad. And I shouldn't ask it of you, either. I think we both see each other as something a little less than real." She looked down at her gloved hands, at the loose threads of her sleeves, picked apart during moments of thwarted anger. "I can't promise that I'll be what you want me to be at the end of this," she said quietly.

He started to disagree, but then he stopped and looked at her, and he sighed. "You may be right," he said. "I suppose I wanted to remember what it was like—to live in a palace, to be a part of a court, to feel like a hero again."

"Again?"

He ran a hand through his curls, his shoulders tensing, and Soraya felt like she was seeing him for the first time—not as a brave hero or her dashing rescuer, but as a young man with burdens of his own.

"This isn't the first time I've moved up or down in society," he said, bitterness lacing his words. "I told you, I think, that my father was a merchant. He was a very successful one, and he was often a guest in the palaces of satraps and the estates of the bozorgan.

Sometimes he would take me with him, and I suppose I began to feel like I was one of them, like I *belonged* there. But then my father made some bad investments and fell out of favor. We were cast out. I lost everything I had, everything I believed I was."

"Your father," she said, "is he . . ."

"Dead?" He looked her in the eye, not flinching from the word. "Yes. He died shortly after our disgrace. I lived on my own in the village we ran to until the divs came and slaughtered half the villagers." He paused, his eyes flickering to the ground. "It seems wrong, but sometimes I still feel such anger toward him, for all the things he couldn't be. For the ways he failed me."

His fists clenched at his sides, and Soraya saw the veins on his knuckles stand out as he fought down his anger. She wanted to trace them with her fingers, to feel the shape of someone else's anger, someone else's pain. She thought of the look they had shared after he had struck Ramin, the sense of connection between them. It was when they let each other see their harsh edges that they both felt real.

Azad shook his head, breaking himself out of his reverie. "That first time I saw you on the roof, I felt like that young man again. I suppose I wanted to regain what I had lost through you. I'm sorry for that." He reached forward, slowly enough not to startle her, and carefully—so carefully—brushed his knuckles against Soraya's hair. "But I'd still like to help you, if you'd let me," he said. "I like the person I am when I'm with you. And I'd like to help you be whoever you want to be."

He had touched her hair before, but this time felt different. She had hardly breathed last time, certain that he'd fade away or disappear under the weight of a single breath. But now, after what he had told her, after seeing the veins in his hands and hearing the harsh edge in his voice, Azad seemed . . . touchable. A bolt of heat went through her at the thought, like a spark suddenly ignited. That was how she felt—like she was transforming from smoke to flame under his gaze, his touch. She could have echoed his words and meant it: *I like the person I am when I'm with you.*

She leaned away, letting her hair slowly unwind from his finger. "Tonight, then?"

His lips curved into a smile that was both fond and a little sly. "Tonight," he agreed.

9

For what must have been the fifteenth time, Soraya drew her shawl more tightly around her face, hoping that the shawl and the steadily dimming light would make her appear little more than a shadow. She could have been any young woman sneaking off with a handsome soldier—or so she hoped.

Her own personal handsome soldier was waiting for her outside the walls of the golestan, as they had arranged. As soon as she left behind those familiar walls, he was at her side, taking her arm.

"Are you ready?" Azad whispered to her.

She pretended not to hear. It wasn't even the thought of the dakhmeh that scared her most—simply leaving the palace where she had spent her entire life was enough to send her heart racing. She was about to step off the edge of the world she had always known. Could anyone ever be ready for that?

Their timing was convenient, she supposed. The garden was alive with music and celebration tonight, the night before the shah's wedding. The crowd wasn't as large as the one on Nog Roz, since only members of court were attending, but it was large enough to let Soraya and Azad blend in as they made their escape.

Soraya gripped his arm tightly as they walked through the garden, trying not to flinch every time someone passed by them. She kept looking around her, sure that her mother would appear, or that someone would collide with her and accidentally touch her skin. She almost felt like she was walking through a painting or a tableau on a tapestry—like she was intruding in a world where she didn't belong and didn't quite fit, and it was only a matter of time before someone noticed her. But Azad confidently steered her around the celebrants as they danced or laughed or ate together, and no one paid the two of them much notice.

Finally, they neared the palace gates, and Azad told her to wait as he approached the guards standing watch there. She knew why he didn't want her to hear him—she could tell what Azad must be saying from the knowing smirks on the guards' faces. But whatever Azad had said evidently worked, because soon he was waving her forward, and she was hurrying past the guards to join him.

And then they were through, looking down the steps cut into the small hill that would take them into the center of the city. It really did feel like stepping off the edge of the world. Or was it the other way around? Was she finally stepping *into* the world? Soraya turned her eyes above, to the stars that were beginning faintly to appear. Looking out at the city made her feel disoriented and exposed, but when she looked up, she could imagine herself swimming in the stars, sinking beneath the surface of the sky to some hidden depth. Maybe in a world turned upside down, she wouldn't be poisonous anymore.

Azad was standing motionless a few steps ahead of her, and she tore her eyes away from the sky to see what was occupying his attention. But it was *her*—he was watching her, his eyes brighter than the stars. She returned his gaze, and her fingertips tingled through her gloves.

"Are you ready?" he asked for the second time, and reached slowly for her hand.

She closed the gap, letting her gloved fingers entwine with his. "I am now."

Azad led her into the emptying streets. The city was beginning to quiet down for the night, but there were still enough people out to make Soraya cautious—though not so many to overwhelm her, as on Nog Roz. And as they neared the city square, the streets widened, and she began to breathe more freely.

It was when they reached the square that it struck her how strange it was to be inside this space that she had only seen from above and afar for so long. Here were the block-shaped homes and buildings whose roofs had lit up for Suri, and there were the archways that led into and out of the square. Everything was both familiar and foreign, both known and unknown.

Azad must have noticed the way she was looking up and around, and he paused to point out a tall, imposing building. "That's the courthouse," he whispered to her. "We're about to go through the bazaar now."

Soraya peered down the long avenue at the people closing down their stalls and shops, imagining how it must look and sound during the day with bustling crowds and merchants calling out to potential customers. Only the scents of the bazaar lingered; she thought she caught a hint of rose water in the air, and a little while later, the coppery tang of blood mixed with leather.

"Is this where the tanning bazaar is?" she asked Azad, and he looked at her in surprise.

"The butchers and the tanners are down there," he said, pointing to a set of steps that led to a narrower alley. "This is where the rug bazaar would be."

These stalls were all empty now, but she imagined this street lined with rugs and tapestries—the bright colors of the dyes, the sound of looms clacking as they turned bolts of raw silk imported from the east into the beautiful patterns of the rugs Atashar was famous for.

"I wish I could see it," she whispered into the night.

The night didn't respond, but Azad did. "You will. I'll show it to you when your curse is gone."

He led her down another set of streets, past flat-topped houses with walled orchards. She heard the sound of children laughing from behind one of them.

"We're almost at the city walls," Azad said. His grip on Soraya's hand was tight, his gaze focused ahead, his gait steady and quick. Soraya's heart lurched. It had been easy to forget their real destination—that they were leaving this hub of life and light for a place of death and shadows.

But Soraya wasn't capable of fear right now. She had been afraid to come into the city at all, but this outing had quickened her blood and quieted her fears. She was here, outside the palace, in the world, and she had harmed no one. She could *live* without someone or something dying for it.

"You're not tired, are you?" Azad asked her, his pace slowing slightly.

"No," she said. "I've never felt less tired in my life."

She thought she saw a flash of a smile, and they continued on.

They moved toward the setting sun, and by the time they reached the large wooden door set into the eastern wall of the city, that sun had nearly dipped below the horizon. The night guard took a glance at Azad's red tunic and let them pass without question.

It would be another hour's walk to reach the dakhmeh, which stood alone on a low hill, a safe distance from the living. Azad had brought a lantern with them, and as the sun disappeared, he lit and raised it to light their way. The light didn't extend to the dakhmeh, however, and so all it did was illuminate the dry, cracked ground around them.

Soraya had thought moving through the city would be the hardest part of this journey, but with each step that took her farther away from the city walls, her breathing became more and more labored, as if a weight were pressing down on her chest. She tried to look back to see how far they had come, but the city was lost to the night now. Outside the lantern's wavering ring of light, there was only darkness all around them, stretching on without end.

On the roof, the whole world had been laid out in front of her, and she had been able to map the distance from the city to the dakhmeh easily. But now that she was no longer watching from above, she felt like she had shrunk down to the size of one of the insects in her garden, walking an impossibly long trail in a world that was too big for her. Had she found the boundaries of her room and her garden suffocating before? Had she felt she couldn't breathe in the passages behind her walls? She could have laughed at herself—first it was not enough, and now it was too much.

Azad must have heard her increasingly ragged breathing, because his voice broke through the silence and the darkness, saying only, "Tell me a story."

His words brought her out of her head, and she looked at his profile, lit softly by the lantern light. He was trying to distract her, to make the journey shorter, and she was grateful to him for it.

And so she told him the story of the princess who let down her hair for her lover to climb, and when it was over, Azad asked for another. This time she told the story of a brave hero stronger than ten men who bested dragons and rescued a foolish shah from the hands of divs.

She waited to hear him ask for yet another story, but this time he said, "Tell me your favorite story. The one you've read over and over again."

Soraya wanted to protest that the first story she'd told *had* been her favorite—but it wasn't the one she'd revisited the most over the years. It wasn't the one that haunted her dreams night after night. It wasn't the one that she felt was a part of her, so much so that she hesitated now, in case it would reveal too much of herself.

But as always, once the Shahmar entered her mind, she couldn't think of anything else.

"There was and there was not," she began, in a voice that seemed both hers and not hers, "a prince who was what every young man should be. He was handsome and courteous and brave, but he was also proud and curious. One day, the prince captured a div, but he didn't vanquish it. Instead, he kept it locked up in a cave, and visited it every day, demanding the secrets of its knowledge."

She paused, knowing both of them must be thinking of Soraya's visit to the div locked away in the dungeon.

"Before long, the div convinced the prince that he would make a better ruler than his father or his elder brothers. And the young man agreed—after all, didn't he know even the secrets of the divs? And so the prince slew his father and brothers, and took the crown for himself.

"The prince—now the shah—ruled for a time in peace, despite his bloody coronation. But he still visited the div, and over time, the prince noticed that he was changing. His bones shifted, his skin grew scaly and rough, and his heart grew violent. He hungered for war, for destruction, and he began to rule by terror and force, demanding the senseless sacrifice of two men every month to quench his desire for bloodshed. The act of murder that had made him king had now also twisted him into a div himself—"

Her voice broke, and she froze where she was, trying to collect herself, her throat burning as she tried to hold back angry tears. From beside her, she heard Azad say, "I've heard the rest. You don't have to go on."

The rest of the story was about her ancestor, the adopted son of the simorgh, who had led a rebellion against the Shahmar and chased him off into exile, where he was either killed by other divs or lived long enough to take his revenge against the simorgh, depending on which version you believed. And yet, even though that was her family's origin, that wasn't the part of the story Soraya felt most connected to.

"Why does that story affect you so?" Azad asked her, his voice gentle.

She didn't want to answer, but she wouldn't have begun the story at all if she hadn't been prepared to face this question.

She held her arms out to him, pulling back her sleeves so they both could see the dark green veins running down her wrists. "Do you have to ask?" she whispered. "Doesn't it sound familiar to you?" She pulled her sleeves back down. "Ever since I was a child, I've wondered if the same thing would happen to me—if the poison was only the beginning, if I was going to grow more and more dangerous until I wasn't human anymore." She had thought she would have to fight to get the words out, but she found now that it was easy to say them. They were less frightening aloud than they were in her mind.

"And so I told myself," she continued, "that as long as I was *good*, never angry or envious, I wouldn't become a monster like the Shahmar."

Azad swallowed, his eyes moving over the veins on her face and neck. "And have you been successful?"

She lowered her head, looking for reassurance from the cracks in the earth. But the way they branched out reminded her too much of her veins and the poison inside them. "I don't know," she said. She thought of all the dead insects in her garden, of the night she had been tempted to hurt Ramin, of amber eyes staring in the dark. "I try to hold myself back from doing any real harm, but sometimes I feel like my thoughts are steeped in poison, and that it's only a matter of time before I lose control over them . . . or over myself. I dream about it sometimes—I see myself transforming

into something else, and the Shahmar stands over me, laughing—"
She shut her eyes, but in doing so, she only conjured up the image
of the Shahmar.

She hadn't realized she'd been plucking at her gloves until Azad
put his hand over hers, stilling her anxious movements. "Look at
me, Soraya."

Her eyes opened, and instead of the Shahmar's triumphant face,
she saw only Azad. His gaze was focused on her with an intensity
that made her breath catch, the flame from the lantern flickering
in his eyes in a way that reminded her of Parvaneh. The furrow in
his brow made him seem almost angry, and she tried to look away,
but his hand tightened over hers and she held still. "Stories lie," he
said, his voice low and urgent. "You're not a monster."

She shook her head. "You don't know me," she said, even though
he knew her better than most by now. "I must seem so small to
you, so insignificant, hiding behind walls and layers of fabric, more
a story than a person. But there are parts of me you don't know,
parts you haven't seen."

"I don't think you're small or insignificant," he said. His gaze
softened, solemn rather than fierce. "I think you have so much
power within you that it scares you, and that you make yourself
small on purpose because you don't know what you'll become if
you ever stop."

He let go of her hands, and neither of them spoke as they continued on toward the dakhmeh. Their trek was almost over, and
before long, Soraya saw the shadowy cylinder on a hill up ahead.
The sight of it should have filled her with dread or disgust, but she
barely paid it notice. She was repeating Azad's words to herself
over and over again until their cadence matched her heartbeat.

It was only when they had come to a stop at the foot of the hill that
Azad's words lost their enchantment. The dakhmeh loomed over

them, and Soraya's stomach lurched in revulsion. The *wrongness* of being here—of being here *alive*—settled over her, coating her skin like fine grains of sand. She was breathing shallowly, not wanting to inhale the contamination of death in the air.

As they neared the top of the hill, Soraya saw a pale orange light glowing from inside the dakhmeh. *I was right*, she thought. She supposed it could be a different yatu, someone other than the false priest, but she couldn't help feeling that whoever was inside had been waiting for her all along.

She kept expecting Azad to tell her she could turn back, that she didn't have to go through with this, but he didn't, and she wasn't sure she wanted him to. Instead, to her surprise, she was the one who offered a way out. "You should wait here."

Azad shook his head. "I can't do that. We both go in or we both go back."

There was the excuse she'd been waiting for to turn back, but Soraya knew she couldn't take it, not when they had come this far. "My curse will protect me," she argued. "I *want* to go in alone." As soon as she said it, she knew it was true. There was an intimacy to this unraveling of her life that she didn't want to share with anyone else.

He frowned at her, but he must have believed the resolve in her voice, because eventually he nodded. "I'll stay close. If you need me, call for me."

Soraya agreed, and after taking one last breath of the cool night air, she continued onward. She had never seen the inside of a dakhmeh, of course—only the corpse-bearers came inside—and so she walked in expecting the worst. Would there be corpses laid out, decayed or half eaten by scavenger birds? Would a yatu be committing some unholy ritual with parts of the dead? Every story meant to scare children away from the dakhmeh swam through her mind. *If you step into the dakhmeh, or if you linger too long around a dead body, then the corpse div Nasu will find you and make you fall ill.*

But as soon as Soraya stepped inside the dakhmeh, she no longer felt any terror or disgust—the only sensation was one of overwhelming emptiness.

The dakhmeh had two layers, she discovered, and she was standing on the top one, a jutting platform that formed a ring around the dakhmeh's perimeter. And all along the platform were rectangular indentations, the right size for a grave. To her intense relief, each of the shallow graves was empty. There was no roof, of course, in order to grant access to the birds, and so the air was not as stale and foul as she had expected, and the stars still shone overhead.

The platform gently inclined downward to a pit at the center of the dakhmeh. Soraya carefully made her way down the footpath between the graves. There were three rows of them, and when she passed the third row, with the smallest graves, she realized these must be for children.

At the end of the platform, she hesitated. She saw a fire burning in the pit below, the source of the light they had seen from outside. But otherwise, she saw nothing and no one, and she began to regret telling Azad to stay behind.

Why should you ever be afraid of anyone? she heard Parvaneh's voice asking her. And she was right, wasn't she? Soraya was always the most dangerous person in any room. With this surge of confidence, Soraya sat on the edge of the platform and slid forward to land on the ground below.

A fine white powder rose up from the ground with the impact of her landing, and now Soraya knew what happened to the bones once the vultures finished their meal.

In the firelight, Soraya could make out the shapes of grates set into the wall—drains, she supposed, for rainwater. She went closer to the fire and found a waterskin and an empty bowl with the remains of some kind of stew. As Soraya began to wonder where the owner of these objects was, she heard a voice, like stone scraping against stone, from behind her.

"Who are you?" came the voice—a voice she recognized. "What are you doing here?"

Soraya turned at once to face it. In the shadow under the platform was a grizzled man, his gray hair and beard unkempt, his eyes red. He was not as tall as she remembered, but still, the sight of him made her want to shrink back, to escape the judgment of both him and the Creator. *Why should you ever be afraid of anyone?* she reminded herself again, and her fists clenched at her sides, grounding her.

"Do you remember me?" she asked him in a steady voice.

He stared at her blankly at first, but then he sucked in a breath and said, "Show me your face." He came toward her. "Show me if you are who I think you are."

Fear returned to her, but still she turned toward the firelight, removed her shawl with shaking hands, and pulled her hair away from her face to show the old man the rivers of poison under her skin, made visible by her rapidly beating heart.

His eyes shone when he saw her face, and he nodded slowly. "I remember you, shahzadeh," he said. "I remember that night." He snickered. "I frightened you, didn't I?"

Her face burned with anger. *I could reach out and touch him right now,* she thought, *and then see which one of us is more frightened.* But no, she couldn't harm him. She still needed him. "Have you been hiding away here all this time?" she said. "I thought yatu were more powerful than that. Can't you use your magic to help you escape?"

His smile turned sour. "Why do you think no one has ever found me here?" He spread his arms wide. "I lay a spell on the dakhmeh's boundaries, to keep away those who mean to do me harm." His arms fell. "But without my books, I can do little else but cast petty curses on the villagers using the remains of their relatives."

The word *curses* echoed in her mind like the hissing of a snake, reminding her of her purpose. "I could find your books for you, if they haven't been burned," she said.

He let out a skeptical snort. "I assume you want something in return," he said.

"As high priest, you would have known the location of the simorgh's feather. Tell me where it is."

If her request surprised him, he didn't show it. He only briefly considered her offer before nodding. "The simorgh's feather is the heart of the Royal Fire," he said.

"It's inside the fire?" Soraya thought of the iron grate shielding the fire, of the priests who stood guard day and night to ensure no one extinguished it. If she could find a way to be in the fire temple alone, then perhaps Soraya could use some tool to take the feather from the fire. Parvaneh had said she would be able to return the feather once she was finished with it—Soraya could discreetly re-place it once she knew the answer to lifting her curse. She could be free without betraying her family. Something like joy was begin-ning to ripple through her.

But as if he could hear the direction of her thoughts, the yatu was shaking his head. "You don't understand. The feather is not *in-side* the fire. It's *part* of the fire. In any other fire, the feather would simply burn, but in the Royal Fire, it becomes part of the flames, giving the fire the power to protect the shah."

Soraya frowned. "The *fire* protects the shah?"

The yatu nodded. "As long as the feather is part of it."

Already her joy was fading away, replaced by a cold, creep-ing dread making its way through her limbs, her body under-standing before her mind did. "And so the only way to take the feather . . ."

The yatu said what she could not: ". . . is to put out the fire."

Those words extinguished Soraya's last hope. Even if she re-placed the feather, it wouldn't matter. The feather alone couldn't protect her brother, and the fire, with its many ritual sources, couldn't be rebuilt immediately, leaving her brother vulnerable to attack for a dangerously indefinite period of time. The only way she could learn how to lift her curse was by endangering her brother and committing a crime the yatu had been sentenced to death for attempting.

The yatu was watching her. "Ah," he said with mocking pity. "I didn't tell you what you wanted to hear. Does that mean you won't search for my books after all, shahzadeh?"

"Maybe you can still earn them," Soraya answered, her voice hard. She had almost forgotten her distant hope that the yatu would know a way to lift her curse. If he knew the answer, then she wouldn't need the feather after all. "Tell me how to lift the curse that makes me poisonous."

This time, her request surprised him. He shook his head. "I thought you knew, shahzadeh. The feather *is* the way to lift your curse."

Soraya thought she had misheard, her anxiety over the feather twisting the yatu's words. But then the yatu continued: "The simorgh's feather has restorative powers. In your case, you need the tip of the simorgh's feather to break your skin. A prick of the finger would do."

Soraya shut her eyes, her blood churning. "Thank you," she murmured tonelessly, turning her back on the yatu. Something had gone numb within her. She was barely aware of her surroundings, the world blurring around her as if it were all an indistinct dream. *No more thoughts tonight*, she decided. *No more hopes, either.*

"Wait, shahzadeh," the yatu's gravelly voice called out behind her. "I give nothing for free. You owe me for the information I've given you."

She waved a hand listlessly in his direction, saying, "I'll search for your books and bring them to you if I find them, as promised."

"I think you can offer me something better than that."

She started to turn toward him to ask him what he meant, and then all she saw was something blurry from the corner of her eye— all she heard was the thud of an impact—

And as she tumbled to the dirty, bone-littered ground, all she felt was pain.

10

Her vision went briefly dark, but when she came to herself again, Soraya was still on the ground, one hand over her eye, where something blunt had struck her. And then her hand was wrenched away, and she looked up at the chiseled face of the yatu, who was quickly tying her wrists together with a thick cord around her gloves. Between his teeth was a long knife with an ivory handle—he must have used that handle to strike her.

"Stop! What are you doing?" Soraya cried out, trying to jerk her hands away from him. She didn't dare shout for Azad, not when that blade was so close to her face, but if she spoke loudly enough, maybe he would hear and know something was wrong. "What do you want with me?"

The yatu finished tying her hands and retrieved the knife from his mouth. "What do you think your family would give me in exchange for your life? Wealth? An official pardon, even? Far more than just my books, surely. Or perhaps they're more likely to pay me for making you disappear."

Soraya bit down on her tongue to keep herself from calling for Azad. The yatu was working on her ankles now, using the hem of her dress to guard his hands from her skin. Maybe if she screamed quickly enough, maybe if she lunged for him, maybe if she pretended to faint—

But before she could form a plan, something tackled the yatu, throwing him to the ground. The yatu hadn't finished with Soraya's ankles, and so she kicked the cord away, rolling to her side and pushing herself up onto her knees. And now she saw that it was Azad who had attacked the yatu—he had left behind his lantern, allowing him to sneak down the platform—and the two of them were both struggling for control of the knife in the yatu's hand.

Soraya looked in horror at Azad, pinned to the ground by the yatu's weight, the knife's edge dangerously close to his throat. "Go!" Azad called to her.

But of course she couldn't leave him here. Soraya tried not to lose her balance as she struggled to her feet, her bound hands shaking in her gloves . . . gloves that were slightly too large for her. Saying a silent thank-you to Parvaneh, Soraya bent down and stepped on the very edge of one glove, on the tiny pocket of air the glove left above her fingertips. And then she tore her hand from the glove with as much force as she could.

If she had been wearing her usual gloves, her plan might have failed, or she might have injured herself. But thanks to fate, or the Creator—or Parvaneh—the glove was just loose enough to let her pull her hand partly out of it. She pulled again—and again—until her right hand was free from both the glove and the bindings around her wrist. Quickly, she shook the cord off her other wrist.

While she had been working to free herself, Azad had continued struggling against the yatu. But once Soraya slipped free from her bindings, she looked up to see the yatu slam his knee into

Azad's stomach. Azad lost his grip on the yatu's wrist as he cried out in pain.

That cry sparked something in Soraya, a shame that flooded through her whole body. Azad was going to die because of her—because he had agreed to her dangerous plan, because he had come running when she had cried out—and Soraya was powerless to stop it.

And once more, Parvaneh's voice whispered in her mind: *You could wield such power.*

Those words were no longer a taunt but a suggestion—a solution. The yatu had a knife, but Soraya had her own weapon. The firelight glinted on the yatu's raised knife, and Soraya's shame ignited into rage.

He plunged the knife downward—just as Soraya wrapped her bare fingers around his wrist, pressing into his skin with bruising force.

I'm touching his skin. My skin is touching his skin. The yatu's skin was cold, but still it was warm in a way that she had never felt before. Even though the circumstances were unpleasant, the simple sensation of it was so unfamiliar to her that Soraya briefly forgot who and where she was. She forgot what would happen next.

The yatu seemed shocked, as well. He had frozen, his eyes locked on Soraya's hand, on the lines of poison under her skin. They both watched in surprise as the veins in the yatu's wrist became that venomous shade of green Soraya knew so well, the poison spreading down his arm. The knife fell from his hand and clattered to the ground harmlessly beside Azad.

"What have you done?" he rasped, his body slumping to the ground, his wrist sliding out of Soraya's grasp. The poison was now traveling up his neck, and when he tried to speak again, he started to gag.

I did this to him, she thought. *I have the power to do this.* All the times she had felt small and meaningless, all the times her family had lied to her or avoided her, all the times she had folded herself away, hiding like she was something shameful—all of that poison was in the yatu now, and she watched him choke on it, leaving her weightless. Bodiless. *Free.*

Soraya had never seen anything larger than a butterfly succumb to her poison. She didn't know how long it would take for him to die, and she watched it happen with a kind of numb curiosity. He was laid out on the ground, convulsing, the last sparks of life twitching out of him. And then he stilled, the veins fading away, and Soraya knew he was dead.

"Soraya."

He was *dead,* and she had killed him, and he was so much bigger than a butterfly.

"Soraya, what have you done?"

She thought it was the yatu who had spoken, repeating his final words, but then she realized it had been Azad's voice. He pushed himself off the ground and went to examine the body, putting his fingers to the yatu's throat.

After a brief but painful silence, Azad said, "He's dead." He looked at Soraya, mouth slightly parted, eyes wide and round with awe. "You killed him."

I did it to save you, she wanted to say. *I had no other choice.* But even as she scrambled for righteousness, she knew she was lying to herself. She might have found something heavy to knock the yatu unconscious. She might have only threatened him with death without actually touching him. She might have thought of *something* else, except she hadn't thought at all. She had killed the yatu because she was angry with him for what he had said to her all those years ago, because he hadn't given her the answers she wanted . . . and because it was easy. Because a little part of her had always wondered how easy it would be, and then she had had the perfect excuse to find out.

Soraya gagged, putting her hands—one gloved, one bare—over

her face, trying to block out the sight of the yatu's open, glassy eyes. But she couldn't block him out—he was part of her now. That corpse on the ground was hers. She was responsible for it. "I'm sorry," she said, but the words changed nothing. When she lowered her hands, the body would still be there, and she would still be a murderer.

Azad took hold of her wrists over her sleeves, careful to avoid her skin, and pulled her hands away from her face. "Don't be," he said firmly, letting the words echo through her mind, her memory—to the day they'd first met, when he had defended her against Ramin. "You saved us both."

His gaze was as sure and unflinching as his words. Shadows swam over his face, his skin tinted orange in the dim light. Perhaps, if she let him, he could burn the guilt out of her with words, with a look, with a single touch. She started to lean toward him, not even realizing what she was doing until she stopped herself. But still, she felt an undeniable pull toward him, a thread that wound around them, tying them together. Whatever happened now, this moment belonged to the two of them alone, joining them together like a macabre wedding.

Azad's brow furrowed. "Are you hurt?" he asked her.

A laugh escaped her, the sound of it loud and hideously inappropriate in this place of death. "No one can hurt me," she said, a frantic note in her voice. She continued in a calmer tone. "It's over now. The story ends here, Azad."

"What do you mean?" he demanded, his hands tightening on her wrists. "What did the yatu tell you? You can't tell me it's over without any explanation."

He was right. He had endangered himself for her, rushed to save her, comforted her when she was at her worst. It wasn't fair to shut him out now—not until he knew the truth and understood why it had all been for nothing.

"In order to lift my curse, I need the simorgh's feather. That was why I came to the yatu. He used to be the high priest, until he was arrested for treason. I asked him how to find it."

Azad watched her, rapt. "And did he tell you?"

Soraya told him what the yatu had told her about the feather and the fire, how together they gave the shah the simorgh's protection. "Do you understand now? I would have to betray my family."

She waited to see some sign of resignation on his face, but instead he was shaking his head, a stubborn glint in his eye. "Soraya, no. You can't stop now. Maybe the yatu was lying. Maybe if we go to the fire temple, we'll find some way to borrow the feather without endangering anyone."

"No," she said at once. She pulled away from him and looked at the corpse, reminding herself how easy it was for her to lose her self-control. "I don't trust myself to do that."

"I won't give up," Azad said. "Together, we'll find a way."

He reached for her again, but she backed away, looking at him in disbelief. "I don't understand you. I'm a murderer, Azad. You saw me *kill* someone. Why would you even want to help me anymore?"

Azad shook his head slowly as he came toward her. "You saved me, Soraya," he said. "How is what you did any different from what soldiers do on the battlefield? No one would blame you for killing a yatu. You said yourself he was already wanted for treason."

His words sounded reasonable enough, but Soraya knew that what was true for anyone else could never be true for her. If her family found out she had killed, they would see her differently—not as a sleeping serpent, its poison dormant, but as one that was awake and poised to strike. Soraya thought of the Shahmar with a shiver.

"It's different," she said.

"*How?*"

"Because I touched him to see what would happen!" she cried out, her arms wrapping around her waist. "I wanted to see for myself what I was capable of. It wasn't the duty of a warrior. It was . . ." She shook her head, a bitter taste in her mouth. "It was a show of power."

She watched for Azad's reaction, waiting for his disgust for her to show on his face. She saw the movement of his throat as he swallowed, saw his fingers curl slightly at his side—but otherwise he was unreadable.

Her eyes kept flitting between Azad and the lifeless figure of the corpse, each painful in different ways, and so she turned her back on them both, arms tightening around her waist, her back hunching over. But it was too late to make herself small. The damage had already been done.

Gentle hands settled on her shoulders, and as if they had released her from some enchantment, Soraya's shoulders went slack, and her eyes fluttered closed. From behind her, Azad spoke, his voice so low and quiet that it might have been coming from her own mind. "Listen to me, Soraya," the voice said, wrapping around her. "Whatever your reasons, and no matter what anyone else might say, I'm glad you did it. I think you're . . . *extraordinary*."

The last word was an exhale, his breath warm on the curve of her neck. She wanted nothing more than to lean back against him, to let him hold her so close that she would forget everything outside the circle of his arms. She wanted his words to seep into her skin until she believed them. The longing was deeper than she'd ever felt before, a craving for something more than human touch. There was a dull ache in her heart as she opened her eyes.

"We'll leave the body here for the vultures," Azad said. He removed his hands from her shoulders, going to retrieve her other glove.

"No," Soraya said with surprising firmness. "We have to put it on the platform." Dead flesh belonged to the Destroyer, and would pollute the Creator's soil until there was nothing left but bone. She had already broken too many rules tonight; it seemed vitally important to her to keep this one.

Azad looked like he wanted to argue, but he sighed and said, "Fine." He threw the corpse over his shoulder and carried it to the platform, hoisting it up onto the rock. Soraya tried not to focus on the yatu's feet dangling over the edge.

"Now let's leave this place and put it out of our minds," Azad said. He held Soraya's glove out to her. "But our story isn't over yet, Soraya. I promise you that."

She was too exhausted to contradict him—especially when she wanted him to be right. "Take me home," she said softly as she took back her glove. She slipped it on, put her gloved hand in his, and let him lead her out of the dakhmeh, back into the world of the living.

11

Soraya was barely aware of her surroundings as she followed Azad back through the empty city streets to the palace gates. Once again, both the guard at the city walls and the guards at the palace gates let them pass despite the late hour once they saw Azad's uniform, and even through the haze of her guilt, Soraya couldn't help thinking how easy it was for Azad to make his way through the world. With his new status and his air of confidence, he could go anywhere he wanted, while Soraya couldn't even leave the palace without ending up with blood on her hands.

The yatu's face still flashed through her mind, his eyes somehow both blank and accusing at the same time, the poison in his veins spreading up the strained muscles of his neck.

Something touched her shoulder, and she flinched before realizing it was only Azad, his hand dropping away at her reaction. He said something—asked her how she was, if she wanted him to stay with her—and she shook her head, hardly able to understand him over the roar of guilt in her head.

She wanted to cry, to have a measure of release, at least, but she felt withered and empty. The smell of death and dirt from the dakhmeh still lingered on her clothes and in her hair. It was trapped inside her lungs, along with powdered bone remains that also stained her gloves and dress. But Soraya knew that even if she bathed and changed, even if she burned these clothes, she would carry the dakhmeh with her for the rest of her life. That was why the living should never enter the dakhmeh—there was no way to truly leave it behind.

They parted ways outside the golestan. Soraya entered alone, using the key that she had slipped in her sash when she had left earlier this evening, but she couldn't bring herself to continue on to her room. Her body didn't want to move, and she wondered if she would still be standing in the dakhmeh over the yatu's body if Azad hadn't been there to lead her away. She had always thought guilt was an emotion, but now she understood that guilt was a sickness, a fever. It made her feel like all her muscles were being stretched beyond their limits, her body twisting itself around this new and terrible truth.

She was a murderer. She was a monster.

Soraya looked around at her garden. It was the furthest place she could imagine from the dakhmeh—teeming with life, the air fresh and clean with the scent of dew and roses. It was all life that she had nurtured herself, with her own hands. It was life that she couldn't kill.

It was an elaborate and beautiful lie.

Without realizing what she was doing, Soraya shed her gloves, strode over to the nearest rose, and tore it from its stem, crumpling it in her hand. As long as she had this garden, she could convince herself that she was good, that she was not designed solely for wickedness, for killing. But tonight she had learned how easy it was to become something cruel and murderous, how much effort it took to be good. To be small. They were the same thing for her, weren't they?

With a muffled cry, she lunged for the roses and began ripping them all from their stems, not even caring when the thorns pierced her skin. She moved through the entire garden in a frenzy of destruction, pulling the rosebushes apart and crumpling them underfoot until she had laid waste to it all. She knew she'd feel ashamed when she confronted the wreckage in the morning, but now—*now*—she felt nothing but the purest relief. She lost herself, and yet for the first time she *was* herself, more than she had ever been before.

She was breathless when it was done, her hands smeared with dirt and red streaks that were either blood or crushed petals, her dress ruined. The grass was littered with crumpled roses and broken stems. Anyone who saw the golestan now would think a storm had struck.

There was no sound but the rush of blood raging in her ears, but it all went silent as something gray and fluttering landed on a bare stem in front of her. *Parvaneh*, she thought, naming both the creature on the stem and the face that came instantly to her mind.

Even now, Parvaneh was waiting for her, still holding her stolen glove hostage. *Come back for it*, she had said, and Soraya felt the pull of those words as strongly as if there were a cord tied between her and Parvaneh, one monster linked to another. She was the only one here who could make Soraya still feel human. Not even Azad could offer her that. He was too innocent, his hands too clean.

Soraya reached out, one fingertip hovering over the moth's wing. Would it matter anymore if she killed it? What was a moth or butterfly compared to a human being? But before she could make that choice, the moth fluttered away to safety, leaving Soraya feeling strangely bereft.

Come back for it.

Soraya slipped out the golestan door, heading toward the secret entrance in the stairway that she had shown Azad. She understood now that it wasn't the golestan she needed tonight—not the comfort of her roses or even the assuring words of Azad.

What she needed tonight was another monster.

The cavern was almost completely dark, the brazier emitting only a few sparks of light. Soraya was glad. The darkness was effacing; it hid the streaks of powdered bone on her dress, the bleeding scrapes on her hands, and the poison under her skin. Here, she was nothing but a voice.

Or so she believed until she heard Parvaneh say, "You've had an eventful night, I see."

Soraya squinted through the bars until she saw the inhuman sheen of Parvaneh's eyes. "Of course you can see in the dark," Soraya muttered.

Parvaneh walked up to the bars, more visible now that she was closer. "You came back. Does that mean you have the feather?"

A wave of anger burned through Soraya, warming her cold hands. "You knew from the beginning that the feather could lift my curse," she said, her voice little more than a tired rasp.

Parvaneh's face fell, her shoulders slumping. "So you found out," she said, her voice dull with disappointment.

"Why didn't you tell me?"

"Because you never would have brought me the feather if I had."

"You were *using* me, then?"

"And what were you doing with me?" Parvaneh said sharply. "If I had told you from the start how to lift your curse, you never would have come back here or spared me another thought. We owe nothing to each other except for the deal that we made. You would bring me the feather, and I would tell you how to use it to lift your curse. I would have kept my promise."

Soraya shook her head in disgust. "This was all a game to you."

"*No*," Parvaneh said, her voice ringing through the cavern. Her hands clutched the bars so tightly that her veins stood out. "This is no game to me, Soraya. I need that feather. I don't know why you bothered coming back without it—did you think you could trick me into revealing the divs' secret plans? I've kept far more precious secrets to myself while enduring worse than this dungeon. So if you didn't bring me the feather—"

"I can't bring it to you," Soraya snapped. She gestured to her face, to the veins pulsing under her skin. "Don't you think I would have used it by now if I could?"

Parvaneh held Soraya's gaze, the eerie glow of her eyes becoming stronger as she said, "But you know where it is, don't you?"

Soraya let her silence answer for her.

"It's not that you can't find it, but that you can't take it. Why?"

"If I took it," Soraya said, "I would have to betray my family and everything I've ever known."

"Why should you care about them?" Parvaneh nearly shouted. "Are they truly your family if they've failed to accept you as their own? If they cast you out and treat you with disdain? Why do they still matter to you?" Her face was contorted, her voice frantic, and if Soraya didn't know better, she would think Parvaneh was on the verge of tears. She wondered what was fueling this sudden burst of emotion, but whatever sympathy she felt shriveled up when Parvaneh said, "You'll never lift your curse if you're unwilling to face any hardship."

"Unwilling?" Soraya spat back. "How do you think I found out where the feather is? I stepped inside a dakhmeh tonight. I spoke to a yatu, and he tried to attack me. I had to—"

Her voice broke before the words left her throat, and then, finally, the tears came, pouring out of her with such violent force that she sank to the ground, her forehead resting on the dirt and stone as if she were prostrating herself before some divine authority.

She let the tears come—she felt like she was expelling the dakhmeh from her lungs. And when she was finished, wrung dry at last, she was no longer tense or angry. She was almost drowsy, and she thought she could probably curl up there on the dungeon floor and fall asleep.

She looked up to find Parvaneh now sitting on the floor across from her, watching her intensely. "What happened at the dakhmeh, Soraya?"

She heard Azad saying, *Let's leave this place and put it out of our minds.* But why else had Soraya come here, if not to bury her confession in this dungeon? And who better than a demon to hear that confession and not judge her?

"I went there for answers," Soraya said, the words spilling out as easily as the tears had. "I asked the yatu where to find the feather, but the answer he gave me was . . . impossible." Soraya closed her eyes, not even the darkness of the cavern enough to protect her from the truth of herself. "What I did find out tonight was what happens when I touch a living human being. I found out that I'm capable of killing—not as a mistake, but with purpose, with intent." She swallowed. "With rage."

She opened her eyes then, because she knew she would find no judgment on Parvaneh's face. But what she didn't expect was for Parvaneh to drop her gaze when Soraya looked at her. She seemed distracted, staring at a spot on the ground, her forehead creased in thought, lost in some private conversation that Soraya couldn't hear. Finally, she looked up at Soraya and said, "So you've made your choice?"

Soraya shook her head. "There is no choice. I've always wondered who I would have been without my curse, what kind of person I would be if I hadn't grown up hidden and ashamed. But after tonight, I wonder what kind of person I'm becoming, what this path is doing to me. I was always afraid the poison would make me a monster, but what if trying to get rid of it makes me more of a monster than I was before?"

Parvaneh didn't respond. She was staring at Soraya with something heavy and unreadable in her eyes. And again, Soraya found herself wondering what kind of life Parvaneh had lived before now—what was the "far worse" she had endured? Why did Soraya think she could read her own remorse written in the lines and patterns on Parvaneh's face? A delicate sympathy floated in the silence between them, like ashes falling after a fire had burned itself out.

"Then don't do it," Parvaneh said at last. Her voice rang out in the cavern with the clarity of conviction, and she shifted closer to the bars. "You were wrong when you said there is no choice. You *made* a choice. Now embrace it. You are the most powerful and protected being in Atashar. Why would you want to give that up? Why make yourself vulnerable? This is a dangerous world."

Soraya thought again of the yatu—but this time she saw him not dead but alive, bending over her, tying her wrists together while her eye throbbed. Hadn't she thrilled with the power of her curse when she had grabbed his wrist? Hadn't she marveled at how easy it was to bring her attacker to his knees? Without her curse, he would have killed Azad and held her for ransom—but without her curse, she wouldn't have been there in the first place.

"It's because of you and all your talk of power that I killed the yatu," Soraya snapped. It was an unfair accusation, but it comforted her a little. "That was what ran through my head tonight. I thought I was being powerful when I killed him, but all I've done is lose a piece of myself. It's not power to be *dangerous*, to have to hide away behind walls so you don't shame your family while everyone you've ever known leaves you behind. I want my family. I want companionship. I want—" But the word *love* refused to move beyond her lips, too new and precious to lay itself bare for mockery.

Parvaneh thought a moment, and then said, "Perhaps you're simply keeping the wrong company. You would be welcome among my sisters. If you freed me now, I could take you to them. You could have a new family."

Soraya let out a disbelieving laugh. She thought at first that Parvaneh was toying with her, but her tone had been solemn, her words sincere. "You want me to forsake my family and join the divs?"

"Not the divs—the pariks."

"I still don't understand the difference," Soraya muttered as she pushed herself up from the ground.

"You should ask your mother. She knows."

Those words made Soraya freeze. "What do you mean by that?"

Parvaneh rose from the ground, her movements more labored than Soraya would have expected. What happened to a div who was exposed to esfand for this long?

"Haven't you wondered why your mother lied to you about your curse? It's because she's the one who did this to you."

"You're lying," Soraya said. "You said the pariks did this to me."

"At your mother's request. She brought you to the pariks wrapped in a blanket of stars and asked for this curse. Are you curious to know how it's done? It's the blood of a div that made you poisonous. If a human bathes in blood from a div's heart, that human takes on properties of that div. You must have had only a few drops."

Soraya tried to soak in the words like they were rain and she was parched earth, so little did she know about her own history. And yet, each word was a tiny stab, further confirmation that she shared a link to demons. "My mother would have no reason to want such a thing."

"Go ask her why," Parvaneh said at once, an urgent note in her voice.

Soraya shook her head, which was throbbing in pain. "I shouldn't have come back here. Neither of us can help the other now." She turned to go.

"Soraya, wait!" Parvaneh called. "This belongs to you." She reached her arm through the bars, holding out something dark.

Soraya stepped closer, but she was too afraid to reach out with bare hands.

Understanding the source of her hesitation, Parvaneh said, "Don't be afraid. Take it. I'll be careful enough for both of us."

Soraya slowly lifted her hand, reaching through the shadows until she felt the soft, familiar fabric of her glove. She took hold of it, remembering that if Parvaneh was the reason she had killed, she was also the reason she had been able to save herself and Azad.

Parvaneh didn't let go of it. Her mouth was a thin line, tense with unspoken words, her eyes burning with some unknown fire. But then she shook her head and let the glove slip out of her fingers. "There's much you don't know, much I can't tell you," she said. "But trust me when I say that if I were you, I wouldn't shed my armor for the sake of a kind word or a gentle touch. That's my advice to you, from one monster to another."

She retreated back into the shadows then without any word of farewell, as if certain that Soraya would return again.

12

The next morning—the morning of the wedding—Soraya's mother arrived along with her breakfast. Tahmineh was already dressed for the wedding in a gown of purple silk, her hair braided with jewels, and next to her, Soraya felt haggard and unkempt. She'd slept for maybe an hour at most, and those brief snatches of sleep had come with terrible dreams. In a way, she was glad she wasn't attending the ceremony.

Her mother took one worried look at her and carried the tray of food to the low table in the room. "I thought it would be nice to sit together this morning," she said as she and Soraya settled on cushions across from each other at the table. "I know I haven't had as much time to spend with you this year because of the wedding, and I'm very sorry for that. But after today, I'll make up for it."

Soraya put a date in her mouth so she wouldn't have to respond. It wasn't true, of course. Even after the wedding, Tahmineh would want to help Laleh settle into her new role as shahbanu, and in a few months, they would all move on from Golvahar without her.

Perhaps Tahmineh expected Soraya to be sullen today; she continued talking, filling her in on court gossip without expecting Soraya to say much in return. This suited Soraya; all she could think about was Parvaneh's claim that Tahmineh was responsible for her curse, and she was afraid that if she spoke, the question would come tumbling out.

Soraya was fairly sure that Tahmineh had lied about the details of the curse, but she had never imagined that Tahmineh had *wanted* her daughter cursed. There was no logical reason for it. Soraya was a constant threat to their dynasty. She would be much more valuable to her family if she could appear at court or marry well or simply not be a terrible secret they needed to hide. Parvaneh's accusation didn't make sense.

Go ask her why, Parvaneh had commanded, as if doing so would be as simple as posing the question. But Soraya knew that a question like that would be the same as an accusation, and to accuse her mother—to accuse the *shah's mother*—of associating with divs and meddling in forbidden magic was disrespectful at best and borderline treasonous at worst.

And what if Parvaneh is wrong? Soraya thought. What if she ruined her relationship with her mother for nothing? Already, she felt a gulf far wider than the table between her and Tahmineh—a gulf large enough to fit the dungeon and the dakhmeh, the yatu's body lying at the bottom of it. What if there was a loneliness even deeper than the one she felt now?

When Tahmineh finally stood to leave, Soraya couldn't help feeling relieved. "I need to check in on the bride and make sure she'll be ready," Tahmineh said. She tried to sound as if it were an obligation, but Soraya heard the pride and excitement in her mother's voice. This was the kind of relationship she wanted to have with a daughter—why, then, would she have condemned her own to the shadows?

At the doorway, Tahmineh turned back to Soraya and said in a lowered voice, "I know how disappointed you were about the div, but I know it wouldn't have helped you. You can't trust anything they say."

"I know, Maman," Soraya said.

Tahmineh smiled. "I'm glad you understand. And even if you don't, trust me now and you'll understand one day."

Soraya nodded, but once her mother was gone and the door was shut, she felt a scream building inside her chest. *How can I trust you,* she'd wanted to say, *when I don't know what the truth is anymore?* And yet, her mother was right—Parvaneh had destroyed her with a single word, a single suggestion. Soraya would never fully believe Parvaneh, but she would never be able to stop wondering, either.

Before she even realized what she was doing, Soraya went to the hidden door by her bed and stepped into the passageways. She had to do *something* to either confirm this suspicion or forever dismiss it. Since she couldn't bring herself to ask her mother directly, she would have to go digging through her rooms for evidence instead. Her mother would be with Laleh now, and then they would all go out to the garden for the ceremony—her rooms would be empty, and so Soraya could sneak in and out unnoticed.

Only when she arrived at her mother's antechamber did she hesitate. The room was empty, but her mother's jasmine scent was in the air, and as always, Soraya felt like an intruder.

But she had come there with no other intention but to disturb this room's peace, and so she began her search, beginning with the antechamber. She gingerly turned over cushions and peered inside empty vases, still feeling as if she were contaminating everything in the room.

There weren't many places to hide anything here, so she moved

on to the bedchamber. As her search went on, she grew less careful, less reverent. She looked under beds and chairs and even rugs,
inside drawers and jewelry boxes and the wardrobe, pushing aside
her mother's gowns with a roughness that felt strangely satisfying.
She looked everywhere, without even knowing what she was looking for.

She was searching for some sign that her mother knew what had
happened to her, but apart from a written confession, she couldn't
imagine what that sign would be. And perhaps that was the reason
she had chosen to snoop through her mother's things: not to prove
Parvaneh right, but to prove her wrong.

And only when she realized this did she find something.

In her search, Soraya had taken down a tapestry hanging
against the wall across from her mother's bed. As she went to replace it, she noticed that one of the stones on the wall was different
than the others—it was scored, like someone had chipped at it.
She went to her knees and examined it more closely. It was loose,
and so Soraya removed it, still telling herself that it was simply a
loose stone her mother had covered with the tapestry because it
marred the beauty of her room.

She was halfway convinced of this until she found something
inside the wall—something her mother had clearly wanted to hide.
Whatever it is might not be hers, Soraya told herself. *It might have
been here for hundreds of years before us*. Soraya reached into the wall
and pulled out what appeared to be a bundle of rags—bloodstained
rags.

Soraya unwrapped the bundle and laid it out flat on the ground.
And then she let out a moan and covered her face with her hands.

It was a blanket, and yes, it was stained with blood. But beneath
the blood, dust, and grime, she saw the fading pattern on the soft,
thinning cotton: a pattern of stars.

She breathed in, and the smell of esfand seemed to be all
around her as she heard Parvaneh's voice saying, *She brought*

you to the pariks wrapped in a blanket of stars and asked for this curse.

The pieces began to join together in Soraya's mind. The pained, guilty look Tahmineh always wore when she saw her daughter. Her insistence that Soraya not see the div in the dungeon, and her panicked insistence at knowing what Parvaneh had told her. Her dismissal of all of Soraya's questions when she was a child. *The ways of divs are mysterious and unjust,* she had always said, to cover up any cracks in her story.

Soraya heard her own breathing, sharp and quick, as she tried to read a different message in the pattern of stars. But they spelled out only one truth, over and over again: *She did this to me. She knew all along.*

Soraya still didn't understand why her mother would bring such suffering onto her daughter, but she couldn't deny this blanket, still stained with blood from a div's heart.

Why me and not Sorush? She couldn't help asking the question that had plagued her since childhood. Why was she cursed, but not her twin? Why did she have to hide in the shadows so that he could grow in the light? Why had she chosen not to take the feather for his sake, when her family had never once done anything for hers?

She heard Parvaneh saying, *Are they truly your family if they've failed to accept you as their own? If they cast you out and treat you with disdain?*

She heard Azad's gentle voice promising, *Our story isn't over yet, Soraya.*

She heard their voices so clearly, but when she tried to think of her mother, her father, her brother, or the people of Atashar—all she heard was silence.

In the stars of the bloodstained blanket, she saw her choice laid out in front of her. She could choose to cut these ties that had never done anything but strangle her so that she could be free to live the life she had always wanted. All she needed was a feather to drain this poison that her mother had given her.

With shaking hands, Soraya folded the blanket under her arm and left the room, not bothering to replace the tapestry on the wall. Her blood pounded a relentless rhythm throughout her whole body as she made her way back to her room, the path ahead of her clearer than it ever had been. She felt like she'd been struck by lightning, and now there was a fire crackling all through her. If she waited too long to take the feather, then the fire would go out, and she would become nothing but ashes before she could lift her curse. It had to be today, before she could talk herself out of it. Everyone would be in the garden, including the priests, which meant that the fire temple would be unguarded.

In her room, Soraya hid the blanket deep under her bed, then rummaged through her gardening tools for the urn she used to water the roses. She filled it with water from the pool in the golestan and went out through the garden door—and nearly tripped over Azad's outstretched legs.

Some of the water in the urn sloshed as she recovered her balance. Azad had been sitting with his back against the garden wall, and he leaped to his feet at the sight of Soraya. "I've been waiting here all morning, hoping to see you," he said. "I wanted to check on you after last night."

"I'm fine," she said flatly, and kept walking.

He followed, of course, and she knew it wouldn't take him long to realize what she was carrying and where she was going. "Shouldn't you be in the gardens for the wedding?" she said.

"I don't care about the wedding. Soraya, what are you doing? Did something happen?"

He took hold of her arm, forcing her to stop if she didn't want to spill more water. She looked up at him, wondering how much to tell him. He might find her plan abhorrent—treasonous, even—

but he had seen the worst of her last night, and he had stayed by her side. And in any case, he would know soon enough.

She looked around them to make sure no one was listening. The air was pungent with meat and herbs, flowers, and spices, but this part of the grounds was empty today—everyone was either inside the palace or in the gardens. "I'm going to the fire temple," she said. "I'm going to free myself."

He held her gaze, and then he shook his head slowly and said, "Whenever I think I finally know you, you surprise me. But Soraya, are you sure this is what you want? Your family—"

"My family *did this to me*," she snapped, clutching the handles of the urn so hard her knuckles hurt. "My mother had me cursed and lied to me about it for years. So tell me, what do I owe my family? My loyalty? My affection? When have they ever given me either of those? They sacrificed my life and my freedom—I'm only taking back what they stole from me."

For the first time in their acquaintance, Azad looked scared of her. His hand dropped from her arm and he took a step back, his mouth falling open in shock. But then he spoke, and she understood that *she* wasn't the cause of his growing horror. "Your mother did this to you?" he said. "Did she tell you why?"

"No," Soraya replied. "I haven't spoken to her. I don't *want* to speak to her. All she's ever done is lie to me."

"I understand," Azad said, stepping closer to her again. "Trust me, I know that anger. I've felt it before. But are you sure you want to do this? Are you ready for the consequences?"

"Yes," she said at once, but truthfully, she hadn't thought much of the consequences. She wanted to strike now, without worrying about what came after. The yatu had been sentenced to death for attempting to put out the fire. Soraya knew she would receive no less severe a punishment—unless she escaped, as he had. "Yes," she said again. "I want this. And then I want to leave Golvahar and never come back." She shifted the urn's weight to rest in the crook of one arm, and then shyly, uncertainly, she put her gloved hand on Azad's chest, fingers curling over his heart. "Would you come with me?" she asked him in a whisper.

She didn't know what she was asking—for him to come to the temple with her, or to run away with her, or to stay by her side for as long as she wanted him. All of them, she supposed. The idea of freeing herself from her curse only to lose Azad seemed cosmically unjust when he was the one person she wanted to touch most of all.

He took a hesitant breath, but Soraya knew he would agree. She knew he must feel the same bond that she felt, that unspoken promise from the dakhmeh. She had become a murderer to save his life—and in return, he had agreed that there was nothing she could do that would drive him away. They would rise or fall together.

"Soraya." He put his hand over hers, and she felt the heat of his skin through the fabric of her gloves. "I dreamed of you for so long. I would do anything to be with you. Even this."

"I know I'm asking much of you, to sacrifice your position so soon after you earned it."

He shook his head. "I've already learned how suddenly that can be taken away. I lost my family and my social standing a long time ago. I have nothing else to lose now—except for you." He brought her hand to his lips and kissed her gloved fingers, a promise of things to come.

She wanted to linger, but she took back her hand and said, "It has to be now, while the priests are occupied and the temple is unguarded."

They went together to the low hill behind the palace. Azad offered to take the urn from her, but she refused; she wanted something to hold on to. They did encounter a few palace attendants on their way, but they were all so preoccupied with the wedding that they hurried past Soraya and Azad without a glance, never noticing the way Soraya's hands were trembling, or the dark green lines spread out over her skin.

They ascended the stairs cut into the hill, and when they reached the top, they came face-to-face with the only other two people in Golvahar not attending the wedding.

Soraya had been right that the priests would be in the garden, but she hadn't considered that there would be guards watching over the fire in their stead.

Azad, however, didn't seem surprised at all. "I'll handle this," he murmured to Soraya, and he went forward with a wave to approach the two guards. Soraya exhaled in relief, thankful once again for Azad's special status among the azatan. He was better than any key.

She watched Azad greet the two men, putting his hand on the shoulder of the guard on the right as he continued speaking. And then she saw him reach for something at his side, something tucked away in the folds of his tunic—something that glinted sharply in the white spring sun.

Azad struck so quickly, so smoothly, that when the guard on the right let out a cry of surprise and clutched at his side, staggering to his knees, the other guard didn't realize what had happened. He hadn't seen the edge of Azad's dagger find its way in the gap between the first guard's armor plates, digging into his flesh. But Soraya had—and she was frozen in horror even as she knew what would happen next.

The second guard knelt down to inspect the first, and before he could see the blood seeping through the injured man's fingers and know that he'd been stabbed, Azad struck again—this time for the throat.

The second guard fell to the ground instantly, and while his life bled out of him, Azad finished the first guard with another slash to the throat. By the time he returned to Soraya's side, both men were dead.

Azad put a hand on her shoulder, and she flinched violently and rounded on him. "What did you *do*? I thought you were going to *talk* to them and get us inside the temple, not slaughter them!"

"And then what would have happened?" Azad shot back. There was a smear of blood on his cheek, but he was otherwise unaffected—there was only conviction in his eyes, cold and determined. "Do you think they would have let us simply walk away once they found out what we had done? I asked if you were ready for the consequences, Soraya. And some part of you knows I'm right, or else you wouldn't have stood there and let me do it."

Whatever argument she wanted to make died on her tongue. He was right, of course—she had seen him take the dagger from his tunic, and she had said nothing, done nothing. She had let it happen as if it were unavoidable, because she knew that if she stopped him, they would fail before even entering the temple. No, it wasn't that he had killed them that bothered her—it was that he had done it so *well*.

She nodded to him in concession, and without speaking again of the dead men on the ground, they continued into the fire temple.

Soraya saw the flicker of the Royal Fire in its silver urn behind the iron grate, and she felt the flame inside of her, too, burning her from the inside out. *This is a mistake,* the fire was warning her, but if she turned back now, those two guards would have died for nothing. It was too late for regrets.

Azad remained outside the temple entrance, both keeping guard and giving Soraya some privacy, as Soraya walked up to the grate and slid it open. The smell of esfand and sandalwood was almost overpowering as she stepped onto the pedestal and felt the heat of the fire on her face. She looked into the heart of it, searching for some sign of the simorgh's feather embedded in the flames, a mother's protection for her son.

The thought made her bristle, and her anger from this morning flared up again, replacing the dread that had begun to creep over her when she saw the fire. All these years, she had tried to be a good daughter, a good sister. She'd made it so easy for her family to forget and ignore her existence, folding herself away without complaint. Even as she had tried to find a way to lift this curse, she had told herself that she had been doing it in part for her family, so she would no longer be a shadow over them. But she could no longer lie to herself. If she put out the Royal Fire, it would be an act of pure selfishness, designed to benefit herself and no one else.

And just this once, she wanted to be selfish.

She raised the urn full of water over the fire and poured. The water hit the fire with the hiss of a serpent, and steam immediately billowed around her. When it cleared, the fire was gone, leaving only ashes. The urn fell from Soraya's shaking hands and shattered on the ground. Before she could think too hard about what she had done, Soraya dug her hands into the ashes, her gloves becoming streaked with soot.

And there, buried under the ashes, was a flash of color. Soraya brushed aside the rest of the ash and uncovered the simorgh's feather, mostly green but tipped with vibrant orange. It was unburned and unstained, as if it had just been plucked from the simorgh herself.

Soraya removed her gloves and gently lifted the feather, holding it across her palms like it might crumble into ash—as punishment, perhaps, for this ultimate betrayal.

But no, she wouldn't think of that. She couldn't think of it now, when she was so close to freedom.

Soraya remembered the yatu's instructions. Hardly breathing, she pressed the pad of her finger against the sharp tip of the feather, hard enough for a bead of blood to appear, like a single pomegranate seed.

At first, she felt no different, and she wondered if this entire ordeal had been for nothing. But then a shudder ran through her, and her heart began to beat so fast—faster than the usual rapid pulse of fear or exertion—that she couldn't catch her breath. Colors blurred around her, and she felt like she was blurring, too, her body losing its solidity, her insides draining away. It wasn't painful, but it wasn't comforting, either, and she wondered if anything would be left of her once the poison was gone. Light-headed, she held up her hands and watched as the dark green lines running down her wrists faded to a faint blue-green tinge under her skin.

As her veins finished fading, her heart gave a last lurch and returned to normal, a steady beat in her chest that echoed through her ears. Her vision steadied, her blood stilled, and she knew it was over. The poison was gone.

A strange, muffled sound between a sob and a laugh bubbled out of her. She could *feel* the poison missing, but to her surprise, the absence felt cold, like a draft blowing through an open window, like the chill of regret. Soraya shook the thought away. She wouldn't regret this decision, not once she told Azad or tried touching something. She tucked the feather into her sash in case she needed it again. When she was sure its effects were permanent, she would find a way to send it back.

Stumbling down from the pedestal in her haste, Soraya ran to Azad, who turned at the sound of her footsteps.

"Your face," he said, his eyes wide. He took a step into the temple. "Your veins . . ."

"I think it worked," she said, fighting to keep calm, to think rationally. "But I have to test it first, I have to touch something and see if—"

But before she could finish speaking, Azad had taken her face in his hands and crushed his mouth to hers.

Oh, Soraya thought. *Oh.*

It was the first touch she had ever known, and it consumed her. There were too many new sensations—his lips on hers, his hands on her face, his heart beating against hers, the heat rushing through her veins—and so she couldn't focus on just one. It would have been like trying to feel a single raindrop during a storm. Instead, she gave herself up to it—to *him*—and stopped thinking at all, letting long-dormant instincts take over. Her hands did what they had itched to do from the beginning, and wound around Azad's beautiful neck, pulling him flush against her. And all the while she was thinking, *He's still alive. I'm touching him but he's still alive.*

There was a sudden flash of pain like a pinprick on her bottom lip, and she let out an involuntary muffled cry—whether from pain or pleasure, she didn't know. Her skin felt raw and sensitive, like it had been scoured clean, and so the line between pain and pleasure didn't exist anymore. There was only *touch*, so overwhelming that it was almost unbearable.

But Azad must have thought he hurt her, because he drew her away from him, untangling himself from her hungry grasp. Soraya tried to catch her breath, and her eyes slowly fluttered open as she looked up at—

No.

The blood drained from Soraya's face as she looked up, *up*, at a figure a head taller than Azad, a creature that wasn't Azad but was horrifyingly familiar.

Her first thought was that she had done this to him. She had transferred her curse to him somehow. But the hideous scaled monster standing before her wasn't at all surprised by his transformation. That neck that she had always admired was covered in patches of coarse green and brown scales. The hands that had just been on her skin were now longer, with spindly fingers tipped by sharp, curved nails like the claws of a lizard. His hair was gone, his head ridged and scaled like the rest of him. From his back emerged two large, leathery wings. And his face—his face was smiling, sharp, curved fangs showing between thin lips.

Soraya's knees buckled, but she fought to remain standing, not wanting to be on her knees in front of this creature from her nightmares. "What are you?" she said, her voice escaping in a gasp.

He tilted his head, the curve of his neck painfully familiar to her. "I'm hurt, Soraya," he said in a mocking tone. It was the same voice, the same cadence, but deeper now, like she was hearing

Azad calling up from the bottom of a well. "I would have thought you'd know exactly who I am."

Yes, she knew who he was. She knew even before she had asked. She knew when she had looked up and seen him in place of the young man she had expected.

But he still told her anyway.

"I'm your favorite story," said the Shahmar.

13

Soraya prayed that she was dreaming, that this was yet another nightmare. After all, she had never heard of a div being able to appear as human, or to resist the effects of esfand. But in her dreams, she always woke soon after the Shahmar appeared—just when the dream turned into a nightmare.

This time, the nightmare didn't end.

Azad—the Shahmar—took a step toward her, and for the slightest moment, she forgot to be scared. She forgot that she no longer had poison to protect her. And then the memory of Azad's hands on her face, his mouth on hers, came back to her, and she shuddered—not from repulsion or regret, but from a fear she had never known before.

For the first time in her life, she was completely defenseless.

The Shahmar lifted one clawed, scaled hand to hover over her cheek, and Soraya froze, years of habit forcing her to stay still when someone came too near. She looked for the eyes she had known before, but now they were yellow, the pupils vertical slits—the eyes of a serpent.

"Brave, ruthless Soraya," he said, an oddly tender note in his deep voice. "I'm much fonder of you than I thought I'd be." His hand fell away from her face, and she fought down the instinctive disappointment she felt, her traitorous skin still longing for touch, even from a monster. "I have other matters to attend to," he continued, turning away from her. "Stay out of the way, and you'll be safe."

Before she could find her voice, he had stepped out of the fire temple. His wings spread out to their full span, each one the length of a human body, and carried him up into the air.

Soraya recovered at last and ran outside, looking up at the shape of the Shahmar soaring overhead. A shadow fell over the palace—he had paused in front of the sun, his wings blocking its light. She gazed up with a mixture of terror and awe, wondering how this fearsome creature had ever contained himself in the shape of a human, how he could have fooled her so utterly. . . .

Then the screaming began.

The screams seemed to surround her, a wave of terror crashing over her from every direction. And soon she knew why. From her vantage point on the hill, she could see the northwest quarter of the city. She saw the fissures running down the streets, splitting open to release a horde of divs in a kind of hellish earthquake. She saw people run screaming through the streets, trying not to be trampled underfoot or crushed by falling rubble from overturned buildings.

He promised he would show me the city during the day, Soraya remembered. But would there be anything left to see?

She had been frozen, numb with horror and shock, but now she ran. Soraya tore down the hill and around the side of the palace, going in the direction of the nearest screams—to the wedding party in the garden where the most important people in Atashar were all currently gathered like a herd of sheep. She had been so shocked by the revelation of Azad's identity that she had forgotten the reason for the entire pretense. *He made me put out the fire,* she thought. Never mind that she had put it out willingly, that in fact she had convinced *him* to come with her—the truth was that he had been leading her to this moment step by step. He had been waiting for her to find the feather so that he could strike.

And now Soraya's family—her entire *country*—was in danger because of her. Because of her one selfish action.

Even as she ran, her chest stinging from breathlessness, she wondered what use she would possibly be now that her only weapon was gone. She could do little more than warn people of a threat that was already upon them.

As if echoing her thoughts, a shadow fell over her, and she didn't need to look up to know it was the Shahmar, circling the palace like a vulture over the dakhmeh. He was signaling the divs, she realized, purposefully making himself visible to let his accomplices know when to strike. But how had they been able to attack from below?

Soraya heard the answer to her question in her own voice— an innocent, thoughtless remark from nearly a month ago. *There used to be tunnels underneath the entire city,* she had told Azad. Either he had already known from the days of his reign, or she had handed him a way for the divs to infiltrate the city. He had planned everything so thoroughly, and it all depended on Soraya, on his certainty that she would make the wrong choice again and again. He had made a traitor of her, and she hadn't even known it.

Soraya tore through the orchard that bordered the garden, then stopped to catch her breath and observe the damage she had caused.

At first glance, the garden seemed to have descended into chaos.

Large pits spotted the garden where the openings to the water channels had been, and divs appeared from these enlarged tunnels as well as from the now-battered palace walls. Tables of food had been overturned, entire trees uprooted, and rugs trampled over. The panicked wedding guests were running in all directions, but none of them made it beyond the garden borders, because at every turn, a div was there to stop them.

Not even Soraya's visits with Parvaneh had prepared her for seeing a div attack. None of these divs were pariks, with their mostly human forms. Instead, they were beastly in appearance, like the illustrations she had seen in books. They were as varied as they were terrifying, some with scales and fangs like the Shahmar, others with long tusks and bristling fur growing over their bodies. Though some were of human height, many towered over the guests like giants. A few had wings like the Shahmar, and they hovered overhead or scaled the walls of the palace, throwing down chunks of stone to block the paths of the panicked guests.

Soraya ran farther into the garden, trying not to notice the corpses—crushed and broken bodies of soldiers and palace guards, their skulls caved in and limbs snapped to reveal the white of bone, their torsos ripped open, staining the grass red with blood. People kept brushing past her in their attempts to run to safety, reminding her of what she had done—of the price she had willingly paid to be able to stand here in a crowd and be harmless.

She heard the sounds of battle and turned to see one of the remaining soldiers lunging at a furred, fanged div with his sword. His back was to her at first, but then she caught a flash of his profile and inhaled sharply in recognition. *Ramin.* His expression was fierce and focused, but the div easily blocked the sword with a large plank of wood torn from one of the banquet tables and used it to wrench the sword out of Ramin's hands. Defenseless and unarmored, Ramin began to retreat, looking around him

for a weapon, and his eyes caught Soraya's. In that brief, surprised pause, the div struck, his claws raking against one side of
Ramin's waist. Soraya's hands covered her mouth to hold back a
scream as Ramin fell heavily to the ground, his life's blood flowing out of him.

Soraya turned away, feeling no right to witness his last breaths.
Hadn't she fantasized about killing him only weeks ago? Wasn't
she responsible for his death now? He never would have fallen so
easily in a true battle—none of the azatan would—but today the
azatan were outnumbered, unarmored, and unprepared, while the
divs moved with perfect certainty. Soraya remembered what Sorush
had told her about the recent div raids, that the divs seemed to be
practicing for something bigger.

The memory cut through her haze of guilt and fear, and Soraya
began to notice something about the ensuing chaos—that it *wasn't*
chaos at all. She had learned enough about div raids to know that
their main goal was destruction and carnage, but most of the dead
among them now were soldiers and guards. None of the divs made
any move to enter the palace, though a few were still crawling over
the surface and the walls, and a group of them was barricading
the entrance. She watched as one div with a horn and skin plates
like those of a rhinoceros roughly grabbed an elderly man who
was trying to sneak inside, but all the div did was add him to a
group of people huddled together under the watchful guard of another div. In fact, all around the garden, the divs were herding the
wedding guests into small groups, preventing them from escape
but making no other move to harm them. And Soraya understood
now why she had managed to escape their attention so far—she
was neither running away nor fighting, and so they didn't care
what she did.

The div guarding a group of people near the palace steps moved
to the side, and Soraya saw the agonized face of her mother, her
composure fallen away. Soraya didn't think—she ran toward her,

seeking comfort or forgiveness or simply some reassurance that she hadn't brought on the death of her entire family.

As she reached the palace steps, she tripped over her dress, landing on her hands and knees in front of her mother—a fitting position, she thought, to beg for forgiveness.

"Soraya? What are you doing here? You shouldn't be here!" Tahmineh's voice was shrill with panic and utter dismay.

Soraya looked up at her mother—the purple silk of her gown was torn, the jewels in her hair were tangled in her elaborate braids, and her face was swollen from tears. Soraya had always wondered what her mother would look like undone, and now she wished she didn't know. "I'm sorry, Maman," she said, reaching up to her. "I'm so sorry."

For the first time in her memory, Soraya touched her mother's hands, taking them in her own as if that would explain everything.

Tahmineh didn't flinch or pull her hands away from Soraya's grasp—instead, she immediately gripped Soraya's hands more tightly, like they were locking into place. She didn't even seem to know anything was amiss until she looked down at the bare, smooth surface of Soraya's hands and realized there was no poison under Soraya's skin.

"No," she said, the word escaping her like it was her last breath. She lifted her head and looked Soraya in the eye. "Soraya, what have you done?"

The words rang through Soraya's head, an echo of the question she had been asking herself from the moment she had stepped back from her first kiss to see the creature from her nightmares.

Before she could answer, something wrenched her up from the ground, its grip tight around her upper arm. The div towered over her, long tusks emerging from his mouth. "I don't remember you," he growled at her.

"You can't harm me," Soraya said with more confidence than she felt. All she could think was that if she were still cursed, the div would be dead by now.

The div narrowed his eyes. "I can't *kill* you. I can still—"

But before the div could explain in any further detail what he could do to Soraya, a shadow blocked the sun again, and all heads turned up to see a winged silhouette descending from the sky.

The Shahmar landed at the head of the palace steps, wings outstretched, framed by the ayvan behind him. He was still dressed in Azad's clothing—the red tunic and trousers stretched over his scaled form in a mockery of humanity. The garden was hushed as he walked down the palace steps.

He stopped in front of the div that was still holding on to Soraya's arm. "If you touch or threaten her again, I'll tear out your tusks myself," he said in a low, calm voice.

The div's hand instantly fell away from Soraya's arm.

The Shahmar turned to Soraya, holding her gaze. And then— to Soraya's surprise—his eyes moved away from hers, to rest on something right behind her. When she turned her head, she saw her mother standing close to her, her face bloodless, returning the Shahmar's gaze with cold recognition.

But before Soraya could begin to make sense of what she was seeing, the Shahmar turned away from them both and swept forward into the center of the crowd. Even the placement of the captive guests in small groups around the garden had been deliberate—the divs had formed an audience for the Shahmar, who now stood on the trampled rug where the bride and groom should have been sitting.

"You know who I am," he bellowed in his deep, sonorous voice, his arms and wings both outspread to address the crowd. "Many of you have thought me dead, or merely a story to scare your children. But the legend of the Shahmar is real, and I have returned to take back my crown from the line that usurped mine all those years ago. The descendant of that line is among you now. Bring him forward."

There was a flurry of movement among the crowd as everyone looked around them for the shah. Soraya let out a long, relieved exhale. If the Shahmar wanted to see her brother, that meant he wasn't dead.

"Here, shahryar," one of the divs called out. He was standing by the line of cypresses, and she saw that the humans the div was guarding were the injured remains of the king's guard. They all rallied themselves now, but before a fight could ensue, a figure both familiar and strange stepped out from their midst and came forward. Soraya knew that handsome, boyish face, but it was now haggard and ashen. She knew his easy yet dignified gait as he walked out to the center of the garden, but now he seemed so small, so dull, especially as he drew closer to the imposing form of the Shahmar.

"Sorush, the young shah," the Shahmar said, circling him. "You wear my crown. You live in my palace. You use my title."

Sorush shook his head. "You lost your right to the throne. None of this belongs to you any longer."

The Shahmar halted, looming over Sorush, but Sorush kept his gaze ahead of him, not even looking up to meet the Shahmar's eye. "Is that so?" the Shahmar hissed. "And yet *you* were the one to welcome me to your home. You called me a friend and thanked me for saving your life."

Only now did Sorush's regal mask start to crack. He glanced up at the Shahmar, brow furrowed in confusion—and then his eyes widened in understanding. "Azad?"

The Shahmar put his hand to his chest and dipped his head in a mocking bow. "I owe this victory in part to you." He pitched his voice louder, so all could hear. "Even now, an army of divs is storming your city. And they won't stop, not until they've laid waste to your entire kingdom—or until I tell them to stop."

He paused, and there was a low buzzing of murmurs all around the garden, people looking up and noticing the plumes of smoke overhead, wafting from the direction of the city. Sorush's jaw tensed as he tried to remain impassive.

"You've noticed," the Shahmar said, still addressing the crowd more than the shah, "that the divs listen to me. They obey my commands. Over the years of my exile, I have taught them what it means to band together under a king, to follow a vision—*my* vision. The simorgh will not come to your rescue this time, I promise you that. Only I can end this violence. I can return you to your lives of wealth and influence. But first—first you must accept me as your new shah."

He knew when to speak and when to fall silent—to allow the full meaning of his words to sink deeply into the minds of every person present. And they weren't just any people gathered here for the wedding of the shah. They were the bozorgan and satraps from all across the country, the people who chose the shah and those who governed the provinces in his name.

This was why the divs had been instructed not to seriously harm or kill anyone apart from soldiers—the Shahmar didn't want to destroy Atashar. He wanted to rule it.

"Well, then?" the Shahmar said to Sorush. "Will you give up your crown to protect your people? Will you bend your knee to me in supplication?"

Sorush lifted his head to look his enemy in the eye. "The Creator will protect us," he said, his voice quieter than the Shahmar's, but no less powerful. "And you will fail."

The Shahmar didn't respond, staring down at Sorush with deadly stillness. And then, with one fluid movement of his graceful neck, he turned his head and looked directly at Soraya.

"No," Soraya breathed. She didn't think she'd spoken aloud, but then she felt her mother's hands clasp around her arms.

The Shahmar began to walk slowly in her direction. "I understand now," he said. "You refuse to surrender to me because you still believe that the simorgh's protection will shield you." The closer he came to Soraya, the more her mother's grip tightened. He came to stand directly in front of her, shaking his head in disapproval. "So many lies in this family. Perhaps it's time to bring everything to the surface." He wrapped his scaled hand around Soraya's wrist, and with one sharp tug, he tore her from her mother's grip.

Soraya and her mother both cried out together, but the tusked div prevented Tahmineh from following, and the Shahmar effortlessly dragged Soraya to the center of the garden, directly across from her brother. Sorush didn't look at her or show any reaction to his mother's and sister's cries, knowing the Shahmar would use any emotion against him.

But then Sorush's eyes widened as he realized the Shahmar was touching Soraya's bare skin—a subtle movement, but one the Shahmar noticed as well.

"Do you want to tell him, or shall I?" he said to Soraya, his hand still encircling her wrist.

Soraya looked up at the Shahmar, her eyes pleading—and for the first time, she noticed that there were patches of skin visible between the scales that covered his face. She saw the shape of Azad underneath the Shahmar, the boy he had once been before his corruption, the boy she had come to trust and had wanted to run away with. And at the sight of him, a lightning flash of rage pierced through the thick gray fog of her guilt.

"Don't touch me," she said through gritted teeth, wrenching her wrist out of his grip. It was the worst insult she could think of to say to him—that no touch at all was still better than his.

The Shahmar let out a low growl as he stared down at Soraya. He grabbed her wrist again and swung her around to face the encircling crowd.

"People of Atashar," he called to his audience, "I'm sure you've heard tales of the shah's mysterious sister. Perhaps you've wondered why she remains hidden, why she never appears with her family."

Soraya tried to pull herself out of his grip again, but his claws were piercing her skin.

"Allow me, then"—he looked down at Soraya, the beginning of a smile on his thin lips—"to tell you the truth of the shahzadeh's curse."

The Shahmar pointed directly at Tahmineh, who was still in the grip of the div. "When her children were first born, your beloved queen mother—then, the shahbanu—took her infant daughter to the divs and asked them to grant her protection."

Protection? Soraya froze, no longer struggling. She had told Azad that her mother was the cause of her curse, but not even she had known the reason for it. But if he knew the reason, then he'd known the truth all along, watching her stumble from the dungeon to the dakhmeh to the fire temple, looking for answers while her hands grew more and more stained with blood. But even as she hated him for it, she longed to know what he would say next.

"And the divs agreed," he continued, "because the shahbanu had helped them once, and they owed her a debt. They laid a curse on the child and filled her veins with poison, so that she would be deadly to the touch."

The crowd's murmuring was louder now, like the furious roar of a wasp nest. How could the shah's mother have committed such an atrocity? How could the shah have kept his sister's curse a secret from the court all this time? What else was this family hiding?

But Soraya knew the worst was still to come.

The Shahmar spun her around again, holding her in place by her arms, so that she couldn't look away from her brother's grief-stricken face. "And so this girl decided to take her revenge on the family that had cursed her. She waited until the day of her brother's wedding, and then she went to the fire temple, slew the guards, and put out the Royal Fire, because she had discovered that inside the fire was the one object that could free her from her curse—the simorgh's feather."

The Shahmar didn't have to explain further. He put one hand under Soraya's chin and held her face, so that all could see him touching her bare skin without consequence.

Soraya couldn't even turn her head to look away from her brother's broken gaze. "I'm sorry," she tried to say, but the words were so mangled by the sob trapped in her throat that they were barely audible.

The Shahmar released her then, and she fell immediately to the ground, crushed under the weight of her guilt, her brother's shame, and her mother's secrets. She managed to lift her head and see the Shahmar approach her brother slowly, with the same elegance that she had so admired in him when she thought he was hers.

"Well?" he said. "Do you still believe your Creator will keep you safe? Do you think you can protect Atashar better than I can? Or will you kneel?" He turned to the crowd. "Will you kneel," he called out, his arms outstretched, "to save your land from ruin?"

Soraya didn't know who was the first to kneel. She didn't know if it was done out of anger at her family or out of hopeless despair. But all around her, one by one, the most influential people in Atashar went to their knees and chose a new shah. She didn't blame them; pride or loyalty would only lead to more destruction.

Soon, all the bozorgan were kneeling except for relations of the shah—aunts and uncles and cousins Soraya had never really known. Laleh and her wounded father, huddled together. Tahmineh. And Sorush.

From where she lay on the ground, Soraya watched her brother, waiting to see if he would look at her. But Sorush kept his eyes on his usurper as he slowly went down on one knee, then the other, before pressing his forehead to the ground in supplication.

The Shahmar had won.

14

For years, Soraya had thought of herself as a prisoner in the walls of Golvahar, but now, she actually was one.

Her prison was luxurious, certainly—one of the rooms in the new wing, usually reserved for the shah's most important visitors. Its beauty was slightly tarnished, though, since the divs had stripped the room nearly bare, removing anything that could be used as either weapon or escape route—bedding, letter openers, and vases, as well as practically any piece of furniture that could be lifted. When the div had first locked her inside, Soraya had almost longed for the shadows of the dungeon—they were more comfortable to her than a room where there was nowhere to hide.

But more important, there was no way to escape. Soraya didn't need to wonder why the Shahmar had chosen such a gilded prison for her and her family. She already knew the answer:

These tunnels run all through the palace?

Everywhere except for the newer wing on the other side.

Still, the first thing Soraya did was check the walls for hollow spaces. It was something to do other than wonder how long the Shahmar planned to keep them all alive. She had expected him to execute her brother on the spot once Sorush had bowed his head, but the Shahmar had simply ordered his div soldiers to herd together the shah's family and anyone who hadn't kneeled, and keep them confined to the new wing. Soraya didn't think it was mercy—she assumed the Shahmar wanted to kill them later in secret, so as not to upset his new subjects.

Around the room she went, putting her ear to the wall as she knocked, listening for the echo that would tell her she was wrong about there being no passages linked to these rooms. But all she heard were the words echoing in her head to the rhythm of her knocking: *Your fault. Your fault. Your fault.*

Just as she reached the doorway, the door opened and she froze, one fist still in the air. The beaked head of a div poked into the room, took one look at Soraya, and then flung Tahmineh into the room before shutting the door on them both.

Was it a coincidence that they were locked up together? Or did the Shahmar hope that they would tear each other apart and save him the trouble?

They stared at each other, neither of them speaking or moving. They were both bedraggled, their faces tearstained, their hearts heavy. Soraya didn't know whether to beg forgiveness or demand an explanation. Even now, she didn't know how to speak to her mother candidly, without layers of courtesy and formality.

Finally, Tahmineh stepped forward, eyes glistening, and reached one hand to touch Soraya's face. Soraya backed away, more from habit than anything else, but she could tell from her mother's wince of pain that Tahmineh believed the movement had been a rejection.

With a weary sigh, Tahmineh turned away and moved to the

window. Soraya had already checked the window and found that it was too small to fit through and too high up to jump from without breaking bones. She started to say so when her mother turned to her and said, "You weren't surprised when he told everyone I did this to you. You already knew."

"I knew you did this to me, but I still don't know why."

If Tahmineh heard the implied question, she ignored it. "How did you find out?"

"The div," Soraya said. There seemed little point in keeping that secret anymore. "The one in the dungeon."

Tahmineh arched her eyebrows. "You spoke to her?"

"At Sorush's request. He wanted me to report to him if she told me anything useful."

Tahmineh shook her head with a wry smile. "I should have known better than to think I could control my children. At least now you know why I was so insistent that you not speak to her. But what I don't understand," she said as she stepped forward into the center of the room, still leaving plenty of space between her and Soraya, "is why you didn't come talk to me after you found out."

Her hands were open, her eyes entreating, and Soraya wondered if she would have gone to Tahmineh first if *this* had been her image of her mother—open and honest. But how could Tahmineh ask her that question when every time Soraya had ventured too close to forbidden topics, that one worried line would appear on her forehead, and her body would tense as if ready to receive a blow?

"Tell me honestly," Soraya said, her voice shaking slightly. "If I had come to you and told you what the div had said, would you have told me the truth? Or would you have denied it and said the div was lying?"

Tahmineh was silent, which was all the answer Soraya needed.

"And I still don't understand *why*," she said, the last constraints of formality falling away. "The Shahmar said you did this for my protection, that the divs owed you a debt. *He* knows more about my life than I do. It's no wonder he—" She stopped, not even sure how to finish. What had Azad done? Before she had taken the feather, what had he done that she did not want him to do? Soraya wrapped her arms around her waist and turned away from her mother, ashamed of her outburst. She wasn't sure she had any right to anger anymore.

From behind her, Tahmineh placed a tentative hand on her shoulder. "Did he make you do this?" she asked in a low voice.

Soraya shook her head, wishing she could answer otherwise. "He didn't make me take the feather. But he always knew what to do, what to say, to make me trust him."

"So you didn't know what he was? What he was planning to do?"

Soraya turned to her mother in surprise. "Of course not!" she said. "I didn't want any of this. I only wanted to be free from my curse."

Tahmineh let out a brittle laugh that didn't reach her eyes. "And now by breaking one, you've fallen into the other."

"What do you mean?" Soraya asked. "What other? Will you ever tell me the truth?" The last question came out harsher than she'd intended, but there was no point in hiding her feelings now.

Tahmineh went to the wall beside the door and leaned back against it, her eyes pointed up to the ceiling. "You're right. It's time for you to know the full story," she said. "It's *past* time. Maybe if I had told you before, I could have prevented this from happening." She smiled sadly. "Or maybe you would have just learned to hate me sooner." She slid down to sit on the floor, her knees bent in front of her. Soraya had never seen her sit so casually, without her perfect posture. It felt like being in the room with a stranger. She sat on the bare floor across from her mother and, as she had done so often as a child, waited for her story to begin.

"The first part was true," Tahmineh said. "I did wander into the forestland near Mount Arzur when I was little more than a child, and I did find a woman wrapped in a net. But the woman wasn't human. I didn't know that at first—I couldn't see her clearly enough in the net, and she looked so close to human—but when I freed her, she unfurled her wings, and I understood. She was a div—a parik. She gave me a lock of her hair, and told me that if I ever needed a favor in return, I should burn the hair and breathe in the smoke, and then that night I could speak to her in my dreams. She flew away, and I was alone."

She paused, her lips clamped shut, as if it physically pained her to speak.

"And then the Shahmar found me," she said.

Soraya's heart gave a lurch. "The Shahmar was the same div who found you in the forest?" But even as she asked it, she knew it was true—she remembered the look of recognition that passed between them in the garden.

"The Shahmar found me," Tahmineh repeated, her voice louder, like she was trying to scare away her own fear. "I didn't know who he was at the time. I just thought he was a monster. He told me I had taken something of his, and so now he would take something of mine."

Soraya frowned. She knew this part already. "But—"

"He told me he would wait until I had a daughter, and when that daughter came of age, he would steal her away and make her his bride."

Tahmineh's words hovered over them like a blast of cold air, and Soraya let out a low moan of regret, because now she understood why her mother had wanted her to be untouchable. She had spent these years believing Tahmineh had hidden her to protect their family or the safety of others—but Soraya had been the one Tahmineh was trying to protect all along.

"For years, I tried to forget what he said," Tahmineh continued. "I didn't know if he had meant it or if it was an empty threat. But I prayed—I prayed every night from that day on—that I would never have a girl. When Sorush was born, I thought my prayers had been answered—but then you were born, minutes later, and I loved you and feared for you at the same time."

"The parik's favor."

Tahmineh nodded. "I had kept the lock of her hair all those years, knowing this day might come. I burned it the night after you were born, and I dreamt I was in a forest—but not the same one where the Shahmar had found me. It was a forest I had never seen before, lush and green. The parik was there, and I told her I needed protection for my daughter, so that no div could ever touch her. She told me to meet her at the dakhmeh near the palace the next night, and to bring you with me."

"You went to the dakhmeh?"

Tahmineh bowed her head in shame, but Soraya felt an unexpected tenderness for her mother, knowing they had both made the same choice to brave the dakhmeh. But her mother was even braver, because she had gone alone, undefended. *For me*, Soraya thought. *She did that for me, and I betrayed her.*

"I was desperate," Tahmineh continued, "and so I did as the parik asked. She was there with a few others of her kind, and she had brought a basin large enough for an infant, filled with water. She had a vial of some red liquid and told me that a few drops of it mixed in the water would make you untouchable. Any human, beast, or div who touched you would die almost instantly."

Tahmineh looked directly at her, a fierce glint in her dark eyes. "And I agreed," she said, her voice firm—defiant, even. "I agreed because I didn't know how else to protect you in such a dangerous world. There were times when I even envied your curse, because I thought you would never know the fear that I knew when the Shahmar found me in the forest. I kept you hidden away in Golvahar and forced myself to leave you here, because I didn't want to draw the Shahmar's attention to you in case he ever sought me out. But I wish I could have kept you with me. I wish I had told you the truth sooner."

"Why didn't you?" Soraya asked at once. A curious mixture of remorse and resentment swam inside her.

"At first I didn't tell you because I didn't want you to be afraid," Tahmineh answered. "How could I tell my child that a monster might steal her away? And how could I explain what I had done without letting you know why? I didn't want you to grow up with that shadow over you. And when you were older . . ." She looked down at her lap, avoiding Soraya's eye. "I didn't want you to hate me. I saw how unhappy you were, and I couldn't stand knowing that it was because of my actions—because I couldn't protect you myself. I felt so guilty every time I left you here on your own." She lifted her head, her eyes swimming with tears. "Soraya, can you forgive me?"

Soraya's eyes were stinging, her throat closing up. A part of her wanted to say that she was the one who should be asking for forgiveness—she was the one who had brought ruin on them all with her choices. And another part wanted to say no, she couldn't forgive Tahmineh, because by trying to protect her daughter from one kind of danger, she had left her completely vulnerable to another.

But instead of saying either of those things, Soraya did what she had wanted to do since she was a child. She inched closer to her mother and laid her bare hand on Tahmineh's. In the space of a breath—a sob, really—Tahmineh had enclosed Soraya in her arms, laying her daughter's head on her chest and stroking her hair as she rocked them both slowly back and forth.

They wept, forgiveness neither granted nor denied for now. Perhaps they both were to blame, but they both also knew the kinds of terrible choices a person made when at the mercy of the Shahmar. It was a curse they shared, a curse that Soraya had inherited—and in a strange way, it was the first time she truly felt she was her mother's daughter.

The heavy, formless guilt that had been threatening to suffocate her was now taking shape, becoming something she could *do* rather than feel. "I started this," Soraya said, her voice thick with tears. She lifted her head. "And I have to end it—for all of us."

Tahmineh put her hands on Soraya's face, one palm on either cheek, and for a moment, they remained like that, enjoying a simple pleasure that had so long been denied them. Then she dropped her hands and said, "He started this, not you. But you *are* the only one who can end this. If anyone can find a way to sneak out of the palace, it's you. And once you've escaped, you have to find the parik with the wings of an owl. She already paid her debt to me, but maybe she'll help us again. The pariks are against him, I think. If I can get you out of this room, will you do the rest?"

"Of course, but how—"

Tahmineh shook her head and held a finger to her lips. "Not now. Later, when it's dark." She gestured to the window, which was letting in the warm orange light of sunset.

They waited together until the light slowly faded away, and then Tahmineh whispered to her, "Wait behind the door. As soon as it opens, and the div enters, run out of here as quickly as you can. Don't hesitate, Soraya, do you understand me?"

Soraya nodded, but she still didn't know what her mother was planning. She stood with her back flat against the wall so that when the door opened, it would hide her. Tahmineh went to the window, curled her hand into a fist, and slammed it into the glass pane, shattering it with a loud crash.

Both Tahmineh and Soraya let out loud cries of alarm—though Soraya's was genuine, while Tahmineh's seemed calculated. Her eyes never left the door, not even as she pulled her bleeding arm back in through the window. Soraya wanted to run to her, but Tahmineh held up a hand, and she remembered her mother's order not to hesitate.

Mere seconds later, the door slammed open with such force that

Soraya was nearly crushed by the impact. The beaked div came forward, going across the room to where Tahmineh was holding out her bleeding arm while making garbled pleas for help. And despite her mother's orders, Soraya did hesitate—because how could her mother know if the div would help her or if he would let her bleed to death? How could she be so sure that the Shahmar cared if she lived or died?

But if she didn't go now, then Tahmineh's actions would have been for nothing. Soraya had already wasted one of her mother's gifts—she wouldn't make the same mistake again.

With the div's back to her, Soraya slid out from behind the door—and ran.

15

She began to veer right, but there was another div standing nearby, mercifully facing the other end of the hall, so Soraya skidded to a halt and changed direction. She wasn't familiar with this part of the palace, but after making another turn, she found a narrow stairwell that would almost certainly be too small for most of the divs to fit into.

It was fortunate that the div had blocked her first instinct to turn right. When Soraya stepped out of the stairwell, she realized by the narrowness of the corridors and the unadorned walls that she was in passageways used mainly by servants, at the back of the palace. Soraya went to the end of the hall and turned down the only way open to her—a long hall that would take her from the new wing back to the main structure of the palace, where she could more easily disappear into the walls.

The long hallway led to a round, colonnaded vestibule with large, arched doorways that opened out to the grounds behind the palace. But the doorways were guarded, of course, by two equally large divs, and Soraya stayed in the shadows of her hallway, trying to remember the closest entrance to the passageways.

Her heart was beating frantically in her chest, and she took a breath to calm herself. *If anyone can find a way to sneak out of the palace, it's you,* she thought, finding comfort in her mother's words. Even though the poison had been drained out of her, she was still an expert at sneaking through the palace unseen and unheard. With one last inhale, she looked out across the vestibule, at the hallway opposite hers. Inside the second door on the right down that hall was an office for scribes, and inside that office was a hidden door that would take her into the passageways—if nobody caught her first.

Soraya stepped out into the vestibule, slowly enough that the soles of her slippers made no sound against the marble floor. With painfully slow steps, she reached the first column without the divs noticing her. She peered out from behind the column, waiting for the divs to look away before she dared move out into the center of the room, directly into their line of vision. She watched them . . . waiting . . . and finally, something made them turn their heads to look out onto the grounds.

Soraya ran, no longer bothering to take slow, quiet steps. The slapping sound of her slippers against the floor must have drawn their attention, because she heard a gruff shout, followed by the sound of footsteps running in her direction.

She was in the opposite hall now, and she made it to the second door just as one of the divs squeezed himself into the hallway, barreling after her while she fumbled with the door handle with damp hands. *If I had my gloves, this would be easier,* she thought, but she managed to get the door open and shut it behind her, hoping that would buy her enough time to disappear before the div saw where she had gone.

In the scribes' dark, windowless office, Soraya moved by instinct, finding the opening of the door in the wall behind the writing desk. The door to the office began to open—Soraya stepped into the passageways—

And swung the door shut behind her as the div burst into the room. From the narrow seam in the wall, Soraya watched the div look around the empty office, confusion on his furred and leonine face. He let out an angry snort and then he was gone.

Soraya collapsed against the wall in relief—but her relief didn't last long. She was safe for now, but still had to find a way out of the palace, and it was only a matter of time before the Shahmar discovered she was missing. He would likely guess she was in the passageways, and he already knew one of the entrances.

And then there was her mother's advice, that Soraya find a parik with the wings of an owl. But even if Soraya managed to escape the palace, how would she ever manage to find the parik on her own?

You would be welcome among my sisters. If you freed me now, I could take you to them.

The solution was both obvious and ridiculous. Parvaneh would know how to find the other pariks, of course. She probably even knew the owl-winged parik her mother had mentioned, since she had known so much about Soraya's curse. But why would Parvaneh ever agree to help her? *The feather,* Soraya remembered, putting a hand to her waist, feeling the outline of the feather inside her sash.

She began to walk in the direction of the chamber that would take her to the dungeon, but even though she knew Parvaneh was her best option, she worried she was making yet another terrible mistake. Parvaneh was a div—she would surely be in league with the Shahmar.

As if Parvaneh were in the same room with her, Soraya could clearly see the insulted look on her face and hear the irritation in her voice. *I'm not any div,* she had once told her. *I'm a parik, and my purposes are my own.*

Soraya remembered, too, that Parvaneh had last urged her not to take the feather at all, to live with her curse in peace—and to ask her mother why she had wanted her daughter cursed. If Soraya had followed any of her advice, the Shahmar's plan might have failed.

Even as Soraya argued with herself, every step she took led her closer to the dungeon. When she emerged into the round chamber where she had once stood with Azad, she knew there was never a question of whether she would return to the dungeon, not truly. Even if she didn't need help finding the owl-winged parik, Soraya would still want to look into those amber eyes and see for herself if Parvaneh had been a part of this plot from the beginning.

The familiar and reassuring smell of esfand surrounded her as soon as she stepped out into the dungeon. If the smoke was still this strong, then no other divs had been here—which meant, possibly, that Parvaneh wasn't a part of their plot. Soraya reminded herself that the esfand hadn't had any effect on Azad, but she supposed that was because of his former humanity.

Letting out a slow breath, Soraya crept down the stairs to Parvaneh's cavern. The light was stronger this time, and so she could clearly see Parvaneh restlessly pacing the length of her cell. As soon as she saw Soraya, she froze and walked up to the bars. Her gaze immediately went from Soraya's face and neck to her bare hands. "You did it, didn't you?" she said. Her eyes snapped back to Soraya's face with an urgent gleam. "Do you have the feather?"

Soraya stepped forward, ignoring Parvaneh's question. "Did you know? When you saw him here with me that first day, did you know who he was—and what he was planning?"

Parvaneh didn't need to speak her answer aloud. The glow of her eyes dimmed, her shoulders sagged, and her hands fell away from the bars. Everything about her spoke of defeat.

Soraya shook her head in disappointment. She didn't understand why she was so surprised, so betrayed. Parvaneh was a div, wasn't she? "You knew and you said nothing."

"I said plenty. You didn't listen."

"You were a part of this from the beginning, weren't you? When you attacked my brother—that was all part of the plan to get both of you into the palace. What a wonderful spy you've been for your king," Soraya sneered.

Parvaneh's eyes flashed with anger. "He's not my king," she said, her voice a snarl. "He's my captor. If I had told you everything, would you have believed me? You barely believed a word I said as it was. If I had told you that your handsome new friend was secretly the leader of the divs, you would have denied it at best. At worst, you would have told him, so he could reassure you that I was a liar, and then he would have punished me and my sisters."

Soraya heard the echo of her own response to her mother's question of why Soraya hadn't confronted her sooner, and so she couldn't deny that Parvaneh was probably right. Soraya's voice softened a little as she repeated, "Your sisters?"

"He hunts us for sport. Many of my sisters are his prisoners."

Like the parik my mother freed in the forest, Soraya remembered. "The other pariks—does one of them have the wings of an owl?"

Parvaneh's head tilted in surprise. "Parisa," she said, with a glimmer of a smile. "She's the one who made you what you are."

"I need to find her. Do you know where she is?"

"Captured, or so he told me. But . . ." Parvaneh's eyes flickered to a spot behind Soraya's shoulder—the source of the fragrant smoke all around them. "If you let me out, I could take you to her and the others, and we could free them. We both have families to save."

Soraya considered in silence. She didn't know whom to trust anymore—she had trusted Azad completely, and she had been wrong. Was it possible, then, that she had been wrong to think that Parvaneh was her enemy? Or would she be even more of a fool to trust her now?

Parvaneh nodded in understanding. "You still don't trust me. But maybe if I show you what he's done to me, you'll believe that I'm no friend of the Shahmar." Parvaneh turned, her back facing Soraya, and lifted her worn shift over her head. Startled, Soraya began to look away, but then she understood what Parvaneh was showing her.

Her mother had thought she was freeing a girl until the parik unfurled her wings—the wings of an owl. Parvaneh's wings were, of course, the wings of a moth, bearing the same patterns as the ones on her skin. Or at least Soraya thought they were the same patterns—it was difficult to tell because Parvaneh's wings were slashed and torn, hanging like ribbons down her back.

Without thinking, Soraya came closer, all the way up to the bars. From here, she saw the tears in the wings more clearly, long, clean lines as if from a dagger—or claws.

"He did this to you?" Soraya asked in a small voice.

Parvaneh put her shift back on and turned around to face her again. "Bit by bit over time, yes. I had hoped the simorgh's feather could restore them."

Soraya listened to her, but it wasn't the words that spoke to her loudest. In the hollow sound of Parvaneh's voice, the dimmed glow of her eyes, the tired lines on her face, Soraya recognized someone who had lost not just her family, but a piece of herself.

Soraya pulled out the feather from her sash, careful not to hold it out of Parvaneh's reach. Parvaneh's eyes locked on the feather with a hungry, desperate look. "You have it," she breathed.

Soraya turned away from Parvaneh and went to the lit brazier hanging from the wall. Perhaps she was a fool to trust Parvaneh, but images kept swimming in her mind—images of destruction and despair, of sharp claws and leathery wings, of a terrified girl in the forest and a young shah on his knees. Soraya couldn't undo any of the Shahmar's actions—except that she could free Parvaneh.

For the second time that day, she put out a fire, upending the brazier and sending the coals to scatter over the ground.

Parvaneh didn't need an explanation. As soon as the esfand smoke began to disperse, she wrenched two of the bars apart with unearthly strength and walked through them—free.

Soraya wondered if she had made another mistake, if Parvaneh would snap her neck and go join her master, where they would both laugh at the naive girl they had fooled. But Parvaneh made no move toward her. She closed her eyes, lifted her head, and took a deep breath. "Thank you," she said.

"You said you would help me," Soraya reminded her.

"And I will," Parvaneh said. Impossibly, her eyes were even brighter than they had been before. "But I won't be much help until my wings are restored." She turned and lifted her shift again, her movements more fluid now that the smoke had cleared. Soraya took an involuntary step back. The idea of someone baring their skin for her was still unthinkable, and she looked from Parvaneh's back to the feather in her hand as if she didn't quite know how to bring them together.

After a lengthy pause, Parvaneh shot a pointed look over her shoulder at Soraya and said, "You'll have to come closer."

Her sardonic tone broke Soraya out of her trance, and she moved toward Parvaneh, observing the damage of her wings without touching her. She brushed the tip of the feather along the largest tear, and instantly, the wing stitched itself back together. But there were many tears—not just the long, clean ones, but also smaller, jagged ones that probably happened on their own. It was delicate work, and so neither of them spoke as Soraya continued to tend to Parvaneh's wings, one tear at a time.

It was calming—the soft brush of feather against wings, the hushed sounds of their breathing, the feeling of putting something together. It reminded Soraya of working in her garden, pulling away vines and plucking away dead petals so that her roses could bloom and thrive. She wasn't even aware of what she was doing when she first touched Parvaneh's wing with her other hand, meaning to smooth out the surface so she could better attend to it. As soon as she realized what she had done, she drew back, but then her instinctive fear drained away, and she brushed her fingers against the wing again, thinking of that first butterfly from so long ago.

She continued her work, but her eyes kept drifting to the strip of bare skin between wings—to the matching patterns swirling like shadows on Parvaneh's back, the soft down near the base of her neck, the curved ridge of her spine. It was almost like wanderlust; her fingertips yearned to explore new landscapes, new textures that they had never known before.

Only when she had finished repairing the last tear did Soraya allow herself to reach out with one faintly trembling hand and brush the pads of her fingers against Parvaneh's skin, tracing one of the whorls on the inside of her shoulder blade where the wing was knitted into her back. Soraya was amazed at how soft Parvaneh's skin was—softer than the petals of Soraya's roses or the wool of her gloves. She let her fingers glide to the top of Parvaneh's spine, and felt the strength of bone and muscle underneath the fragile layer of skin. She pressed down lightly, exploring the rise and dip of the ridges there, and she heard Parvaneh inhale sharply, her back arching.

Soraya pulled her hand away at once as if she'd been burned. She had forgotten herself—forgotten everything except her hunger for touch.

Parvaneh glanced over her shoulder at her, and Soraya tensed, expecting mockery. But Parvaneh's expression was serious, and her voice soft—almost apologetic—as she asked, "Are you finished?"

"Yes," Soraya said. "I think I repaired all of them."

Parvaneh slowly opened her wings out to their full length, then closed and opened them again, and Soraya heard the barely restrained joy in her voice as she said, "Yes, you did." Her wings collapsed, lying flat along her spine, and she put her shift back on. "Thank you," she said, turning to Soraya. A hint of a smile played on her lips. "You have a gentle touch." She headed for the stairway, leaving Soraya speechless behind her.

Once they ascended from the cavern, Parvaneh let Soraya lead the way through the dungeon. Soraya brought her to the secret entrance to the passageways, then paused to consider. She didn't know if the Shahmar had noticed yet that she was missing, but if he had, he would likely be waiting for her to emerge from the passages—and he already knew about one of the doors. She wondered if it would be safer to use the regular entrance to the dungeon, but that, too, seemed too exposed, too risky. Better to take Parvaneh in through the passages and surface somewhere behind the palace—near the stables, if possible.

Soraya pulled open the door to the passageways, and told Parvaneh to follow.

She took them back to the circular cavern, though she ventured cautiously in case any divs were lying in wait. From there, they continued on down the central tunnel, Soraya heading toward the far western corner of the palace. There was a door there that would open onto a terrace that overlooked the training grounds. From there, they could run for the stables. Parvaneh's presence behind her was an unexpected comfort—Soraya wasn't alone now. She had someone powerful on her side, and soon the other pariks would join them. Her promise to her mother wasn't bluster or desperation. It was possible. She could still undo what she had done.

As they neared the terrace, the passage became narrower, and Soraya had to duck her head. She was relieved when her hands met the low, square door at last. She pushed it open, letting in the crisp night air and the light from the stars, and began to crawl out through the opening in the palace wall onto the white stone of the terrace.

And then something sharp clamped around her arm and dragged her out the rest of the way.

The beaked div stood alone on the empty terrace, as if he had been expecting her. "The Shahmar said I would find you here," he said. "He's waiting for you."

Soraya didn't have time to wonder how the Shahmar had known where to find her. She needed to be ready to make her escape—because she noticed at once that the beaked div was alone, and she had Parvaneh with her.

Except that when she turned to look down the tunnel, Parvaneh was gone, and Soraya cursed herself for trusting yet another div.

The div led her into the palace, down halls that were now lined with other divs. She had expected him to take her back to the new wing, but instead, he went all the way down the hall to the entrance of the throne room.

The throne room was exactly as she had last seen it on Nog Roz—except that a different occupant lounged on the throne, his posture relaxed and arrogant. The beaked div brought her to the center of the room, where Sorush was standing rigidly on the image of the simorgh.

A ring of divs circled the room, and Soraya cursed silently as her eyes went to the door hidden in the right wall. One of the divs was positioned directly against it, blocking any escape. *The Shahmar knows about the door,* Soraya thought at once, but that was impossible, wasn't it? She had never shown it to him, or even told him about it.

Following her gaze, the Shahmar said, "You're looking for the door, aren't you?" His voice rumbled with amusement. "I should have known better than to try to keep you prisoner here. You know these walls even better than I do. And I know them quite well myself—I built those passages that have hidden you away from me for so long, and so I knew which one you would likely take to escape. Don't you find that poetic?"

A paranoid shah, Soraya remembered. *Paranoid but clever*, Azad had insisted. She was beginning to think there was no way to detangle her life from his, or his fate from hers.

The Shahmar continued: "I would have retrieved you soon anyway. I want you to be here when I kill your brother."

Her stomach lurched, and she tried to find Sorush's eye, but he kept his gaze straight ahead. Instead, she faced the Shahmar and said, "Why kill him? Isn't it enough that he's your prisoner?"

It was a weak argument, and they both knew it. The Shahmar shook his head. "I won't make the same mistake I did last time, Soraya. As long as he lives, people will have hope that he can rise against me, and I won't be overthrown by your family again." He rose from the throne and descended from the dais. At once, Soraya stepped in front of her oddly passive brother.

"I won't stand and watch," she said to the Shahmar as he stepped closer and closer. "I won't let you—"

"Soraya, stop." Sorush's voice rang clear, his hand firm on her shoulder. "It doesn't matter."

She spun to face him in astonishment. His face was blank and unfeeling, but somehow his calm demeanor only made her feel more frantic, more desperate. "How can you say that?" she said to him. "That is your throne. Those are *your* people!"

He gave a slight shake of the head. "Not anymore. You saw to that."

The chill in his voice made Soraya shiver. "Sorush, I'm sorry," she said to him, her throat dry. "I never thought this would happen. When I put out the fire, I didn't know—"

"And I didn't know you hated me this much. I didn't know you were capable of this."

Soraya's hands clenched at her sides, and before she could stop herself, she snapped, "Of course you didn't know. How would you know anything I feel, or what I'm capable of, when you've barely spoken to me since childhood? After you became shah, you left me behind."

This was wrong—she wasn't supposed to be angry with him, not now, not after what she had done. But her old wounds hadn't disappeared just because she had struck him a new one, and Sorush's coldness toward her only reminded her of what had driven her to the fire temple in the first place.

Sorush's eyes flickered, but only briefly. "You're right," he said. "I left you behind, and I worried about you often—but I had to worry about everyone else in this country as well. And now you've had your revenge on all of us—a very thorough one."

The Shahmar's scaled hand came down on her shoulder before she could respond. "As much as I enjoy seeing you like this, I think we're finished here."

He gestured to one of the divs, who came forward to lead Sorush away.

Soraya started to follow, but the Shahmar kept her in place. "Where are you taking him?" she asked hoarsely.

"I've changed my mind about the execution," the Shahmar said, circling around to stand in front of her and block her view of Sorush's retreating back.

"Why?"

"Perhaps your tender plea has moved me." His hand encircled her wrist, and he pulled her alongside him as he strode out of the room.

Soraya fought to keep up with his determined stride, which only halted when they were both outside the main doors of the palace. The wreckage of the garden was masked by the darkness of night, but still, Soraya couldn't bear to look at it.

"Where's Sorush?" she demanded. "What are you going to do with him?" Her voice was growing ragged with the start of tears.

"You needn't worry about him for now."

"And my mother?" she said, Tahmineh's pained cry still fresh in her mind. "Is she . . . ?"

"Is she alive, or did I let her bleed to death after creating a distraction that allowed you to escape?" the Shahmar finished for her with a sneer. Soraya waited, hardly breathing, until he said, "She's alive and safely bandaged."

"Let me see her."

"No," he said without hesitation.

"Fine," she said, weariness draining her remaining resistance. "Return me to my room."

"No," he repeated with a note of amusement. His lips twitched as he tried not to smile.

It was that hint of a smile, so maddeningly familiar, that shattered her last remnants of composure. "What more do you want from me, then?" she shouted at him as she ripped out of his grip. "You're like a cat with prey, the way you've toyed with me all this time."

The Shahmar's smile was gone, but his eyes gleamed in the dark. "It's strange, isn't it? I thought I would surely kill you once you handed over the feather." He reached for her, hooking one claw into her sash and using it to drag her toward him. When he withdrew his hand, he pulled the feather out from its hiding place, too, enclosing it in his scaled fist. "And yet, as I told you, I've grown quite fond of you, Soraya. You impressed me greatly during our time together. I find that I don't want to kill you—I want to keep you." He took hold of her again, his long fingers encircling her upper arm in a firm grip. "But I clearly can't keep you here. You would escape me eventually. I'll have to take you elsewhere."

Before Soraya could respond, he swept her up in his arms and beat his massive wings until they were both high up above the palace.

In fear, Soraya clung to him, her eyes squeezing shut. She had read a story like this once, about a girl who was carried away by a monstrous bird to Mount Arzur. But the bird was enchanted, and when the girl kissed him, he turned into a handsome young man. It was fitting, Soraya supposed, that she would kiss a handsome young man and turn him into a monster.

She risked opening her eyes again, looking down as her conquered home and the charred outline of the city became smaller and smaller. Her breathing grew thin, and she gasped for air before her terror and exhaustion were finally strong enough to make the world go dark.

16

Soraya woke with a gasp. The last thing she remembered was moving up toward the stars and seeing Golvahar disappear below her. She remembered the beating of wings and the sharp points of claws digging into her skin. But these were all just memories. She was lying on something solid now—a bed?—and she was alone. Or at least she hoped she was alone. The light was dim, wherever she was.

Soraya sat up cautiously and squinted in the low light. When she touched the wall beside her for leverage, her hand met cool, uneven stone. What had the Shahmar said? That he couldn't keep her in Golvahar, and so needed to take her elsewhere. She tried to keep her breathing even as she considered the possibilities—was she in a cave somewhere in the forest? Did he intend to keep her locked up here until he tired of her? She still wasn't entirely convinced he didn't plan to kill her.

She rose from the bed, and went toward the source of light. As her eyes adjusted, she saw that she was in a windowless room hewn out of rock. The light came from an iron candelabra set on a table, alongside a jug of water and a bowl of fruit. Everything in the room seemed cobbled together and slightly worn, from the rickety wooden bed frame to the chipped marble of the table to the moth-eaten rug beneath it. It seemed more like a mismatched collection than anything else, and it did nothing to alleviate the feeling that she had been buried alive.

But she let out a breath of relief when she saw a door set into the wall. The door, too, seemed misplaced—a rectangular wooden panel jammed into an arched opening—but more important, there was no keyhole beneath the handle. She wasn't trapped, then . . . unless it was a different kind of trap. What would happen to her if she opened that door? What would be waiting for her on the other side?

Soraya went toward the door, and as she neared it, she noticed deep grooves made in the wood around the handle—the kind of grooves claws might make.

She was still staring at the door when the handle started to move and the door started to open. She braced herself for the sight of the Shahmar, that face from her nightmares.

But it wasn't the Shahmar who stepped through the door. It was Azad. Soraya glanced at his hands, at his eyes, at his hair, but there was no sign of the monster she knew him to be. He was as beautiful as the day she'd first seen him.

He smiled when he saw her. "Good, you're awake. Now we can—"

"No." Her voice echoed slightly.

He tilted his head. "What do you mean?"

"Don't pretend. Not anymore." Her throat clenched painfully as she tried to hold back angry tears.

"I'm not pretending, Soraya." He stepped forward and reached for her hands, thumbs tracing the line of her knuckles. Soraya wanted to pull away, but it was still so *new*, so strange to feel bare skin on hers, and she couldn't make herself deny something she'd wanted for so long. It was harder to remember to hate him when he looked like the boy who had comforted her at the dakhmeh. *That boy never existed*, she reminded herself, but when he slid his hands up her arms, when he cupped her face and began to lean in, she wanted so much to let herself forget.

"*No*," she said, forcing the word out of her with all her strength. She tore away from Azad before he could kiss her, and she wrapped her arms around herself, curling inward as she always used to do. "No," she said again, unable to look up at his face, though she could imagine the look of hurt and surprise—the vulnerability that he had cultivated to draw her in. "Your voice, your face, your hands— they're not real. They're not who you are." She lifted her head, forcing herself to look at him and still deny him. "Show me who you are."

His eyes narrowed, and when he spoke, it was with that other voice, his *real* voice. "Fine," he said. "If that's what you prefer." Azad began to fade away like smoke, and the Shahmar emerged.

But now that she had seen his transformation, she could find the points of commonality more easily—he had the same bone structure, the same athletic grace. The shift from Azad to the Shahmar wasn't a complete change; it was the burial of one underneath the other. She still didn't understand how he was able to appear as human—she had never heard of any other div doing such a thing—but she knew with certainty that when he did so, he was taking the form of the prince he had once been, before his corruption.

"Are you satisfied now?" he said in a low growl. He seemed insulted by her demand—embarrassed, even. Perhaps he had been as eager to forget as she was, and these past weeks had been a fantasy for them both.

But he had been the one to end it, not her.

"Satisfied?" she said in disbelief. "You've usurped my brother's throne and imprisoned my family, and now you're holding me captive. You've lied to me at every turn and gained my trust while guiding me toward my family's destruction." Her voice was growing louder as she spoke. There was no poison in her veins anymore, no one to hurt as a result of her anger, and so she let herself revel in it, knowing the Shahmar was a worthy and deserving target. "You threatened my mother all those years ago," she continued. "You're the reason I was cursed. You're the reason for *all* of this!"

The words came so easily to her that she knew, as soon as she'd said them, that she wanted them to be true a little too much. How easy it would be to lay all of her guilt on the Shahmar's scaled shoulders.

She was afraid he would challenge that last statement, or remind her of her role in this disaster. But instead, he only asked, "So your mother told you the truth at last? Did she tell you everything?"

Soraya heard her mother's voice saying, *He told me he would wait until I had a daughter, and when that daughter came of age, he would steal her away and make her his bride.* He had certainly stolen her away—but did he mean to keep the last part of his promise as well? She watched the flickering candlelight, unable to look directly at him, as she said, "Is that why I'm here? Because of some petty grudge you have against her?"

"No," he said, taking a step toward her. "I didn't bring you here because of the threat I made to your mother. That was only ever meant to scare her. If she hadn't made you poisonous, I would never have given you another thought. I wouldn't have known about you at all, except that a parik told me about you after I captured her. In exchange for her freedom, she told me that the shah's sister was a girl with poison growing inside her, waiting to be unleashed. As I heard her story, I realized who you were—who your mother was—and I knew you were the key, the ally I needed to take Golvahar.

And . . ." His voice softened into a low hum. "I couldn't resist seeing you for myself." He reached for her, brushing his gnarled fingers against her hair. "I felt as if I already knew you, as if you were already mine. Didn't you feel the same?"

It was all too familiar. *He* was too familiar—the cadence of his voice, the intensity of his gaze, even the way he touched her hair. And worst of all, she *had* felt from the beginning as if she had known him, as if she had dreamed him into existence. *As if you were already mine.*

But if familiarity weakened her resolve, it also saved her. In some corner of her mind, a knowing voice whispered, *He's doing it again.* And she knew at once that the voice was right. In either form, Azad or the Shahmar, he knew the exact words she wanted most to hear, the exact gestures that would stir up desires that she had long ago put to rest. Even now, he was playing on her as easily as if she were an instrument, hoping the chord he struck would be louder than the screams from the garden.

He must have seen something harden in her expression, because his eyes narrowed and his hand fell away.

"Did you think the same tricks would work on me again?" she said coldly. "What do you even want with me? Why did you lock me up here instead of killing me?"

He stared at her in silence for the space of a heartbeat, then another, like he was waiting or searching for something, and Soraya realized, *He doesn't know, either.* He had meant it when he said he'd planned to kill her. But for all his planning and manipulating, Soraya must have managed to surprise him. That gave her hope—it meant there was still a part of her that he couldn't possess or predict.

Finally he said, "You're wrong about one thing, Soraya. There's no lock on the door. You can step outside anytime you'd like." He gestured to the door, and Soraya tried to find some hint of his intentions in those cold eyes. But whatever was beyond this room, she had to know, and so with a last suspicious look in his direction, she went to the door and pulled it open.

She blinked, thinking that she was still unconscious, that this was a cruel dream, because she could have sworn she was standing at the threshold of Golvahar's secret passageways. But then she noticed the differences—mud-brown rock instead of tan brick, wider walls and a higher ceiling, and a lit torch in a sconce on the wall.

"Go on," the Shahmar urged from behind her.

Soraya stepped out into the tunnel, unnerved to be in a setting that was familiar and yet foreign, and to know that the Shahmar was behind her at every step. There was only one path to take, so she followed the tunnel until it opened out into a larger one, at which point the Shahmar grabbed her by the arm and pulled her back.

"Don't leave my side," he said. He led her out into the larger tunnel, still holding on to her arm, and soon Soraya realized why.

Divs roamed this tunnel—though Soraya didn't feel like she was in a tunnel anymore, but rather in a hallway that might have been lifted from Golvahar. High above her head was a vaulted roof, and the torches illuminated a series of carvings along the wall, all of the Shahmar victorious in battle. She might have been in a nightmare version of Golvahar, complete with monstrous inhabitants.

But Soraya knew where she was, and a soft groan escaped her lips. She recalled the feeling of being buried alive, and she had been almost right, except she wasn't underground. She was inside Mount Arzur, the home of divs. And now she understood why there was no lock on her door. She was trapped inside a mountain, and every div here was her jailor.

"It took me years to achieve this," the Shahmar said with pride as he led her down the hall. Every time a div approached them, Soraya tensed in fear, but none of them noticed her. Instead, they bowed their heads in deference to the Shahmar, passing her by without a glance. As much as Soraya hated to admit it, the Shahmar's presence beside her was almost like having her curse restored, a shield of safety that made her untouchable. "First to win the divs to my side," the Shahmar continued, "to make them understand that they would be more powerful united under my command—then to carve this mountain into something worthy of a king. But it was only something to occupy me until I found a way to return to my true home—" He looked down at her. "Until I found *you.*"

His words stung, reminding her of her role in her family's downfall. But before she could respond, he turned her to the left, through a rounded opening that brought them into a massive cavern.

They were standing on a narrow rock bridge that spanned the entire cavern, and Soraya might have stumbled over the edge if the Shahmar hadn't held her back. "Careful now," he said.

A metallic smell filled the air, the smell of blood and weaponry. Above her was the mountain peak, allowing no escape except for a few holes carved into the rock that let down beams of silvery moonlight. Below, inside a shallow, rectangular pit in the center of the cavern, two divs—one female with sharp horns, and the other male with bristling gray fur and the snout of a wolf—were locked in fierce battle, their battle-axes clashing loudly against each other. Soraya would have thought they were sparring, except they swung their axes wildly, without concern for limbs lost or blood shed. All around the pit were other divs, some cheering, some shouting curses, while yet others were occupied by sharpening weapons on grinding wheels, or performing drills.

The Shahmar kept his hand wrapped around her arm as he led her to the center of the bridge, where another div was watching the training below. He resembled the Shahmar more than the other divs—his build was leaner, closer to human, and his skin was covered in a kind of shell, like a scorpion. But what caught Soraya's attention the most was the large, bloodstained club in his hand. *Aeshma,* she remembered from her books. *The div of wrath.*

"Aeshma," the Shahmar said to him as they approached. "Is all as it should be?"

Aeshma turned at the sound of his voice and quickly bowed his head. "Yes, shahryar," Aeshma said in a voice like a rattle. He gestured to the fight below. "Please, watch the battle below and see if your soldiers are as fierce as you wish them to be."

"Thank you, Aeshma. Leave us now."

Aeshma bowed again and retreated to the other side of the bridge.

"Shall we watch?" the Shahmar said, positioning Soraya in front of him for her to see the fight below. "These are *my* training grounds, and the kastars are my soldiers," he said with pride.

"Kastars?" Soraya echoed, remembering the word from before—something Parvaneh had said about different kinds of divs.

"Kastars are large and brutish divs, their methods of destruction more obvious, as you can see below. The div you just saw—Aeshma—is a druj. I use the drujes as my generals. They're smaller in build, but their minds are sharper and more strategic. Before I united them, the divs rarely worked together, their powers limited, which is why they were never able to accomplish more than petty violence and short-sighted raids. But joined under one vision, they can conquer kingdoms. As you've seen."

"What about the pariks?" Soraya snapped, irritated by that last remark.

His hands tightened around her arms. "The pariks are spies, and cannot be trusted."

With this new knowledge, Soraya surveyed the cavern once more, noticing that the divs practicing the drills were all larger than the divs who barked orders. Her gaze went back to the pit where the two divs were fighting—both of them kastars, large and menacing, showing no restraint.

Soraya had never seen a female soldier before. She had read stories of women who had donned armor and fought in armies, but she had never seen any herself, and so her eyes kept returning to the horned div and the pure, relentless fury of her movements. Soraya felt the impact of each blow that the horned div struck somewhere deep in her chest, as if the battle below were an extension of herself, the sound of metal against metal the scream that she had been holding inside her lungs for her entire life.

"Do you want to know why I brought you here, why I can't bring myself to kill you?" the Shahmar said from behind her, his voice low and soft. "Because I know *this* is where you belong. I knew it the night we went to the dakhmeh. Before then, I thought you would merely be useful to me. But when I heard my story from your lips, when I saw you unleash all your fury on the yatu, I knew you deserved more than what your family had given you—as I once did."

"I'm not like you," Soraya said. She stared straight ahead, wishing she could tear her eyes away from the violence below and prove him wrong. "I won't be like you."

"That's not what you told me that night, on the way to the dakhmeh." He placed his hands on her shoulders, the tips of his claws brushing against her collarbone. "And do you remember what *I* told you? I said you were extraordinary—and I meant it. You came alive that night."

Of course she remembered—he had stood behind her then, too, just like this, his hands on her shoulders, and she had wanted nothing more than to sink back against him.

Soraya twisted to face him, and his claws raked against her skin, leaving thin red scratches. "Then what good am I to you now?" she said in a rasp. "I'm not deadly anymore."

He shook his head. "It isn't the poison that makes you deadly,

Soraya. It's *you*. The poison was only a tool, a weapon like any other. But your will, your fury—that was what I saw in you. And I knew then that you were capable of anything. You proved that to me at the fire temple."

At the mention of the temple, Soraya's face went hot from shame. He kept using her words and actions against her, and she had no power to deny them. But before she could even try, a loud cry went up from below, and she spun to see the cause.

At first, she only saw the blood staining the dirt in the sparring pit below, and then she found its source: The gray div had buried his ax into the horned div's arm. The horned div was bellowing in pain as blood spurted out of her like a gruesome fountain, while all around, the other divs cheered. The gray div removed his ax, and turned his back on the horned div, holding the ax above his head to the delight of the crowd. The horned div's arm dangled uselessly from its socket, hanging on only by a few threads of muscle and skin, and her ax clattered down to the ground. Then the horned div ripped off the remains of her arm with a sickening tearing sound, threw it aside, and charged forward with a yell. Still boasting his triumph, the gray div didn't notice the horned div's attack until those horns went clean through his torso, impaling him.

Soraya put a hand over her mouth, afraid she would be ill, and turned away from the spectacle. Her hands were shaking, her eyes trying to blink away what she had seen, but along with the disgust and the nausea was a flood of relief that she was horrified at all—that she took no delight in the carnage, the way the other divs did. *He's wrong,* her twisting stomach assured her. *You don't belong here.*

The Shahmar silently led her away, back to the hallway. When they were in her room again, he told her he was returning to Golvahar, and so would not see her until the following night. Soraya heard his words in a daze, still trying to erase what she had seen.

"I would suggest you remain here until I return for you," the Shahmar said, and he didn't need to explain why.

He started to turn for the door, but Soraya gathered enough of her wits to call out, "Wait!" He stopped and looked at her expectantly. "What are you going to do to my brother?" she said.

"Why do you still care about any of them?" he asked, genuine curiosity in his voice. "Why are you still fighting me at all? Don't you have everything you wanted? You wanted revenge against your family. You wanted to lift your curse. You wanted to be far away from Golvahar—with *me*."

She shook her head. He wasn't right. He couldn't be right. As long as she fed the spark of hatred for him and let it spread through her, there would be no room for him to be right.

"I don't want you," she snapped. "I never did."

"That's a lie," he said at once, and she hated that she couldn't deny it. "And . . ." He took a hesitant step toward her, and in a voice she almost recognized, said, "And there's no reason you shouldn't want me still. My name truly was Azad, once, before it became lost to time and legend." He held out his arms and looked down at his hands. "The face you knew was what I looked like before . . . before I became this." His eyes met hers, and they were hopeful, almost human despite their color. "The gulf is not as wide as you think," he said quietly, like he was telling her a secret.

I know, she almost replied, but to admit that was to admit that she had looked hard enough to see those remnants underneath.

"All that means," she said, "is that I never should have trusted you in the first place. Now tell me what you've done with my brother."

At once, his eyes went hard, and his hands clenched into fists. "I have plans for your brother, but you're not ready to hear them yet."

"If you harm him," Soraya began, not even sure what she could threaten him with, "if you harm anyone in my family—"

"Don't be naive. You know I can't allow him to live for much longer."

"If you expect me to ever speak to you again, you'll allow it."

A low growl escaped him. "I'll return tomorrow night," he said before he turned and left, nearly breaking the door in the process.

17

And now she was alone, with only her treacherous thoughts for company. Different walls, different furnishings, but in a way, she was exactly where she had always been.

She hadn't wanted to take anything that the Shahmar offered, but her stomach demanded otherwise, so she ate the fruit on the table and wondered how she was supposed to pass the time until he returned. Perhaps that was the point—to leave her here long enough that she would be pleased to see him when he returned for her, hungry for any company. The thought made her shudder, because she knew that plan would work in the end. She had been lonely enough at Golvahar to be susceptible to his charms, and now her isolation was even worse.

Without windows, there was no sense of how much time had passed since he'd left her here. Soraya looked at her bowl of fruit, now missing one pear and several grapes. She had eaten without thinking, but now she realized she would need to ration herself more carefully. She had no idea if she would be fed again before Azad's return. She would have to preserve her water, too. At least at Golvahar, she had never had to worry about food or drink—she had lived in comfort, lacking nothing except company. Soraya buried her head in her hands, guilt and regret turning the taste of the fruit sour in her mouth.

Her mother's voice came to her, gentler than she deserved: *He started this, not you. But you* are *the only one who can end this.*

Soraya lifted her head. She had promised her mother she would make up for what she had done, and to do that, she still had to find the owl-winged parik. But she would never be able to keep that promise if she stayed here, day after day, at Azad's mercy.

It took several tries to pry open the tightly wedged door, but as soon as she did, some of her worries faded. She was comfortable with tunnels, after all—they had practically raised her. If she kept heading down, she'd eventually reach the mountain's base, where maybe she would find a way out. She just had to evade the divs, as she had done in the palace.

Soraya moved silently down the tunnel, waiting until the large hallway beyond was empty before daring to take another step. This time she noticed that the ground was built on a slight incline. Soraya went in the direction inclining downward, which was the opposite of where Azad had taken her, staying close to the walls and moving from shadow to shadow. Along the hall were smaller openings that led to side passages, and she paused before crossing them, making sure nothing was going to jump out at her. She noticed, too, that the hall was rounded, and she hoped that this one tunnel wound itself all the way up the mountain in a large spiral. If it did, she could follow it down until she reached the mountain base.

And perhaps she could have, if the hall had remained empty.

She felt the vibration of heavy steps under her feet before she saw the divs themselves, giving her enough time to duck down one of the side tunnels before three large divs came into view. She waited a little longer to make sure no other divs would pass, but she waited too long, and soon another passed in the opposite direction.

She kept waiting, and the longer she did, the more divs she saw moving in both directions—and the more she realized how futile and foolish this decision was. Every time one of them passed her hiding place, Soraya held her breath and shrank back, knowing that eventually one of them would turn this way. She couldn't stay here, but she couldn't continue on the main path. She was fortunate that she had managed to make it even this far. Conceding defeat, she followed the tunnel she was already in.

Soon, she found a stairway, and she went down, knowing she would be trapped if she met anyone or anything in this narrow space. She found herself in another, smaller tunnel, but there were no torches here, nothing to light her way as she stumbled along in the darkness, one hand on the wall. She was breathing so heavily that she worried someone would hear her, and so she put her other hand over her mouth to silence the frightened wheeze her lungs were making.

But even with her mouth covered, she could still hear the sound of breathing behind her—and it wasn't her own.

Soraya ran, all hope of escaping the mountain abandoned in favor of merely finding a safe place to hide. As soon as her hand no longer felt solid rock, she bolted in that direction, moving down another hall that took her deeper into the mountain. The torches began to reappear, though they were few and far between, as Soraya threw herself into the labyrinth of tunnels, trying to outrun approaching shadows and the echoes of footsteps. She didn't know where to find safety or when to catch her breath. Her heart was racing, the way it had when people kept brushing against her on Nog Roz, never giving her time to recover. Except now she was the only one in danger.

She should have listened to him. She should have stayed in her room. It was only a matter of time before she was too slow or took a wrong step.

Down, she told herself. *Just keep going down*. It was too late, and she was too lost, to retrace her steps to her room. The only hope she had was to keep heading downward until she eventually reached the base of the mountain.

She kept moving until she found another set of stairs and hurried down them, but instead of leading her into another tunnel, they brought her to a cavernous room—empty, thankfully, except for a fire in the center of it. And beside the fire was something that smelled delicious.

After catching her breath, Soraya went toward the fire. The smell was coming from a piece of meat spitted on a stick—some kind of bird, from the look of it. Thinking of the finite supply of fruit in her room, Soraya took the stick and sank her teeth into the wing of the cooked bird. She gave an involuntary sigh as she swallowed and took another bite.

But before she could swallow again, she heard footsteps coming from the stairs behind her. Soraya dropped the stick at once and looked around for another exit, but the stairs were the only way in or out of this cavern. She should have already known that. She should have turned back at once as soon as she saw this was a dead end, but the smell of the food had been too tempting to resist. She had allowed herself to be caught in a trap.

As the steps grew louder, Soraya moved away from the fire, into the shadows. She pressed herself flat against the wall right beside the opening to the stairwell, hoping she could repeat her trick from the palace and sneak past the div.

The steps slowed, then stopped, and Soraya waited for the div to appear.

And then a large fist slammed into the wall above her head.

Soraya ducked as the div lunged out from the stairway, bits of rock raining down onto the top of her head. He had only missed her because he had struck without looking, and she knew he wouldn't miss again. She ran for the stairs, but it was a last, hopeless attempt at escape, and she wasn't surprised when the div clutched the back of her dress and pulled her back into the cavern, throwing her to the ground.

"I heard you breathing, little thief," the div said in a rumbling voice. He had the torso of a man, his skin deathly white, but the legs and head of a wildcat. "I can smell my dinner on your breath. But that's no matter—I'll just eat you, instead."

"I'm the Shahmar's guest!" Soraya cried, reaching out an arm as if that could somehow stop him from killing her. *It would have, before,* she thought with a strange pang. Once, she could have killed him easily, with only a touch. She would have been deadlier than he was. And she wouldn't have to use the name of her captor as a shield. "He would be displeased if you harmed me."

The div chuckled. "I don't know what you're doing here, human, but it doesn't matter to—"

He never finished, because two hands appeared on either side of his head and viciously snapped his neck to the side with inhuman strength.

Before the div fell dead to the ground, Soraya's rescuer jumped lightly off his back and stood with her hands on her hips.

"*There* you are," Parvaneh said.

Soraya remained frozen on the ground at first, her mouth hanging open. "I thought you left me," she said as she rose. "You disappeared."

Parvaneh shook her head. "I transformed. Pariks all have one other form they can take." To prove her point, she suddenly vanished—or so Soraya thought until she noticed a dark gray moth hovering where Parvaneh had been standing. In another moment, the moth was gone, and Parvaneh reappeared. "I followed you all the way here."

"You've been here the entire time," Soraya said, more to herself than to Parvaneh.

"I lost track of you for a while, and by the time I found you again, you were sneaking through the tunnels—which was very foolish, by the way." She gestured to the dead div on the ground. "If I hadn't heard you, he'd have eaten you by now."

Soraya looked from Parvaneh's disapproving stare to the div. And then, to her own surprise, she began to laugh. She didn't know why she was laughing, exactly—because she'd almost been eaten, or because she was being lectured by a demon, or because she still had an ally and wasn't trapped alone in this mountain with only Azad for company after all. She was laughing so hard that she couldn't breathe, and tears began to stream down her cheeks, and now she wasn't sure if she was laughing or sobbing.

She only stopped when she felt Parvaneh's cold hands on either side of her face, shocking her into silence. Would she ever become used to something as simple as the feel of someone's hands on her skin? It seemed impossible.

Soraya focused on those eyes like glowing embers, even more vivid now in the light of the fire, until the rise and fall of her chest slowed to normal.

"I'm glad you're here," she managed to say.

"We had a deal."

"Yes, but divs aren't known for being true to their word."

Parvaneh lifted an eyebrow. "I must be fond of you, then."

Soraya smiled to herself as Parvaneh returned to the div's corpse and searched it. She pulled off the tattered, voluminous cloak he'd been wearing, her lip curling with distaste. "Here," she said, tossing the cloak to Soraya. "You can hide in this the next time you want to wander through the tunnels."

"I wasn't wandering," Soraya said. "I was looking for a way out of the mountain. I still need to find the parik with owl's wings. You said you would take me to her."

Parvaneh nodded, but she was still staring down at the dead div, avoiding Soraya's eye.

"Az—the Shahmar said he would return tomorrow night," Soraya continued. "Can you take me to her before then? Can we go now?"

Parvaneh lifted her head. "That depends," she said. "Did you bring the simorgh's feather with you?"

Soraya's hands went to her sash, but then she remembered that Azad had taken the feather from her before bringing her here. Parvaneh must not have seen it happen when she was following in her moth form. Still, she hesitated before telling this to Parvaneh. Why did Parvaneh need the feather in order to take her to the other pariks? If she knew Soraya didn't have it, would she refuse? Soraya wanted to trust her—Parvaneh had become, in a strange way, her confidante as well as her ally—but she was still living the consequences of the last time she had been too eager to trust someone.

"Yes," she said, her hand pressed down over her sash. "I have it. But I'll give it to you *after* we find the parik."

Parvaneh started to argue, but then she nodded, a wry smile on her lips. "Fair enough," she said. "I won't need it till then anyway."

"Why do you still need it at all?"

Parvaneh hesitated, and Soraya supposed she was also deciding how much they could trust each other. "We can't defeat the Shahmar without the feather," she said.

Soraya couldn't help scoffing. "How is a single feather going to stop him?" But Parvaneh's expression remained grave, and Soraya felt a twinge of worry as she again remembered the feather in Azad's fist.

"That feather," Parvaneh said, "is the only thing that can make him human."

Soraya shook her head. "He can change form at will—I've seen him do it."

Parvaneh again hesitated, as if trying to determine how much to say. "I mean permanently," she said. "The feather will make him human, as he once was, before he became a div—just as it removed your curse. And only then can we kill him."

In the silence that followed, Soraya wondered for the first time how Azad had become a div. The stories made his transformation sound like some kind of divine punishment—he acted monstrously and became a monster. *Stories lie,* he had told her. She wondered, too, if he knew that the feather could restore his humanity. If he did, why hadn't he used it? He must have already known what Soraya hadn't understood—that the price of humanity was vulnerability.

Soraya's fingers curled over her waist. "Is there no way to defeat him while he's still a div?".

"It would be difficult to strike any blow—his scales are like armor," Parvaneh answered. "But even then . . . there's something you don't know about divs. It would be easier to show you."

Parvaneh took the tattered cloak from her, looking from its length to Soraya with an appraising eye. "We can both hide under this," she said. She stood beside Soraya and threw the cloak over Soraya's shoulders, drawing it forward over both their heads to create a makeshift hood. "Hold it tight," she said.

Soraya drew the edge of the cloak in toward herself, and she and Parvaneh huddled close under the fabric. It was long enough to hide their feet, and thin enough that they could see where they were going.

"Something's wrong," Parvaneh said. "Can you not breathe?"

Soraya's breathing *was* quickening, but not because of lack of air. "I'm not used to this," she managed to say. Parvaneh's shoulder was flush against hers, and every time their hands brushed against each other in the close proximity under the cloak, Soraya felt an instinctive jolt of panic.

"Give me your hand," Parvaneh said. Soraya shyly threaded her fingers through Parvaneh's, and then they waited—waited until

Soraya adjusted to the presence of touch, until her heart slowed and her breathing became normal. It was like sinking into a hot bath, the water gradually becoming bearable against sensitive skin.

"I'm ready," Soraya said.

Parvaneh led the way through the tunnels, using their joined hands to indicate which direction she wanted them to go. Soraya kept her eyes down so she wouldn't trip over the cloak's hem. They passed other divs on their way, but none of them glanced at the unwieldy shape beneath the cloak.

Once they had returned to the long hallway, Parvaneh led them down—the way Soraya had been planning to go before she'd become lost. But when they reached the end of the path, at the base of the mountain at last, Soraya saw that she would never have managed to make it out of the mountain alive.

At the base of the mountain was the largest cavern that Soraya had seen yet—it was larger than the palace gardens. They stayed close to the wall, still hidden under the cloak, and Soraya's hand tightened around Parvaneh's. Through the fabric, she saw mostly shapes and shadows, but it was enough to let her know she was looking into the hellish heart of this mountain.

There were divs lounging throughout the massive cavern, some drinking or eating, many sleeping, and others just watching. In the center of the cavern was a wide pit, and from its unknown depths, more divs climbed out at irregular intervals.

"Is this some kind of test?" Soraya asked, thinking of the training grounds.

"This is his throne room," Parvaneh said, gesturing to the far wall of the cavern. There, a massive throne had been carved into the rock. It was empty, of course, its usual occupant currently visiting a different throne. "And *that*," she said, pointing to the large pit, "is Duzakh."

Soraya shuddered at the word. "That's the home of the Destroyer," she said, remembering the yatu.

"When the Destroyer releases us into the world, this is where we emerge," Parvaneh said. "When a div dies, the Destroyer feels it, and he sends out a replacement, a druj for a druj, or a parik for a parik, and so on. That's why the Shahmar always captures pariks but never kills them."

Soraya's eyes were locked onto the mouth of Duzakh as a wolfish head emerged from it. A div similar but not identical in appearance to the one who had perished in the sparring pit crawled his way out. As soon as he was fully above the surface, a wiry druj came to his side and led him away—recruiting him to the Shahmar's cause, Soraya guessed. She thought of all the battles her brother and the shahs before him had led, all the divs they had killed, not knowing that each victory was only temporary.

"Will the same thing happen if we kill the Shahmar?" she asked. "Another div will rise to take his place?"

"Not exactly," Parvaneh said, her voice strained. "Some of us tried to kill the Shahmar in the beginning. But something about his human origins has interfered with the usual process. When he's struck a mortal blow, he doesn't die—he regenerates. His scales spread out and close over any wound. I think the div in him only grows stronger with each attempt. In order to truly defeat him, we must make him human first—and to do that, we need the simorgh's feather."

Soraya's hand went to her sash again, a hollow feeling growing in the pit of her stomach.

18

From Azad's throne room, Parvaneh led her back into the tunnels. She mentioned something about a secret escape route known only to pariks, but Soraya only half listened. She was too busy arguing with herself.

Tell her about the feather, one part of her was saying. *Tell her now.*

If you tell her now, she'll never help you, the other insisted. *She'll leave you here in the tunnels to be torn apart.*

They stopped in front of a blank wall, Parvaneh looking around before she dug her fingers into a crease and pulled open a heavy slab of rock. She removed the cloak from around their shoulders, and both of them took a breath. "Watch your head," Parvaneh warned, and they ducked into a narrow passage. Once they were inside, Parvaneh pulled the hidden door back in place, leaving them in total darkness.

Soraya tried to straighten up, but her head met the rock above with a dull thud. This passage was clearly smaller than any of the others; she felt more like she was inside the passages of Golvahar than the finely carved halls of Azad's mountain palace. But the darkness of Golvahar's passages was far more familiar to her, and she tried to find the wall with her hand to give her something solid in the nebulous dark.

Something brushed her hair, and she let out a small yelp.

"It's me," Parvaneh said in a hushed voice. Parvaneh's hand found Soraya's, and Soraya gratefully latched on to it. "We're in a part of Arzur that only pariks know about," Parvaneh explained. "Keep your head down and don't let go of my hand."

They continued on, and when the ground beneath them started to incline upward, Soraya hoped they were near the end. The air here was thin and stale, and not being able to see made her feel untethered, with Parvaneh's hand as her only anchor.

Finally, Parvaneh told her to wait as she took back her hand. Soraya heard the sound of rock scraping against rock, and shortly afterward, a stream of air and moonlight bathed her face, as pure and refreshing as any river.

Parvaneh emerged first, and Soraya followed. Outside the mountain at last, Soraya stood with her head back and filled her lungs with the night sky. And then she looked around her and was convinced she had stepped into a different world.

"Where are we?" Soraya asked with a mixture of alarm and awe.

"The forest, of course," Parvaneh said flatly.

But Soraya had never seen forestland like this before. She had never been inside a forest at all. From the roof of Golvahar, she could see the sparse forestland at the south of the mountain— where her mother had first encountered a div. But the land there was dry, with clumps of trees scattered across the landscape, more brown than green. That was not the forest Soraya was standing in now.

The trees here were so tall, so densely packed, that Soraya could barely see more than a short distance in their direction. She didn't even recognize these trees, with their long vines and leaves hanging down and their trunks twisted into different shapes. Even in the moonlight, she could tell how green it all was—it *felt* green. It smelled green. The air was thick with moisture, and everything around her felt vivid and alive, like she was standing on a pulse. It reminded her of being in the golestan, except the golestan was only a shadow of the lush forest around her.

"I didn't know such a place existed in Atashar," she said, walking toward the forest. She took slow, hesitant steps, like she was afraid of waking something up.

"This is the forest to the north of the mountains," Parvaneh said behind her. "Few humans have walked here." That explained why Soraya had never seen it from the roof. The mountains had always blocked her view of anything farther north.

A sound like fabric tearing made Soraya turn back to Parvaneh, and again, she was struck with awe. Parvaneh's face was tilted up to the sky with a look of pained joy, like she thought she'd never see it again—and Soraya understood now why keeping her buried in a dungeon had been a terrible punishment for her. Parvaneh seemed to be made of the night. She wore it like a gown, draped over skin that shimmered in the moonlight. The sound Soraya had heard must have been Parvaneh making a tear down the back of her shift, because now her wings were free and unfurled. The moth patterns on her face were almost luminescent, not dull and faded as they appeared in the dungeon. Strands of moonlight caught in her black hair like ribbons of silver, and her eyes—those hawk's eyes—burned like firelight. Soraya had never seen her look so inhuman—or so beautiful.

That could have been me, she thought. If she had stopped trying to hide the veins of poison under her skin, if she had pulled back her hair and shed her gloves and not been ashamed to look anyone in the eye, then would she have had this same aura of majesty? She felt a pang of resentment toward her mother, not for cursing her, but for hiding her away and not telling her the real reason why— for letting her think she was made of shame instead of beauty.

But resentment was a familiar path, one she had already taken further than she had ever thought she would, and it had brought her to this prison. If she kept taking it, where would it lead her next? As if answering her question, she heard Azad's voice: *Do you want to know why I brought you here? Because I know this is where you belong.*

"Where should we go now?" she asked loudly, trying to drown out that insidious voice in her head.

"I'm not sure," Parvaneh said with a note of worry. "I know he keeps the pariks here, but this is a large forest, and we don't have much time."

"We don't have to find them tonight," Soraya offered. "Az—the Shahmar won't know I'm gone until he returns tomorrow night."

Parvaneh shook her head. "You haven't considered something. When the Shahmar returns to the palace, he'll likely notice I'm missing. And once he does, he won't leave the pariks unattended, or he might move them somewhere else entirely. This is our only chance."

Parvaneh charged into the forest, and Soraya was glad to let her take the lead, because as soon as the trees enveloped her, she knew she could easily forget her purpose and wander deeper and deeper into this forest until it swallowed her whole. The beams of moonlight filtering through the canopy draped over the trees like pale silk or cobwebs, giving the forest the impression of being ancient and untouched. *But I can touch it,* Soraya thought. The leaves and roses of her golestan had cradled her since childhood, never refusing or shying away from her touch, and so when Soraya reached up a hand to pass through the leaves dangling above her head like diamonds, she felt like she was greeting a dear friend.

Ahead of her, Parvaneh seemed to feel the same. She had dived into the forest with purpose, but now her pace was slower, and she often reached out to lay her palm against the thick, knotted tree trunks that they passed. Her dark wings and hair blended into the forest, and she moved around trees and over roots without pause, already knowing where they would be.

Soraya didn't have the same confident familiarity, and yet she didn't mind when she stumbled over the uneven ground or when her hair became tangled in the slender branches of a birch tree. These brief stumbles only brought her into closer contact with the forest, allowing her to know the paper-like texture of the bark under the pads of her fingers, the rich, earthy smell of the soil, the brush of leaves against her cheek—the forest returning her caresses.

They started to pass through rows of trees with twisting trunks, their thick, ropy branches reaching across to each other, creating a kind of latticed arch overhead, when Soraya called for Parvaneh to stop.

Parvaneh turned to her. "What happened? Is something wrong?"

Soraya shook her head, but she couldn't speak, the tears stinging her eyes threatening to overflow. She only gestured to the scenery around them—to the clumps of moss glowing in the moonlight against the dark wood of the trees, and the silhouettes of the branches tangled with one another. Somewhere in the distance, an owl was hooting, low and reverberant.

Parvaneh's face softened, and she nodded. "I understand."

A few stray leaves had wound themselves into Parvaneh's hair, and her eyes glowed with bliss and moonlight. Her wings fluttered behind her, the sound as soft as the rustle of wind through the trees. If Parvaneh told her she was the forest made flesh, Soraya would have believed her.

Unable to look away from her, Soraya murmured, "I've never seen anything so beautiful."

Parvaneh started to come toward her, the air around them heavy with dew and silence—but then she stopped and turned to her right, suddenly alert. "The wind just changed," she said.

"What do you mean?" Soraya asked, feeling slightly breathless.

"Can't you smell it?"

Soraya lifted her head and inhaled deeply, and a familiar feeling of safety wrapped around her. *That scent . . .*

"Esfand," Soraya said, her excitement building. "If the pariks are being held prisoner—"

"The Shahmar would need esfand to weaken them and keep them from transforming," Parvaneh finished for her.

Parvaneh took the lead again with renewed purpose, and Soraya followed, struggling to match her quickened pace in the dark. But even though her skin was damp from perspiration and the humidity in the air, and she kept scratching herself on branches and shrubs, and she heard the ragged sound of her own breath, Soraya wasn't tired. On the contrary, she was invigorated, like she was coming to life with every step deeper into the heart of this forest.

"We're getting closer," Soraya said. "The smell is getting stronger."

"I know." Parvaneh panted beside her. "I feel weak. You have to go on without me."

Soraya spun in the direction of her voice with a disbelieving glare. "You're going to leave me?"

"I'll wait right here. But you have to put out the esfand first—I can barely breathe. As soon as you do, I'll find you. I promise."

It was foolish to trust the promise of a div, but Parvaneh hadn't broken a promise to her yet, and Soraya was the one with a secret. Soraya nodded and walked ahead, following the scent of the esfand.

To her immense relief, she went only a little way farther before she stepped out into a clearing where the moonlight streamed down unfettered. But there was more than moonlight floating in the clearing. *Smoke,* she thought. The entire clearing was thick with smoke and scent.

And yet it was empty. Soraya walked to the center of the clearing, waving the smoke away, but there was nothing there for the smoke to be coming from. *Help me,* she asked the forest. *Show me what doesn't belong here.* But the forest didn't answer, of course, and she made it to the other side of the clearing without finding the source of the esfand.

And then she heard a strange noise from above, like a sigh, and she looked up.

The smoke was thicker here, but through it, she saw an iron cage hanging from the high branches of a tree. Hanging below the cage was a brazier, the smoke wafting upward to surround the cage. The brazier was clearly the source of the esfand—although it couldn't have been the only one, given the amount of smoke and the strength of its effect on Parvaneh—but it was the iron cage that caught Soraya's gaze, because through the veil of smoke, she saw someone asleep inside it.

Soraya backed away toward the center of the clearing again, and now that she knew where to look, not even the smoke could hide the truth from her. All around the edge of the clearing was a ring of cages. There were a dozen of them, each hanging from a tree, and each with a brazier of esfand pouring smoke from below it. And inside each cage was a sleeping form. Long hair spilled from some of the cages, and Soraya thought she saw the shape of wings in others.

The pariks. She had found them.

19

Twelve sleeping figures in twelve iron cages, wrapped in smoke and moonlight. Soraya felt like she had stepped into one of the illustrations in her books. She wondered how she was supposed to climb up and free them, but then she remembered that she only had to put out the esfand before Parvaneh could come and help her.

When she went up on her toes, she could reach the brazier enough to overturn it, sending a shower of coal dangerously close to her head. One by one, she went around the ring and put out the braziers. As the last coals came tumbling down and the smoke dispersed, some of the pariks began to stir, awakening from their forced slumber. Soraya moved away from the cages, hoping that Parvaneh would appear soon. She didn't know how the pariks would react to her, or if they would believe her when she claimed to be their ally.

"*You,*" came a voice to her right. Startled, Soraya turned and met the gaze of one of the pariks. She was still curled up from her sleep, but she lifted her head and peered at Soraya through the bars with wide orange eyes. She appeared mostly human, except for the feathered patterns on her skin. "I know you," she said.

Soraya shook her head and began to explain, but then she heard a rustling of leaves, and Parvaneh appeared among the trees, glowing and healthy once more. Soraya gestured for her to look up, and Parvaneh let out a long breath as she looked around to see her family returning to life.

The pariks were awakening, a few of them calling out Parvaneh's name in confusion, and Parvaneh unfurled her wings and rose up into the air to help them bend the bars of their cages enough to slip through.

Soraya watched but tried to keep to the shadows, away from this reunion she had no place in. They all had wings, though of different kinds, some feathered and others translucent like Parvaneh's. One had the leathery wings of a bat. And though they were more human in appearance than other divs, their eyes all glowed with an inhuman sheen.

But human or demon, one thing was clear: the pariks were a family. As soon as one was free, she would go to help her sisters, until they were all joined together on the ground, laughing and talking and embracing, or adjusting each other's hair or wings. Soraya felt a familiar ache in her chest, the same one she'd felt when she saw Sorush and Laleh and her mother together on Nog Roz. That sense of belonging and rightness was the same—and again, Soraya stood apart from it.

Soraya looked away, and to her surprise, found Parvaneh standing near her. She thought Parvaneh would be at the center of this joyful reunion, but she was lingering at the edge of the clearing, watching the other pariks intently with her wings flat against her back and her hands fidgeting in front of her. Even when she was held captive in the dungeon, she had never seemed so cowed, so unsure.

"Parvaneh," a voice said, and Soraya turned her head in its direction. The pariks all stepped aside as one of them strode forward—the one with the orange eyes that had spoken to Soraya when she was waking. At the time, Soraya hadn't noticed her wings, but now they were more visible: tawny brown, with serrated edges like the wings of an owl.

Soraya wanted to address her at once, but the parik's gaze was locked on Parvaneh, and from the way the other pariks had parted for her, the way they all waited silently now, Soraya knew better than to interrupt.

"Parisa," Parvaneh said, the word little more than a breath.

"You've returned," Parisa said. Her voice was soft, but Soraya heard every word. "Does that mean you've completed your task?"

Parvaneh's eyes flickered to the ground, and she gave a quick shake of her head. "Not yet."

Parisa's wings fluttered in what Soraya could somehow tell was disapproval. "Then why are you here?"

"I have something that can help," Parvaneh said, her voice growing louder now. "I have something that can stop the Shahmar." She turned her head to look straight at Soraya, and Soraya again felt that hollow sensation as she realized what Parvaneh was talking about.

"The simorgh's feather," Parvaneh announced with such certainty, such confidence.

An excited chattering erupted among the pariks until Parisa held up a hand to silence them. "Show it to me," she said.

Parvaneh came to Soraya's side, and Soraya felt a wave of nausea as all eyes turned expectantly to her. She shook her head lightly and whispered to Parvaneh, "I don't have it."

She hadn't meant for the others to hear, but instantly, there was an uproar of angry voices and fluttering wings. Parvaneh clasped her hand around Soraya's wrist. "You said you had it," she bit out between clenched teeth.

"He took it from me before he brought me here," Soraya said. "I didn't know that . . ." She couldn't finish the thought aloud. *I didn't know that they wouldn't welcome you without it. I didn't know you were an outcast.*

But now she remembered Parvaneh's furious outburst when she had told Soraya to abandon her family. *Are they truly your family if they've failed to accept you as their own? If they cast you out and treat you with disdain? Why do they still matter to you?* Perhaps Parvaneh had wanted Soraya's answer so she could know it herself.

Parisa called for silence again. "We thank you for freeing us, Parvaneh, but it's not enough to meet the conditions for your return."

Parvaneh's head was turned away from Parisa and the others, but Soraya saw the clench of her jaw, the dimming of her eyes. She felt Parvaneh's shame and humiliation as if it were her own, because it had been—it still was.

"She doesn't have the feather yet, but she will," Soraya called to Parisa.

The pariks all fell silent in surprise. Parisa looked at Soraya now as if she had only just noticed her. Parvaneh placed a hand on her arm. "Soraya—"

But Soraya ignored her. "The Shahmar took it from me," she said, stepping forward, "but I can find it again." In her mind, she imagined green veins curling over her skin like vines, and the image made her feel bold.

"How?" called out the bat-winged parik from behind Parisa.

Parisa inclined her head, approving of the question. "How can you get close enough to the Shahmar to do such a thing?"

"The Shahmar is fond of me," Soraya answered. "He brought me here rather than killing me. If I pretend that I want to join him, he'll keep me close enough to learn his secrets. I'll find the feather, and when I do, I'll give it to Parvaneh—*only* to Parvaneh."

Soraya didn't know when she had become so comfortable making bargains with divs, but she managed to hold Parisa's steady
gaze as she spoke, her voice never wavering. The words came to her
as if she had planned them, because as soon as Parvaneh had told
her why they needed the feather, some part of her had known that
she was the only one who could retrieve it again.

"How do we know we can trust her?" said another parik, her
gossamer wings twitching.

Parisa came to stand directly in front of Soraya, studying her face
closely. "I know you," she said again. Now that the smoke had completely faded, the feathered pattern on her skin was clearer, her
eyes even brighter. "You saved me once before, in the forest to the
south. You freed me from one of the Shahmar's traps."

"That was my mother," Soraya said. "My mother freed you when
she was a girl."

Parisa's eyes widened in recognition. "You're the child," she said.
She raised a hand to brush aside Soraya's hair, but then she shook
her head. "But you can't be her. I gave that child a gift that you
don't have."

"I did have it," Soraya said. Grief and bitterness mingled on
her tongue, her words both an accusation and an apology. She
knew that Parisa would never understand that her gift had been
a curse to Soraya—and Soraya wasn't even sure of it herself anymore. "I had poison in my veins," she continued, "but I rejected
it, and in doing so, I put my whole family—my people—at risk.
My mother told me to find you and ask for your help to defeat the
Shahmar."

Parisa tilted her head, the movement so much like Parvaneh's
that Soraya almost smiled. "Are you like your mother?" she asked.

Soraya flinched inwardly. Was she like her mother, a woman
who was determined and ruthless enough to go to a dakhmeh at
night, who had freed a parik and tried to thwart a div, who had let
her shame fester inside her until the consequences spiraled out of

her control? "Yes," Soraya said, her voice thick with a mixture of pride and regret. "I'm very much like her."

Parisa called back to the others, "We can trust this one. If she brings us the simorgh's feather, we will stand with her and the humans against the Shahmar." She turned to the other pariks. "Does anyone disagree?"

The other pariks all shook their heads. "No, Parisa. We trust your judgment," the bat-winged parik said.

"We must leave this clearing at once." Parisa turned back to Soraya. "You will return to Arzur, of course."

Soraya swallowed down the lump in her throat. It was unthinkable that she should leave behind the freedom of the forest and the open sky to crawl back inside that prison of a mountain. But she nodded, accepting the task she had given herself.

Parisa looked to Parvaneh now. "When you have the feather, you know where to find us."

The pariks all began to move deeper into the forest, and Soraya watched them go with a feeling of loss she didn't quite understand.

When they were alone, Parvaneh said, "Why didn't you tell me you didn't have the feather anymore?" There was no anger or resentment in her tone, only curiosity.

Soraya turned to face her. "I didn't know if you would keep helping me if you knew. Why didn't you tell me you weren't welcome among the pariks?"

"I didn't know if you would give me the feather if you knew," Parvaneh answered.

Standing face-to-face, it was almost as if they were in the dungeon again, trading pieces of the truth through the bars. "Why did they cast you out?" Soraya asked.

"I made an error in judgment that they still haven't forgiven me for. They were lenient with me because of my age."

"I thought divs didn't age," Soraya said with surprise.

A weak smile crossed Parvaneh's face. "Not as humans do. I

was never a child, but at that time, I was the most recent parik to emerge from Duzakh. By div standards, I'm not much older than you are." Before Soraya could ask anything more, Parvaneh continued hastily, "We shouldn't linger here, either."

She set out in the direction they had come from, leaving Soraya with no choice but to follow.

The forest felt less liberating to her now that it was the path back to her prison, but still, Soraya tried to absorb it into her memory, breathing in the smell of wet soil. She hoped one day she could come back here in the sunlight.

"Thank you," Parvaneh said, breaking the silence between them. She kept her eyes ahead of her as she continued. "Not just for freeing them, but for what you said. What you offered. It's a dangerous task you've given yourself."

"There's not much else I can do," Soraya muttered as she tried not to trip over her dress. "I'm not strong enough to fight a div, I can't see in the dark, I'm not even—"

She tripped over a root, but Parvaneh caught her before she fell. Soraya straightened, but Parvaneh didn't move away, still holding Soraya's arms. "You're not even what?" she asked.

Soraya had spoken without thinking, but now she faced the truth directly. *I'm not even poisonous anymore*, she had meant to say. But when she tried to say it aloud, her throat closed up. She had betrayed her family to be rid of that curse; she had no right now to mourn its absence.

But Parvaneh heard the words anyway. "You miss it now, don't you?"

The lump in Soraya's throat began to loosen at hearing the truth from someone else's voice. Why was it that all of her secrets came to light whenever she was alone with Parvaneh? Was it her, or was it the darkness, the feeling of being so far from her old life that anything seemed permissible—or forgivable?

"You must think me such a fool," Soraya said, her voice wavering. "You warned me, but I didn't believe you. And yet I believed *him*. I trusted him so completely."

Parvaneh's hands tightened around her arms, and her eyes flashed in the darkness. "He gave you reason to trust him—and then he abused that trust. Don't waste your anger on yourself. Save it for him." Her hands fell away, and she stood there for a moment, watching Soraya before she stalked off in a different direction. "Follow me!" she called back.

Soraya quickly followed, not wanting to lose sight of Parvaneh in the dark forest. "Where are we going?"

Parvaneh slowed down for Soraya to catch up and said in an impassioned flurry, "You've lived your whole life with this curse because of him, and you can't even enjoy yourself once you're *free* of it because of him. Why should you suffer for what he did?"

Parvaneh stormed ahead again, and Soraya followed, muttering to herself, "But where are we *going*?"

Somewhat abruptly, Parvaneh stopped, and Soraya nearly collided with her. Parvaneh sniffed the air, put her hand on a nearby tree, and nodded. "Hornbeams," she said. She led Soraya a little farther ahead, into a patch of moonlight that managed to pierce through the canopy. "Wait here," she said, and then walked over to one of the trees. *Hornbeams*, she had said. Soraya looked around at the not-quite-identical trees around her, all of them with thick, sinewy trunks.

When Parvaneh returned, her hands were sticky with tree sap. "Roll up your sleeves."

Soraya considered questioning her, but something about the excited glow of Parvaneh's eyes and their sudden rush through the forest made her want to play along. She rolled up the sleeves of her dress, which were hopelessly dingy by now, and said, "Now what?"

"Hold out your arms."

Soraya obeyed, her stomach already flipping in anticipation, because she could guess what would come next. Parvaneh stepped

forward and brushed her hands along the insides of Soraya's forearms, and Soraya's entire spine straightened at once, her breath
catching in her throat. "What are you doing?" she said in an exhale.

"Hush," Parvaneh said. "You'll see."

Once Soraya's forearms and her palms were coated with tree
sap, Parvaneh stepped away, leaning her back against the nearest
tree trunk. "Now wait," she whispered.

Ordinarily, Soraya might have felt ridiculous standing in the
middle of a forest with tree sap on her outstretched arms. But the
forest was *alive*. She felt it pulsing all around her. And so she knew
she wasn't simply standing, but waiting, with arms open to embrace whatever envoy the forest was about to send to her.

She didn't have to wait long. She heard it first—a fluttering
sound that seemed to come from the air—and then something tick-
led her arm. When she looked down, she saw a gray-brown moth
settled on her left forearm, wings opening and closing leisurely.

Soraya barely breathed, afraid she would scare it away—or
worse, that it would go still and fall dead to the ground, as that
first butterfly did so many years ago. But her skin was covered in
tree sap, not poison, and so the moth didn't die, and soon it was
joined by others. One—two—a third that landed on the very center of her palm. To them, she was no different from one of the
trees, a source of nourishment and life, not death or destruction.
Soraya laughed, and her eyes went blurry with tears.

Now she understood why Parvaneh had brought her here. Here
in the forest, far enough away to forget about Azad and the divs
and her family, Soraya allowed herself to enjoy the absence of her
curse without guilt or complication. She would return to Arzur,
and she would find the simorgh's feather, and she would help save
her family—but for now, she would marvel at the brush of moth
wings against her skin.

She looked up at Parvaneh, suddenly self-conscious. Parvaneh
was still leaning against a tree trunk, her arms crossed over her

chest, watching Soraya with a small smile on her lips. It was the first time Soraya remembered seeing her smile in earnest, and she wondered if the same was true for her, if this was the first time she had seen Soraya genuinely smile.

"Thank you," Soraya called to her. The words felt weak compared to the gratitude she felt.

Parvaneh came over to her, moving slowly so as not to startle the moths. As she approached, Soraya felt a strange kind of fluttering in her stomach, as if one of the moths had flown inside. It reminded her of something—something she hadn't felt since she was a child.

"In the dungeon, I used to like making you angry," Parvaneh said. She reached down to scoop up one of the moths and held it up to her face, brushing its wing against her cheek with a tenderness that only worsened the fluttering in Soraya's stomach. Parvaneh let the moth fly away and looked Soraya in the eye. "But I think I like making you laugh even more."

"Why did you like making me angry?" Soraya asked in mock offense.

Parvaneh grinned and swept aside Soraya's hair, her fingers brushing Soraya's cheekbone. "To see your veins, of course," she said. Her hand moved down to trace the dull claw mark on Soraya's collarbone with her fingertips. "I always thought you . . . I thought they were beautiful."

The fluttering—she had felt it before. Not with Azad, though he had ignited a fire of his own, as sudden and scorching as lightning. This was more like the gradual, steady warmth of a summer day, a heat that spread all the way down to the tips of her fingers and her toes. She remembered that day—not summer, but spring—lying on the grass beside Laleh, feeling that fluttering as she told Laleh she wished she could marry her. Then Laleh had laughed, and it had died away, never to return.

But she felt it now, and when Parvaneh lifted her eyes to meet Soraya's, neither of them was laughing.

Parvaneh's hand was still curled against Soraya's collarbone, and she was standing so close that Soraya felt her breath warm against her face. She was so keenly aware of all these points of contact—skin, breath, gaze—but most of all she was aware of the way her pulse slowed and quickened at the same time, giddy yet languorous.

Speak, Soraya willed herself. But she felt like she was lost in a maze, unsure how to find her way out. Deep at the center of the maze was the truth she didn't want to acknowledge, that she had cared for Azad, and he had betrayed her so terribly that she had been unsure she would ever trust her heart again. In a way, it was a relief to know that the feel of Parvaneh's fingers brushing along her skin could still stir something in her—it meant Azad was not her only choice, her only chance.

Speak. She could say that she had come to treasure their conversations in the dungeon, even if they had made her angry, because they were the only time she had ever fully allowed herself to drop all pretense and be herself. Or that now she realized it wasn't the dungeon that had given her a strange sense of refuge all this time, but Parvaneh herself, with whom she had been even more honest than she had with Azad.

Speak—but it was Parvaneh who spoke first.

"We shouldn't dwell much longer," she said, looking up with concern at the lightening sky.

The moths had all flown away by now, and Soraya rolled down her sleeves. The sap was still sticky on her arms, but she could use the jug of water in her cavern to wash them later.

Parvaneh led her back in silence, stopping at the mouth of the hidden tunnel to drape the cloak over both her and Soraya. When they found her room, Parvaneh removed the cloak and told Soraya to hide it in case she needed it again.

"I'll return tomorrow at dawn," Parvaneh said. She looked around the room, forehead wrinkled in concentration. "Here." She went to the table and lifted the candelabra. "If he leaves again and it's safe for us to talk, keep the light on this end of the table. If he hasn't gone, or if it isn't safe for any reason, move it to the other end of the table."

Soraya nodded, twisting the fabric of the cloak in her hands. She didn't want Parvaneh to leave her alone here again, but she had made a promise—to her mother, to the other pariks, to Parvaneh— and she didn't intend to break it.

There was nothing left to be said, but Parvaneh lingered, looking at Soraya with concern. She came toward her, rested one hand on Soraya's shoulder, and kissed Soraya's cheek. "Until tomorrow," Parvaneh said, her lips brushing the corner of Soraya's mouth as she spoke. Before Soraya could react, Parvaneh was gone, a moth similar to the ones in the forest fluttering in the air where she used to be.

Soraya watched her go through the gap between the door and the wall, and gently touched her cheek. Even after everything she had seen—demons and sorcerers and curses—there was nothing more astonishing or magical to Soraya than being able to touch Parvaneh.

20

Exhaustion set in, allowing Soraya to sleep before Azad's return. She woke to the scent of cooked meat, and found that the fruit on the table had been replaced by a plate of skewers and warm bread. It unnerved her to know that someone had come and gone without her knowledge, but she still ate ravenously, assured now that Azad didn't plan to starve her into submission.

She didn't know how much longer it would be until his return, but in the time she had, she formed a plan. She couldn't ask Azad directly about the feather without making him suspicious, and so she would have to approach the topic from a different path.

Pacing around the room, she rehearsed the words in her mind, until finally she heard a rap at the door. *How courteous of him,* she thought dryly.

As soon as he entered—as himself, not human—he frowned at her. "Your dress," he said.

Soraya looked down at the pale turquoise gown she had first put on the morning of the wedding. By now, it was filthy—the hemline ragged and completely black, the arms and torso stained and torn in places. Her hair was probably a nightmare too. She would have changed before he'd arrived if she'd had the option, but as it was, she didn't think he would suspect the grime came from the forest instead of the mountain. She faced him boldly and said, "I don't know what you expected. You've given me no opportunity to change or bathe since stealing me away."

He was draped in a robe of purple brocade himself, stolen from the royal wardrobe she had no doubt, and the contrast between his splendor and her disheveled appearance apparently disturbed him. "I'll remedy this," he promised. "For now, though, I've assured your mother that you're alive and in my care."

Soraya didn't know if he meant this as a kindness or a taunt, but her heart sank a little imagining her mother's reaction to that news. Every choice Tahmineh had made, misguided or not, had been for the purpose of keeping Soraya away from the Shahmar, and now she would think it had all come to nothing. She wanted to tell him what a monster he was, to wound him in some way in return for her own pain, but she reminded herself of her plan to gain his trust, and she held her tongue—she had plenty of practice doing so.

But still, she couldn't stop herself from asking, "And my brother?"

He crossed his arms and said, begrudgingly, "Still alive. For now."

"Thank you," she said, her relief audible. "Truly, I'm thankful, and . . . I'm relieved to see you again."

He smiled, but there was a spark of suspicion in his eye. "Are you?"

"You knew I would be," she said. "You left me here with no company, no occupation, except to think of you and wish for your return."

He took a step closer to her. "And have you thought of me?" he asked, his voice a low rumble.

Soraya ducked her head and nodded. *Was I this easily fooled as well?* she wondered. She was thankful now for the lesson he had taught her in those early days together—that if you told people what they most wanted to hear, they would almost certainly believe you.

"I keep remembering what you said to me before—that there isn't much difference between who you are now and the young man you once were. The young man I knew." She glanced up at him shyly, thinking of the way he had been so hesitant in those early days, feeding her lies while making her think she was drawing them out of him. "I want to know more about him," she said, her voice almost a whisper.

He was watching her warily, eyes slightly narrowed, as if trying to determine whether she was leading him into a trap. But then he simply said, "Come with me," and turned for the door.

She followed at once, remaining close to his side as he led her back out into the tunnels. It was too much to assume that he would take her to the feather at once, but if she could keep him on the topic of his lost humanity, she hoped he would mention the feather himself in time.

As he led her down the winding path through the mountain, he said, "I forgot to ask you something. Do you remember the div that was locked up in the dungeon at the palace?"

Soraya's step faltered only slightly. "Of course I remember. You planted her there, didn't you?"

"I did, but when I went back to retrieve her, she was missing. When did you see her last?"

She tried to push away the memory of Parvaneh's hair shining in the moonlight, of her lips brushing the corner of Soraya's mouth, as if Azad might somehow be able to read her thoughts. "The night we went to the dakhmeh," she answered. "She must have escaped after I . . . after the fire went out."

"Yes, I would have assumed the same, except for the esfand burning in the dungeon."

Soraya kept pace with his stride and said nothing.

"And you're sure you haven't seen her since before the fire went out?"

Soraya nodded.

"How interesting," Azad continued in a voice like silk. "Then either the pariks have found a way to resist the effects of esfand, or they have a human helping them."

Soraya abruptly halted, forcing Azad to stop and look back at her. "Are you accusing me of something? Please let me know what it is you think I've been able to do while tucked away in the room you put me in, unable to leave without fear of losing my life." The words came out harsher than she intended, but the only way she could think to avoid his suspicion was to face it directly.

He held her gaze, then shook his head and kept walking. When Soraya was at his side again, he said, "No, I suppose you couldn't have done anything. But if you see her or if she comes to you, let me know at once."

She didn't respond, hoping he would take her silence as agreement.

"Turn left here," he said after they had continued a little longer. They went down a different passage and stopped at a door in the wall. But unlike the door to her room, this one was pure metal, with no space between the edges of the door and the wall. The door also had a keyhole, which Azad used the tip of one claw to unlock.

The security of this room gave Soraya hope—perhaps he was going to take her to the feather now after all.

But when the two of them stepped inside, all thought of the feather briefly fled Soraya's mind. Everywhere Soraya looked were relics of the past—vases and painted jars, goblets and gold-rimmed dishes, tapestries and piles of coins. And all of them bore the image of the same man—Azad, before his transformation.

She walked up to a tapestry hanging on the wall to study the image of a young man hunting. She recognized him from the profile that she had found so beautiful, her eyes tracing the curve of his neck up to his face. He was riding a horse, a bow pulled taut in his hands, with a fierce look in his eye—a hunter tracking his prey. She knew that look. She had seen it on that first day, when he had spotted her on the roof.

When she turned to face him again, he was watching her. And even though he was as monstrous as ever, he seemed pathetic to her then, standing in the middle of this shrine to his lost humanity.

"Look around you," he said. "What do you see?"

"You."

"What else?"

She walked around the cavern, eyes glancing over the hoard of useless treasure, at the image of Azad engraved and carved and painted on each relic. She found a plate on the ground, chipped around the edges, but with a clear image of Azad in the center, and she picked it up, frowning. It was a garden scene, etched in gold. Azad was seated on a rug, under the shade of the pavilion, and all around the pavilion were rosebushes. She brushed one of the roses with her thumb, and the indentations of the petals felt like a spiral.

What else?

I see a selfish child who betrayed his family.

I see a demon in the making.

Soraya's hands clenched tighter over the plate. She had the urge to throw it to the ground or dash it against the wall. She wanted to destroy everything in this room, not stopping until the images were unrecognizable and there were no longer any surfaces in which to see her reflection.

She didn't hear Azad coming nearer, but he was suddenly in front of her, prying the gold plate from her grip as if he sensed what she wanted to do to it. "You'd like to know more about who I am, who I used to be? You already know him. You *are* him."

"Why did you do it?" she asked, looking up at him. It was one of the questions she had planned to ask to guide the conversation, but now she found that she truly, desperately wanted to know the answer. "What made you decide to destroy your family?"

He sighed and turned away from her, moving toward a pile of rolled-up rugs and tapestries. He knocked the pile down with one wave of his arm and picked up the tapestry at the very bottom. He gestured for Soraya to come see, and unrolled the tapestry along the ground.

Soraya came to his side and looked down at the woven image before her. A shah, middle-aged and full-bearded, sat in a throne at the center of the tapestry. Surrounding him were five younger men of different heights and ages. Soraya looked at each one in turn, but none of them resembled Azad. All along the edge of the tapestry were dark singe marks, as if someone had decided to burn it but then changed his mind, several times.

"Are . . . are those . . . ?" Soraya couldn't finish the question, unsure of what reaction it would draw from him.

"My father and brothers," Azad said.

"Was this before you were born?"

He snorted. "No," he said. "I was the youngest, still a child, but that's not why I'm missing. All five of my brothers were destined to rule—the eldest as shah, the younger four as satraps of rich provinces. But I was born under bad stars. The astrologist told my father that if I ever ruled even the smallest province, dire consequences would follow. My father took this advice very seriously. While I watched my brothers become the princes they were meant to be, I was allowed no battle training, no education in affairs of state, no sense of my future at all." He kicked the tapestry aside, letting the edges curl up over his dead brothers' faces. "I wanted so much to prove the stars wrong. I used to stay up through the night and read in secret or practice on the training grounds on my own, desperate for any opportunity to impress my father. He was never cruel to me, but I knew how he must have seen me. I knew that I was . . ."

He trailed off, unable to find the words, and so Soraya provided them: "You were your family's shame." No wonder he had found her so easily at Golvahar. He knew where to look for someone who felt unwanted.

Something strange happened then. Perhaps Soraya only imagined it, but for a moment, Azad's eyes changed—no longer cold and yellow, but the rich brown she remembered. And in that brief time, she saw in them the kind of self-loathing that seemed exclusively human. Once more, she became aware of the patches of skin showing through the scales, the pieces of Azad that refused to be swallowed up by the demon. She wondered if his transformation was even complete, or if he still woke sometimes to find another patch of skin covered in scales, another piece of himself gone.

"And then I met the div," he continued, his voice hardening. "It's much as you once told me—one night, when I went out riding in secret, I caught a div. But I didn't want to take her to the palace with me yet. Instead, I kept the div trapped in a cave, and I returned every night to learn her secrets, hoping that I would discover something invaluable to present to my father. But you know as well as I do that when you learn a div's secrets, the div learns your secrets, too. The div became my most constant companion, and so when she began to tell me that I would be a better ruler than my father or any of my brothers, I believed her. When she told me how furious I must be at my treatment, I became furious. She made me question whether the astrologer's warning was even true, or if my father was lying to me for his own purposes." He took a halting breath before continuing. "And so I approached a faction of powerful nobles and soldiers opposed to my father's rule, and suggested they should help me replace him. I had decided that if I could not rule with the blessing of my father or the stars, I would defy them all, no matter whose blood I had to spill."

Soraya didn't know where to look—everywhere, she saw Azad, and so everywhere, she saw herself. She shut her eyes, but in the darkness behind her eyelids, she saw the young man she had known with blood on his hands, slaughtering everyone in his path to the throne. She tore her mind away from the image, reminding herself of her plan to find the feather.

She opened her eyes and asked, "And how did you . . . When did you become . . . ?"

He hesitated, and when he spoke, his voice was hushed, like that of a child telling a secret. "I asked for this," he said. "After my father's and brothers' deaths, I was afraid I wouldn't be able to keep control of Atashar. I had so little education on the subject, so I asked the div what I should do. She told me to tear out the heart of a div, and to bathe in the blood from that heart. I didn't want to kill the div I had, and so I hunted down another, one with scales and claws and wings. I didn't realize what would happen. I didn't know . . ." He looked down at his hands—clawed and scaled, gnarled and bloodstained—and then looked up at Soraya, eyes pleading for understanding.

And she did understand, of course. It was so easy to imagine their places switched. She knew, too, why he had been so affected on the night of the dakhmeh, when she told him his story. Because it was not just his story that he heard, but his fears, his own strangled heartbeat, echoing back to him from someone else for the first time.

"You appeared as a human to me," she said, returning to her plan. "Why don't you do so all the time? Why would you choose to live as a div instead of a human?"

From the way Azad avoided her eye, she could tell he didn't want her to know the answer. "I tried, for a time," he said. "But the effect is temporary, and the price is not always easy to obtain."

She shook her head. "I don't understand."

"The blood from a div's heart made me a div. I thought, then, that the opposite might be true as well."

"The opposite—?" Soraya's eyes widened in understanding. "Blood from a human heart?"

"Yes," he admitted. "And it did work, but as I said, only for a short time. Little more than a month before I would need to repeat the process."

Soraya grimaced and covered her mouth with her hand, remembering one of the more gruesome parts of the Shahmar's story—that he would demand the sacrifice of two men every month, seemingly for no reason. And in a strange way, Soraya was grateful for the knowledge. The image of the ill-omened boy had become too strong and too familiar in her mind. She needed a reminder of his blood-soaked reign.

But then an even more unsavory truth occurred to her. "That means that before you returned to Golvahar, before I first saw you, you must have . . ."

He nodded. "I can still change form, but it will wear off soon." He had been avoiding her eye, but now he looked at her, and he bristled at the revulsion on her face. "Besides, to live as a human would mean living as no one, as nothing, the way I once was. If that's a human life, then I prefer to live as I am. As the Shahmar, I have the power to command a shah to his knees."

The image of Sorush kneeling before him sent a welcome burst of anger through her, and before she could stop herself, she said, "And as the Shahmar, you lost your throne."

One of his hands clenched and unclenched at his side. In a cold voice, he said, "There's something you haven't asked me yet, Soraya."

Soraya's pulse quickened. Had he seen through her line of questioning? Did he know she was going to ask about the feather next? "What question is that?"

"Ask me for the name of the div who turned me into the Shahmar."

If Soraya felt a prickle of foreboding at his words, she ignored it in favor of relief that he didn't know her true purpose. "Fine, then. What's the name of the div who turned you into the Shahmar?"

His mouth twisted into a thin, cruel smile as he pronounced the name that Soraya should have expected, because it was the only name that would have meant anything to her, the name that would hurt her most:

"Parvaneh."

21

In her room once more, Soraya tried to erase Azad's words from her mind.

Ask me for the name of the div who turned me into the Shahmar.

She had wanted to deny it, but the more she considered it, the more it made sense. This was why Azad hunted down and captured pariks. This was why the other pariks shunned Parvaneh—and why she was so desperate to defeat the Shahmar. Parvaneh had done to Azad what Azad had done to Soraya. Soraya wasn't surprised, then, that he still hadn't forgiven her.

Azad had returned her to her room, promising to return again the next night. And now Soraya sat at her table, the candelabra on the end closest to her, waiting for Parvaneh to appear.

"Any luck?"

Soraya's head snapped up at the sound of Parvaneh's voice. She was no longer wearing the worn shift from her captivity, but a shimmery gray tunic with a slit in the back for her wings. Had she been Azad's prisoner ever since he had been a young prince, still human? No wonder, then, that there was an effusive energy around her now that she was free, her eyes bright and smiling.

"No," Soraya said. "Not yet. I think he's beginning to trust me, though. He told me a great deal about himself."

The smile in Parvaneh's eyes wavered. "Did he? Anything useful?"

"In a way."

Parvaneh turned away from her, arms crossing over her chest as she looked around the cavern. "Being here makes me feel like a prisoner again," she said. "Is it safe for you to sneak out to the forest?"

She almost said no to be contrary—or to punish Parvaneh for her deception. But she knew staying here would be more of a punishment for herself. Unlike Parvaneh, Soraya couldn't come and go anytime she liked.

They left the mountain the same way as before, using the cloak and the secret escape tunnel. When they were outside, Parvaneh led her through the trees, back to the grove of hornbeams. There, a small fire was burning on the ground, and a number of dark moths fluttered around it, drawn to its light. Soraya hadn't known Parvaneh would bring her back to this spot, and her face warmed from the memory of last night. Was she destined always to grow close to people who would betray her? Or perhaps the problem was that she wasn't growing close to *people,* but to demons.

A mossy log lay beside the fire, and Soraya sat down at one end of it, watching the moths dance around the flames. Parvaneh sat beside her, close enough for their shoulders to touch and said, "I have something for you. A gift."

Soraya was tempted to say that she didn't want anything Parvaneh offered—or to ask her whether she had thought she was giving Azad a gift, too, when she convinced him to murder his family. But before she could say anything, Parvaneh was holding out the gift: a sprig of white hyacinth.

"That's from Golvahar," Soraya said, reaching to take it. She instinctively brushed it against her cheek, the familiar scent and feel making her eyes sting with tears. "You went back?"

Parvaneh nodded. "I wanted to know what the Shahmar was doing during the day—he's been holding audiences with the nobility, offering them gifts and land to solidify their loyalty. Some of them have refused, but the ones who agreed are granted more freedom of movement. Some have even been allowed to leave the palace with their families. He's also been sending divs out into the city to patrol the streets. Many of the buildings are damaged, but the people are safe for now. I think they're trying to go about their days without attracting any attention." She paused, and glancing at the hyacinth in Soraya's hands, she said, "I checked to make sure your family was safe too. They're locked in a wing of the palace, but they seemed unharmed from what I could see. And then I couldn't resist bringing something back for you."

Soraya looked at her in surprise, forgetting Azad's revelation and her feelings of betrayal. Parvaneh had risked returning to the place of her captivity, risked doing so when Azad was still there, even risked changing forms, to bring Soraya some peace of mind— and a reminder of home. She stared down at the hyacinth in her hands, unable to look at Parvaneh. "You endangered yourself, your freedom, for—" *For me.*

Parvaneh brushed some of Soraya's hair away, her fingertips lingering on Soraya's neck. "You have faith in me," she said softly. "It's been a long time since anyone has. I wish I could give you more."

Soraya lifted her head and froze as she found Parvaneh closer to her than she had expected, their faces mere breaths apart. Parvaneh's eyes were on Soraya's lips, and Soraya couldn't bring herself to move away as Parvaneh leaned closer—as their lips met.

Her kiss with Azad had been devouring, almost violent, but this was different, delicate—as delicate as a moth's wing. Soraya felt like a cat stretched out in a patch of sunlight, luxuriating in the softness of Parvaneh's mouth, in the slow drag of Parvaneh's fingertips along the length of her neck. Parvaneh seemed to be trying to memorize the feel of Soraya's skin, and Soraya, remembering the sight of her tattered wings, wondered when Parvaneh had last experienced any kind of touch that was not in violence.

But that thought only made her remember the violence that Parvaneh herself had done.

Soraya broke off abruptly, standing and practically bolting to the other side of the fire, away from Parvaneh.

"Is something wrong?" Parvaneh asked with a tilt of her head. Her voice went cold as she asked, "Do you wish I were him instead?"

Soraya shot her an incredulous glare. "Of course not," she said. "I only wish you were who I thought you were."

"And who is that?"

"Someone without blood on her hands."

Parvaneh hesitated before replying, "What is this about?"

Soraya shook her head. "You're only asking me that because you don't want to give away your secret unless you have to. But maybe if you had *told* me, if you hadn't let me hear it from *him*—"

"Hear *what*, Soraya? The Shahmar is a liar, in case you haven't noticed. He might have told you any number of terrible things about me. He and I have known each other a long time, and we've seen the worst in each other. I didn't know you expected me to give you a full account of so many years."

"Not a full account," Soraya said. "Only the beginning. You were the div who convinced him to murder his family. You were the div who turned him into a monster in every way. *All* of this is your fault!"

"I know it's my fault!" Parvaneh snapped, rising to her feet. "Why do you think I'm trying so hard to fix my mistake? I'm the reason my sisters have had to go into hiding. They won't even take me back until I've repaired the damage I've done. And this is the first time I've even come close to stopping him, because I've been his prisoner for over a century!" Her anger dissipated, her face contorting in pain as her wings drooped behind her. When she was composed again, she said, "At first, I didn't tell you because you were my only chance at freedom, and at stopping the Shahmar. Then you defended me to Parisa and the others . . ." She looked away, avoiding Soraya's gaze. "I didn't want you to regret that decision, or to look at me the way they do. I wanted you to keep looking at me the way you did last night."

Soraya wrapped her arms around her waist and looked down at the ground. She didn't know what Parvaneh would see on her face right now, and so she didn't want to look at her at all, not until she sorted through her feelings. "What made you do it?" she said to the ground, an echo of the question she had asked Azad. "Why did you tell him to kill his family?"

"I didn't tell him to kill anyone, not directly. He had captured me, bound my wings so I couldn't transform, and refused to release me until I told him something useful. So I did what any div would do—I tried to destroy him, however I could. I sought out his weaknesses, his insecurities, and I reminded him of them at every opportunity. I didn't know what he would choose to do."

Soraya lifted her head to ask, "But did it matter to you? Once you knew what he'd done, did you feel any regret for all that bloodshed?"

Parvaneh held her gaze. "Do you want me to lie to you?"

"Never."

"No, it didn't matter to me. And if you think it would, then you're right—I'm not who you think I am." She turned away, running her hands through her hair in frustration. Her shoulders softened and she stepped around the fire, coming to stand in front of Soraya. "I may not care about him or his family," she said, "but I do have my loyalties, and I am true to them. I care deeply about my sisters . . . and I care about you. Why do you think I tried to stop you from taking the simorgh's feather toward the end? It was because I couldn't do the same thing to you that I did to him, even if it meant being his prisoner forever."

A chilling thought occurred to Soraya then. "Were you the one who told him about me? About my curse?"

"No," Parvaneh said at once. "I was still his prisoner when your mother took you to the pariks. But I was there when he interrogated the parik who told him. That was how I knew about you."

Soraya's arms tightened around her waist. "But you *were* the one who told him to use the div's blood. You must have known what would happen to him."

Parvaneh shook her head, mouth pursed in disgust. "I was angry. He had become shah and he still refused to let me go—and then had the gall to ask me for help. I knew about the properties of a div's heart's blood, but I had never seen a full transformation. I didn't realize how *complete* it would be, or what kind of div he would hunt down.

"After he was deposed, I managed to escape and return to the pariks for a time. But when he grew in power and began to hunt us down, I had to tell them what I did. They exiled me, and told me I could only return to them when I had undone my mistake. The Shahmar caught me soon after that, and I thought that he would kill me, but instead he took his anger out on me in other, smaller ways." Her wings twitched. "I told myself then that I would stop at nothing to defeat him and undo my foolish, reckless mistake."

The words resonated more deeply than Soraya wanted to admit, and she stared down, hunching over into herself as she had always done before to find comfort when there was no one to give it. Parvaneh's bare feet approached her, and then Parvaneh's hands gently unwrapped Soraya's arms from around her waist, and held Soraya's hands in her own.

Soraya lifted her head to meet Parvaneh's intense, amber stare. "Do I have your forgiveness?" Parvaneh said. "Are you still with me?"

It seemed a simple enough question, but Soraya found it to be as tangled and impenetrable as a thicket. She and Parvaneh and Azad—their choices, their mistakes, their ambitions—were all entwined, inseparable from each other. How could she forgive Parvaneh without forgiving Azad? But how could she forgive Azad without forgiving herself? Maybe they all deserved nothing but one another, a constant cycle of betrayals.

"I don't know," Soraya said hoarsely. It was the truest answer she could manage.

Parvaneh waited for her to continue, and when Soraya didn't, she nodded and looked away, letting Soraya's hands slip out of hers.

22

Soraya was beginning to become as nocturnal as the divs, sleeping through the day to make the time pass faster. She woke groggy and irritable after having another one of her usual nightmares. But this time, Soraya was the Shahmar, scales spreading down her arms instead of veins, and when she looked up, it was Parvaneh who was watching her transformation with a satisfied gleam in her eye. Parvaneh opened her mouth, and Soraya thought she would laugh, but instead she only said, *Are you still with me?* before dissolving into a flurry of moths that surrounded her and then fell one by one, dead to the ground, as soon as they touched her.

With a weary groan, Soraya rose from her makeshift bed and tried to run a hand through the tangled mess of her hair. She went to the table, toward the smell of food, but her eyes passed over the dishes laid out for her, distracted by the sight of something more familiar.

Draped over the table was one of her gowns from her wardrobe at Golvahar. It was one of the finest she had, delicate purple silk brocade etched with gold roses. She had never worn it, but she took it up in her hands and breathed in the slightly stuffy scent of her wardrobe as if it were the fragrance of roses from her garden. *Home.*

On the floor was a pair of matching slippers. Beside the gown was an array of jewelry that also came from her collection, as well as a glass bottle of rose water and a folded note leaning against it.

There will be a banquet in your honor tonight. Ready yourself
and I will send someone to accompany you.

She crumpled the note, the sound of it reminding her of crushed wings, and sat down to eat. *I won't dress for him,* she told herself as she folded a piece of lavash over quince jam. *But it would be nice to have a change of clothes, especially clothes from home,* she thought after one bite. *And until I find the feather, I still need to play along with his games.*

By the time she finished eating, she decided to compromise. She would wear the dress as a welcome change, as well as the slippers since hers were nearly worn, but not the jewelry, which felt too ornamental. After another internal debate, she uncorked the bottle and scented her hair and wrists with rose water. She wore it not to please Azad or anyone else, but because when she closed her eyes and took a breath, she could almost fool herself that she was standing in the golestan. Since she had no sense of time, she kept a nervous eye on the door as she changed out of her old dress and into the gown.

After she finished dressing, she didn't have to wait long until the door to her room opened unceremoniously, without even the courtesy of a knock. Soraya stood tall, ready to reprimand Azad for being so uncivil, but it wasn't Azad who had opened her door.

It was a div with sharp quills all along his skin. In a flat voice, he said, "The Shahmar sent me to fetch you."

Soraya followed the div out into the long pathway. Whenever other divs glanced at her with curiosity as they passed by, Soraya huddled closer to the div beside her.

"Here," the div said at last. They emerged from the tunnels into another enormous cavern, much like Azad's makeshift throne room. Soraya braced herself, but this time, she didn't see anything like the div training grounds or the pit from Duzakh. What she saw felt like . . . home.

Long trestle tables holding plates of food were set out through-out the cavern, and Soraya inhaled the smell of lamb and buttered rice, along with mint and saffron and wine—the kind of meal she would expect at Golvahar. A bonfire burned at the center of the cavern, filling it with light, and rugs were scattered over the ground around it. Azad had promised her a banquet and he had given her one, exactly as she would have imagined it, except that every guest here was a div.

They were seated on the rugs, eating their food, or milling about the banquet tables with goblets of wine in their hands. Soraya rec-ognized those goblets—as well as the tables and plates holding the food—from the palace, and the sight of them enraged her. As soon as she had found her clothes laid out for her, she had known that Azad was trying to give her pieces of home to make her more com-fortable here, to confuse her into a sense of belonging. But that was only half of his plan. Because he had brought her a dress that she had never had occasion to wear before. He had issued her an invi-tation she would never have received. And now she was the guest of honor at a banquet that she would never have attended. This was a version of Golvahar that had never existed, because it was a ver-sion of Golvahar where she was allowed to exist. He was trying to tempt her with the promise of a life she had never had.

And Soraya was furious because it was working.

None of the divs reacted to her presence, but now the cavern began to grow quiet and the divs shuffled aside, parting to form an aisle that was heading straight toward her. Even before he appeared in the crowd, Soraya knew who was approaching.

She held his gaze as the Shahmar came toward her, striding down the aisle formed for him with singular purpose. When he was directly in front of her, he held out a hand as if he were still a heroic young prince. She wondered briefly if Sorush had ever greeted Laleh in this way, and she almost laughed, because if this entire banquet was a demonic version of the real thing, then it seemed right that she and Azad should echo Sorush and Laleh's tender courtship. *What a twisted version of them we would make,* she thought.

His eyes swept over her dress with a smile, and only then did she notice that the rich purple of her gown matched the color of his robes. She placed her hand in his, and he led her back down the aisle, the divs murmuring as they passed, until they reached a raised platform like a dais cut into the rock at the other end of the cavern.

He guided her up onto the dais and turned her to the crowd, lifting their joined hands. "Here is your champion, divs of Arzur," he called out, his voice booming through the cavern. "It is because of Soraya that we have taken the palace and dethroned the shah."

The truth of Azad's statement sent a chill through her, and she tried to wrench her hand away, but he held it fast. He turned his head toward her, watching her as he again addressed the divs. "Show her your thanks for our victory," he said, "and let it be known that no div shall ever do her harm. From this moment on, she walks freely through the halls of Arzur, a friend to the divs."

As one, the divs let out a mighty cheer and raised their goblets to Soraya.

The sounds of adulation were so unfamiliar to her that she wasn't sure if they were cheering or protesting Azad's decree. She tried to retrieve her hand again, tried to step backward, away from all those eyes, but Azad kept her in place, and soon the panicked fluttering in her chest began to slow. Now she could acknowledge the meaning of Azad's decree and see the benefit in it—if she could wander Arzur freely, then she could more easily search the mountain for the feather during the day when Azad was gone. She wouldn't have to rely on a cloak to hide her—or on Parvaneh, for that matter.

She took a long breath, and as she exhaled, she felt a part of her flowing out into the crowd, and she was no longer afraid. She knew Azad was watching her, waiting for her to react or say something, and so she stubbornly kept her eyes straight ahead, looking at this cavern of monsters who had accepted her more easily than her own people ever had.

A rough, scaly finger pressed under her chin, moving her head to the side to face Azad. "It's rude to ignore your host," he said, a touch of humor in his voice. "Especially after I went through so much trouble to make you feel at home."

"Why are you doing this?" she asked him, her voice thick with emotion.

"You've been hidden away long enough," he said with unexpected tenderness. "It's time for you to become who you were meant to be."

She looked out at the divs and back at him, uncertainty furrowing her brow. "This isn't— I'm not—"

But before she could figure out what she was or wasn't, he began to lead her off the dais. "Come, meet your new people," he said.

They walked out together into the crowd, dressed in the color of royalty, and the divs all stepped aside to make room for them. As she swept past, many of them kneeled down, placing their heads against the ground or reaching out to touch and kiss the hem of her dress, as she had seen people do for her brother, her mother, her father. And yet, Soraya did not feel moved by these gestures. She had seen the divs bow for Azad, and she had thought it was out of deference, but now there was something about these exaggerated gestures that felt mocking or insincere to her. Azad was walking with his head held high, and so he didn't see the glimpses of amusement in the divs' eyes before their heads touched the ground, but Soraya did, and they made her uneasy.

Before Sorush, the shah was always set apart at Golvahar, and Soraya wondered if that distance was too cold or unnatural for the divs, who lived in such close proximity inside a mountain. She wondered what would happen if that distance were closed.

Her head was spinning from being so close to so many, and so she hardly thought as she slipped her hand out of Azad's and moved ahead of him, drawing closer to the crowd. A murmur of excitement went through them, the divs lifting their bowed heads to regard Soraya with new interest. She reached out one arm, letting the divs brush their scaled and furred and plated hands against hers, a new variety of sensation to experience. Some of them were bold enough to reach out and touch her hair or her dress, and they began to close in more tightly around her, but strangely enough, Soraya wasn't afraid. Div blood had once run through her veins— divs had shaped the course of her life—and so it seemed right to her that she should belong to them, and them to her.

There was a tearing sound, then a flash of pain, and she looked down to see a rip in her sleeve, a thin line of blood welling up. The divs were surrounding her so completely now that she could barely move, and she felt another bite of pain, this one on her scalp, as strands of her hair were pulled away. She felt something else tugging at the hem of her skirt, fingers around her ankle and curling in her hair, breath against the back of her neck, claws scraping her skin like the prick of thorns in her garden when she didn't wear her gloves. Tears were filling her eyes, but Soraya didn't resist. She simply offered herself up to them, wondering what would happen if she allowed the divs to claim her as their own. Would they rip her apart and rebuild her in their image? What would it mean to surrender? What would she become?

"Enough!"

At the sound of the Shahmar's voice, the divs fell away, leaving Soraya both relieved and bereft. Azad's arm came around her, and he guided her through the rest of the crowd, as he had done on Nog Roz.

At first, Soraya was afraid—more afraid than she wanted to admit—that Azad's stern command would make the divs reject her, but if anything, the contrast between Azad's almost paternalistic distance and Soraya's full surrender brought the divs closer to her. Many of them nodded to her as she passed with sly smiles or knowing looks, as if they were conspirators, as if they shared something that not even the Shahmar could understand.

Once they had crossed the cavern, Azad raised his arms to keep the divs' attention and announced, "It's time now to give Soraya the gift we have prepared for her." He beckoned to two of the divs, who separated from the crowd and went toward the cavern entrance for their unknown task.

Even through her intoxicated haze, Soraya felt a chill run down her spine. *Parvaneh*, she thought, suddenly afraid that he had captured her again. "What gift?" she asked him.

"You'll see," Azad said with a grin. "I promise you that you'll enjoy it."

Soraya tried to take a breath, but the air seemed trapped in her chest, unable to find its way out. "Please, just tell me."

But instead of answering, he held out his arms once more to silence the noise of the cavern. "Some entertainment," he called, loud enough to echo. "Bring him out."

Him? Soraya looked to where he was gesturing, and saw the same two divs pushing their way forward, dragging something through the crowd. It was a man, his hands bound in front of him and a sack over his head. He was bare from the waist up, revealing a vicious wound cutting through his side, the skin caked with dried blood. He dragged his feet every step of the way, forcing the divs to practically carry him down the aisle until they stopped in front of Azad and Soraya. Azad nodded his head, and one of the divs pushed the man to his knees, while the other lifted the sack from his head to reveal Ramin, furious and very much alive.

"Well?" Azad whispered to her. "Aren't you pleased?"

23

I saw him die, Soraya thought as she stared down at him. She hadn't, though, she reminded herself. She had only seen him wounded, and assumed that death would shortly follow. But other than the wound at his side and a few scrapes and scratches on his face and torso, he appeared unharmed.

Soraya wasn't sure how to feel at the sight of him—relief that he was alive, or pity for his current position . . . or satisfaction at knowing he was her prisoner, and that he was utterly alone when he was the reason she had felt so alone. Soraya couldn't help seeing the justice in that.

"Do whatever you want with him," Azad said from beside her, low enough so only she could hear. "He's yours to control. No one else may intervene unless you wish it."

Of course this was Azad's gift to her. He had met Ramin on Nog Roz. Azad had struck him, and Soraya had thanked him for it. That was the first time she and Azad had felt a pull toward each other, their first shared act of violence. And now, in this room of demons, she knew no one would stop her, or even care, if she did something to hurt him. More likely, they would cheer her on.

She couldn't help the flicker of excitement this ignited in her blood. She no longer had poison in her veins, but she still had—what was it Azad had said?—her will, her fury. *It isn't the poison that makes you deadly.*

But no, she wasn't thinking clearly. She had to think like Parvaneh, to see what use she could make of this situation. Ramin was the only other human here, the only other possible ally outside of the pariks. If she could somehow convince him that he could trust her, then maybe they could work together to find the feather.

Soraya went toward him. Her pulse was slow, like her heart had been sealed in ice. Ramin glared up at her as she approached, his jaw locked in defiance. "I always knew not to trust you," he spat at her. "I warned my father a hundred times, but he never believed me."

Aware of Azad's watchful stare behind her, and of all the other divs in the cavern waiting for violence, Soraya circled around him, placed one hand on his shoulder, and kept her voice as low as possible. "I came here the same way that you did—by force."

He scoffed at her. "The Shahmar told us who he is—who we all thought he was. But you knew all along. You were with him on Nog Roz."

She buried her hand in his hair and pulled his head back with a violent jerk, causing a snicker of delight to go through the room. "I didn't know," she murmured to him. "He fooled me, too. I'm a prisoner here like you. We can help each oth—"

"A prisoner like me? Is that so?" Ramin's eyes were so cold, his voice so biting, that Soraya knew he would never trust her, no matter what she said to him. His lip curled with disdain. "Will he give me clothes as nice as yours? Or do I have to pay for them with my family's blood like you did?"

She was too hurt to react at first. But that had always been her instinct—to freeze, to retreat, to cradle her anger in her hands until the flame went out safely. That was what she would have done before. That was what she *had* done before, a thousand times over the years, during every encounter with Ramin. Even surrounded by divs, powerless, he still thought he could say whatever he wanted to her. He thought she wouldn't strike back.

And now, her blood still singing after her surrender to the divs, all Soraya wanted was the pleasure of proving him wrong.

With one hand still grasping his hair, she bent down and dug her nails into his chest, causing him to hiss in pain and the divs to let out a cheer.

"You think you can speak to me that way," Soraya whispered to him, her head bent beside his, "because you never believed I would fight back." She was herself and not herself—she didn't know what she was, except that she was free. "I could have shocked you into silence with a single touch so many times over the years, but I always let you win. That's why you were never afraid of me. That's why you mocked and insulted me. But you should have been afraid, Ramin. You should have been afraid of me from the start." She dragged her nails up his chest as she straightened, tearing through skin, and leaving an angry scratch on his chest.

The divs cheered for her again, as if she had scored a blow in a sparring match, and she couldn't fight the flush of satisfaction that went through her—nor did she want to. When she looked up, her eyes met Azad's, and it was the same as it had been on Nog Roz, a crackle of energy passing from one to the other like lightning.

Ramin had bent his head, and his shoulders convulsed in what Soraya thought was pain—until she realized he was laughing. He looked up at her and said loudly, "You think I wasn't afraid of you? You're deluded, Soraya—I've *always* feared you. But I promised myself I would never show fear in front of you, because how could I protect my sister from something I was scared of myself?"

She didn't want to hear Laleh's name or anything that would stop her from enjoying Azad's gift to her. But still, she asked, "What do you mean?"

"Why do you think I trailed along after you and Laleh? I couldn't stand to leave you alone with her. I saw the way your eyes followed her when she and Sorush would leave you behind in your dismal passageways—that jealous, hateful look."

"That's not true," Soraya snapped, but whether it was true or not, she knew Ramin didn't think he was lying. He couldn't fall back on his usual arrogant posturing anymore, and there was raw emotion in his face and voice. This was a confession: he had feared her—and he feared for Laleh.

"I've seen that look grow sharper over the years, seen the poison in you grow stronger," Ramin continued. "I told Laleh to stay away from you, but she was too kind, or maybe she pitied you too much, so I found other ways to separate you. I knew you would hurt her one day."

"Enough," Soraya ordered. Each word that he spoke threatened to dim the glow of satisfaction that came from her control over him. She couldn't lose that glow—without it, she would be left in darkness.

But Ramin's voice only became louder. "I thought that would be enough to keep my family safe from you, but clearly, I was wrong. My sister spent her wedding day in tears because of you and your—"

"I said, *enough!*" Soraya shouted as she stepped forward, pulled her foot back, and aimed a hard kick at his side—at the wound.

The shout of triumph from the divs was so loud that she almost didn't hear Ramin crying out as he slumped forward. But she *did* hear it, and the sound of that cry, so agonized, so primal, brought her back to herself.

Oh no.

She had been so desperate to keep his words from reaching her, from letting him win *again*, even when he was her prisoner, that she had barely thought before reacting. Now as the words were sinking in, Soraya looked at Ramin, his eyes shut from the pain, and saw him anew. All this time, she had thought of him as her persecutor and herself as the maligned victim of his pride, intimidated into submission because she refused to hurt him. But Ramin had been living in a different story, with himself as the hero, protecting his family from a demon in their midst that only he could recognize.

Standing here in a cavern of divs with blood under her nails and on the hem of her gown, Soraya was no longer sure which story was true.

Once more, she moved toward Ramin—but this time, she bent to undo the cords around his wrists.

"What are you doing?" he asked her with surprise.

"I'm sorry," Soraya responded, unable to look him in the eye.

Before she could even begin to loosen the cords, a hand came down on her shoulder and she froze. "Stop at once," Azad hissed at her under his breath. "You mustn't show any weakness in front of the divs."

She looked up at his stern face. "You said I could do whatever I wanted with him. I choose to free him."

He shook his head. "I won't allow that. *They* won't allow that."

Soraya looked up at the crowd of murmuring divs, craning their necks to see what violence Soraya would inflict next. "Then I want him returned to Golvahar unharmed." She faced Ramin now, who was staring at her with a bewildered frown. "Look after them all," she said to him in a hushed voice. "Protect them as much as you can."

Azad took her arm and lifted her to her feet. "Go wait for me in that hall," he whispered to her, gesturing to one of the tunnels leading out of the cavern. With a last guilty glance at Ramin, Soraya did as he said, hurrying through the crowd. As she pushed her way through to the tunnel, she heard Azad call out, "Your champion has wisely decided to let her prisoner recover before she causes him further injury. . . ."

As soon as she was alone in the tunnel, Soraya leaned her head against the stone wall, taking deep, shuddering breaths. Ramin's cry of pain was still in her ears. How could she have let herself lose control like that? After so many years of holding herself back, she had lost that skill. It seemed to her sometimes that she could only ever be one thing or the other, a mouse or a viper, with nothing in between. And if that were true, then she didn't know which she would choose. Either way brought her misery and shame.

"Soraya." Azad's hands wrapped around her arms and turned her to face him, his grip surprisingly gentle. "I gave orders for him to be returned unharmed to Golvahar."

"Are you lying to me?"

"I swear on my throne that I'm not lying to you."

Soraya supposed she'd have to be content with that—Azad was already leading her farther down the tunnel, away from the cavern. "Where are you taking me?" she asked.

"Somewhere you can rest safely," he said. "I was hoping you would be pleased with my gift, but it seems to have upset you. Perhaps I gave it to you too soon."

Not too soon, but too late, she thought. She never would have hurt Ramin like that before the fire temple, before the dakhmeh—before she'd first learned the pleasure of lashing out.

She had assumed he would return her to her room, but they passed the now-familiar tunnel that would take them there. They kept going, higher up the mountain than she had been before. Only when he finally stopped and opened a thick iron door wedged into the door frame did Soraya understand where he had taken her.

She was in a room much larger and more lushly furnished than her own, with a daybed and several chairs. The hard stone floor was covered in overlapping rugs, their threads worn and colors faded. A crystal chandelier lit with candles hung above a large, oval table of polished wood. A map of Atashar was laid out on the table, with carved wooden figures painted in red or white set out in different arrangements. There was even an ornate fireplace carved into one wall. A cool breeze chilled her face, and she looked up in surprise to see a window in the wall opposite. It was no more than an uneven rectangle carved into the rock, no glass to keep out the wind.

Compared to the rest of Arzur, this was a room fit for a shah.

Azad put his hands on her shoulders, and she stiffened. "Why did you bring me here?"

"I thought the fresh air would do you good," he said. "There are no other windows in the mountain."

She went to the window, wanting to put distance between them, and in truth, she did find the fresh air a relief. She thought she saw the dark outline of Golvahar's dome in the distance, past the brush on the south side of the mountain. The sight of it made her ache.

"That night at the dakhmeh," Soraya said, turning to face him, "when I killed the yatu, you comforted me. You told me I had done right, that I shouldn't be ashamed. Are you going to try to do the same for me now?" She hadn't meant the question to sound like a plea, but the wavering final note in her voice was unmistakable.

He studied her, and then he said, "Is that what you want? For me to absolve you? It's easy enough. That boy deserved what you did to him tonight. They all deserve it. That's why . . ." He stopped, but his eyes were alight with some unknown excitement. "That's why I want you to be the one to execute your brother."

Despite all the horrors around her, Soraya barked out a shocked laugh. "I would never kill my brother," she said, aghast.

"That's what I once believed. But during all the time we've spent together, Soraya, one thing has become increasingly clear to me."

He began to walk toward her, taking slow, measured steps across the room as if he would frighten her away if he moved too quickly. "I can never show myself as human in front of the divs. I don't want them to remember my origins, my weaknesses. I want them to see me at my full strength. And so I forget him sometimes, the man I used to be. I forget what he looked like, how it felt to be human. But when I'm with you, I remember." As he continued walking toward her, the scales on his skin began to recede, his body slimming into the familiar form of his human self. "You and I don't belong fully to either world. We know what it is to be something between human and div. We know what it means to turn against families who have hurt us. That night in the throne room, I truly meant to execute your brother. But when I saw you fight back against him, I couldn't bring myself do it, because I knew that it should be you. I *want* it to be you. I've been waiting all this time for you to want it as well. Once you do this, you'll know that there's nothing you can't do. You'll be free." He was in front of her now, fully human, vulnerable in a way Soraya hadn't understood until she had seen the veins under her skin fade away, her own armor dissolved. "And you'll rule with me, at my side, as my queen."

She shook her head. She had heard him wrong, she thought, too distracted by seeing him human again—by the curl of his eyelashes, the bridge of his nose, the shape of his upper lip. "What are you asking me?"

His eyes were so bright, so young, as if he truly were a young prince again. "To be mine. To love me, as I love you."

"You don't love me," Soraya said at once.

A melancholy smile passed over his face. "It's easier for you to believe that, but you know it isn't true, and I can't deny it anymore, either. I've loved you since the dakhmeh, when you showed me who you are. You're the part of me that I had forgotten, Soraya. And I'm the part of you that you could be—unrestrained, unburdened."

Soraya turned from him, gulping in the night air like it was water as her arms wrapped around her waist. It was too difficult to remember all that he had done to her and to the people she loved when she saw him like this.

From behind her, Azad's hands—his soft, smooth hands—rested on her shoulders. "I understand if you can't strike down your brother," he said, his voice low and sympathetic. "I was the same once. After I killed my father and brothers, I thought I had done wrong. I agonized over it, over every death that brought me to my throne. But before long, all that pain and doubt burned away, and there was only the knowledge of what needed to be done. You'll see in time, but until then . . ." His hands glided from her shoulders down her arms and found her own hands, his fingers entwining with hers. "Until then, let me be your hands. Let me be your rage. Tell me you'll be mine, and I will do what needs to be done."

Soraya leaned back against him, letting him bear her weight, as he promised to do. Was there any point in fighting him anymore? Wasn't he right that they were alike, that his past was her future, that a different kind of poison still ran through her veins? Hadn't she proven that herself when she had struck out at Ramin?

I couldn't stand to leave you alone with her. I saw the way your eyes followed her when she and Sorush would leave you behind in your dismal passageways—that jealous, hateful look.

How simple it would be to close her eyes and only open them when all of this was over. *It would be like falling asleep,* she thought as she felt the rise and fall of Azad's chest against her back, his pulse in time with her own. And when she awoke, the world would be new and different. Sorush would be gone, along with the memory of his final harsh words, and Soraya would take his place in a world turned inside out. She would grieve for him, but as Azad had said, all that guilt and grief would soon burn away.

A sigh escaped her, and Azad slid his hands out of hers and swept her hair off the back of her neck, fingers grazing the sensitive skin at her nape. And yet, Soraya felt nothing at his touch, neither re-vulsion nor pleasure, only a kind of numb relief. When she didn't stop him or pull away, his hand moved lower, dipping below the collar of her gown to the ridges of her spine. A memory ran through Soraya's whole body—the smell of esfand; the feeling of soft skin under her fingertips; the sound of breathing in the dark-ness; a whorled pattern on a patch of skin between shoulder blades. *Between her wings.*

The sight of those wings, torn to shreds, hanging down Par-vaneh's back.

Soraya flinched away from him with a vehemence that surprised them both. The vividness of her memory paired with the visceral touch of Azad's hands on her spine had made her react, as if hers were the wings he had torn.

She had spun to face him, and they stared at each other now in mutual confusion. Soraya could still feel the pressure of his touch along her spine, but it only made her think of being in the dun-geon, of wanting to brush her fingertips against Parvaneh's spine as she carefully stitched her wings back together, repairing what Azad had destroyed.

And he had destroyed so much. She thought of Parvaneh, of the other pariks sleeping in cages, of her mother as a terrified child confronting a monster in the forest, of Laleh's ruined wedding and her brother on his knees . . . and she wondered how she could have ever trusted Azad to absolve her of anything.

"I didn't mean to startle you," Azad said, his voice hoarse.

She felt like she was waking from a dream, the world taking solid shape around her. "I'm sorry," she said, edging away from the window, so she wouldn't be cornered. "I need time to think."

Her plea sounded like the stall for time that it was, and so he tensed with frustration as he nodded. "I understand," he said, com-ing forward to close the gap between them. "But I can't leave your brother alive for much longer, Soraya." He was backing her toward the fireplace now, and she looked behind her anxiously as she tried to think of how to further placate him. "I need you to make your choice."

There was a cold glint in his eye, and Soraya almost thought he was going to transform again. But he remained human, and just as she had once been startled to see the eyes of the boy in the Shahmar, she now saw the eyes of the monster in Azad.

The gulf is not as wide as you think. It had been a plea when he'd said it before, but she heard it now as a threat.

"It's not *my* choice," she said, her voice strained, "when I'm still your prisoner."

With a dismissive shake of his head, he said, "You're not a prisoner, Soraya."

His tone made her bristle. "I'm not a prisoner? Because I'm not locked up in a cage hanging from a tree? Because you said I can now move freely through Arzur? As long as you have my family, I'm under your control and you know it."

She swept past him and headed toward his door, ready for this night to end. But as she started to pull open the door, a powerful, scaled hand pushed it shut, trapping her inside. Soraya turned to find the Shahmar standing over her, transformed.

"How did you know where I imprisoned the pariks?" he asked, his voice dangerously low.

24

Soraya went cold as she realized her mistake. She had let herself become angry, and so she'd spoken without thinking over her words first, without considering how much she was supposed to know. "I don't—I didn't—"

"You lied to me when you said you hadn't seen Parvaneh." He took her chin in his hand and tilted her head up to look at him. "I thought it strange that Parvaneh could have resisted the effects of the esfand after all this time. But of course, if she had a human accomplice, that would explain everything. You've been working against me this entire time."

She shook her head. "No . . . no, I . . ."

He sighed impatiently. "Choose a lie more quickly, Soraya."

Her mind was working frantically, trying to find a lie that he would believe, but it seemed pointless. He wouldn't believe her, not enough to trust her again—certainly not enough to tell her where he kept the simorgh's feather.

The truth, then. As much of it as she dared.

"I did free her," Soraya said, her voice wavering from fear. "I needed a way to escape the palace, and when she showed me what you had done to her wings, I thought she would help me. But you caught me first."

A low growl escaped his throat. "When did you find the other pariks? You freed them, too, didn't you?"

Soraya nodded. "The first night, after you left. Parvaneh took me into the forest and we found them . . . and I freed them."

"And where are they now?"

"I don't know," Soraya said, thankful it was true. "They all left together, but I don't know where they went."

He released her face and turned away from her with another heavy sigh, his hands running over his head where his hair had once been. "I don't know what to do with you now, Soraya," he said, a note of regret in his voice.

Soraya was on the verge of tears. She had spoiled everything because of one thoughtless moment. How had Azad managed to fool her for so long without letting his mask slip? She had started to see it at one point—she had realized that he was playing a part, telling her what she wanted to hear. Then he had told her the story of his merchant father, and she had believed him again—because even though the details weren't true, his resentment was. That was the trick of it, then—to sharpen lies with the truth.

She swallowed down her fear and approached him, her hands resting on his back. He went rigid under her touch, but she took a breath and said, "When I freed her, I didn't know what she had done to you. She lied to me, fooled me as she fooled you." He didn't respond, but he didn't pull away, either, and so she moved around him so that they were facing each other. "I was furious with her when I found out. Whatever alliance we once had is over."

From his long silence, his searching stare, she knew that he wanted to believe her. Finally, he said, "Why should I trust you?"

Soraya shut her eyes, the flickering flame of a candle appearing in her mind. "Because I can give her to you," she said, the words scraping her throat. It was the worst betrayal she could think of, but it was also the only solution to make Azad trust her again.

She opened her eyes to find him watching her with curiosity. "How?" he said.

"She always comes to my room after you leave for Golvahar. If you hide there, you can catch her when she appears."

"And you would be content with this?"

Soraya nodded, thankful now that she had become so adept at pushing down her emotions over the years. "I don't care what happens to her."

Azad abruptly left her side and went to an iron chest against the wall. He retrieved something from it, and when he returned, Soraya saw he had a coil of rope around his arm. *He had captured me, bound my wings so I couldn't transform,* she remembered Parvaneh telling her. Azad went to the door and gestured for her to follow.

"*Now?*" Soraya said, her voice going up an octave.

He looked at her coolly. "Why not? The time for her arrival is near. If you meant what you said, there's no reason to wait."

Soraya followed him out into the tunnels, walking quickly to keep up with his determined stride. "What are you planning to do with her?" she asked.

"You said you didn't care what happens to her," Azad answered, and Soraya went quiet.

He won't kill her, she reminded herself. Parvaneh had told her that he always captured pariks rather than kill them. He probably would keep her unconscious, as he had done with the others. But what if she was wrong and he preferred to kill Parvaneh rather than risk her escaping again? What if he kept her alive but tore her wings, or found other ways to harm her? Soraya's stomach twisted with nausea. Perhaps if she used the candle to signal to Parvaneh that it wasn't safe, then she would understand not to appear, and

Soraya could tell him that they'd fought, and that Parvaneh had abandoned her.

Soraya practiced the conversation in her head, and by the time they reached her room, she was calmer.

Before Azad's banquet, she had left the candelabra at the far end of the table—the signal for Parvaneh not to appear—and it remained there still. As long as Soraya didn't move it, she could pretend that Parvaneh should have come by now. She gestured to a shadowy part of her room beyond the table where Azad could hide, and he nodded, tightening the rope between his hands.

"She may not come," Soraya said quickly. "We fought the last time we spoke. I told her I was finished with her."

Azad laughed softly and took Soraya's head in his hands, the rope around his wrist scratching her cheek. "I hope that isn't the case, Soraya. Because if she doesn't appear tonight, I'll think you were lying to me, and I'll have to take measures to ensure that you don't betray me again. What was it you said before? That as long as I have your family, you're under my control? I'll make you a deal, then. If I capture Parvaneh tonight, I will let your family live—other than your brother, of course. But if Parvaneh doesn't appear tonight, or if she escapes me, then I will start to kill them one by one every time you defy me, beginning with your brother's pretty bride."

He released her face and went to conceal himself in the shadowed alcove, only the yellow of his eyes revealing his position. Soraya fought to control her breathing as she counted one, two, three seconds. She stepped forward and slid the candelabra across the table to rest in front of her.

A few seconds passed, and Soraya felt more and more ill with each one. Her vision was blurring, and her mouth was bitter with the taste of bile. She kept hearing Parvaneh's voice in her mind, asking, *Are you still with me?* She wished she had said yes—fullheartedly, in every way possible, yes. She wished she had one more memory of joy between them before she would have to see the hurt and betrayal in those eyes that had captivated Soraya from the start.

From the corner of her vision, Soraya saw a flutter of wings, and then Parvaneh appeared beside the table, her back—her wings—to Azad.

Soraya wanted to say something to warn her, or to apologize at least, but any indication of loyalty to Parvaneh would make Azad suspicious.

Parvaneh shook her head slightly. "What's the matter, Soraya? Are you still angry with me?" At the same time, Soraya saw Azad peel away from the shadows, approaching silently with the rope taut between his hands.

"Of course I'm still angry with you," Soraya said. Despite her effort to muster some conviction, her voice sounded lifeless. "You lied to me."

As if he had been waiting to hear Soraya say those words first, Azad struck, lunging forward to bind Parvaneh's wings with the rope with expert speed. Parvaneh thrashed and struggled against him, but he used the rope to pull Parvaneh back against him as they tightened around her wings, and one of his hands came to encircle her throat, holding her head still.

Soraya couldn't stop a tear from running down her cheek as she stood rigidly apart from the two of them, her hands clenched at her sides. She couldn't speak—if she opened her mouth, the words *I'm sorry* would spill out.

"Parvaneh," Azad said, the name a low growl in his throat. "Haven't you missed me? We've been together so long, I can't imagine what you would do without me."

With his hand still around her throat, Parvaneh choked out a laugh. "Do you think I care what you do to me? I've freed my sisters from you. That's all that matters to me."

"I'll simply hunt them down again. It's been at least a year since I caught one of you—I was starting to grow bored."

He pushed her forward, and she landed on the ground in front of Soraya, her wings tightly bound behind her, still connected to the rope in Azad's hand. *I could unbind her,* Soraya thought. *If I do it quickly enough, she can transform*—and then Laleh would die, followed by the others.

Parvaneh pushed herself up and looked at Soraya through a sheet of black hair. "You've made your choice, then," she said. "I knew you would join him in the end."

Soraya frowned, her confusion genuine. "What do you mean?"

Parvaneh laughed again but her eyes were hard and cold. "You're too alike. I've known it since the dungeon. Every time I spoke to you, it was like speaking to him, all those years ago. I thought I could stop you from making his mistakes, but I should have known it was pointless." Her face twisted into a grimace. "You deserve each other."

"On your feet." Azad tugged sharply on the rope, and Parvaneh hissed in pain. "You've said enough."

"Congratulations, Azad," she said, his name sounding like an insult on her tongue as she rose to her feet. Even though she addressed Azad, her eyes remained on Soraya as she spoke. "You finally found someone as wretched and despicable as you are. I would keep her close if I were you."

The sting of Parvaneh's words was all the more painful considering how close Soraya had come to succumbing to Azad tonight. Was there truth in what she was saying, or was she only speaking out of anger, lashing out because she had been betrayed? Soraya trembled with the effort of not speaking, knowing that if she challenged Parvaneh now or told her how wrong she was, Azad would know her true loyalties.

"I'm sorry it happened this way," was all she could trust herself to say in a small, shaky voice.

"I'm sure you are," Parvaneh replied with a sneer.

Azad held her by the back of her neck and guided her toward

the door. Anger spiked through Soraya as she watched his smug, retreating form. He owned her now. The only way she could ever escape him was to cut her heartstrings and abandon all the people she had betrayed.

Before he led Parvaneh out, Azad turned back to Soraya and said, "You've proven yourself to me tonight, in more ways than one. I'll return tomorrow." He left her then, taking Parvaneh with him.

Soraya couldn't move. She stood rooted to where she was standing, as if time would stop if she simply never moved again. Her anger had faded now, snuffed out as soon as Azad and Parvaneh were gone. She had always wanted to extinguish the persistent spark of anger that burned deep in her heart, so sure that it would turn her into a monster. She hadn't realized that her anger could only exist because she still had hope. Once hope was gone, there was no point in fighting, and so she had no need for anger anymore.

Soraya finally found a reason to move. She went to the table and blew out the candles, leaving her in darkness.

Without even the candles to help her determine the passage of time, Soraya had no idea how long she had been lying curled up on the ground, hot tears pouring out of her tightly shut eyes. She wished for sleep, for a temporary reprieve from thought and memory, but instead, she spent the time sinking into a kind of waking nightmare, too awake to find peace, but too exhausted in every possible way to pull herself out of it.

After what must have been hours, Soraya managed to open her eyes and found two round orange beams pointed at her.

She sat up in a flurry of groggy confusion, her head aching. It was too dark to see anything except for the orange lights glowing at her from the direction of the table. The orange lights emitted a low, hooting sound, and Soraya understood.

"Parisa?" she whispered.

The lights went out, and a dim, shadowy figure stood at the table. Parisa lit the candles with the flint beside it and, newly illuminated, faced Soraya with an accusing stare. "Where is Parvaneh?"

The name made her wince. "You shouldn't be here," Soraya said as she rose to her feet. "He might return."

"It's still day. He never returns until dusk. Where is Parvaneh?"

"Why do you even care what happens to her? You cast her out."

The eerie orange glow of her eyes dimmed a little, her wings bristling behind her. "She's still our sister," she said with a note of irritation. "We keep track of her movements. She entered Arzur last night by the pariks' passage, but she never returned." Parisa took a step toward her. "*Where is Parvaneh?*" she said again, emphasizing each word.

Soraya had to look away from her insistent stare before she could answer. "I don't know," she said. "He captured her." *I betrayed her.* "I don't know where he took her—or if she's even alive."

"She's alive," Parisa said, and Soraya looked up at her with the first semblance of hope she'd felt since last night. "We would know if she had died, or if another parik had risen."

Soraya let out a heavy sigh, relief bubbling through her—until Parisa stepped closer to Soraya and held out her hand, palm upward. "Here," she said. "Take this and use it to find her."

In the dim light, Parisa's hand appeared empty, and Soraya had to squint before she saw the few dark tendrils of hair across her palm. *Hair?* She was confused until she remembered what her mother had told her—how she had burned a lock of Parisa's hair to speak to her in a dream. Soraya's chest tightened. "No," she said in a rasp. "I can't. You do it."

Parisa shook her head. "It will only work with a human."

Soraya started to reach for the lock of hair, but the memory of Parvaneh's furious, glowing eyes burning at her through a sheet of that same hair made Soraya physically recoil from Parisa's outstretched hand and sink back into herself the way she had always done. Her arms wrapped around her waist, her shoulders hunched over, her hair falling down around her face. *Poison,* she thought. *I'll always be poison.*

"She won't want to speak to me," Soraya said. "I'm the reason she was captured."

She peeked up through her hair, expecting Parisa's eyes to go cold or angry, for her fist to close, but she mostly seemed impatient. "Yes, and Parvaneh is the reason we were captured, but that never stopped her from trying to find us again." With her other hand, she took Soraya's chin and lifted it, so they were eye to eye. "Even if she's upset with you now, if you do right by her, she will forgive you."

"Maybe I don't want to be forgiven," Soraya said, pulling away from Parisa's hand. "Maybe I just want to be forgotten."

And now Parisa's frown deepened into a look of disgust. "Then what do you plan to do?" she asked, her voice stern. "Are you still going to bring us the simorgh's feather?"

Soraya looked away. "Every mistake I've made has come from trying to find that damned feather at any cost. I'm finished planning."

Parisa was silent at first, then shook her head slowly. "You should be angry."

Soraya laughed harshly and shrank even further into herself. "Do you think that would do any good? I've been angry my entire life, and all it's done is twist me into something as terrible and violent as *he* is." Memories flashed through her mind—the yatu's face draining of all life, her brother on his knees, Ramin's agonized scream. And at the heart of it all was a little girl with green veins looking at an illustration in a book, seeing a prince with scales growing over his skin, and knowing that they were the same. *You deserve each other.*

Shame flooded her, and she buried her head in her hands, trying to make the memories stop. Parisa took her hands and brought them down from her face. She held them tight, her gaze as sharp and knowing as that of the bird she resembled.

"You say you've been angry, that you've hurt others, that you've become something violent like him," Parisa said. "Very well, then. *Be* angry. Be violent. But not for his sake. Not to do as he commands. Be angry for yourself. Use that rage to fight him."

Soraya shook her head. "It's too late. My mother was right to make me poisonous—I see that now. I can't fight anyone like this."

"Your mother fought him. She outsmarted him by bringing you to me and asking me for protection. If you truly are like her, as you told me you were, then you'll find a way to outsmart him, too. Be clever. Be patient. Keep that anger close to you, nourish it like a flame, and when the time is right, fight him however you can. No one is untouchable, Soraya."

Her hands slipped out of Soraya's and she turned and went to the door, opening it before becoming an owl and flying into the darkness of the tunnels.

Soraya stood there alone awhile longer, looking down at her hands—open but not empty.

25

As the smell of burning hair filled the cavern, Soraya inhaled deeply, breathing in the smoke. She had spent several minutes staring down at the strands of hair that Parisa had left for her, but in the end, she knew that the only thing more unforgivable than betraying Parvaneh would be to give up without even trying to free her.

When the hair had finished burning, Soraya lay back on her straw mattress and tried to will herself to sleep. Eventually, her breathing slowed and her thoughts became hazy and disconnected as her dreaming mind took over. *Parvaneh*, she thought. *I have to speak to Parvaneh.*

She knew where her dream had taken her before she even opened her eyes again. The air around her was chill and slightly damp, and when she breathed, she smelled esfand.

Golvahar. She was in the dungeon of Golvahar. She kept her eyes shut tight, not yet ready to face the home she had betrayed, but they filled with tears anyway. Tears of relief or regret, she wasn't sure. She wasn't even sure she had a right to call Golvahar home anymore.

She pushed self-pity aside, reminding herself that she had come here with a purpose, and that Parvaneh would find no comfort in being locked up in her former prison. Soraya opened her eyes and sat up from the cold, stony ground. She couldn't see much—the entire cavern was swirling with misty gray smoke, so thick that it obscured her vision, though strangely enough, she had no trouble breathing.

When her eyes adjusted enough to see the shape of bars in the distance, she rose and went toward them. As she came up to them, though, her foot met something hard. When she looked down, she found a row of dim orange lights hidden deep under the layers of smoke. She bent down, hoping they were the braziers with the esfand. There were at least five of them, enough to ensure that Parvaneh would be completely weakened, if not fully unconscious. Her hand met the metal of the brazier, but to her surprise, it wasn't hot, or even warm, to the touch. It was solid under her fingers, but it didn't *feel* like anything at all, as if she were touching it in a dream—which, she supposed, she was. When she tried to lift or move it, it wouldn't budge, and so she gave up on trying to put out the smoke and went on toward the bars, feeling for them with her hands.

Two of the bars were still bent from when Parvaneh had freed herself, and Soraya stepped through them, into the cell. "Parvaneh?" she called out. Even if Parvaneh were unconscious, Soraya thought, she might still be awake in this uncertain dreamscape. There was no response, though—or maybe Parvaneh didn't *want* to respond.

The smoke closed in on Soraya from every direction, making her feel disoriented and slightly drowsy, even within a dream. She kept wandering with small, uncertain steps until she saw a shadowy outline on the ground near the far end of the cavern. She went toward it, and as she neared, the smoke began to clear slightly, as if it knew what she was looking for and wanted to oblige. And then Soraya saw her.

Parvaneh lay on her back, her wings hidden from view, her hands folded over her stomach, her eyes closed. Surrounded by tendrils of smoke, she looked like an apparition, or a mirage in the desert, the air shimmering around her. Soraya bent down beside her and looked at her face. She had always thought people were supposed to look peaceful when asleep, but Parvaneh's forehead was lined with distress. Soraya reached with one uncertain hand to smooth the line away, but as with the brazier, she couldn't make any change to her surroundings, nor even fully feel anything under her touch. She had thought she would be afraid to speak to Parvaneh again, but this silence, this sleep that was almost death, was far worse. Soraya would have endured the angriest of diatribes if it meant seeing those eyes open again.

"I'm sorry," she said, the words swallowed up by the smoke. "I promise I'll come for you. I won't give up. I won't let him win. I'll show you how wrong you were about me."

Before she willed herself awake again, she brushed her lips against Parvaneh's forehead, a kiss neither of them could feel.

Soraya woke with her fists clenched at her sides, her whole body coiled and ready to act. She rose at once and checked the candle. It was only a little shorter than it had been when she'd gone to sleep, which meant she probably still had time before dusk. When Azad returned, she would have to think of a way to guide their conversation toward the simorgh's feather again, but in the meantime, she finally had a place to search.

Her cloak was bundled up under the straw of her mattress, and she retrieved it now, even though she hoped that after Azad's decree, no one would trouble her. Her caution was unnecessary—as soon as she stepped out into the main tunnel, she encountered a div who passed by her with a simple nod of the head. There were fewer divs passing through than she had seen before—probably because it was day—but each div that she passed as she made the climb up to Azad's room paid her similar treatment. A strange thrill went through her on each of these occasions. Unlike their exaggerated deference to Azad, these gestures of recognition were small and subtle—a quick nod, a flash of a smile, a knowing look. *We see you and know you,* they said, *and you are welcome here.* After a short while, Soraya found herself returning the gestures, and the cloak dropped from her hands.

When she thought she was near Azad's room, she began to slow and peer down tunnels, looking for an iron door. Most of the rooms and caverns didn't have doors at all, and the ones that did were either made of wood or were simply curtains, so it was easy enough to find the one she was looking for. Unlike the door to his treasury, this one had no lock—his attachment to his humanity was his only secret—and so Soraya opened it and went inside.

She had thought that returning to this room, where she had nearly given in to her worst instincts, would be unbearable. But the room around her was nothing like the one from last night. She would have thought she was in the wrong place except for the cool breeze coming in through the window, the only one in all of Arzur, Azad had said. Because the breeze wasn't the only visitor to the chamber—sunlight also streamed through the window, trans-forming the room entirely. It was the bright orange light of a slowly dying sun, which meant she didn't have much time until dusk, and yet she stood enraptured at seeing and feeling the sunlight for the first time since she had been taken from Golvahar. She had never realized how easily hope died when there was no sunlight, how hard it was to believe that another day was worth fighting for when there was only night.

But that sun was also a measure of how much time she had left until Azad's return, so she quickly recovered herself and started rummaging through the room as she had once done in her mother's chambers, not long ago. She began with the chest where he had retrieved the rope last night, but it held only tools that were appropriate for living in a mountain—chisels, pickax heads, more rope.

She overturned all the rugs next, careful to replace them when she was finished, then went to the table where the map still lay. She could look at the wooden figures on the map more clearly now, white and red figures clashing at various points along the borders of Atashar. She dimly remembered seeing a similar map, with the same areas marked. *Those marks are where the divs have attacked in the last few years*, Sorush had explained to her. *It's almost as if they're practicing for something*. Soraya was tempted to knock the map off the table, but she restrained herself, instead carefully lifting a corner to look underneath.

There was a short hall off to the side of the room, which Soraya followed to a doorway at its end. Inside was a smaller chamber, roughly the same size as her own, and nearly as simple—a table, some candles, and a pallet that served as a bed, without even a blanket. *This is where he sleeps*, she thought. She couldn't make herself go into the room. There was too much of him there.

Back in the main chamber, though, she had run out of places to search. She walked through the room carefully, checking for anything she may have missed, and stopped at the massive fireplace. *Would he have—?*

With a growing sense of dread, Soraya knelt down in front of the fireplace and began to sift through the ashes. Would he have destroyed his only chance of becoming human again? He had said he had no interest in living a human life, but his treasury of mementos from his reign said otherwise. Soraya's fingertips were becoming gray, but she kept digging through the soot, until a flash of green caught her eye, reminding her too much of the last time she had dug this same feather out of the embers of a fire.

Soraya uncovered the remains of the simorgh's feather, a few green barbs that became ash as soon as she touched them.

It was over, then. Their only chance at defeating the Shahmar—Soraya's only chance at saving her family and Parvaneh—had crumbled into nothing.

Soraya remained kneeling by the fireplace, looking at the ashes that had once been the simorgh's feather as if they would regenerate through whatever magic gave the feather its power. It seemed ridiculous that the feather had the power to heal anything except itself. But the yatu had warned her, his words more prophetic than she had known: in any fire other than the Royal Fire, he had said, the feather would simply burn.

She shut her eyes, letting the breeze cool her face, the back of her neck . . .

Her face *and* the back of her neck?

Soraya's eyes snapped open, and she acknowledged that yes, she felt the breeze from two directions at once, both from the window behind her—and from the fireplace in front of her.

She reached a hand out to the back of the fireplace, trying to find the source of the air. Her hand touched brick, and when she pushed at the surface of the wall, it budged. The fireplace was large enough that she could stand inside it at her full height, and so she rose to her feet and walked into the mouth of it, then pressed both hands against the brick wall with all of her strength. The wall moved inward, revealing a dark passage beyond.

A secret passageway, Soraya thought, *built by a clever and paranoid shah.* She shouldn't have been surprised.

The breeze was stronger now, clearly coming from the passageway, which meant that there was likely an opening beyond. An escape route would do her no good at this point, but curiosity and desperation led her farther down the passage, keeping her hand to the wall so she wouldn't lose her way.

It was not as dark as she would have expected, and not just

because of the light coming from the window in the room—there was another light source beyond, again confirming her belief that there was an opening at the end of the passage.

There was only the one path, and the light was growing stronger as she continued. Before long, the passage opened up into a cavern, lit from above by a stream of pale orange light coming in through an opening in the rock. Soraya thought the chamber was empty until she heard a sound like the clinking of chains, and saw something moving against the far wall.

Parvaneh, she thought at once, a flutter of hope in her chest. Perhaps she had performed the ritual with the hair incorrectly, and her dream had been nothing more than a guilt-induced fantasy. She stepped forward, toward the beam of light, and the prisoner in the shadows.

And then she saw it—saw *her*, the shape of her becoming more distinct as Soraya drew nearer. She was so familiar that Soraya knew her at once, even though the truth of it seemed impossible. Green feathers tipped with orange, a long and graceful neck, her head and body shaped like a peacock's, while her wings had the majesty and breadth of an eagle. All of the theories about her disappearance had been wrong; none of them had prepared Soraya to find the simorgh hidden in this chamber inside Mount Arzur.

Heavy chains around her legs kept her bound to the rock, and the only items within reach were a bowl of water and another bowl that was currently empty. All this time, Azad had been holding her captive, keeping her alive—but why? Why not kill her as some people believed he had done? Parvaneh had wondered the same during her captivity, and her words returned to Soraya now: *He had captured me . . . refused to release me until I told him something useful.* What did the simorgh have that Azad would find useful? If he wanted a feather to retain his humanity, he could have taken it and killed the simorgh long ago. But perhaps it wasn't the feather itself he wanted, but the security it could provide him—if freely given.

He wants the simorgh's protection, Soraya realized, *and she's re-fused him all this time.*

Soraya tentatively moved closer, wondering if the simorgh knew that Soraya was of her lineage, a lineage that Soraya had rejected and betrayed. The simorgh ruffled her feathers slightly, but showed no reaction to Soraya's presence. In her eyes was an intelligence that was far beyond any bird Soraya had ever seen—but it wasn't human, either. It was as if she already knew all that would come to pass, and was simply waiting for events to unfold. If Soraya detected a touch of reproach in the curve of her brow, she wasn't sure if it was real or if her own guilt was making her see it. *I've been expecting you,* the simorgh's eyes seemed to say. *And you are very, very late.*

"Can you understand me?" Soraya whispered, moving slowly toward the simorgh.

The simorgh didn't speak, of course, but simply bowed her head in a slow nod.

Soraya held up a shaking hand, revealing her seal ring, the sim-orgh's image etched into it. "Do you know who I am?"

It was a question with many answers, but the simorgh's fierce, unblinking stare made Soraya think that she knew all of them. *I'm your descendant. I'm your betrayer. I'm your rescuer.*

The simorgh nodded again, this time emitting a low-throated cooing sound that Soraya thought she could understand. *One of mine.* With a rattle of chains, the simorgh came forward as far as she could go, bringing her a step away from Soraya. She was the size of a large dog or small horse, her head level with Soraya's chest, and yet Soraya felt engulfed by her presence. The simorgh made another gentle cooing sound, and then she stretched out her long, beautiful neck and fluttered her wings, as if in welcome.

Soraya's chest tightened painfully, and she let out a broken sob as she fell to her knees and wrapped her arms around the simorgh's neck. The simorgh nestled her head against Soraya's as Soraya wept into her feathers. She felt undeserving of this affection, unworthy to have been the one to find the simorgh, the root of her family, after so many years. And yet, wasn't that the story of her family's beginnings? The simorgh had found an unwanted child and decided that he belonged to her now, and that she would love and raise him as her own, even if others found him unworthy. If only Soraya had seen herself in that child instead of the Shahmar, then maybe she would have found her place in her family line long ago. She would have known that what defined her lineage was not blood or duty or obligation, but a single act of compassion, of protection, granted freely.

Soraya pulled away. Her eyes were still wet with tears, but she felt lighter now than she ever had. The patch of sky overhead began to darken, and she knew she couldn't stay much longer, even though the idea of leaving the simorgh here was unthinkable. *I could take a feather*, she thought, with a glance at the simorgh's brilliant plumage. But even to ask for such a gift felt wrong to her—the feather was something the simorgh should give of her own volition, not something to be taken. Maybe that was why every time Soraya tried to take the feather for herself, the result had been disastrous.

"I'll come back," she told the simorgh. "I need something to help me with the chains."

The simorgh bowed her head in understanding, and with an aching heart, Soraya went back through the passage. She left the false brick wall as she had found it, slightly open, then brushed off the soot from her gown before stepping out of the fireplace. She looked hesitantly from the chest of tools to the swiftly darkening sky out the window. Did she have time to free her now?

She took a step toward the chest, but then a shadow filled the room, and she turned her head to find Azad standing in the window.

"Soraya," he said with surprise as he stepped off the ledge into the room. "What are you doing here?" He tried to keep his voice light, but she could hear the undercurrent of suspicion.

"I'm here to see you," she said at once, grasping for something she knew he would be happy to hear. "Now that I can move freely through Arzur, I saw no reason why I should wait for you in my room like a prisoner."

He laughed softly. "Fair enough. Have you given thought to my offer from last night?"

"To kill my brother or let you do it for me?"

"I could decide for you, if you'd prefer."

"No," Soraya said at once. "I've already made my decision."

She had spoken without thinking, simply wanting to stop him from losing patience with her, but now her mind was working like an overactive hummingbird, trying to figure out what came next.

Azad studied her with narrowed eyes, and Soraya returned his stare with all the resolve she could muster. She weighed the options in her mind, and she knew there was only one choice she could make now.

"And what have you decided?" he asked her with some skepticism.

"I've been thinking of what you told me before," she said, "when I asked you why you never chose to live as a human. You said it was because of power, but I think that's only part of the truth."

He walked toward her, stopping when he was close enough that she had to turn her head up to look him in the eye. "Is that so?" he said, his mouth twisting in amusement. "Then what's the real reason?"

"Because if you chose to stop fighting for the throne and live a quiet life as a human, then everything you did to your family would have been for nothing."

His smile faded. His eyes darkened. "Soraya—"

"And if I keep holding myself back, then the same will be true for me."

His mouth hung open with whatever unspoken reprimand he had been about to speak. "What are you saying?"

"I'll kill Sorush myself." She turned her eyes up, looking at him through her eyelashes. "And then I'll be yours."

Is this cruel? she wondered. Was she being as cruel to him as he had been when he'd pledged himself to her outside the golestan, knowing that he was about to betray her? *If I* am *being cruel,* she decided, *then it's because he taught me how.*

Azad was studying her again, searching for the trap that he was clever enough to suspect but didn't want to find. "Are you toying with me?" he said, his voice a low growl.

"I'm done playing games," she said. "I've felt more myself here among the divs than I ever have at Golvahar. I want what you promised me last night. I want to be free."

And even though she had no intention of killing Sorush, the words were true enough that she knew Azad would believe them.

His hand came to rest on her shoulder, and he brushed his thumb along the curve of her throat. "Is that the only reason?" he said, his voice softening into something almost wistful.

She knew what he wanted to hear, and she took a breath, preparing the lie on her tongue. "I miss you," she said. "I miss working with you instead of against you. I miss what we once had. I want to know if I can find it again."

His hand tightened on her shoulder. "You will," he said. "I promise you."

The conviction in his voice made her wonder if it were true—if, given time, she would one day look at him and see only that young man again, the one who had noticed her on the roof and come to her rescue on Nog Roz. But no—that young man had never existed, and even if he had, she didn't want him anymore. She didn't want someone who always told her what she wanted to hear. There was something better than that, something truer and more alive, and it was currently waiting for her, asleep in the dungeon of Golvahar.

But first, she needed to free the simorgh. "That was all I came here to tell you," Soraya said, turning away from him and moving toward the door. "I wanted you to know my decision before you returned to Golvahar."

"Before *we* return to Golvahar," Azad corrected.

Soraya turned, the hummingbird in her mind taking flight once more. "What do you mean?"

"There's no reason to delay. We can leave for Golvahar at dawn— or sooner, if you'd prefer."

She had thought he would wait at least another day before insisting on her return—on Sorush's execution—and then she could return for the simorgh. *I can still delay him*, she thought. She just needed to make him leave Arzur again.

"You seem surprised," he said. "Did you think I wouldn't hold you to your promise?"

"I simply thought you would need more time to make arrangements. I don't want to return the way I came, carried over your shoulder like a prisoner."

He bowed his head and said, "Then you shall return on a golden litter down the city streets, my queen."

"And I want something else," she said, thinking of how to delay him, how to make him return to Golvahar before her.

"You know I would give you anything," he said.

Except my family. Except Parvaneh. Except my freedom. "When we return to the palace, I want my old rooms back."

He hesitated. "Soraya, I want to trust you. . . ."

"But you'll need to board up the door to the passageways first. I understand. Do what you must. But I want something familiar. Something to remind me of my old life." More gently, she added, "I'm sure you can understand that."

He nodded. "Very well. I'll prepare your room tonight, and you'll begin your journey at dawn."

He insisted on accompanying her back to her room in the mountain, and Soraya's heart pounded with a mixture of fear and excitement. It had worked—she would wait until her candle was halfway burned before setting out for his room again, and this time, she would bring tools with her to free the simorgh.

But instead of turning toward her room, Azad gripped her arm and led her farther down the passage. "What are you doing?" Soraya said.

"When I announced that you could move freely through the mountain, I hadn't yet known about your outings with the pariks. They're very loyal—if they learn what you did to Parvaneh, they may come for you and take their revenge. I'd prefer to keep you secured more safely tonight."

It was such a blatant lie that Soraya nearly told him about Parisa's visit just to catch him in it. But she had made that mistake once before, and she kept her anger—and her tongue—in check as he led her to his treasury, the only room with a lock on the door.

"You can't keep me here," she said, attempting to pull out of his grip as they neared the door. "There's no bed."

"You've seen for yourself that there are plenty of rugs that you can pile up."

"What about food?"

"You'll be fine until morning. Sleep, and the time will pass quickly."

He unlocked the door and dragged Soraya across the threshold.

"But what if I—"

He silenced her with a finger against her lips. "Think of this as a test of your loyalty to me. Because if this is another ploy, Soraya—if I discover that you're deceiving me in any way—then there will be no more bargains or exchanges. I will slaughter your family in front of you as easily as I slaughtered mine."

26

Soraya's mother had told her once that it was almost a day's journey from the city where she had spent her childhood to Golvahar. And so Soraya knew she had roughly from sunrise to sunset to figure out what she should do once she arrived at the palace.

Sometime before dawn, Azad had retrieved her from the treasury and brought her to the entryway of the mountain. As promised, a golden litter awaited her there, along with two smaller divs on horseback. Once Soraya was in the litter, and the litter securely attached to the horses, Azad took off, promising to greet Soraya at journey's end.

And what would she do when she reached her destination? The simorgh was chained up inside the mountain. The pariks were hiding somewhere in the forest. Her family and Parvaneh were imprisoned. What had Soraya managed to accomplish during her time here? She cursed herself now for not simply plucking one of the simorgh's feathers when she had the chance, but some part of her knew that nothing good would have come from such a theft. The feather had to be granted freely or not at all.

As they traveled through the scattered woodland of the mountain steppe, and the sun began to rise, Soraya saw city walls in the distance to the south. That was where her mother had been born, where she had returned one day after meeting a div in these same woods. She imagined what it would have been like to grow up there, in the shadow of Arzur, constantly under threat of a div raid. Her mother had lived so close to danger all her life—it was no wonder, then, that she had seen Soraya's curse as a reasonable price to pay for her safety.

When they moved closer, Soraya noticed the large gaps in the mud-brick walls, where something had battered it down. She wondered if it was from a recent attack, or if the people there had simply given up repairing it over the years, knowing that the divs were so near.

They stopped when the sun was at its highest overhead. There was still enough grass for the horses to graze, and so the div in front unlatched the litter and led the horses out to where the grass was thicker. Soraya wondered if they planned to feed her, too.

She tentatively stepped out of the litter, unsure if she would be allowed to do so, but wanting to stretch her legs.

"Don't worry," said a thin, reedy voice from behind the litter. "We have food for you as well."

The div came toward her and held a basket out to her. Soraya hadn't been able to look closely at the divs accompanying her in the morning, when it had still been dark, and so she was struck motionless. The div standing before her resembled a human in appearance—more accurately, she resembled a human corpse, wrapped in a gauzy white garment like a shroud. Her hair was long, gray, and stringy, her skin sallow and leathery, worn tight over protruding bones. A familiar smell accompanied her—familiar, because it reminded Soraya of the dakhmeh. A name formed in her mind, but she didn't dare speak it.

With a nervous bob of her head, Soraya took the basket and retreated back to the litter.

"You don't have to stay in there, either," the div said. "We both know that if you run, I'll catch you."

Soraya didn't want to admit that she found the div's appearance unsettling—more so than any of the beastlike divs she had seen in Arzur—and so she remained standing while the div regarded her with an amused expression.

"You've been to the dakhmeh," the div said. She leaned forward and sniffed the air. "I can smell it on you."

Soraya's stomach clenched, and finally she gathered the courage to say, "You're Nasu, aren't you?"

The div only smiled, pleased to be known and named.

And yet now that she had this confirmation, Soraya felt no fear—only confusion. "Why do you follow him?" she asked.

Nasu's eyes widened in surprise at the abrupt question. "The Shahmar?"

"You're one of the most feared and powerful divs among humans," Soraya said. "How did the Shahmar come to inspire such loyalty among divs that you would all follow his commands and treat him like a shah?"

Nasu reflected a moment, and then she said, "If you've been to the dakhmeh, then you understand the nature of scavengers— vultures, jackals, and the like. Why hunt for prey when someone else will do it for you, and you can enjoy the spoils? The Shahmar has his uses. He thinks that without him, divs would have no purpose, and he's wrong about that. But he understands human instinct, and he knows how to exploit human weaknesses." She gave Soraya a pointed look, and Soraya's face warmed with shame. "We simply go through the doors that he breaks down for us," Nasu continued. "And if he wants us to bow our heads as he passes in return, it's a small enough price to pay. It's become a bit of a joke among us, the way he believes in such human formalities."

Soraya listened in fascination, understanding now the secret that the divs had been sharing with her ever since the night of the banquet, the one they reflected back to her in their nods and smiles. The Shahmar thought he ruled the divs—that they were instruments of his vision, his purpose—but in truth, the divs were using him.

"Now *you*, on the other hand," Nasu said, drawing Soraya's attention back to her. "The divs are all very interested in you."

"Because I betrayed my people?" Soraya said, her throat tight.

Nasu shook her head. "I was there the night of the banquet, when you stepped out into the crowd and let them tear off pieces of you. Even those who weren't there have heard of it by now. It was . . . rapturous. You gave yourself to us that night." She took a step closer to Soraya and raised her hand to hover over the base of Soraya's throat. "There's something restless growing within you. We're all very curious to see what happens when it breaks free."

Soraya looked down at the hand that was not quite touching her, fighting a primal instinct to flinch away from it. But it was surrender that the divs demanded. Soraya had felt that pull not only at the banquet, but in the pariks' forest, too. That was the other secret that Azad didn't understand. There was no ruling the divs—there was either surrender or destruction. She wondered which would befall him in the end, and then her head snapped up, her eyes meeting Nasu's as the thought struck her: If the divs were more aligned to her than to him now, perhaps she could use that to her advantage. "Would the divs be willing to help me? To fight him?" she asked urgently. But she regretted the words as soon as she'd spoken them. What if Nasu told Azad she was plotting against him? His final threat still rang loud in her ears.

But Nasu didn't seem shocked or aghast at her questions. She only shook her head with a confused frown as her hand fell away.

"We aren't finished with him yet. Why would we want to fight him? Why would *you* want to fight him? He wants you to rule with him, doesn't he? Isn't that why we're delivering you to the palace?"

"He'll kill my family if I refuse him."

"Then don't refuse. You'll be in a far better position to protect anyone you want to protect if you're his consort. The choice seems simple to me. Either you're his prisoner while he does as he pleases, or you're by his side, with the power to influence him. Perhaps he could be useful to you as well."

Soraya didn't respond. The advice chilled her, because she heard the truth in it and knew that she might have no better choice. The other div returned with the horses then, and Soraya returned to her litter with the still-untouched basket of bread and cold meats that Nasu had given her.

They didn't stop again until they reached Golvahar.

Soraya had shut the curtains of her litter to block out the sun, but when she could no longer feel the sun's heat, she pulled back one of the curtains and saw the walls of the city approaching, the shape of Golvahar rising up at its center.

She hadn't known how she would feel upon returning to Golvahar, but when she saw the city, she heard screams in her head, and a knot of guilt formed in her stomach. *I'm going to put it right again,* she promised the terrified voices in her mind. But she still had no idea how she would manage to accomplish that, and the more time that slipped away, the louder Nasu's voice grew in her head.

She kept the curtain open now, wanting to see if the city had changed since Azad had taken control. She had hoped the damage wasn't too severe, but as they wound their way through the city streets, the knot of guilt only tightened.

The last time she had gone through these streets, she had been struck with a sense of possibility. The world had seemed so wide, so expansive, that she thought surely there must be room for her in it. But now . . . now there was rubble crowding the streets, remains of the damage done on the wedding day. Some of the homes were charred and half burned, with chunks of wall or roof missing. It reminded Soraya of the way melted wax figures might look right before they collapsed into shapelessness. The air was full of dust and ash, and Soraya had to cover her nose and mouth to keep from coughing.

And then there were the people. Azad had promised Sorush that if he bowed to him, the townspeople would return to their ordinary lives. He hadn't lied, exactly. The townspeople were free to go where they pleased. Shops were still open, and vendors still set up their stalls in the bazaar. But Soraya noticed that they all walked quickly through the streets with their heads down, not wanting to attract the attention of the divs who patrolled the streets as the new city guard. Their faces were ashen, and on the few occasions when people did look up to see who was being carried through the streets like royalty, there was a haunted look in their eyes that soon hardened into anger when they saw her. Soraya didn't think they recognized her by sight—few people had ever seen the mysterious princess—but they saw a human treated like a queen by the divs, and that was enough for them. They knew a traitor when they saw one.

Soraya wanted to let the curtain fall, but she couldn't make herself do it. She had to see—both because she deserved their scorn and because she needed to remember why she couldn't let Azad win.

As they reached the center of the city, Golvahar loomed ahead, and Soraya's eyes went to the roof, wishing she were still standing there alone. Would it always have happened this way? Even if Azad had never come, if she had never spoken to Parvaneh, would she still have reached the threshold of her patience one day and lashed out at her family? *Yes,* said a voice from deep within. She couldn't have lived that way forever, not without understanding why or how. It was inevitable that she would have begun to rattle the bars of her cage, and that all her buried frustration would have found a way out. That girl on the roof was gone, and though Soraya wished over and over again that she had chosen differently, she knew that the girl she had been would never have been able to love her family or her people the way Soraya did now. She had been too full of poison, too afraid to let herself feel anything.

The gates of Golvahar opened for her, and she was relieved to find the gardens unchanged. Still, the sounds of screaming in her head grew louder here, and she could see invisible bodies on the lawn, where soldiers had fallen.

They'll never forgive you, said a voice in her mind. But she hadn't returned here for forgiveness. She had broken something, and now she had to fix it as best as she could.

The divs set the litter down at the palace steps where Azad stood tall, waiting for her. He came forward to help her up, and remembering what he had said to her last night, she tried not to let her contempt show on her face.

He asked about her journey, to which she replied politely in turn and told him she was tired and wanted to rest. He led her to her room—a path that felt unfamiliar to her, because she was so accustomed to using the passageways.

The room was as she'd last left it. She had told Azad she was tired so he wouldn't expect her to make conversation, but at the sight of her bed, she realized how true it was, how inexpressibly tired she felt. She wanted to sink into this room like it was a bath and let it strip away all memories of the mountain.

She waited for Azad to leave, but he was staring at her expectantly, until finally he said, "Don't you want to know when the execution will be?"

"Of course," she said. "I'm just so exhausted, I can barely think."

His gaze softened. "Yes, I understand. But everything will be easier from now on—you'll see. Tomorrow, before sunset, we'll take care of your brother, and this ordeal will be over."

She managed a smile, which seemed to satisfy him, and then he left. She heard the click of a key in the lock after the door was shut.

When she was finally alone, she went first to the hidden door in the wall on the slightest chance that he had forgotten to seal it shut. But he hadn't forgotten, of course, nor had he forgotten to bar the doors leading out to the golestan. A beam blocked the handles from the outside, so that she could only push the doors open a crack.

At first sight, she had thought nothing in the room had been changed since she was last here, but as soon as she began to scan the room for anything useful, she saw that wasn't true. Her hand mirror was gone, as were her bottles and vials of fragrances and a crystal vase. Anything breakable—anything that could create shards or sharp edges—had been removed, so that she couldn't use them as weapons.

My gardening tools. Soraya hurried to the bed and knelt down, reaching underneath to see if Azad had been thorough enough to find her shears and other tools wrapped in leather under the bed. The tools were gone—but Soraya's hand met something else instead. Something soft and made of cloth, like a rag . . .

Or a blanket.

From beneath the bed, she pulled out the blanket of stars that had set her on her path of destruction. She laid it flat in front of her, remembering now that she had taken it with her from her mother's room and buried it under the bed. Her fingers brushed over the stiffened patches of blood on the fabric. And then her hand froze as she realized that Azad had mistakenly left her the most powerful weapon of all.

Are you curious to know how it's done? It's the blood of a div that made you poisonous. If a human bathes in blood from a div's heart, that human takes on the properties of that div. You must have had only a few drops.

Would it be enough? The stains on the blanket were old and long dried. She would have to soak the blanket to get any use out of the blood, and even then, she had no idea if it would still be effective. If it were, though, then she could curse herself anew and become poisonous once more. *But what if I can't reverse it again?* The simorgh was not in such easy reach that she could safely depend on using her feathers to lift the curse—and she knew better now than to take one of the simorgh's feathers without her permission. What if the simorgh found her unworthy of such a gift? Would Soraya still be willing to make this choice?

Soraya's mouth went dry, her eyes locked on the blanket with such focus that the stars began to blur. Would her poison be enough to stop the Shahmar? Parvaneh had told her previous attempts to kill him had failed, or even made him stronger, but her mother had trusted in this poison to keep her daughter safe from him. Before she had used the feather, Azad had always been careful not to touch her . . . and at the very least, she would have a way to defend herself against the other divs. She had no other plan, no other option. If she didn't do this, she would very likely have to kill her brother and rule with Azad, or else watch her family die.

She was running her fingertips over the fabric without even realizing it, as if her hands knew what she was thinking and were trying to remind her of what she would be giving up. Her mother's arms around her. The flutter of moth wings against her skin. *Parvaneh.*

But Parvaneh would sleep forever if Soraya didn't do something to help her. As for her mother, Soraya already knew what choice she would make. And Tahmineh was the only person Soraya knew who had beaten the Shahmar at his own game.

Are you like your mother? Parisa had asked her.

Soraya clutched the blanket in her hands. *Yes,* she thought. *Yes, I still am.*

She shoved the blanket back under the bed, went to the door, and began pounding her fists on it as loudly as she could. Within seconds, the door opened, and a div with spotted fur like a leopard's stood frowning at her. "Yes?" the div said.

"I'd like a bath," Soraya told her.

The div nodded once and shut the door on Soraya.

She paced nervously as she waited, wondering if the div had simply nodded to appease her, when the door opened again, and the same div brought in a metal tub and two buckets of steaming water.

Cold water would have worked better for her purpose, but she didn't know how to ask for it without warranting suspicion, so she thanked the div and waited for her to leave.

Once Soraya heard the click of the lock again, she dragged a chair to the door to block the handle as an additional precaution. If anyone tried to enter and Azad questioned her about it, she could say she wanted privacy for her bath.

After retrieving the blanket, she poured the steaming water into the tub. She focused on the task like it was something routine—like when she was working in her garden—concentrating on each action so that there was no room for thought. Otherwise she might forget that she had chosen this—that at one time she had even missed seeing those green veins under her skin and knowing she was untouchable.

She dipped the blanket into the water and watched the water slowly turn pink. When she thought the water was as pink as it would ever become, and the water cool enough to touch, she removed the blanket, undressed, and stepped into the bath.

The water came up to her knees, and she looked down at her feet, wondering if even now, they were becoming steeped in poison. It had only taken a few drops to curse her the first time, but she didn't know if the blood would lose some potency when it was diluted with water. This was the best she could do with her limited time and resources: submerge herself entirely in the blood-tinged water, and hope that it would have some effect.

Soraya sat in the tub, letting the water cover her entirely except for her head. Her heart was beating wildly, urging her to flee, but she ignored it. She tried to ignore every thought and every impulse, every doubt and regret. This was the choice she had made, and even now, it was possibly too late to change her mind. She drew in a long breath, closed her eyes, and dunked her head under the water so that every bit of her skin was submerged.

She counted to ten, and when she surfaced again, the breath she'd been holding came out as a sob, loud and almost painful. She buried her face in her hands, tears spilling from her eyes, her body heaving, like something was trying to escape from inside her.

When the tears slowed, and her breath no longer felt like it was being torn from her body, she looked down at her wrists. The veins there were not dark green, or even particularly noticeable at all. Maybe it would take time before the curse took hold, she thought, and she stood and used the other bucket of water to rinse the blood off of her. She wrapped herself in one of her dressing gowns, her wardrobe still intact, and looked down at the pink water in the bath with a frown.

Would a div notice or care that the water was pink? Soraya could say she had cut herself by accident, but there was nothing in the room sharp enough to make the lie believable, and she was ill at ease not knowing what would happen to the rest of the bloody mixture, assuming it did still work. Perhaps that was why her mother had kept the blanket all these years instead of trying to burn or dispose of it.

In the end, she decided to drag the tub to the garden doors and pour the water out into the golestan. It streamed through the crack in the door, down the steps, and onto the grass below. If anyone asked her why the tub was empty, she would say she used it to water the golestan, unsure if anyone had done so since she'd been gone. It was true, in a way.

As she waited for her attending div to return, she kept sneaking glances down at the insides of her arms, but she still found no change.

At last the div came, without any comment on the missing water in the tub, and Soraya murmured something polite as she came forward to help. She handed the div one of the buckets, allowing their knuckles to brush against each other, sucking in a breath as she waited to see what would happen in this final and most definitive test.

The div took the buckets and the tub without a word and left the room very much alive.

Soraya's last resort had failed.

27

A beam of sunlight woke her the next morning—which was strange, because her curtains had definitely been closed the night before.

Soraya blinked, shading her eyes from the sun streaming through her windows. It had been a restless night as she tried to decide what to do now that both of her plans—the simorgh and the blood—had failed. All night long, Azad's words kept returning to her: *I will slaughter your family as easily as I slaughtered mine.* What was the right choice, then? To refuse him, knowing that her family might die for it, or to kill her brother in order to save everyone else? Was Nasu's solution the only one left? She had drifted into sleep eventually, but still without an answer.

She sat up, looking toward the source of the light—and saw that the golestan had come to her rescue.

One of the double doors to the golestan had been forced open, allowing the light to spill in, along with a tangle of thorns and roses that wound around the door and stretched across the floor. Soraya climbed out of bed and went to look more closely.

The last time she had seen the golestan, it had still been a ruin from when she'd destroyed it. Now it was more than restored—it was overflowing. The rosebushes had spread out across the length of the garden and were climbing up, so thick that the walls were almost entirely covered. But it wasn't the roses that caught Soraya's attention—it was the thorns. Her rosebushes had always had thorns, but the thorns growing from them now were longer and sharper than they had been, more like needles than the stubby thorns she remembered. Soraya bent down to examine one of the roses that had spilled into the room, cupping it in her palms. She almost dropped it immediately, because she could have sworn the rose was pulsing against her skin, like a misshapen heart in her hands. And there was something else, something that made her know without question what had caused this sudden overgrowth. The veins on the underside of the rose's petals, usually white, were now a dark, venomous green.

She had disposed of the bathwater by pouring it into the garden—and now the garden was imbued with the blood of a div.

Soraya opened the door and walked outside, careful not to touch any of the wicked-looking thorns. She knew with a certainty she couldn't explain that those thorns would be poisonous to the touch. *Like I should be*, she thought. But then, was it possible that the blood had simply needed time to take effect? The golestan had grown overnight; perhaps she had been too hasty to call her plan a failure.

Her veins were still normal, but she immediately began to look for some stray insect to touch. Navigating the golestan was difficult—the thorns left little room for safe passage—but she was used to shrinking herself down and moving through narrow spaces. She found a patch of uncovered grass and knelt, digging until she found a wriggling pink worm. She brushed her finger against it, waiting several breaths to see if it would stop moving, but her touch had no effect at all.

Soraya let out a frustrated sigh, looking at the thorns around her with envy. But her disappointment didn't last long, because through the thorns, she could make out the shape of the garden door.

Escape. Not from Golvahar—she would never make it that far, and she couldn't abandon her family to their fates. But if she could make it to the dungeon without being seen . . .

Soraya returned to her room and quickly dressed. It was still early—too early for Azad to send someone with food for her, she hoped. She didn't have much time, but she had to be slow and careful as she moved aside the thorns and roses blocking the door. A few of the thorns snagged on her sleeves, but they didn't touch her skin. When the door was clear enough to open, she tried the handle, relieved when it gave way.

She opened the door only a little, peeking through to make sure no divs were patrolling the grounds. She wedged a rock into the doorway so that she wouldn't be locked out and slipped through the door, ignoring the temptation to run as fast as she could. Instead, she stayed close to the garden wall, moving alongside it until she had come all the way around to the palace walls. Even then, she moved slowly and deliberately, thankful for all her years of slinking through shadows. There *were* divs patrolling the grounds—she saw one pass by in the opposite direction—but divs' senses were keener at night, and tucked away as she was, making no sudden movements, the divs didn't look her way or notice her.

Only when she had painstakingly edged her way to the dungeon steps did she allow herself to move quickly. She had no worry of divs here—she could already smell the esfand as she went down the steps—and so she tore through the dungeon, following the smoke to Parvaneh's cell.

The cavern was thick with smoke, and as she had seen in her dream, five braziers filled with coals were set out in a row in front of the bars. This time, though, Soraya could kick them over, scattering the hot coals over the ground. She waved some of the smoke away and saw the outline of bars, finding the two bent ones. She stepped into the gap between them, and as the smoke began to clear, she found Parvaneh's sleeping form on the floor. Soraya knelt beside her and waited for her to awaken.

Parvaneh's eyelashes were the first things to move, twitching against her cheeks. And then her eyes slowly opened, liquid amber glowing in the darkness. She blinked a few times and started to cough.

Soraya had wanted to keep her distance, unsure if Parvaneh would still be furious with her, but now she helped Parvaneh sit up as she finished coughing the smoke out of her lungs. When Parvaneh looked at her in surprise, Soraya quickly removed her hand from Parvaneh's back. Her wings were still intact, Soraya noticed with relief.

Parvaneh pushed herself up to her feet. "Soraya?" she said, her voice still scratchy.

"Please listen," Soraya said with urgency as she rose as well. Since the dream, she had wondered what she would say to Parvaneh, how she would explain her actions, but the words spilled out of her now with no plan or preparation, a torrent of remorse. "I never meant to betray you, but I misspoke and Azad figured out that I had seen you, and he wouldn't believe me when I said I didn't know where you were, and I didn't want him to know I was working against him the entire time, and then he threatened my family and I had no choice, but I would never have given you to him otherwise, I'm still with you, I'm still your—"

"*Soraya*," Parvaneh interrupted, silencing Soraya with a hand on her arm. "I know."

"What?"

"I know you didn't mean to betray me. I was already in your room when the two of you entered. I heard what he said to you, that if he didn't capture me that night, he would start killing off your family. I knew it was a trap."

Soraya was stunned. "All those things you said to me about knowing I would choose him, about deserving each other—"

"Those were all for his benefit, not yours. I wanted him to believe that you were loyal to him, that he should keep you close so you could finish your mission."

"But if you knew it was a trap . . ." Soraya shook her head. "You were his prisoner for so long. Why didn't you fly away unseen? Why show yourself at all?"

Parvaneh hesitated, like she was trying to find the right words. Her voice solemn, her eyes full, she said, "I told you before. I have my loyalties."

Soraya absorbed the words and their meaning—both spoken and unspoken—and then she stopped thinking at all and threw her arms around Parvaneh's neck, finding her lips with her own.

Parvaneh made a muffled sound of surprise as Soraya crashed into her, but it didn't take her long to respond. Soraya had never initiated a kiss before, and so she was happy to let Parvaneh take control, one of her hands twisting in Soraya's hair while the other guided her backward until Soraya's back thudded against the cell bars. Soraya wrapped her arms around Parvaneh more tightly, as if she could absorb everything that was fearless about her into herself. She ran her thumb along the nape of Parvaneh's neck, moving down to the space between her shoulder blades, that patch of skin she found so tempting.

They were pressed so tightly against each other that when Parvaneh withdrew, Soraya felt like a piece of her had been peeled away. But Parvaneh remained within the circle of Soraya's arms, her own hands gripping the bars on either side of her, and she whispered into the crook of Soraya's neck, "What were you going to say before?"

"When?" Soraya asked, breathless.

"Before I interrupted you. You said you were still with me, that you were still my . . . my what?"

It seemed ridiculous that she could still blush in her current position, and yet she felt an unmistakable heat warm her face. "I don't remember," she said.

Parvaneh lifted her head, eyes sparkling. "Liar. You're still my friend? My ally? Tell me. We have no secrets in this dungeon."

"Yours," Soraya said, looking Parvaneh in the eye, as if the word were a challenge. "I was going to say I'm still yours."

Parvaneh arched an eyebrow. "Interesting," she said. She leaned in again, brushing her lips against Soraya's shoulder. "And how long have you been mine?"

Soraya tugged lightly on Parvaneh's hair, making Parvaneh look up. "It was when I healed your wings," she said, "when I touched you for the first time."

Parvaneh smiled in response, but the memory of using the feather made Soraya think of the captive simorgh.

"What's wrong?" Parvaneh said, drawing away as she noticed Soraya's suddenly rigid posture.

Soraya shook her head. "It's always so easy to forget the rest of the world, or the passage of time, when I'm here with you. I have to go back before I'm discovered, but first I have to tell you what I've found." She told Parvaneh everything then, from her discovery of the simorgh to her failed attempt at restoring her curse.

Parvaneh listened in rapt attention, and when Soraya was finished, she said, "I can do it. I can free the simorgh and return with her."

"Not just her," Soraya said. "The pariks, too—we need them all."

Parvaneh went silent, her mouth a thin line. "I don't know if they'll listen to me," she said at last. "Even with the simorgh, I don't know if they'll receive me again. I don't think they'll ever . . ." Her voice broke, leaving the thought unfinished.

Soraya held Parvaneh's hands tightly in her own. "They will," she said. "The day after you were captured, Parisa came to me and asked where you were. She said you're still their sister."

Parvaneh soaked the words in like they were moonlight, her eyes wide with longing. She straightened and said, "How much time do we have?"

"He said the execution would happen before sunset today."

Parvaneh nodded, but her expression was serious. "It's not much time."

"I know," Soraya said. "But even if"—*even if I have to kill my brother first*—you're not back in time, we can still put an end to this."

"I'll make it in time," Parvaneh promised. She kissed Soraya's cheek and whispered in her ear, "And then I'll deliver that bastard to you on his knees."

It had been tempting to slip into the passageways from the dungeon—to let Golvahar hide her away until she disappeared. But her family was still beyond reach in the new wing, and if Azad found her missing, she may as well have condemned them all to death.

After watching Parvaneh fly away as a dark gray moth, Soraya returned to her room. As she made her careful way back through the golestan, she noticed that the garden had further expanded since she had last seen it—the vines and roses were now climbing up the palace walls. But she didn't have time to contemplate this; almost immediately after she returned, her door opened, and it continued to open and close several more times over the course of the day.

First there was breakfast, and afterward the leopard-spotted div brought a very frightened human seamstress carrying an ornately embroidered gown. Azad had planned ahead, apparently, ordering the seamstress to make a new gown for Soraya using the measurements from the clothes in Soraya's wardrobe. Now the seamstress nervously asked Soraya to try it on so she could make any adjustments.

Soraya didn't bother arguing. She didn't want the seamstress to be punished for her own stubbornness. The gown fell over her skin in waves of green and gold—the same colors as the dress she'd worn on Nog Roz, when she'd first spoken to Azad. He was feeling sentimental, apparently. When she looked closely at the pattern of the brocade, she flinched, causing the seamstress to prick her with a needle by accident. The pattern that repeated on the gown was of a rose entwined with a snake.

When the fitting was over, more human attendants were brought to bathe and groom her—and only then did Soraya realize the point of the gown. *He's acting like this is a wedding.* An execution and a wedding together—they would be married in her brother's blood.

Again, Soraya didn't protest while the attendants performed rituals that would ordinarily be performed in the bathhouse the day before a wedding ceremony. And as they scrubbed the dead skin off of her with a rough stone and shaped her eyebrows using threads, she realized with begrudging acceptance that she didn't *want* to protest. Her mother and Laleh would have been used to these ministrations, but no one had ever braided Soraya's hair or painted her face. Not even her mother had ever been able to do this for her.

Azad would have known that, of course. He was once again offering her something that her family had never been able to give her—a reminder that she should choose him over them. But there was one thing he hadn't foreseen, one element that spoiled the relaxation of being pampered. Whenever she looked at her attendants, their eyes quickly dropped, but Soraya still saw the traces of fear and resentment in them. They were not here by choice, and they would not forget that fact, even if Soraya could. Did they recognize her? Did they think she had joined the Shahmar willingly? If so, then they must hate her. Their hands were gentle, but their eyes were as sharp as thorns.

Another meal, and then the seamstress returned with the gown. Once the gown was on, Soraya couldn't stop herself from asking the spotted div, "Could you bring me a mirror? Just for a short time?"

The div considered this, then nodded. She guided the seamstress away and returned several minutes later carrying a full-length mirror.

Once the div set down the mirror, Soraya walked up to it, hands trembling in anticipation. This was the first time she would see herself since lifting her curse, the first time she would see her face unmarred by a web of veins waiting to spread.

In the mirror was a young woman in a dress that fit her perfectly, her hair braided with jewels, her eyes rimmed with kohl. Soraya wanted to hate the sight of herself—but she couldn't. She looked more like her mother now, the promise of her poise and beauty finally fulfilled. She looked like the queen that Laleh should have been. She looked like everything that had ever been taken from her. This was who she would have been if she had never been cursed.

And as the leopard-spotted div drew her away from the mirror and led her out of the room, Soraya wondered—what would she do if Parvaneh didn't return in time? What would she allow herself to become?

28

Soraya stepped into the shade of the ayvan, shielding her eyes as she looked out into the garden. She could recognize some of the divs gathered there—Nasu was the first to catch her eye, but she noticed others who seemed familiar to her from Arzur. Interspersed among them were members of court, glancing nervously around them. Did they know what this gathering was for? Did they regret buying their freedom in exchange for accepting Azad as shah? Soraya supposed she should have felt disdain for them, but she was in no position to judge their self-preservation, and mostly she hoped they wouldn't all die tonight because of her.

Kneeling at the head of the steps were three bowed figures, their hands tied behind their waists. First Sorush, then Laleh, and then Tahmineh, their backs all to her. Soraya's eyes locked on them immediately, so intently that she didn't notice when a long shadow removed itself from the wall and came to her side.

"You're even more beautiful than I imagined you would be," Azad whispered in her ear. "You look like a queen already."

Soraya looked up at him and forced a smile. "It's a beautiful gown, but executions are messy, and it would be a shame to spoil it. I should go back and change."

He brushed one knuckle against her cheek. "Soraya, the only thing that could make you more beautiful to me than you are now is to see you covered in that young man's blood."

She had no response to that.

He took her hand and led her to the head of the steps until they were standing beside the bound figures of her loved ones. Azad had chosen the position carefully—from here, Sorush's blood would run red down the white marble stairs.

"Tonight, you shall have a queen," Azad called out to the crowd. "But first, you will have blood."

The divs cheered at this, while the humans in the crowd all looked faintly ill. Soraya kept her eyes on them, not yet ready to see how the three figures beside her were looking at her. Did they think she had agreed to this? Could she blame them if they did?

Azad drew a sword from his side and wrapped Soraya's hand around its handle. "Soon it will be finished," he murmured, too low for anyone else to hear. "It will be easier than you think."

She turned, sword in hand, to look down at her brother's hunched form. She could still hear his vicious words from the throne room, and she had been afraid of what she would find in his eyes now. But she hadn't expected that he wouldn't look at her at all. He kept his gaze straight ahead, his spine as straight as his bindings would allow. He would die a king.

Beyond him, Laleh wasn't looking at her, either, because her eyes were too full of tears, her head bowed so she wouldn't have to witness Sorush's death. But why wouldn't Sorush look at her? Why wouldn't he look up and see if she had some hidden message for him, some silent reassurance that all would be well? Soraya's grip tightened on the sword handle. This was what he had always done—turned away from her when the sight was too difficult to acknowledge, or when it would damage the royal image he wanted to project. He had known how unhappy she had been, and yet he had done nothing to help her. Again, Soraya found Nasu in the crowd, and as their eyes met, Nasu gave her a small nod of approval.

She raised the sword, laying the flat of it against the nape of Sorush's neck. He flinched at the feel of cold metal against his skin. *You can't ignore* that, *can you?* "Bow your head," Soraya said coldly—because Azad was watching, and she couldn't show too much hesitation, or he would suspect. *It will be easier than you think.*

Sorush bowed his head, and as he did, her mother's face came into view. She was the only one of the three prisoners who was looking at Soraya, her eyes red but dry. When Soraya's eyes met hers, Tahmineh mouthed two words: *I'm sorry.*

The sword wavered in Soraya's hand, and she felt the urge to cry—to throw the sword to the ground and crawl into her mother's lap, as she had always wanted to do when she was a child. Instead, she looked down at the curling hair at the base of Sorush's skull, at the ridge of his spine, and wondered if she would have the strength to kill him in one blow.

Because she would have to kill him—there was no way around that now. She was using the drama of the occasion to stall for time, hoping Azad would think she was trying to torture her brother, but she couldn't do so for much longer. Parvaneh wasn't coming, and if she didn't kill Sorush, then Azad would murder him anyway, along with everyone else in her family. This was not an execution, but a sacrifice. And if Sorush would only have *looked* at her, she could have tried to tell him that, so he would know he was dying for a worthy cause.

She raised the sword . . .

. . . and almost dropped it as a piercing cry filled the air. It wasn't a human sound, but the battle cry of a bird of prey. Soraya looked up and found the majestic form of the simorgh swooping down over the cypress trees. *A mother coming to protect her young,* she thought with a wave of relief.

Every head in the garden turned upward—and the first rain of arrows fell from the sky.

"What is this?" she heard Azad shout, and as he spoke, several of the divs in the garden—all of them with wings, Soraya noticed— fell to the ground, arrows lodged deeply in their chests. Above, at least twenty winged figures remained out of reach as they let loose more arrows. *Parvaneh found the pariks,* Soraya thought with a burst of pride.

Soraya acted quickly, kneeling beside Sorush and cutting through the rope around his wrists with her sword. "Here," she said, putting the sword in his now-freed hands. "Be their shah again."

"Soraya—" He finally faced her, mouth hanging open for a moment before his eyes hardened into a determined stare. And for the first time since he had become shah, Soraya saw herself reflected in those eyes, the two of them in perfect understanding. He gave her a short nod and rushed into the fray.

Next, Soraya freed Laleh, who didn't need Soraya to tell her what to do. She grabbed Soraya's head, kissed her cheek, and then ran into the palace, where her father and the other captured azatan were waiting.

"I knew it," Tahmineh was saying as Soraya began to undo her bindings. "I knew you would find them."

But before Soraya could completely free her mother's hands, she felt a grip like iron clamp down on her wrist. Azad pulled her up from the ground like she was weightless and spun her around to face him. "You knew," he said, and even in the growl of his voice, she could hear a note of hurt. "You deceived me."

"You taught me how."

His grip tightened around her wrist. "Remember that I warned you, Soraya."

He might have said more, but then an arrow hit his shoulder, lodging in the armor of his scales. With a cry of surprise, he released Soraya and took a staggering step backward. "*You,*" he snarled, looking at someone behind Soraya. "But how—"

"Did you think I wouldn't be here to see you fall?" Parvaneh said, stepping forward to Soraya's side. Her bow was still drawn, a fresh arrow pointed at Azad. "Nothing could have kept me away."

Azad wrenched the arrow out of his shoulder and tossed it aside, drawing a dagger from his belt. "Stay back," Parvaneh said to Soraya. "I'll keep my promise to you. On his knees, remember?"

Soraya gave Parvaneh's shoulder a quick squeeze and hurried back to Tahmineh. "Look at them," Tahmineh said quietly, her eyes fixed on the battle in the garden. "They're fighting back."

Soraya followed her mother's gaze and saw that she was right. The simorgh and the pariks were still fighting the divs both from above and on the ground, but they weren't the only ones. The other humans in the garden, perhaps rallied by Sorush's example, had retrieved weapons from the fallen divs and were now doing their best to strike against the divs while they were distracted from above.

Tahmineh's hands were free now, but when Soraya looked back to check on Parvaneh, she went cold with fear. Parvaneh's bow lay in two pieces on the ground, and beside it was Parvaneh on her back, Azad poised above her with his dagger. *Just like the dakhmeh,* Soraya thought, only now Azad was in the place of the yatu. She had saved Azad then, but she'd had poison in her veins. What did she have now?

From above, the simorgh gave another fierce cry, and when Soraya looked up, she saw something floating down toward her. It was a green feather, tipped with orange—her birthright, granted to her freely.

Soraya leaped to pluck it from the air, then rushed toward Azad.

She didn't think she would have the strength to plunge the feather deeply enough to break through the scales and pierce his skin—but Parvaneh certainly did.

Azad was lifting his dagger over Parvaneh, and Soraya knew that she would need to do more than grab his wrist, as she had done with the yatu. She threw herself down over Parvaneh, shielding her with her body, and looked up at Azad with all the defiance she had been holding back.

His arm still in the air, Azad froze, his slit pupils becoming razor-thin. Slowly, he lowered his arm. "You care for her, don't you?" he said, sounding despondent. "All this time, you've been working against me."

Still keeping her eyes on Azad, Soraya's hand found Parvaneh's, waiting until she felt Parvaneh's fist close over the simorgh's feather. "Are you truly surprised?" she said. She started to rise from the ground, keeping herself between Azad and Parvaneh. All around them was violence and destruction, and yet the two of them might have been far from it all, Azad's attention focused purely on her. "You've used me from the start. You used me to hurt my family—"

"You made that choice on your own. All I did was refuse to hold you back."

"*No*," she said forcefully, satisfied when he took a startled step backward. She had blamed herself so many times for what had happened, for the choices she had made, but at the root of every misguided choice, every terrible consequence, was one name. "If I have to bear the blame, then so do you. I thought it was my fault for trusting you, for being such an easy mark for you," she said, moving steadily toward him, her fists bunched in the skirt of her gown. "But you were the one who betrayed that trust." With each step she took, he retreated back from her, and it made her feel dangerous again. "I put out the fire, but you were the one who attacked Golvahar and made my brother kneel in front of you. My mother cursed me, but you were the reason why. Everything that happens to you now is your own—"

"Enough!" Azad barked, reaching to grab her by the shoulders. "None of this matters," he said to her through clenched teeth. "You won't win. Every div killed here today will be replaced in my army. All you've done is sentence your family to death."

Soraya offered him a cold smile. "Your army won't follow you for much longer."

"And why is that?"

But she didn't need to answer, because while they were speaking—while Soraya had kept him distracted—Parvaneh had risen from the ground and begun to circle around them. Soraya saw her now behind Azad, a flash of green in her hand. And immediately after Azad spoke, Parvaneh leaped onto his back and plunged the sharp end of the feather into his neck, burying it in a patch of exposed skin not covered by scales.

Everyone in the garden—div and parik and human alike—went still as the Shahmar let out a scream of rage and pain before falling heavily to his knees at Soraya's feet, just as Parvaneh had promised.

As he'd fallen, Parvaneh had pulled out the feather and jumped down from his back, breathing a sigh of relief, her mission finally fulfilled. But now she was watching Azad in awe along with Soraya and the rest of the garden—because something was happening to the Shahmar. His scales rippled over his skin like they were eating him alive, and then, slowly, they began to recede, leaving him a mottled mixture of scale and skin, demon and man. He covered his face in his hands, and Soraya watched as those sharp nails became blunt, and the scales on his head were replaced with hair. He still had his wings, but when he looked up at her in despair, his eyes were human.

He looked so exposed, so vulnerable, kneeling in front of Soraya without his armor. She remembered that strange sense of emptiness when she realized the poison had left her, and she couldn't help feeling a twinge of sympathy.

He rose on unsteady legs, and even though his transformation was still incomplete, he was human now in a way she had never seen him before. There was a murmur of discontent coming from the garden as the divs realized that their leader had become useless to them, but Soraya kept her eyes on Azad, willing him to ignore the divs. She held out her hand to him, and when she said his name, he looked at her, eyes wild and pleading. "It will be over soon," she said softly. It was not a boast of victory, but an assurance, an attempt at comfort. His fight—with her, with himself, with fate—was over, and he could be free.

Soraya never knew what choice Azad would have made, because the silence between them was interrupted by sounds of battle coming from the back of the garden, near the palace gates.

People were surging onto the grounds—people from the city, bearing torches that shone against the darkening sky, bearing weapons they had forged and hidden away. The simorgh's cry must have let them know that the time had come to fight. Soraya thought of the people she had seen in the city, seemingly defeated but in truth waiting for the right time to strike, as she had done, and she felt a surge of pride at their boundless resilience. The battle began anew, but it was clear now that the divs would be outnumbered.

She had lost her tentative connection with Azad, whose eyes were wide with panic. "Azad," she said again, but when he turned to look at her, there was a familiar cold glint in his eyes. *Ah, there he is,* Soraya thought. She unconsciously recoiled from him, which seemed to awaken his remaining predatory instincts. Soraya saw the flash of his dagger in his hand before he lunged toward her. Parvaneh immediately bolted for him in response, but before either of them could reach their target, someone roughly shoved Soraya to the side.

Tahmineh now stood where Soraya had been, and so it was Tahmineh who ended up in Azad's chokehold, with his dagger poised across her throat. "No!" Soraya shouted, and behind Azad, Parvaneh froze, afraid to provoke him.

"Don't follow," Azad snarled as he began to back both himself and Tahmineh toward the palace doorway. But as he began to retreat under the ayvan, figures appeared in the doorway with swords bared. Soraya recognized the spahbed—his waist was still bandaged, but he stood firm, sword pointed in Azad's direction. Beside and behind him were other wounded soldiers recovered enough to fight.

Cornered again, Azad let out a cry of frustration. And then, with a flourish of his still-powerful wings, he rose up into the air, taking Soraya's mother with him.

29

"No," Soraya kept saying under her breath, that one word over and over again. She watched in terror as the two figures flew up over the roof. But the effort of flying had used up the remaining force of Azad's wings, because when they were barely over the palace, his wings began to crumble like dry leaves, and he and Tahmineh crashed down onto the surface of the roof.

"Go!" Soraya shouted to Parvaneh, but Parvaneh was already flying up to the roof, and Soraya ran past the soldiers into the palace.

She'll be safe, Soraya told herself. *She's always been able to outsmart him.* But Azad's promise to slaughter her family still rang in her ears as she rushed toward the stairwell to the roof. Just as she reached the stairs, something with claws grabbed her by the back of her dress, a low growl coming from above her. Soraya let out a frustrated cry and wildly thrashed against the div that held her, but soon the div let out a yelp of pain and the claws released her.

Soraya spun to find the div's severed right arm on the ground. And behind the div was a familiar soldier, his sword red with the div's blood.

"Go!" Ramin called to her, not taking his eyes off the div, which was moving toward him.

Soraya silently thanked him and began to climb. She ran breathlessly, but halfway up the stairs, she had to stop, because she felt sudden sharp stabs of pain all along her body. She put a hand on the wall to brace herself, waiting for the inexplicable pain to pass, then continued.

She had to pause again when she reached the final flight of stairs, which brought her onto a balconied platform on the outside wall of the palace. At first, she had only stopped because she had been startled by the unexpected flash of green, but then she realized what she was seeing, and her jaw dropped in awe.

The golestan was still growing. Twining through the bars of the balcony were thick green vines lined with thorns. When Soraya looked up at the wall, she saw more of the vines growing over the palace walls, covering nearly the entire facade. Again, she felt a stab of pain that took her breath away, but as soon as it passed, she continued up the last flight of stairs, careful to avoid the vines and their poisonous thorns.

At last she stepped up onto the roof. She rushed toward the edge near the front of the palace, where Azad was backing away, still holding his dagger to Tahmineh's throat. Parvaneh stood several paces away from them both, alert but very still.

Soraya ran to Parvaneh's side and called out, "Let her go, Azad. She has nothing to do with this."

Azad's head jerked in her direction, and Soraya felt a wave of dread. She had expected to find him frantic and afraid, still halfway between monster and man. She had thought she could appeal to him again, as she had tried to do on the steps below. But Azad's eyes were cold and calm, his scales—and any other sign of the Shahmar—completely gone. He wasn't using Tahmineh to protect himself—he knew he had lost his throne, as well as any command he had over the divs. All he had left to do was punish Soraya for his loss.

"Nothing to do with this?" he echoed coolly. "She's the reason we're all standing here now. It's time for her to atone."

"He's right," Tahmineh called back, eyes fixed on Soraya. "You shouldn't be the one who has to stop him, Soraya. It should have always been me." To Azad, she commanded, "Do it, then. Do what you should have done to me thirty years ago."

Soraya balked at her mother's words. But then Parvaneh put her hand on Soraya's shoulder and whispered so only she could hear, "She's doing you a favor," and Soraya understood. Tahmineh's life was the only thing standing in between them and Azad. And so she was offering that life as a sacrifice, so that her daughter could put an end to their family's great enemy once and for all.

Tahmineh gave Soraya a small, subtle nod, and Parvaneh's hand tightened on her shoulder. *Let him do it*, they were both saying to her. Another sacrifice, another exchange. She had put out the fire and endangered her brother so that she could lift her curse. She had given Parvaneh to Azad to save her family. She had nearly killed Sorush for the same reason. But now, just once, Soraya didn't want to trade one life for another. She wanted her family safe, her mother alive, her people protected, Parvaneh free—she wanted it all, and she wouldn't let Azad take a single one from her. Not again. Not anymore.

The stabbing pain was returning, only now she couldn't feel each individual stab, but a constant sense of pressure all over her skin—all *under* her skin, like something fighting to break through. Ignoring it, she stepped forward, letting Parvaneh's hand fall away from her shoulder. "Azad, listen to me, please. You're fully human now, aren't you? You can find a new life for yourself somewhere else, somewhere far from all of your worst memories. You could forget the past and begin again."

The dagger in his hand wavered slightly, but his face remained impassive as he said, "Would you come with me if I did?"

Soraya hesitated for half a breath, then forced herself to say, "Yes."

He laughed wryly. "I was hoping you would say that. I wanted to hear you lie to me one last time. But even though you never keep your promises, Soraya, I always do."

His arm moved in one quick motion, the blade slicing across Tahmineh's throat, and Soraya screamed.

But Azad's reflexes were human now, and as his arm began to move, Soraya saw a flash of movement beside her—a flash of wings—and Parvaneh knocked his arm aside. The dagger flew out of his hand and skittered across the roof.

Soraya ran to her mother, the woman who had both cursed and saved her, and knelt at her side. Parvaneh was already removing the sash from her tunic and wrapping it tightly around the wound to stop the blood from seeping out. "It's not deep," she said. "If we bind the wound—" Her hand went to her waist, where her sash had been, and then her head shot up. "I must have dropped the feather when I flew up here, but if I can find it—"

"Go!" Soraya cried. She was holding her mother's hand, but it was cold—too cold. "Go quickly."

Parvaneh glanced up at Azad, who had been knocked to the ground during her attack. She hesitated, but then she rose and dove off the edge of the roof, her wings carrying her down.

The pressure under Soraya's skin was building, but she paid it little attention, too concerned with her mother's pain to worry about her own. Tahmineh's eyes were still open, and she raised a hand to Soraya's cheek, her lips parting to speak. "Don't let him win," she said with her remaining strength before her eyes fluttered closed.

She was still breathing, but Soraya thought of all her mother had endured—of the shadow she had lived under since childhood, the sacrifices she had made—and her vision went black for a moment. And then it burned red.

Her heart was pounding so strongly she felt the blood in her veins rushing to the surface of her skin. She knew this feeling, and so she knew what she would find when she looked down at her hands, her wrists.

Dark green veins were spreading over her skin, but even without seeing them, Soraya felt the poison inside her. She welcomed it like a friend, like a savior. At this point she had always stepped back from the cliff's edge—she would take deep breaths, calm her beating heart, wait until the spread of her veins slowed. But words were turning over and over in her mind.

Be angry for yourself. Use that rage to fight him.
Don't let him win.

The pressure was unbearable now, and her skin felt tight on her bones, like something was trying to burst out of her. It was the same feeling as in her nightmares, just before she awakened. *Surrender or destruction,* she thought. That was the way of divs. She could surrender to the div's blood inside her, or she could let it destroy her.

For so many years, Soraya had tried to fight down the poison inside her, but this time . . . this time, she surrendered.

The sky was a vivid orange now from the setting sun, and she turned her head up to it and let out a cry of rage and pain and release. And as she did, the pressure began to fade, the pain dissipating.

Something was happening to her—something new.

All along the lines of her veins, thorns were beginning to pierce through her skin, sharp and long like the ones in the golestan. She held her hands in front of her, watching in silent awe as the greenish-brown thorns appeared along the backs of her hands. They pushed out through the fabric of her dress, and when she touched her face, she felt more of them trailing down in two lines along her cheeks, down to her neck. This was what she had always feared: that her transformation wasn't complete, but was waiting for the day she could no longer control the poison within her. But instead of feeling horrified by the change that had come over her, Soraya felt whole.

She could sense the poison inside her now more keenly than she ever had before—but more than that, she could *control* it, directing its movement through her veins until she chose to release it through her thorns. If she had only given in to this transformation years ago, she could have had this power and protection without having to forgo touch—but there was no point in dwelling on the past now. That was what Azad had done.

At the thought of Azad, her head jerked up, and Soraya briefly thought she had been transported somewhere else. Azad was still there, backed into one corner of the roof, and he was looking at her in awe—and unmistakable jealousy. But all around him, climbing over the edge of the roof, were vines from the golestan. They were spreading out along the surface of the roof like a green web, moving closer and closer to Azad, surrounding him until he had nowhere to turn. Soraya could feel the golestan in her blood—in the div's blood that joined them both. There was something alive about it, and it seemed to know what she would want, what she would do, like an extension of her thoughts.

After checking her mother's pulse, Soraya rose, slowly approaching Azad. He looked nervously at the vines that kept inching closer to him, creating a cage of thorns around him.

"I wouldn't touch them if I were you," Soraya said.

He looked up at the sound of her voice and spoke her name under his breath. He tried to move toward her, but the thorns only grew closer around him.

"Don't you like me this way?" she said. The vines parted for her, creating a path to him. "Beautiful yet deadly, remember?"

"I remember," he said, his voice strained as he tried to keep the thorns from touching his skin.

She stood directly in front of him, close enough to touch. Here was the great Shahmar, that monster of her nightmares, the demon who had terrorized her mother and deceived her into betraying her family. He was nothing now but a defenseless young man, fragile and exposed, so easy to destroy. Soraya reached a hand out to him, the thorns on the back of her hand moving closer to his throat . . .

"Soraya."

Parvaneh's voice was clear and loud behind her, but Soraya couldn't make herself turn away. "My mother?" she said.

"I found the feather. She'll heal now."

Soraya did feel relief, but it was buried under something else, something sharp and hungry. Her eyes never leaving Azad's throat, she said, "Does that mean you think I should spare him?"

"No."

Her voice was closer now, and Soraya felt Parvaneh's hand rest on her shoulder, her fingers fitting around the thorns. If Parvaneh wondered at her changed appearance, she must have decided that now was not the time for explanations. "I won't stop you," Parvaneh said, "but I don't want you to do it like this, in anger, so quickly that you barely realize what you're doing. I struck at him like that once, without thinking of the consequences, and I regretted it long after. If you're going to kill him, you should want to do it even with a clear mind. So I'm asking you—are you sure you want to do this?"

Of course I do, she wanted to say, but she forced herself to lower her hand. She pulled away some of the vines encaging Azad, letting them wind around her arm in a kind of caress, as she considered the question more carefully. "What do you think, then?" she said to him. "Should I kill you, or should I do to you what you did to me and Parvaneh? Should I keep you locked away with nothing but your guilt for company? It would be fitting, wouldn't it?"

Azad kept his eyes on her, his fear hardening into defiance, like liquid metal becoming a blade. "Lock me away if you will, but don't think that you'll break me so easily. I waited for over two hundred years to take back my throne—what makes you think chains and thorns will stop me this time?" He shook his head. "I won't stop, Soraya. I won't surrender, and I won't stop fighting you until I see every single member of your family dead and—"

It happened so quickly that Soraya didn't understand at first. Parvaneh had pulled her aside by the sash around her waist, and something blurred past her, and Azad was gasping in pain, the handle of his dagger sticking out from just below his ribs.

"Enough," came a voice from behind them, and Soraya turned to find Tahmineh staggering to her feet. The blood-soaked feather was on the ground beside her, and there was nothing left of her wound except for a silvery, feather-shaped scar across her throat. Parvaneh must have noticed her moving for the dagger and pulled Soraya away so that Tahmineh's aim would land true.

Tahmineh came to them, her eyes never leaving Azad. He had slumped down to the ground, his back against the parapet. While Soraya had gaped at her mother, Parvaneh had already retrieved the dagger, and Azad's bloodied hands tried to cover the expanding circle of red above his stomach.

"You were right about me," he said, his words labored. "In the mountain, when you told me why I never lived as human—that it would have all been for nothing—"

Soraya knelt beside him and nodded in understanding. His words to her before Tahmineh's blow had been true, but they had also been spoken with purpose. He had wanted to goad her into killing him, rather than leaving him to face all his failures in the dark. *I forget him sometimes, the man I used to be,* she remembered him telling her, and she wondered if he already considered himself dead, if he had died with the Shahmar, and no longer knew how to be just Azad.

She glanced at her mother, who had finally faced her own nightmare and won, and nodded again. "Enough," she agreed. Perhaps he didn't deserve the mercy of her thorns, a quick end to his pain, but she would grant it to him nevertheless. Soraya moved one of

Azad's hands away from the wound and pressed the back of her knuckle against his palm, piercing his skin with her thorns as she released the poison into him. He shuddered as the poison spread through his veins, his eyes remaining on Soraya until at last they went glassy and still.

Soraya let out a long breath and dropped Azad's hand, peace settling over her like gentle snowfall. She heard the same soft exhalations from her mother and Parvaneh, as if they were free to breathe for the first time.

Soraya rose, and she tensed as she faced her mother directly, not knowing how Tahmineh would respond to her daughter's new appearance. But when Tahmineh came toward her and saw this final manifestation of her gift, her eyes were wide not in fear or revulsion, but in amazement. She raised a hand to touch an unmarked space on her daughter's cheek and said, "It suits you."

"I agree," Parvaneh said, and Soraya laughed.

But the battle wasn't over yet. Soraya went to the edge of the roof and looked down at the fighting below. The divs were even more outnumbered than before now that so many of them had fallen, but Soraya knew their deaths were only a temporary relief. She took in every div corpse on the ground and saw a new div rising from Duzakh to fight and die, around and around without end. Until now.

"Come," Soraya said. "We have to put an end to this."

Soraya stepped up on the parapet, and the golestan wrapped itself around her arms and waist to carry her down to the platform below. Tahmineh came the same way, as well as Azad's body, wrapped tightly in the vines, while Parvaneh used her wings.

Their descent was striking enough to pause the fighting, and Soraya took advantage of this attention to step forward and address the crowd.

"The Shahmar has fallen," she announced loudly, gesturing to the prone figure of Azad on the steps. She thought of everything

Nasu had told her, and chose her words carefully. "Your leader is gone, and can offer you nothing more."

Soraya descended the platform and walked out into the garden, winding her way through the crowd without fear, as she had done the night of the banquet. The divs regarded her warily, but they knew better than to touch her now. "If you continue to fight," she said, "you will lose again and again, because this land—these *people*—are now under my protection." As she went from div to div, the vines from the golestan followed her, circling around each and every div's feet in silent threat. "But if you lay down your weapons and surrender to me," she continued, "I will let you return to Arzur without further harm."

The vines continued to climb up to the divs' ankles as she spoke, and now she began to reach out and lay a hand on each div she passed—a scrape of nails against an arm or cheek or shoulder, a gesture to remind them of the banquet night, when they had accepted her as one of their own. *Accept me now,* she wanted to say, *and I will protect you, too.*

And as she passed them one by one, laying a hand on each, the divs began to drop their weapons. They did not bow as they had done for the Shahmar, because Soraya would not ask that of them, but simply surrendered.

She circled her way back to the steps and ascended them again. "I ask you—I ask *all* of you, div and human alike—to lay down your weapons tonight and consider this battle ended." But when she looked out at the crowd, she saw something that disturbed her more than any div. Many of the humans in the garden were staring up at Soraya in disgust or horror, likely wondering what made her any different from the monsters they were fighting, and Soraya's resolve began to waver. She wanted to cover her hands with gloves, run into the palace and seek refuge in the passageways—

But then a figure emerged from the crowd, grimy with blood and sweat, but still as radiant as he had always been. Sorush bounded up the steps and stood beside her as her equal. He didn't speak—he didn't *need* to speak. His presence at her side was enough to make it clear that she had spoken for him as well, and that to deny one was to deny them both. He raised his sword for all to see and laid it down on the steps.

And then, finally, the people of Atashar dropped their weapons, and Soraya's battle was over.

30

They had to wait another week before the spring rains came, and longer still before a thunderstorm gave them what they wanted—a bolt of lightning, sent from the Creator.

Shortly before the end of spring, a large crowd gathered outside the fire temple, but within, only the royal family was present, as well as several priests. Soraya stood apart with her mother, the spahbed, and Ramin—with whom Soraya had forged a hesitant truce—while Sorush and Laleh approached the altar. They bowed their heads as the high priest said the words to sanctify both the Royal Fire and the shah it protected.

That protection was mostly symbolic now. Sometime after the battle had ended and the divs had all retreated, the simorgh had vanished once more, not leaving behind a feather this time. Sorush had been concerned about this, but Tahmineh had assured him that the simorgh had only granted her protection before because her son had needed it. Now the Shahmar was no longer a threat, and Atashar had another protector, someone the divs would listen to.

Soraya hoped her mother's confidence in her ability to subdue the divs wasn't misplaced. In the days following the battle, Soraya had visited Arzur, and most of the divs had welcomed or ignored her. A few of the drujes—like Aeshma—had been bitter about their defeat, but they were in the minority, especially after Soraya had poisoned one or two of them who had tried to attack her, to show them that she was as dangerous as she claimed to be.

The first time she entered Arzur and beheld the pit of Duzakh again after the battle, she wondered if she had made a grave mistake in letting the divs live, and if she should send the golestan's vines to cover it entirely, not allowing any new divs to climb out. But she knew they would find a way out of Duzakh somehow. Perhaps it was better to keep control of the divs on the surface rather than attempt to eradicate them entirely. After all, it was only when they were outside of Duzakh, given form in the Creator's world, that they could be seen and recognized and fought.

After the fire ceremony was finished, Soraya began to leave the fire temple, but at the threshold, a gentle hand touched her sleeve, unmindful of the thorns beneath. *Laleh*, Soraya knew at once.

"Soraya?"

Soraya turned to her, fighting the urge to hide the exposed thorns on her face and neck.

"Sorush has to speak to the priests, but he wanted me to ask you to meet him later in the gardens," Laleh said.

Soraya nodded and began to leave again, but she stopped herself and called back, "Laleh?"

Laleh waited for Soraya to continue, but Soraya wasn't sure what she had wanted to say. *Were you ever afraid of me?* maybe, or *Were you only my friend out of pity?* These questions had haunted her since Ramin's confession in the mountain, but standing here with Laleh in front of her again, she found she didn't need to ask them.

Instead, she kept remembering what she had said to Laleh on Suri, when Laleh had first brought her news of the div and set everything into motion—*You were the only person who ever made me feel like I was the one worth protecting.*

Laleh was still waiting for Soraya to speak, and so Soraya took Laleh's hands and spoke the words that suddenly filled her heart: "I'm so happy we're sisters."

The awkwardness that had built up between them for the last several years melted away in an instant as Laleh threw her arms around Soraya's shoulders and held her close, with no fear of Soraya's thorns. "So am I," she whispered.

As she waited for her brother, Soraya walked through the garden with the vines from the golestan trailing behind her. She had coaxed most of the vines back down from the palace walls and clipped a few of them so they could follow her everywhere, often wrapped around her arm or waist.

It was still a luxury for her to be in such a public space without fear. Some of the nobility continued to eye her with suspicion, but Sorush and Laleh's support of her was enough for most of them to accept that the shahzadeh with poisonous thorns growing out of her skin was on their side.

"Soraya!"

She turned back to see Sorush hurrying toward her, and the sight of it felt so impossible to her that she thought she was dreaming. But she brushed her thumb along the edge of one of the thorns on her finger, and she knew it was real.

They hadn't spent much time together over the past weeks. Sorush had been busy reclaiming his throne—with the simorgh's return and the divs no longer a threat, he could finally take steps toward the reforms their father had once hoped for—and Soraya had worked with the pariks to help repair some of the damage the divs had done to the city. But she hadn't forgotten the gesture he had made the night of the battle, and so she smiled warmly when he approached her.

"I've been meaning to speak to you," he said, "but I haven't had the time until today—I'm sorry."

"There's no need to apologize," she said, though they both knew what he was actually apologizing for. "But I'm sorry, too."

They began to walk side by side, sharing an uncertain silence before Sorush said, "It will be summer soon. The court is preparing to leave Golvahar . . . and I'd like for you to come with us."

Soraya laughed. "I would make an interesting addition to your court, wouldn't I?"

Sorush stopped walking, his expression serious. "I mean it. You would be welcome at my court."

Soraya considered his offer, wondering how she would have reacted a year ago, if she would have been grateful or anxious. But whatever longing she had once had to be a part of court life had shriveled away. "I appreciate the offer, truly, but I don't think I'll join you. I love my people—and I will keep my promise to protect them—but I've found somewhere else that feels more like home."

"Where will you go?"

"With us," came a voice from above.

They both turned their heads up to see Parvaneh settled on a tree branch, her legs dangling below.

Soraya couldn't help smiling at the sight of her. "When did you get back?"

"Just now," she said, floating gracefully down from the branch with a small flutter of her wings. "But you both looked so serious, I didn't want to interrupt." Parvaneh walked over to Soraya and kissed her cheek. "We're nearly done, I think," she said. "A few days more, and you'll never know that a horde of demons rampaged through the city."

Sorush cleared his throat and shifted uncomfortably. "Thank

you—all of you—for what you've done for us. The pariks have truly shown themselves to be allies."

"Thank your mother for that," Parvaneh said. "She and Parisa have become good friends, and we pariks always help our friends." Soraya hid a smile, noticing the renewed pride in Parvaneh's voice when she spoke of her sisters, who had fully accepted her back into their ranks. Soraya had wondered why Parvaneh would still be willing to join them again after they had meted out such harsh punishment—but then she supposed that for ageless creatures, their punishment had been a relatively brief one.

"Will they let me come with you, do you think?" Soraya asked her.

"Of course," Parvaneh said. "I told you a long time ago that you would be welcome among us."

To Sorush, she explained, "The pariks live in a forest north of the mountains, and that's where I want to go. I can keep a closer watch on the divs from there, and in the spring, I'll return to Golvahar when the court does."

Sorush nodded his agreement, and Parvaneh excused herself, returning to help the other pariks.

As they watched her fly away, Sorush said, "Isn't she the one who tried to kill me?"

Soraya laughed. "I promise you, it wasn't personal."

The procession leaving Golvahar was much the same as the one that had arrived at the beginning of spring. If anything, it was even grander, in order to show the people that the shah had emerged strong and triumphant from his ordeal. Sorush led the procession beside his general, with Ramin among the azatan, riding stiffly because of his wound, and the people's cheers were surely celebrating their own victory in addition to the shah's. But from the roof where Soraya was watching, it was almost as if nothing had changed.

"So much trouble just to go from one place to another," Parvaneh muttered beside her.

Well, Soraya thought with a hidden smile, *maybe some things have changed.*

Parvaneh turned and leaned back, her elbows on the parapet, with the easy grace of someone who could definitely fly. "Are you sad to see them go?" she asked Soraya.

Soraya shook her head. "This is the first time I've watched this procession without wondering if they'll still remember me when they return." She put a hand on the ledge beside Parvaneh's arm. "And it's the first time I've ever watched it with someone else."

Parvaneh looked down at Soraya's hand, her lips curving into a smile. With the tip of one finger, she began to draw a lazy path between the maze of thorns on the back of Soraya's hand. "I'm glad you're coming back with me to the forest. I don't think I could return there without seeing you in every piece of it."

A pleasurable warmth flowed through Soraya's limbs as she watched Parvaneh. She had thought nothing would be more incredible than the simple sensation of touch, but she'd been wrong: more incredible still was the idea that she could be dangerous, all her thorns on display, and that someone would dare to touch her anyway.

But then her mood darkened, a cloud covering the sun. "You never told me what you thought when you first saw me like this," she said to Parvaneh in a halting voice. "Were you disappointed?"

Parvaneh looked up at her in surprise. "Not at all," she said. "I told you once I thought your veins were beautiful. Your thorns are lovelier still. But more important," Parvaneh continued, drawing her hand away and moving closer to Soraya, "I like seeing you so much at peace."

The words surprised Soraya, and she considered the truth of them. These past months of spring, she had felt unburdened, as if she had been carrying the weight of these thorns all her life—even when her curse had been lifted—and now could finally release them.

"I thought you liked seeing me angry," Soraya said, leaning toward Parvaneh.

Parvaneh nodded in concession. "True. Maybe I just like seeing you." Her hand reached around to the back of Soraya's head to draw Soraya down toward her, and their lips met.

With her eyes closed, Soraya thought she heard the beating of Parvaneh's wings, but Parvaneh broke away with her forehead wrinkled in confusion, her wings still, and her eyes wide as she looked over Soraya's shoulder. The vivid memory of leathery wings made Soraya turn in alarm, but she immediately calmed when she saw the simorgh perched on the roof ledge, above the faded bloodstain that marked Azad's death.

Parvaneh brushed her lips against a patch of skin along the curve of Soraya's neck. "I'll find you later," she murmured before stepping off the edge of the roof, wings outstretched.

Alone with the simorgh, Soraya felt the same shyness as last time. She took a hesitant step toward the simorgh and said, "I thought you had left us again."

The simorgh's feathers all ruffled in response.

"No, you'll never leave us, not when we need you," Soraya said. "Thank you for all you did—and I'm so sorry for what I've done." As she spoke, her stomach twisted with nerves. There was still a hollow space somewhere inside her that filled with guilt whenever she remembered extinguishing the fire. She only hoped that space would shrink in time.

The simorgh stepped off the ledge and came toward her, those all-knowing eyes seeing straight into her thoughts. She blinked once, then dipped her head and started to preen one of her wings. When she lifted her head again, she was holding a single feather in her beak. She stretched her neck forward, offering the feather to Soraya.

Soraya stared at the feather, remembering her fear that the simorgh would find her unworthy of such a gift. And yet . . . she felt no longing for it, no frustrated desire to be free of her poison or her thorns as she had before. She had spent so many years hiding away, trying to bury her emotions and all the poison that came with them, that now it was a relief to wear her thorns proudly, without shame or apology. She had her family. She had Parvaneh. She had a home. Her thorns deprived her of nothing—and in return, they gave her a place and a purpose in the world, her existence undeniable. Soraya no longer had to choose between one piece of herself and another. She could be whole.

"Thank you," Soraya said to the simorgh, hoping she would sense the emotion behind such simple words. "I appreciate the offer, truly. But I don't need it anymore."

The simorgh's eyes glittered with approval. With the feather still in her beak, she spread her wings and flew up into the sky, moving south with the rest of Soraya's family. Soraya remained on the roof and watched the simorgh fly toward the horizon until all she could see was a flash of moving color, a green flame flickering against a clear blue sky.

AUTHOR'S NOTE

Girl, Serpent, Thorn is the result of my lifelong love of fairy tales (particularly "Sleeping Beauty"), a fascination with the concept of a poisonous girl in a garden from "Rappaccini's Daughter," and my more recent desire to know more about the myths and legends of my own culture.

One of the novel's major influences is the legendary Persian epic, the *Shahnameh* (or the *Book of Kings*). The *Shahnameh* was completed in the early eleventh century CE and is a very long account of the history of the Persian Empire, except that the first two-thirds are based more on myth and legend, while the last third is based more closely on actual history. It's in the first sections that you find demons and heroes, snake kings and magical birds, and even a story reminiscent of Rapunzel. I wanted to use this mythical history to create a world that was inspired by ancient Persia (in particular the Sasanian era) and its folklore. Here are a few of the inspirations behind the world of *Girl, Serpent, Thorn*.

LANGUAGE

Most of the non-English terms in this book are a combination of words taken from Avestan, Middle Persian, and modern Persian. For example, *yatu* is the Avestan word for "sorcerer" or "magician"; *Nog Roz* is Middle Persian for "New Year"; and *div* is the modern Persian word for "demon." I chose to use these older versions of the words in order to create a historical mood or to differentiate the terms as they're used in the novel from their modern Persian meanings; however, I also used modern terms based on ease of readability and the mood I wanted to create. Some of the terms' real-world definitions have been altered or simplified for the purposes of the novel.

A quick note on pronunciation: The *i* is pronounced like a long *E*, so *div* is pronounced DEEV, *parik* is par-EEK, etc. The "kh" sound, as in *dakhmeh*, is a kind of throat-scraping sound similar to the "ch" in *loch* (as in *Loch Ness*) or in *Chanukah*.

THE CREATOR AND THE DESTROYER

The novel's cosmology is a fantastical, fictionalized, and truncated version of Zoroastrian beliefs from ancient times. Zoroastrianism is an ancient and complex belief system that has evolved over many years and is still practiced today.

I drew particular inspiration from Zurvanism, an obsolete, heretical version of Zoroastrianism that was popular during the Sasanian period. In the more dualistic Zurvanism, the two key figures, Ahura Mazda (the embodiment of good) and Angra Mainyu (the embodiment of evil) are twin brothers, two halves of an absolute whole, born from Zurvan (the embodiment of time). Orthodox Zoroastrianism is more clearly monotheistic, with Ahura Mazda as the only creator, and Angra Mainyu as a lesser being bent on spoiling Ahura Mazda's naturally good creation with things like sickness and death. Zurvanism also heavily features fate and astrology (as does the *Shahnameh*), whereas orthodox Zoroastrianism emphasizes free will and the choice between good and evil in each person.

The fire temple is the traditional Zoroastrian place of worship. A common misconception about Zoroastrianism is that its practitioners worship fire, but in actuality, the fire is not itself worshipped but is a symbol of Ahura Mazda's creative force. The Royal Fire in the novel is loosely inspired by the ancient coronation practice of lighting a royal fire for each shah, as well as by the Fire of Victory, the highest level of sacred fire, which burns perpetually and has many different ritual sources, including lightning.

The dakhmeh (also commonly spelled dakhma), or "tower of silence," was the traditional Zoroastrian resting place in ancient Persia. Because fire and earth were sacred creations of Ahura Mazda, dead bodies were not cremated or buried. Instead, they were left above the ground in open-air structures to be exposed to the weather and carrion birds. Tombs were also built aboveground for important figures such as Cyrus the Great, whose tomb is still standing in Iran.

DIVS

In their earliest incarnations, divs represent the physical and spiritual evils of the world, such as wrath, drought, or corruption. In later times, and in the *Shahnameh*, divs are monster or ogre figures, often with animal-like features. They are the traditional fairy-tale monster, kidnapping maidens and kings, fighting heroes, and generally causing destruction. In the *Shahnameh*, they can change form or even turn invisible.

Druj (meaning "lie") is one subset of demon and also sometimes refers to female demons. *Kastar* comes from a Middle Persian word for "destroyer" or "wrongdoer," but I borrowed the term to represent another kind of demon.

Divs are traditionally associated with the north and with mountains, with the ridge of Mount Arezur being the gateway to hell (called *Duzakh*).

PARIKS

The pariks of this novel are the middle ground between the pairika and the pari. The pairika (Avestan) were malevolent female demons who could take many forms and were associated with nighttime. Over time, the pairika evolved into the more romantic pari or peri—beautiful, winged women similar to fairies who are benevolent toward humanity. I thought it would be interesting to track the progression of the pairika from foe to friend in the novel, and so the pariks are a little bit of both.

THE SHAHMAR

Azad, the Shahmar (from the words "shah" meaning king and "mar" meaning snake), is based on the *Shahnameh*'s King Zahhak, who is in turn based on the earlier Azhi Dahaka. It's a wild story, so get ready.

Azhi Dahaka is a demon from the start, a three-headed dragon bent on destroying humanity but who is defeated and chained up in a mountain. The *Shahnameh* took this figure and made him a human prince who is persuaded by Ahriman (the Middle Persian name for Angra Mainyu) into killing his father and taking the throne. Ahriman then disguises himself as a chef and requests to kiss Zahhak's shoulders when he is offered a reward for his meals. Zahhak grants the request, and as a result, a snake grows out of each shoulder, and they keep growing back even after Zahhak tries cutting them off. Ahriman (disguised as a doctor this time) tells Zahhak that the snakes will eventually die if he feeds them human brains, so Zahhak orders the deaths of two men every night to feed his shoulder snakes and is generally a tyrant until he is eventually overthrown and chained up inside a mountain.

Azad also bears a resemblance to a character in the *Shahnameh* called Shiroyeh (who corresponds to the historical figure of Kavad II), a prince with an ill-omened horoscope who overthrows his father (and eliminates his brothers) in a military coup and is ultimately poisoned.

There is also a figure called the Shahmaran in the folklore of various West Asian cultures who is a benevolent snake queen, but my Shahmar is not based on that figure.

THE SIMORGH

As in the novel, the simorgh is a mythical bird in folklore. The story in the novel of the simorgh adopting a son is a loose version of the story of Zal in the *Shahnameh*. In the story (which happens after Zahhak's story in the *Shahnameh*, not concurrently, as in the novel), the simorgh adopts an infant boy who has been abandoned by the mountainside because he has white hair (a sign of evil). This boy, Zal, grows up to be the chief adviser to the shah. He is also the father of Rostam, a legendary figure who is similar to Hercules.

Years later, when Rostam is grievously wounded, Zal calls up his adopted mother by burning one of the three feathers she gave him, and the simorgh heals Rostam's wound by soaking one of her feathers in milk and placing the feather over the wound.

SURI AND NOG ROZ

The festival of Suri in the novel is a combination of the festivals of Chaharshanbeh Suri and Fravardigan. Fravardigan was tradition-ally held the five (or sometimes ten) days before the New Year. During this time, people clean their houses and welcome and cele-brate the fravashi (guardian spirits) of their ancestors. Zoroastrians still celebrate a modern equivalent of this festival today.

Chaharshanbeh Suri is celebrated on the Tuesday night before the Persian New Year. On this night, celebrants jump over small bonfires and say, "Give me your red and take back my yellow" (meaning, less poetically, "Give me health and take my sickness"). In this way, they release the negativity of the past year and wel-come the year to come.

Nog Roz is the Middle Persian name for Norouz, the Persian New Year celebrated on the vernal equinox. Norouz has its roots in ancient Zoroastrian times as the most important of several agri-cultural festivals, but it is still celebrated today by people of various religions, inside and outside of Iran.

ODDS AND ENDS

Esfand: A Persian tradition/superstition is to burn esfand (or wild rue) to chase away the Evil Eye and other negative vibes. Don't knock it till you've tried it. (It smells great, too.)

The Pariks' Forest: The pariks' forest is based on the Hyrcanian for-est (also called the Caspian forest) in the north of Iran. The strip of land between the Caspian Sea and the Alborz mountain range is a lush coastal rainforest that you should absolutely look up online because it's gorgeous and so different from the desert landscapes we're used to associating with the Middle East.

There was and there was not: Persian oral stories do have a common beginning, the equivalent of "Once upon a time": *yeki bood, yeki nabood,* which literally translates to "there was one, there wasn't one." This phrase is the inspiration for the novel's more loosely translated "there was and there was not," variations of which can be found in the stories of other cultures as well.

FURTHER READING

To learn more, check out the following sources:

Shahnameh by Abolqasem Ferdowsi (translated by Dick Davis)

Persian Mythology by John R. Hinnells

Wise Lord of the Sky: Persian Myth by Tony Allan

The Circle of Ancient Iranian Studies: www.cais-soas.com

Encyclopaedia Iranica: www.iranicaonline.org

ACKNOWLEDGMENTS

Writing this book was such a labor of love. Thank you to everyone who helped bring it to life:

To my agent, Meredith Kaffel Simonoff, for your insight, empathy, and support.

To my editor, Sarah Barley, for your incredible creative vision and your love for this book.

To everyone at Flatiron, including Amy Einhorn, Patricia Cave, Claire McLaughlin, Caroline Bleeke, Sydney Jeon, Bryn Clark, Brenna Franzitta, Emily Walters, Anna Gorovoy, and Melanie Sanders.

To Tom Mis, Nikki Massoud, and the Macmillan Audio team.

To Sasha Vinogradova, Kelly Gatesman, and Keith Hayes, for that glorious cover.

To Flora Hackett at WME, for your enthusiasm and drive.

To early readers Parik Kostan, Dahlia Adler, Naz Deravian, and Luna Monir.

To Emily Duncan, Patrice Caldwell, Tasha Suri, S. A. Chakraborty, Kat Howard, Gita Trelease, Shveta Thakrar, Cristina Russell, Cody Roecker, Laura Graveline, Kalie Barnes-Young, and Sami Thomason, for reading, loving, and blurbing.

To dear friends, for your support, friendship, and encouragement over the years.

To all the librarians, booksellers, bloggers, reviewers, artists, and readers, for sharing their enthusiasm, their words, and their art with me and others.

And finally, to my family, who have to witness my ups and downs during the writing process:

To Mom, for knowing and loving and understanding me, for always believing in me, and for answering all my random questions.

To Dad, for your constant love and support, and for encouraging me to be proud of and interested in Persian culture.

To Roxanne, for being my confidante, personal cheerleader, and occasional muse.

And to my grandparents and extended family, for being proud of me.

ABOUT THE AUTHOR

MELISSA BASHARDOUST received her degree in English from the University of California, Berkeley, where she rediscovered her love for creative writing, children's literature, and fairy tales and their retellings. She lives in Southern California with a cat named Alice and more copies of *Jane Eyre* than she probably needs. *Girls Made of Snow and Glass* was her first novel.

www.melissabash.com